MW01134724

MAGNOLIA CAFÉ

CHIC GAST

Magnolia Café is a work of fiction. Names, locations, events and characters are products of the author's imagination and are used fictionally. Any resemblance to persons living or dead, events, organizations or establishments is entirely coincidental.

Copyright © 2009 Chic Gast
All rights reserved.

ISBN: 1-4392-3078-1
ISBN-13: 9781439230787

Visit www.booksurge.com to order additional copies.

The author wishes to thank Fritz Henshaw and David Cass for their editing skills and constructive criticism and also wishes to acknowledge the wonderful bevy of readers, Hope Nisson, Jocelyn Gardner and Robbin Gerner for their suggestions and encouragement.

This novel is dedicated to those mental health workers who toil long hours every day with strength and compassion so some desperately ill people may enjoy a more meaningful life. These people are forgotten heroes.

ONE

Like well-trained cattle dogs, they herded Jack Teal across the hot asphalt, never really hassling him but moving with tense joints and clear intention. Unlike herding dogs, they never really looked at him; just shucked and jived across the yard as if he didn't exist. Everyone in the yard found something remote to hold his interest. What was happening had nothing to do with them, but conversation still became muted. The tallest of the three herders was nicknamed Chigger. Leonard, a bigoted half-wit, who had approached Teal only days after he entered the gates referred to him as 'Chigger the Nigger'.

"You better join the Brotherhood boy, or someone will be hankerin' for your ass. You're a big fella, got some size on you, but you're too clean. Clean don't cut it in here; understand what I'm saying? Tats and scars and bad attitudes do. All that – and friends, of course."

Teal knew Leonard and all other eyes in the yard were watching, and, if he lived through this, Leonard would approach him once more spouting his Aryan babble spiked with a sprinkling of 'Ya understand what I'm saying?'

The three men carefully worked Teal along the inner fence and into a corner beneath the west tower where the guard was trying to find shelter from the Texas heat; rifle and boot-heel propped up against the stainless railing in the shadow of the tower. The asphalt was mushy and reminded Teal of walking on the woodland bogs at his uncle's place on the Louisiana coast. Chigger, wearing a black mesh t-shirt, approached him head on while the other two flanked left and right.

Teal had never seen the one on the left who had a scar eyebrow to cheek, highlighting a milky eye. The shorter one on the right was named Monk. He was a giggler. Apparently, as the story went, he giggled when he cut the throat of a convenience store clerk and left him to bleed to death after a botched robbery attempt, which netted fourteen dollars and four corn dogs. The clerk survived and eagerly provided the court with grizzly and unshakable testimony helping to put Monk away for thirty-five years.

"You name Jack, right?" Chigger asked without looking at him while rolling his shoulders; a poseur of a light heavy weight entering the ring.

"You sure are a pretty white boy."

He looked over his shoulder coaxing a giggle from Monk. Waves of rancid body odor resembling the scent of a turkey coop mixed with excitement-spiked testosterone enveloped Teal and stung his eyes. He tried to breath through his mouth scorching his throat with the afternoon heat. Chigger's biceps and forearms were road mapped with huge veins looking like earthworms burrowing beneath his skin and setting up a street fair.

"I never had me a pretty white boy. You just like a big frosty bottle of milk, and this hot old Texas sun is making me mighty thirsty. We come to a little understanding here and see where it leads."

His hands were covered with weight lifters chalk reminding Teal of some long-forgotten actor in a blackface vaudeville routine. Only the eyes, which now pinned his, were not filled with mirth and sly good humor. They were as black and focused as a ferret's.

"And you and me got other issues, know what I'm saying. You selling all that blow an' takin' money out of the pockets of all them little nigga kids on street corners all over the U. S. of A. Shame on you, white boy."

Teal was afraid but not panicked and had no thought of death. His uncle had reminded him on several occasions this day was predestined the moment in entered the prison gates. And had almost gloated.

Teal knew he must try to hurt them before they hurt him, because they *were* going to hurt him. It was the only way he might gain any degree of respect. In high school his boxing coach told him fighting on the street bore no resemblance to fighting in the ring. There were no rules or two-minute rounds or referees to monitor the head butts and kidney punches. On more than one occasion growing up, he heeded the advice.

Teal harbored the naive hope for a moment there would just be fists and shoes but, with mute resolve, realized there was probably little chance of that.

The prison was a treasure trove of sharpened bedsprings or parts of broken cell phones or shards of glass carefully honed and as lethal as straight razors. Teal had heard the oft-told story of a pair of dark glasses frames sharp and strong enough to cut sausage. He had seen a weapon called the fishhook. It was a strong piece of carefully straightened wire with a needlepoint, festooned with tiny barbs and easily concealed between fingers or even, with great caution, nestled next to the gums. It slid through flesh without drawing much attention, but pulling it out was another matter. Some of the most serious, festering wounds had been created by the fishhook.

"I'm not looking for any trouble," Teal said, and Chigger laughed.

"I don't give a shit what you looking for. We talking about what I want," he said thumbing his chest and leaning forward.

Teal, knowing that he had only seconds left, quickly decided to kick Chigger in the crotch and then try for Monk. He knew he would be lucky to unload a couple of solid kicks or punches. At least they would remember him, and it probably wouldn't make the beating any worse.

No-Name was beginning to position himself, and Teal backed up to the fence hoping he could get some leverage or a bounce off the wire. The yard was now as still as a diorama except for a small crowd of Mexicans laughing, chattering and kicking a koosh ball as they unwittingly drifted along the fence line.

Monk was giggling and circling wide to the left a foot or two off the wire and in a slight crouch. Most of his upper front teeth were missing and his eyes were slightly crossed. Under different circumstances, Teal might have stifled a laugh at his bizarre appearance. He quickly revised his plan; kick Monk in the nuts first, since he was closer, and then uncork a roundhouse on Chigger hoping to catch him in the throat. And if he could get in close, he might have a chance to survive long enough for the guards to intervene. He would welcome the rubber bullets and the leaded sticks.

When he shifted his body weight for the bounce off the wire, his muscles pumped with adrenalin, their small group of four suddenly expanded to ten. The group of Mexicans had reined in tightly behind the three black men shielding them and Teal from the yard. To the casual observer, it might appear as if a jokester was preparing to deliver a punch line to a group of buddies. The tallest of the Mexicans threaded through the group and slipped between Teal and Chigger. His right forearm displayed a well-defined tattoo of an eagle with a massive beak and flared wing tips reaching up his bicep to his shoulder. The other Mexicans separated into two groups and isolated Monk and No-Name against the fence, flanking Teal.

"This man is a friend of ours," the Mexican said to Chigger in a voice that was so soft that Teal, standing behind him, could barely understand the words.

"I choose to think you did not know. If I thought you did," he said glancing around at his friends, "it would be a very serious matter."

Several nodded with solemn expressions.

"This man is to be treated with great respect. Do you understand?"

Chigger, still staring at the asphalt, mumbled.

"What did you say? I did not hear you."

"Yeah, I understand," he said with a small dismissive wave of his hand.

"Excellent. Excellente!" the man said, suddenly expansive and generous with his smile. The punch line to the joke had been delivered to the group and there were chuckles and flashes of smiles from the Mexicans. One looked more like a young boy with long lashes framing soft brown eyes and even white teeth. He also had two tiny blue tears tattooed beneath one eye; one for each man he had killed.

"Then we are all finished here. Let us go back and enjoy this fine Texas sunshine before dinner," the tall man said pleasantly as he started to push past Chigger.

On his right Monk suddenly emitted a low growl of pain followed by a sharp giggle. He staggered and started to fall to his knees before Chigger could support him. No-Name quickly sidestepped to help on the opposite side, his eyes wide with fear. The three walked through the cluster of Mexicans

who parted slowly and reluctantly, gesturing and chattering in
Spanish. Monk could barely support his own weight; his right
leg dragging across the hot asphalt and his head bowed. A
thick stream of bright red blood coursed down the inseam of
his jeans and left a thin trail of red, barbequing on the asphalt.

"It looks as if your friend has met with misfortune," the
tall Mexican called after them with concern. "Perhaps he sat on
something sharp – or did something he shouldn't have. He will
have to be more careful."

Four days later Monk was admitted to the prison
hospital, his body racked with a spiking fever dropping him
into a delirious, semi-conscious state. The doctors operated
immediately, but the wound and subsequent infection were
shockingly massive, and Monk's heart stopped beating on the
operating table. They revived him once, but when it reoccurred,
they could not bring him back. Monk would have turned
twenty-four in six days.

That time, and a thousand other cookie cutter days, was
indelibly etched in Teal's brain. As he followed the guard down
'the duce', he feared they would haunt him for the rest of his
life.

The 'duce', called the 'two way' by the older inmates,
was an unremarkable, yet famous corridor where new inmates
entered and parolees or free men exited. Teal felt pity for those
men who would only walk it the one way. The floor consisted
of yellowed linoleum, green in its early life, featureless walls
and clear hundred-watt ceiling bulbs spaced every eight feet
and protected with wire mesh and metal hoods. The bulbs
spotlighted Teal and the guard, creating the illusion of circus
shadow figures chasing each other along the walls. Teal had
never seen the guard who led him down the hall; tall and

gangly with his right arm swinging out from his side as if leading an imaginary marching band.

Teal didn't know *any* of the guards and few of the inmates for that matter.

He had said goodbye to Viejo. "Is there anything I can do for you?"

"Two things," Viejo said quickly. "Don't ever come back and, two, send a battalion of Humvees to get me the fuck out of here!"

The warden was more pragmatic. "You don't belong here Teal. You're far too smart."

The warden was a tough and honest man who wore a silver belt buckle the size of a coffee saucer and left post-it notes all over his desk reminding him of things needing to be done.

Then he said with a grin, "And if you truly believe you're that smart, you probably will end up back inside. Get it?"

"Got it," Teal said, and they shook hands.

Teal had been an anomaly within the system. He was a convicted narcotics trafficker; a broad classification which encompassed the worst type of white slavers pushing black tar heroin to preteens in the projects as well as the fallen gentrified college kids who took the wrong fork in the road and started by selling ecstasy or trading it for sex. The law made little distinction. But he was not black or brown, did not grow up in the projects, was not a homegrown product of a gang and knew both his mother and father, although he was always mystified by what his father expected of him. He had always been difficult to catalog.

The guard stopped half way down the corridor and looked both ways in an exaggerated search for an imagined candid camera.

"You been told that transportation's all taken care of? No
need for a cab or nothing?"

Teal nodded wondering what had been arranged.

"Well then, I'll be sayin' goodbye and take you on down
to the gate guard," he said holding out his hand in which there
was a glint of metal.

Teal shook his hand, pocketed the key transferred to his
palm and followed the man to the main gate where he was
turned over to the gate guard. The first guard turned and
stalked back up the corridor without another word, his dress
khakis whispering like a broom on a concrete floor. The gate
guard checked his release papers and, without uttering a word,
opened the front gate.

Teal walked through and heard it slide shut and
electronically click behind him while he resisted the urge to
turn for a last look. Instead he walked quickly into the lot and,
once sheltered from view by a pickup truck, pulled the key
from his pocket. He grinned and shook his head. The black fob
displayed the symbol of a Porsche.

Shouldn't be hard to find in his lot.

The lot was filled chock-a-block with pickup trucks,
SUVs and generic sedans; all coated with a thin gray film of
East Texas dust making them appear to be a convoy from a
nameless desert nation. The Porsche stood out like a blueberry
in a sand box. It was clean, with bright medium blue paint but
sported a badge of primer on its left front fender. Teal knew
beneath the sheet metal the car would be in perfect condition.
It was the way Koontzman did things. Always first class.

He opened the door and let the waves of heat envelop
him. It reminded him of stepping off a charter airplane in
Phoenix during mid-summer. The coupe's interior was very
clean with soft leather seats and clean looped wool carpets. He

stowed his tiny carryall in the back and slid into the driver's seat. Checking the mirrors, he adjusted them and the seat slightly and keyed the ignition. The engine started quickly and settled to a comfortable burble. For a moment he entertained the bizarre thought of staying there, glued to the seat and playing with the air conditioning and radio until the sunset brought a chill creeping over the bare hills. But he shook the thought with a grimace, slipped the gearshift into first gear and pulled out of the lot and onto the secondary road leading him to the east/west interstate. He accelerated up through the gears and drove through the gentle uphill turns leading him towards the highway.

His knuckles were a red-rimmed white from clutching the steering wheel like a ship-wreck survivor grasping a life preserver. The featureless landscape skidded by at increasing speed while Teal focused on the horizon feeling with wonder the tremors that racked his body. Suddenly, he threw back his head and laughed out loud for the first time in three years. He knew he must sound like a maniac in a teenage slasher movie. But it cleared his mind and soothed his soul and eventually pumped a comforting balm through his veins and arteries while tears streamed freely and dampened his shirt.

* * *

TWO

By the time Teal looked in the rear view mirror, after long heart-aching minutes of denial, all traces of the prison had disappeared. Dry grasses cloaking rounded hills, which edged the asphalt and fled away towards the horizons, had replaced all the cellblocks, administration buildings, outer perimeter fences, towers, parking lot, access roads and halogen lights which never slept. He tried to blot the prison images from his memory but knew they were baggage he would carry forever.

Driving alone had always been a time when Teal could think; work something out, formulate a plan or pick one apart. People who have never been incarcerated often believe there must be ample opportunities to think; being there is little else to do. For Jack Teal that had not been the case – at least not to think clearly. Prison was much more of a 'listen and react' scenario. You were told to do something, dozens of times a day, and you reacted by doing it. If you did not react quickly and correctly, you would be punished, so most people reacted in the prescribed manner displaying adequate survival skills and reasonable intelligence.

But constructive thought? With the exception of time spent in the library, Jack Teal saw little evidence of that process. Strangely enough the renovated library, a project in which Teal had become involved, was likened to a nuclear free zone. Bitter enemies tolerated each other and occasionally sat at the same table – something totally foreign in the yard. Posturing dissolved into natural shoulders, careful gestures and an occasional nodded acceptance or smile.

He thought about the men he had met and avoided or who had avoided him. After the incident in the exercise yard, many treated him as an empty space. He simply did not exist.

"You have very powerful friends," the man who had orchestrated the intervention had said. "They hope that I will assist in providing for you a pleasant incarceration. And I am honored to do that...to a point. I cannot be your shadow every moment of the day, nor do your friends expect that. There are times when you will be alone in the shower or walking that narrow corridor to the library when I cannot hold your hand. A moment is all it takes."

Teal had nodded, and they walked further into the yard. The population parted before them as if ordained, and the tall man led them as if they were strolling down a spit of sand on Padre Island.

"They call me Viejo which means 'old man' in Spanish. I do not mind, and it gives them pleasure," he said with a casual hand flick of his fingers and grin. His teeth were very white and even. "So you must participate in the process and use caution. Then we will all be happy: my friends and I, you, your friends in the free world and, you may find this surprising, all the predators in this hellhole. All of this has been taken out of their hands, and they can concern themselves with other things."

Viejo said something in rapid Spanish to the other men who pealed off like carrier jets and disappeared in the general population.

"I will be available if you need me. But I will not be your friend." He admired the sunset for a moment. "Nothing personal, you understand. Just do your time standing up, and get the fuck out of here."

The horror of nighttime in a cellblock was something else Teal would carry embedded like a tick in his scalp or a tumor in his brain. Nighttime was a calliope of sounds from Hell – men snoring, shouting profanity, crying and farting and one, near the end of the block, quietly praying in Spanish until his plea was drowned out by curses, shouts and laughter. How people were supposed to sleep in this wretched atmosphere was a mystery to Teal. But Teal eventually slept to ease his exhaustion and to hush the recriminations, with which he battled daily.

By the time he reached the interstate, an hour had been deliciously squandered on secondary roads and narrow rancher's lanes, and the freedom of choice was incredibly luxurious.

But he realized that freedom could have subtle shadings and multiple meanings. Freedom to some meant walking through the prison gates, taking the commuter bus to town and a greyhound to Minot or Shreveport or Cajun and a try to reassembling a life that had been torn apart by a moment or months of indiscretion. Others were seduced by that defining moment when they were the masters of their own ship which, unbeknownst to them, had a gaping hole in its hull and was destined to a hundred-fathom resting place. All scripted by the State Police, Highway Patrol, City Police, DEA or their competition. They always thought this time would be different. They were smarter. They had learned the moves from the real pros, never having asked themselves why the real pros were in the next cell over or just down the block.

So Teal wondered exactly where that left him. He was a free man with no restrictions, no ankle bracelet or parole officer whose ass he would have to kiss three or four times a month. He would not have to justify his every movement to anybody or prove that he had a dead-end job with a company paying him far below minimum because, after all, he *was* a con.

Yet, he was driving a car provided him by those for whom he had worked and whose identity he had gone to prison protecting.

"Why won't you accept a lawyer?" his uncle had asked. "He's good and thinks you can beat this." He stormed around the holding room trying to convince and control his temper over something so seemingly simple. "By pleading guilty, you will go to prison. Easy as that. Three to four years. You're breaking your mother's heart. Do you understand that?"

He had slammed his hand against the wall getting stony stares from the guards. "I'll tell you what. I will use this whole affair to scare the shit out of my kids. I never want them to be in your position, and I sure as hell don't want to see something like this destroy their mother's life."

He took a deep breath and looked at one of the blank walls. "You've disgraced the family. I'm finished talking to you."

With the exception of his mother, it was the last conversation he had with anyone in his family. Over three years ago – a lifetime.

When Teal reached the interstate he became restless with its predictability after a few dozen miles even though it would take him to his destination quickly. He took an off ramp without clearly seeing where it led, but that made little difference. The off ramp emptied into a rest stop with the road continuing on past the stop and winding through the dry hills. The stop hardly looked inviting; displaying bathrooms, looking more like portables, two trees (three if you counted the dead

one) and a single semi truck and trailer looking as if had been
parked there for several months.

Teal parked beneath one of the living trees and
stretched outside of the car. It looked like a ghost rest stop.
Nothing moved and heat waves simmered from the roofs of
the bathrooms while the trees appeared to be begging for
a watering. Teal used a bathroom, which was remarkably
clean and returned to the car. He opened the passenger door,
leaned into the car and scooped everything out of the glove
box spreading it out on the slowly cooling car's roof. There
was an owner's manual, an envelope with a sheaf of repair bills
and a second sealed envelope. He slit the seal and shook out
two items – a credit card struck in his name and a California
driver's license bearing a credible likeness of his signature and
a photo taken a few years earlier. The face looked rested and
eyes curious. Teal knew the license would stand any rigorous
checking, and someone he had never met would promptly pay
all the credit card charges. He put them both into his wallet
which contained one hundred and thirty four dollars made
working in the library, and a blurry photo of the house in
which he had grown up. His mother's face was barely visible in
the kitchen window. But he knew all the features of her face –
all her expressions and felt a chill remembering her anguish
when the bailiff led him away for the final time.

On the road again and heading west, he began to feel the
hunger from a skipped breakfast. He had wanted no surprises
in those final hours before his release – a bogus ruckus that
might swarm in his direction or a man stepping out behind a
half closed door or something in his food. Finely ground glass.
Rat Poison. Someone's HIV urine.

He began to watch the highway signs with their familiar service station and fast food logos. When the next off ramp showed a secondary road heading north, he took it without hesitation heading up through rolling hills towards the sharp barren rock teeth of an uplifted ridge, which reminded him of the Flatirons west of Boulder.

A roadside sign gave the mileage to a town, a distance his complaining stomach would survive. He settled into the seat floating through the curves taking him north.

Topping a ridge with a clear view of a small valley running east and west, Teal knew he had made the correct decision. The town was tiny – all of it clearly visible from the pass in the ridge. A small stream cloaked with cottonwoods framed its northern border and alfalfa fields spread to its south resembling a massive green beard. Two roads bisected the center of the town with the buildings dwindling within two or three blocks from where the roads crossed.

Teal coasted down the road and into the town, parking at a raised curb near where the two roads crossed. There was a restaurant bracketed by a small regional bank and a Farmers Insurance office. Across the street was a combination feed store/hardware store/farm equipment outlet. No more than a half dozen cars were within eyesight and nobody on the sidewalks.

He parked the car and entered the café through a glass door displaying the name 'Easy's' in pealing faux gold leaf and found the room almost empty. A young couple sat at the counter chatting with the cook who was framed by a high pass-though, and three elderly farmers with billed caps and coveralls sat at a booth in the rear drinking iced tea and eating chili out of large bowls. One had crumbled in all his saltines making his chili look like a small hill of skree. Two Caterpillars conversing with a ConAgra.

Teal slid into a booth, flipped open the menu and grinned at the two columns of regional road foods. He was well acquainted with generic treats at cafes and roadhouses across the United States. 'Dottie's world famous blueberry muffins'. 'Clair's Gottcha Chile'. 'Mabel's award winning chokecherry pancakes'. And Teal tried them all.

The room was clean and cool and had several faded, sputtering neon beer signs, one a mystery to Teal, a long past county rodeo announcement and a poster touting an upcoming high school dance with 'live music' from Amarillo. The booths had cracked yellow vinyl seats and green tabletops rimmed in scarred aluminum and were duplicated thousands of times across the country.

"Well, do you see anything that rings your bell?" The waitress was tall and angular and had a harvest of red hair that defied containment. Her smile was genuine.

He smiled back and looked back at the menu for reference. "Well, maybe you could tell me about the Pacific Gumbo and the Cowboy Stew."

"If y'all are from the coast, either one, you want to pass on the Gumbo. Lot of frozen crap in it. But the Cowboy Stew might put some heft on you. You're a little on the skinny side."

"I'll take your word on it. Stew and an iced tea, please. Lemon if you got it."

"What – you think you're in Beaumont?' Then she laughed. "Course we got lemon."

She winked, spun and headed for the kitchen.

Teal spread his arms over the backs of the booth and allowed his head to roll back. He was about to relish his first 'free' meal, and it could have been a pile of oyster shells garnished with okra. It would make little difference.

The young couple at the counter laughed over something the cook had said and left holding hands. He waved goodbye with a dripping wooden spoon.

The waitress brought a beaded glass of ice tea and put it in front of him pulling the sugar caddy over for company.

"Name's Bet," she said pointing at her nametag, which was covered with puppy stickers. "Yours?"

"Jack. Nice to meet you, Bet."

He liked the sound of her name. It matched her starched gingham outfit.

"You're not from around here are you?" she asked picking up his iced tea and wiping the ring. "Too pale. You need some good old Texas sunshine to color you up a bit. Looks like you been livin' under a rock. You might even be half way handsome then." Broad wink.

Jack smiled and slipped the menu in the chrome clip next to the window ledge. "Naw, I just drove in from Atlanta. Lost my job there, and thought I'd take some time off to visit the coast."

The lies came easily.

"Nice little Porsche you got there," she said pronouncing the word like something you would sit on during a blazing hot afternoon and have a glass of lemonade. Teal imagined Germans the world over scowling.

"Don't see too many sporty cars around here," she said putting a hand on a cocked hip.

"It's not mine – belongs to a friend."

The cook yelled something from the kitchen, and Bet yelled back. "Hey I ain't deaf, Arnie!"

Jack laughed, and Bet grinned down at him.

"I'll be right back with your vittles."

Jack stretched his arms along the back of the booth again feeling the ridged aluminum trim through his shirt. The men in the booth laughed over a shared moment and waved for another round of iced coffee and tea, and Bet yelled an acknowledgement.

Moments later a police cruiser pulled to the curb in front of the restaurant, and the trooper in the shotgun seat got out and stretched. He had a sweat line down the back of his khaki shirt and his Smokey Bear hat tipped well back on his head. He stared at the Porsche for a moment, stretched a second time and strolled into the restaurant slapping the hat against his pants. Jack pulled open the menu and stared at it blankly, keeping the trooper in his peripheral vision. He saw him glance over, then turn to the counter.

"How's it goin' today, Bet? Got any coffee left?"

A smile and a wink. "Always got coffee for the fuzz." She took two Styrofoam cups over to the coffee bar, filled them and snapped on lids.

"Quiet day, Charlie?" she asked slipping a sweet roll into a separate bag. "I don't suppose we need to tell your old lady about that," she said nodding at the second bag.

Charlie squirmed and his face turned blotchy but didn't turn down the second bag. "Oh, it's pretty quiet out there. Some T-Bar heifers got out on the road and old Leroy Fredricks damn near clobbered one coming around that turn by Two Mile. Went off the road and durn near went on his roof. By the time I got there, his missus, can't remember her name, was still hollerin' at him. Probably did more damage to his eardrums than running off the road did to his pickup.

Bet giggled and tried to tuck an errant strand of hair beneath her cap.

"Gwen. I think her name's Gwen. Generally she's sweet as pie, at least when they come in here, but I hear she can bawl like a calf if she's a mind to."

"Well by golly, that's what she sounded like. Thought I's going to have to arrest her for disturbing the peace."

They both laughed, and Charlie almost tipped over the bag with the coffees. He wiped his eyes, gave Bet a five and waved away the change.

"Take care of yourself, Bet," he said and slapped the counter lightly. On his way to the door, he caught Teal's eye, nodded and swung through the door. Outside he glanced at the Porsche, and Teal could almost sense the calculator in his head putting the two of them together. Several seconds later, an hour it seemed to Teal, the cruiser pulled from the curb and headed south out of town.

Bet slid a plate before him, and he jumped.

"Hey, Jack, you're a little skittish. Been on the road too long."

Teal looked down at the steaming bowl before him. It was roughly the size of a hubcap from a fifties style tour bus. The aroma was heady with spices, and large chunks of meat and sliced vegetables threatened to overflow the rim. Next to the bowl was a platter, not a plate, of large slabs of crusted bread rich with butter and toasted golden.

"Oh my God," was all that Teal could say.

Bet frowned. "You don't like the way it looks or what?"

"Bet, it looks fabulous. It'd be better if I had a family of four to help me out."

Bet threw her head back and laughed. Red hair unleashed in every direction.

"Hey Arnie. He thinks this bowl is big enough for five people."

As Arnie snorted in the kitchen, she slipped into the
opposite seat. "There was an old cowpoke out at Lazy D bar.
He come in here and had two in one sittin' and one to take out.
Lord that man could eat."

"Probably ate himself to death," Teal said rolling a hot
carrot round his mouth trying to cool it.

"Naw. He went a got himself cancer. One day he's here...
next he's gone."

Teal put his spoon down and sighed. "Bet, I'm sorry.
What a stupid thing for me to say."

She put a hand on his arm. "You could'na known, Jack.
But he was a good man. You'd have liked him."

"I'll tell you what, Bet. Why don't you take some time
and tell me about your town. Looks like those fellows in the
rear are happy."

"I'll be right back," she said jumping up, "Don't go away."

She skipped over to the booth, giggled with the men
seated there, ran quickly to the kitchen and then back to Teal's
booth slipping in and fanning her brow. The entire round trip
took about seventeen seconds.

"So why are you interested in this little podunk town?"
she asked looking at him over the rim of a diet soda.

"Oh I don't know. I like small towns and I love hearing
you talk. I haven't had much conversation in my life recently.
I'm starved for it."

She cocked an eyebrow at him and giggled. Then she
told him about the town, past and present, and what part she
and her family had played in it through the passage of half
a century. Teal loved it: the words, her enthusiasm, the hand
gestures and her attempts at containing her unruly hair. Every
syllable reminded him of his freedom. He knew that this day

and these words might be a liqueur to help sooth the fire of the past three years. He relished it.

"You're a funny kind of fella," she finally said with a sigh. "You don't say much but you're one hell of a listener. You know bein' that way you could sweep any Texas gal off her feet? Nobody listens to women when they prattle on."

"Then it's their loss."

She looked at him for a moment, and then shouted over her shoulder. "Hey, Arnie, I think we might have the next town mayor sitting right here eating cowboy stew!"

Teal laughed and put down his spoon knowing his stomach wouldn't accept much more.

"Is that Easy?" he asked nodding his head back towards the kitchen.

"No, no," she laughed, "That's Arnie. Easy's long gone."

"Not dead, I hope?" Teal asked cautiously.

"Not old Easy," she said sliding her diet soda over tabletop. "He just picked up and left. His uncle left him scads of money in a will, and he hit the road. Arnie was working for him, and Easy made him an offer old Arnie couldn't refuse." She wrinkled her brow as if trying to understand why anyone would cut and run. "Can't even remember his first name now," she added.

Jack sopped up more of the gravy even though his stomach was sending him storm warnings.

"So where did he go?"

"To Scottsdale, Arizona," she said, "can you imagine?"

She said it as if Scottsdale bore similarities to the grossest slums outside Mexico City.

"He had a car like yours," she continued. "Except it was some sort of racing car. He raced it all over the place – Texas,

Arizona, California – I don't know where else. Hey, Arnie. You
remember that little racing car that Easy had?"

"Hell yes," he shouted from the kitchen. "Next to that
Daniels kid it was the loudest God damned car I ever hear'd."

"Now I guess he's got a shop there in Arizona and repairs
those cars," she said. "I don't know much about sporty cars, but
it was some sort of a famous old race car, and now he's racing
it in these special things they have for old race cars. Don't that
beat all?" she asked winding up a strand of hair and cramming
it up under her cap.

"I'm a roundy-rounder gal myself."

"Roundy rounder?"

"Yeah, like NASCAR. You know roundy-rounders."

Teal laughed and took a bite from one of the pieces of
toast creating a summer snow melt of butter running down
his chin. His stomach was registering at one hundred and ten
percent full.

"Tell me, Bet. Are there any good motels close by? I need
a good nights sleep."

"Yeah some in Post are okay. And even more in Lubbock,"
she added wrinkling her nose revealing her impression of
Lubbock.

She turned quiet and stared out at the sidewalk and street
for a long moment.

"You don't have any trouble following you do you, Jack?"
she finally asked and then became flustered.

"It's really none of my business."

"What do you mean trouble?"

"Well when old Charlie come in here, you like to turn to
stone," she said not looking at him.

Then she watched him, and her eyes were concerned.

"I've had some trouble, but it's over," he said nodding. "It's over."

"Well I hope so, Jack. You seem to be a nice man, and I don't think you're looking for trouble. I hope it doesn't find you."

Teal reached across the table and took her hand.

"Thanks, Bet. I'll put on some heft and come back to look you up."

She squeezed his hand and grinned.

"You do that, Jack."

As he was walking out the front door with an iced coffee in a bag probably nestled next to an unsolicited sweet roll, she called to him from behind the counter.

"I forgot to tell you. Guy who owned this place? Name was Jason – Jason Easy. I guess I knew that all along."

Teal waved to her through the plate glass window, and she blew him a kiss. Slipping into the Porsche, he put the coffee in a cup holder and idled the Porsche out of town. He felt something else in the bag next to the sweet roll and pulled out several postcards, all with a romanticized rendition of the front of 'Easy's'. Several bushy and impossibly green trees were brushed in and the plate glass was oversized. He grinned and slipped them into the glove box.

Teal's eyelids were drooping by the time he reached Post, although the drive was relatively quick. He was tired of the uniform countryside and the parade of pickup trucks with gun racks and square dance stickers. The rare exception was a truck with high wooden railing extending up from the side of the bed and a saddle horse peering curiously at him as he passed. He spent the next twenty miles wondering how they got the horse in and out of the bed.

He pulled into the first motel on the outskirts of town, paid for the night with his new credit card, which passed the acid test. Half an hour later he was sound asleep in a bed that smelled faintly of room deodorizer and cigar smoke. Tomorrow he would reach his destination.

* * *

THREE

The room was quiet and cool and certain sections were punctuated with muted lighting. On the wall close to the desk was a rosewood and glass showcase containing half a dozen figures highlighted by cones of light from invisible sources. A jaguar was frozen in a muted snarl next to a potbellied man holding something that looked like canes in his left hand. He faced a tall slender figure with protruding eyes and wearing an elaborate headdress. The slender figure shone with a golden sheen while the potbellied figured appeared to have been made of rock hard clay tinted with mottled green and dark red. There were four or five others carved from a translucent green stone.

The name of the man who sat behind the darkly burnished desk was Hector Alviso Koontzman, the son of a woman from a wealthy Mexican family and a penniless German who immigrated to Mexico as a teenager. At six foot three, Koontzman towered over most of his countrymen and was often mistaken for the former President of Mexico, Vinciente Fox. His blue eyes, which highlighted a handsome, deeply tanned face, displayed something disquieting in their depth that made men look away and women to have unsettling dreams interrupting their nights. He wore perfectly tailored clothes and butter-soft leather shoes made especially for him in Milan.

The man facing him across the desk was four inches shorter than his employer but, with his powerful physique, weighed the same. He was known only by the name Rukka. He also was tanned and fit, but his eyes were dark and piercing

and offered little humor and no friendship. The deep pile carpet
sucked sounds from the room like a magician, yet these two
knew each other so well, they spoke softly and punctuated the
air with gestures – some which spoke paragraphs. Both men
had traveled to dozens of countries and knew rich, powerful
men who were used to having their own way in the world. Yet
they acquiesced in Koontzman's presence.

"I am not clear on why you are doing this," Rukka said
drumming his fingers lightly on the upholstered arms of his chair.

There were four fingers on each hand, and the sight of
them had always fascinated Koontzman. Rukka had been born
with a birth defect of having only four fingers on his left hand.
His father, returning drunk from a hard night's boozing with
his fellow mine workers, cut off the little finger of his right
hand with pruning shears when Rukka was four years old.
He said he needed to 'balance him out'. When Rukka reached
his twelfth birthday, his father disappeared under mysterious
circumstances and was never heard from again. Several days
later, Rukka left home and never returned.

"I find him a most interesting person," Koontzman said,
"I've never been quite sure how his mind works."

"Does that mean you are willing to compromise the
company and all your friends?"

Koontzman crossed his legs and bobbed his loafer-clad
foot in an impatient gesture. He wore no socks and his feet
were as tanned as his face and hands. "I don't think that I have
to remind you that he was in a position to do us much harm.
Yet he said nothing. That kind of loyalty is admirable"

"Perhaps it was fear that sealed his lips."

"Fear?" Koontzman thought for a moment, and then
chuckled. "I don't think so. He is not a man who frightens
easily."

Silence filled the room and Koontzman turned to watch a jumbo jet silently making its approach to the San Diego airport, a puppet seemingly suspended in the darkening skies by its landing spots and blinking wing lights and the faint glow from windows.

"Then how long will this be continued?" Rukka asked clearly not finished probing while trying to disguise his jealousy.

"It will be finished when it is finished," Koontzman said quickly, and the stocky man hoped he had not pushed too far.

"He was one of the best people to ever work for me," Koontzman continued as if thinking out loud.

"His group – what did they call themselves? Yes, the Dog Pound. What a strange name, but they were one of the best we ever had."

He shook his head in continuing amazement. "And a bunch of gringos too," he added with a sharp laugh.

"And would he be invited back if he were to approach you?" Rukka asked continuing his tightrope walk.

Koontzman thought about it for a moment and stared at the precious figurines in the showcase. They were mute and held no answers for him.

"We would certainly talk about it. See where it might lead us," he said and seemed pleased with the thought and with Rukka's discomfort.

"What you are doing is not cheap. And we are calling in favors that must be paid back," Rukka said lacing his eight fingers in his lap.

"Are we to worry about a few dollars and a handful of favors that I choose to squander like a bag of peanuts thrown to the pigeons? Now if you are lacking in things to worry about, I can remind you of several things I find much more pressing than this."

Rukka nodded his head, his smile wary. "You are absolutely correct, Hector, and I will attend to them now."

He stood, bowed slightly from the waist and left the room.

Koontzman pivoted his chair to savor the view of twinkling lights and the muted silhouettes of buildings and wondered if he were becoming a sentimental old fool. Perhaps Rukka *was* right, he thought, and this was truly a fool's errand. He picked up the phone, hesitated a moment before punching a number on the speed dial.

* * *

FOUR

Teal woke before sunrise, a longtime habit. As a teenager, when most of his friends were sacked out or whacked out and sleeping in on the weekends, he was up before dawn listening to the birds and chickens and dogs challenge the night.

He looked through the parted curtains at the false dawn and the quiet motel parking lot. Wispy trails of morning dew decorated the neat line of parked cars muting their colors, and the neon sign, humming and sputtering the night before, had gone blank and quiet. Teal watched the restaurant across the street which was just beginning to come alive. A sleepy prep cook accepted an early dairy delivery while balancing a coffee cup and a fistful of receipts.

After showering and dressing in his only change of clothes, he sat at the tiny, scarred desk and pulled the postcards from the bag. The one with the slight butter stain from the pastry he addressed to Bet, taking extra care to highlight the stain. He thanked her for her kindness and vowed to return for a second go-round with the cowboy stew.

The second card he addressed to an old friend from Michigan State. Teal had been an usher in his wedding over six years ago and, although they had been close, had not seen him since.

When he was working in the prison library and helping to set up their computer system, Teal had logged on to the Michigan State web site and printed out the alumni list for his graduating class out of curiosity.

Suzanne Abbot Hunt. Jesus Christ! Suzanne actually married Gary Hunt! What a total dork…but rumored to be hung like Milton Beryl. And rumors only since Gary was a stranger to athletic department showers.

Teal's note to his classmate was short and ambiguous leaving him wondering why he had bothered. But he got some stamps from the desk and mailed both in a box outside the café.

The food was satisfying, filling and completely predictable; Chicken fried breakfast steaks, breakfast scramble (tailored to the region) and pancakes with some topping only available locally and always considered a gamble.

After finishing, he drove to a strip mall and discovered a store called Grundy's Super Mart which seemed to offer a little of everything although the quality was dicey. He bought some toiletries, a stiff canvas duffle and a very sturdy, if not very attractive, locking suitcase. After returning to his room, he packed what few things he had, anxious to get on the road.

The drive to Tucson was fast, compromised only by an Arizona Highway Patrol cruiser with whom he played cat and mouse for almost an hour. When the cruiser tired, Teal cracked it back to between 80 and 90 and made the outskirts of Tucson by early afternoon. He pulled into an enormous truck stop, topped off the Porsche's tank and parked in what precious little shade remained in the simmering lot. Dozens of long haul semis were parked side by side like dozing dinosaurs with their air-conditioning and freezer units humming in a one note chorus.

The attached café was at least twenty to thirty degrees cooler than the baking asphalt, and Teal nearly trampled several slow moving, chatty tourists walking before him when they stopped to catch their breath at the temperature change.

A pretty but exhausted looking dark haired waitress was trying to accommodate the tired, hungry truckers with wallets chained to their belts and the tourists with flip up dark glasses and white, knobby knees peeking out beneath shorts tinted with colors not found in nature. She performed a classic television double take upon seeing Teal, and ten hard years disappeared from her face.

"Jack, for Jesus Christ sakes, is that you?"

She ran from behind the counter and threw herself around his neck. They stumbled backward and almost landed on a table of four.

"Where have you been, you scamp?" she asked after they untangled.

"Hi Peggy," he said with a grin. "You'd never guess."

"Yeah, I probably wouldn't. But you could try tonight over a couple of beers. You've been gone for – what – years."

"Yeah, couple of years," he said holding her at arms length, a little surprised at how she had aged.

She straightened her apron and gave him a sideways glance. "I don't suppose you came to see me."

"Course, I did," he said and pecked her on the offered cheek.

"You are such a bullshitter," she said, and a trucker turned on his stool and barked out a hoarse laugh.

Teal smiled, sat on one of the counter stools and started fiddling with the salt and peppershakers. The air conditioning was starting to give him a headache.

"Is Mister Wonderful in?"

"Oh yeah. Up in his office countin' money or griping at the walls. Go on up – you know where it is."

Teal pecked her on the cheek a second time, although the offered area was a good deal closer to her lips, and climbed the narrow staircase leading to a closed door. He knocked and heard someone bellow from within. It could have been 'come in' or 'get the hell out of here'. Hard to tell with the distorted volume and the roar of the cooling system.

He opened the door and was almost staggered by the blast of even colder air. If the restaurant was cool, this room felt like the polar icecap.

"Get in here and close the door before all the frickin' AC escapes," the fat man behind the desk bellowed and finally looked up from a stack of papers.

"Well you son-of-a-bitch," he said with a tiny down twitch in the vicinity of his mouth, the equivalent of a broad grin from mere mortals.

He leaned back in his chair which elicited a tortuous sound of wood and metal and screws trying to stay connected. The chair was routinely replaced every three to four years.

"You're lookin' buff, Jack," he said, now with a definable grin. Possibly a first.

"Thanks, Roy, but I'm way out of shape. I'll need a whole bunch of fine tuning."

The big man grunted. "I suspect they didn't have much luck punkin' you out," he said and swept the papers into an opened drawer.

"Wasn't because they didn't try," Teal answered and leaned across the desk to shake the man's hand, which was scarred and had knuckles the size of shooter marbles.

"Well, I'm by God glad to see you survived it. No p.o. or ankle bracelet, right?"

"Nope. No counseling or group home or any of that shit. Texas isn't California where they try to kill you with kindness. In Texas, if you live through your full term, they cut you free. None of that progressive, ACLU, help-you-find-God stuff. Fuck ya, and get the hell out of here. They never want to see you again. I'm free and clear and headed to the coast."

The man cupped his chin and nodded.

"Bad in there, right?"

"Not too. I worked setting up a new library with the warden. Pretty good guy locked into a shitty job. And Koontzman had some connections inside. Made things easier."

The big man shifted his weight and grunted.

"So he made it cool for you. And what are you? Like grateful or something? Not thinking about hookin' up again are you?"

Teal looked at the ceiling for a moment and was interrupted before he could answer.

"Shit, man. You don't want to go through that again do you? Plus it's getting rougher and rougher out there. Everyone from the top DEA guys to scout leaders want to bag themselves a dealer and get a ribbon pinned on their chest. And these Colombian cowboys like to shoot the balls off everything in sight. They only stop when they run out of ammo or their gun barrel melts. Me? I like sittin' here and bitchin' about the heat and the Texas Rangers. What a pathetic fuckin' ball club."

"I don't know, Roy," Teal answered. "I'd like to think I'm smarter now."

"That's not the answer I's lookin' for."

"Best I can do, Roy. Simple truth is, I don't know. I just don't know."

He watched the big man in the chair. He knew no one he trusted more, and the premonition causing him to leave a package with the man had been well timed. Three months later he was lying handcuffed on someone's front lawn, and the night was filled with shouts, sirens and swirling lights.

"How 'bout you, Roy? You still straight?"

"Straight as thirty miles of Iowa Interstate," the man said with no hesitation. "And I don't miss it at all. I don't even sell NoDoz to the long distance guys. I sleep like a baby and haven't cleaned my Glock in two years. It's probably full of earwigs."

He chuckled and clasped his hands behind his head. His biceps were the size of burnished pony kegs.

"Don't miss it a-tall."

There were some who had seriously misinterpreted his homey demeanor and considered themselves slick enough to work him with their scams. None tried a second time, and some bore scars.

The chair squealed and groaned again as the man reached into a lower drawer of the beaten desk and brought out a small box wrapped in a brown paper bag with the flap folded over and taped. The name 'Jack' bracketed by two happy faces was scrawled across the top in black marker pen. He skidded it across the desk.

"'Speck you're looking for this. You gonna stick around for a while? Maybe let me buy you a beer?"

"Can't, man. I'll have to take a rain check. Right now I feel like a shark. If I stop moving, I'm going to die. Gonna do some biz in Tucson and then head for the coast later on."

The big man nodded, and Teal sensed a sadness. He leaned across the desk and put his hand on Roy's forearm.

"I owe you, my friend."

"Shit, man," he said waving at the air. "But let me tell you this," he growled with his no-bullshit squint. "When you stop being a shark, maybe you could share some time with your old friends. You know what I'm sayin'? There ain't too many left if what I hear people telling me is true. The Dog Pound is all broke up and scattered. Some dead."

Teal put the small box in his lap and looked at the floor.

"Sorry Jack, but sometime the truth's a bitch. And whatever you may think, Koontzman ain't your friend. Just remember that. You ate shit for that man for – what – three and a half years? No sweat off his butt."

He shook his massive head and stared at Teal.

"You blow in here and spend a whole four minutes with me and then tell me you're down the road."

He snorted and looked at the wall decorated with fading eight by ten glossies of long distance truckers grinning and squinting at the camera.

"Take care of yourself, man," he finally said. "There are people who do care about you. Hector ain't one of 'em."

Teal stood, and they shook hands for a long moment. Then he turned and left the room hearing the chair howl a protest behind him. Peggy Jo watched him walk through the restaurant and out into the parking lot without saying a word. For a moment she thought she was going to cry until the cook hollered that one of her orders was up, and she was back to the hustle. Later, in her tiny apartment, she cried herself to sleep.

Teal arrived in downtown Tucson in thirty minutes and parked in a garage within two blocks of the Bank of Tucson. He tore the paper from the box Roy had given him and slipped off the lid. Teal knew it had not been opened because he knew Roy. The man didn't care what was in the box: carved jade, diamonds or the rarest coins in the world. Someone had entrusted him with its care. Simple as that.

There were almost a dozen keys nestled within: various house keys, one that appeared to belong to a padlock and four safety deposit box keys. Teal had bought them all, with the exception of one, from a locksmith four years before for ten

bucks and had no idea what they opened. He selected one
deposit box key and left the rest in the box.

Dropping the discarded keys and box in a trash receptacle,
he carried the duffel stuffed with several dozen newspapers,
some crushed to give the bag bulk, through the heavy glass
front doors of the bank. The room was large and spacious with
columns supporting a ceiling at least two stories high. The loan
officer's department was fenced off discretely by something a
four year old could easily vault. Somehow the large room was
able to mute the telephone conversations and the click of high
heels on the marble floor. The inside was as cool as the sidewalk
had been stifling. Teal didn't think that temperature changes
this drastic and often could possibly be good for your system.

He walked to the safety deposit cage, signed a slip and
presented his key. The woman checked his name against her
files and led him into the vault. She may have been the same
woman from whom he had rented the box five years before, but
he couldn't be sure. He had a small checking account of less
than a thousand dollars at the bank from which the box rental
was paid yearly.

"Would you like a cubicle?" she asked over her shoulder.
Hearing her voice convinced him she was the same woman.

"Yes, thank you Mrs. Pierce." She seemed pleased that he
remembered her name and smiled.

She almost dropped the box pulling it from the vault
wall, and Teal reached down to help her.

"Good heavens! It's a tad heavy!"

"My wife was going to chuck out my mineral collection,"
he said earnestly. "Had some of 'em since I was a little boy."

She clucked her tongue in understanding.

He carried it into a room, and she closed the door behind
him. After staring at the box for a moment, he looked up at

the open space over his head. Certainly they wouldn't have surveillance cameras watching the cubicles, but old cautious habits die hard. And the one time he had relaxed, cost him over three years of his life.

He couldn't possibly calculate the number of times he had thought of this moment. Some inmates in the prison had dreamt of their wives or girlfriends, or of their mothers and family or even their hunting dogs. But Teal dreamt of this reinforced tin box with the thin wire handles. When times were hard, the image of this box kept him sane.

He flipped opened the lid and turned the box lengthwise on the desk. Picking the heavy bundle off the top, he unwrapped the soft polishing cloth carefully. The SIG P210 nine millimeter parabellum lay nestled in its holster looking as new as the day he had bought it. The gun collector who sold it to him was in a serious financial bind after his wife maxed out four credit cards and split with his Ferrari mechanic. Teal had always thought the SIG was beautiful in a purposeful way, like a Swiss watch or a piece of fine cutlery. It certainly bore little resemblance to the later chunky, stamped out SIG Sauers mass-produced in a licensing agreement with a German firm and now dominating the market. He had fired the SIG three times – once at a tree and twice at a skunk in a field by the side of a country road. He missed the tree but hit the skunk with the second shot and watched it die twitching and releasing its protective spray in futility. Teal had felt so ashamed, he had never fired the weapon again, much to the amusement of some members of the Dog Pound.

Teal stared at the pistol and was swept with the memories of everyone in the crew buying weapons – SIGs, Glocks, AKs, American Eagles, Colt Pythons – automatics with banana clips and revolvers with shoulder holsters and blackout targets of

sinister men in snap brim hats aiming pistols from a crouch.
All the Dog Pound play-acting like they really knew what they
were doing when they were just a bunch of dumbass college
kids sneaking around in the dark.

The rest of the deposit box was filled with money.
Hundreds and fifties carefully banded and lying nestled
like stepping-stones. The SIG had nestled in the only little
pocket left. He had forgotten the number of bundles he had
placed in the box over a two-year period, but he certainly
remembered the total – including the few stacks of twenties.
The total was three hundred and ninety five thousand dollars.
He had visited the bank at least once a month for almost two
years, always driving in from Phoenix or Albuquerque. He
had never flown in to Tucson in his life.

He had convinced himself over the last three plus years,
this is just the beginning. In a year, two at the very most, he
was completely convinced he could increase it ten fold. And
then he would be out for good.

Teal was in a hurry now. He placed the bricks of money,
most hard and sharp edged, and the pistol into the duffel and
replaced them with the newspapers.

After closing the lid and looking quickly around the
room, he opened the door and caught the woman's attention.
Moments later he exited the bank into the sweltering heat. The
bank guard gave him a little hand salute and swung open the
door for him.

Teal drove several miles north of Tucson to get out of
the heat of the basin and checked into an upscale motel with
private view balconies. He gave them the credit card and said
that he would be staying at least a week or two and would like
a nice room with a view of the Western Range.

The third floor room was comfortable and clean with a bland personality and an excellent, unobstructed view of the mountains. He transferred the hundreds and the SIG from the duffel into the suitcase, locked it and placed it on the closet shelf next to the extra pillow and blanket. Taking the duffle with him, he found a shopping center where he bought several changes of inexpensive work out clothes at a sports store. Teal was not, by any stretch of the imagination, a clothes horse. When he found things he liked, he wore them until they suffered death by laundry.

He also bought a bottle of tequila, two packages of beef jerky, some cheese and crackers and a lime at a second store. He let Knootzman's card treat him to the clothes.

Back in his room, he checked the undisturbed suitcase before arranging a small banquet on his balcony where he intended to watch the sunset and entertain the thought of getting a little drunk. When he set the cut limes on the balcony table, he realized that he had forgotten some salt. He frowned hoping some of the crackers were overly salted and sat down to his feast.

With his first tequila, as the balcony began to cool with the approaching night, he started to relaxed, feeling the stiff tension of wariness bleed from his shoulders and back. With the second tumbler, the thoughts of all of them came flooding back – the crew – and where they were or if they were even still alive.

Chris was dead along with Ham and Foxy, all killed in an incredibly violent joint raid with officers from the DEA, local police and FBI on a warehouse in Panama City. They had stupidly tried to shoot it out with the police and had been cut to pieces by a hail of bullets so intense it set the building on fire. Carlito escaped but had been identified by authorities and would be forever on the run. Teal had happened across the short newspaper article on line from the Miami Herald after being in prison for less than a year. Then the story had been smothered with no further information available. It was a clear sign of Garland Bennett's influence and pressure. Chris's father was the most powerful Democratic senator in Washington.

And the rest of the crew? Teal thought the Glitter Twins were probably married and living in Larchmont and playing golf every other day. It made him smile. Crazy Jim was in a Fed lockdown in Wichita and probably wouldn't survive, and the rest had just disappeared – some hopefully back to where they had come from before they had been swept away by the money and madness. What a bunch of dumb fucks, he concluded. But at least he was still alive – and he was way smarter.

The sun had set behind a hill dotted with saguaros and barrel cactus before Teal finished his third drink and half a box of crackers with beef jerky chasers. His stomach was complaining and whining for something more substantial, but he was too tired to listen. Leaving everything on the balcony, he left a jumble of clothes on a chair and slipped into bed. With the sliding glass door open, the Arizona night breeze caressed his skin and eased him into an untroubled sleep.

* * *

FIVE

TJ and Dannie Fitz lived in Marin County, north of San Francisco and anchoring the northern end of the Golden Gate Bridge. The San Francisco Bay graced its eastern flank with the Pacific Ocean defining its western coastline. The geography was dominated by Mount Tamalpais rising twenty five hundred and seventy one feet above sea level with the rest of the county as its apron. From its summit on a clear day you might see the Farallon Islands twenty five miles to the west jutting from the Pacific and clearly demonstrating why they had been nicknamed The Devil's Teeth. On rare occasions a hiker on the mountain might be treated to a glimpse of the majestic snow covered peaks of the Sierra Nevadas some one hundred and fifty miles to the east.

Dannie and TJ had lived in the county for eight years and would be happy in no other place on earth. They loved the cultural and intellectual soup represented by the inhabitants who had turned more than one census taker towards mind-altering substances. There were simply no standards by which the population of Marin County could be measured. And that is precisely why many of its residents lived there. This included billionaires (millionaires being somewhat commonplace), people on welfare, Democrats, Republicans (although all the Republican here were so liberal they were shunned by the rank and file), lawyers, CEOs, shipbuilders, firemen, venture capitalists, gurus, the brilliant and the challenged. For those who craved conformity, this would be a poor place to settle.

Within cities and counties, events will sometimes occur that become defining moments used to describe the heart and soul of an area. Marin County had two such events. One was known to all and well on its way to becoming legendary. The second, a personal event in the life of Dannie Fitz.

The first centered on Sausalito's famous houseboat fleet on Richardson's Bay. The fleet of houseboats, loosely tied together in a floating wad of steel and plastic and wood, was home to people who were more than content to live this quirky lifestyle and probably would chaff in other settings. Children raised here went to school, got into minor scrapes with the law, helped older people work on their boats, learned about sex and, in general, lived through the angst of teenage life. Their only difference from other teenagers was the water. Other teenagers lived on solid ground and could ride their bikes around the neighborhood.

Suffice it to say that the population of the houseboat armada possessed more than its fair share of individualists, and Lyndon Laytell was a charter member. Lyndon was a trust fund baby who had blown through most of his stash with warp speed. When he finally slammed on the brakes, there was enough left to buy a houseboat or live in a trailer park, albeit a very nice one. He purchased his houseboat, repaired and refinished it to his liking and moved in.

Like most of the fleet, the boat he bought had a ballast to keep it upright in turbulent weather. Lyndon replaced the ballast with his sole remaining possession of any value – his wine collection. That done, he settled happily into the rhythm of Sausalito and Marin County.

When he hosted a party, something with which he had vast experience, the empty bottles of wine were carefully saved, filled with seawater, marked with an X and placed back in the hold the following morning. It was a pain in the butt and a nasty job, but he did it anyway. For a while.

But there were so many bottles in the hold, he finally reasoned, that one or two or a dozen certainly could not make any difference. But after two years, they certainly did.

The storm occurred the night after his neighbor had remarked at how high Lyndon's boat was riding in the water. He thought about that, but the thinking never turned to worry, as he was preparing for a party celebrating Ramadan. During the simultaneous peaks of both the party and the storm, the houseboat uttered a burp of displeasure, which quieted the partygoers, and then she sighed reluctantly like a giant sow and began to roll. Partygoers leapt through every opening in the vessel, and the crash of empty wine bottles cascading towards a watery grave was heard a quarter mile away. No one was even slightly injured and, over the ensuing years it became an event, which everyone seemed to have attended – like Woodstock. The QE II could not possibly have handled all the claimed celebrants.

Lyndon Laytell reluctantly moved to a trailer park outside of Sparks, Nevada, the double wide easily accommodating what was left of the wine collection.

Dannie and TJ had purchased their house with every cent they could scrape together and had to deny themselves luxuries to pay the mortgage for the first couple of years. As TJ's job managing a restaurant took on expanded responsibilities with commensurate pay raises, financial security made life more comfortable. Friday night Mexican food was once again an option.

Dannie worked twenty hours a week at a trendy boutique in San Anselmo, which sold scraps of cloth masquerading as bathing suits and t-tops. She rode her bicycle on all days except those threatening hurricanes. TJ could hardly complain since he thought she had the most beautiful legs in all of Marin County. It was always extremely risky for her to wear shorts around the house at night.

The second county defining story happened to her at the store in San Anselmo, and was well on its way to becoming a local legend with its retelling.

The store, in addition to its boutique items, had several tables of knick-knacks like barrettes, bracelets and hand mirrors which Elizabeth, the owner, picked up at garage sales, auctions and flea markets. The problem was their mysterious disappearance – not in wholesale lots, but one here and one there, none of which anyone could remember selling.

Since they were Elizabeth's treasures, she was determined to arrest and prosecute to the fullest extent of the law. The staff set up a hidey-hole in the back room where the entire shop could be surveyed. It's not surprising that no one thought they would capture their thief on the second day and that he would be a full thirty seven inches tall.

David, Davy to them, was in the third grade at the local Catholic school and often dropped in on his way home, dressed in neatly pressed blue pants and jacket, cap firmly in place and carrying a briefcase. The staff tolerated his wandering and thought little about it. He was sort of a mascot. So the shock was profound when someone in the back room watched him slip a stylized comb into his briefcase. It had happened so fast and with such professional aplomb, no one believed her – until they confronted the thief and shook him down.

He cried and blubbered and almost made a dash for the door, but they blocked his escape and called the police. A sergeant arrived in a patrol car, as had always been the plan, although the station was a scant two blocks away. Elizabeth had wanted the full nine yards. Davy was taken away crying and moaning and offering bribes.

"I'll do anything you want," he kept shrieking.

Everyone felt miserable, but the police assured them this was the best way to handle it.

The following day Dannie was returning to the shop from lunch and saw the sergeant returning to the station. He waited for her with a scowl.

Before she could open her mouth he said, "Don't even ask me about that little thief."

She stared in amusement at his fuming. "What?"

"Do you know what your little buddy's full name is?" and when she shook her head, "David Lewis Capelli."

"Capelli?" she asked shaking her head. "Not…"

"Oh yeah! Oh yeah! That Capelli. Lewis Nayland Capelli, defender of the scumbags and immense, gigantic, colossal pain in the backside the world over, is his daddy!"

Dannie had to hide her laugh as the sergeant fumed, then finally laughed.

"We called him up to come down and pick up his boy, and he's up on the sidewalk in front of the station with that damn Bentley of his within forty five minutes. And that's coming from The City; must have been flying! He storms into the station, and guess what the first words out of his mouth were?"

They were both laughing now, and the sergeant supported himself with a light pole.

"He says to me, 'Have you read my son his rights, yet?He's a citizen, you know!'"

People stopped on the sidewalk to watch them collapsing against the walls of the police station in gales of laughter.

"Would you like to see the mail?" Dannie held it down by her side, as TJ relaxed with a cold Fat Tire beer and watched the commute traffic. He loved the honking, the road rage as long as it didn't result in violence (screaming and gesturing were certainly acceptable). He was tired after a long day, but he knew the routine – boring mail was plopped in his lap while interesting mail elicited some sort of routine. This must be interesting mail.

"Yes, I would. Might there be something there to titillate my interest?"

Dannie flipped through the envelopes.

"I don't know. How about a postcard from Jack Teal?"

TJ didn't even try to hide his surprise. "Teal? Jack Teal? You're kiddin'."

"Nope," she said fluttering the postcard before his eyes ready to yank it away.

"Jack Teal," he said leaning back in his chair wondering if in that brief moment he might have missed something interesting on the freeway. "I haven't seen him in – what – six, seven years?"

"Six," she said dropping the rest of the mail on a small glass topped table while dangling the postcard before him.

"Our wedding? That's the last time?"

"Yep."

He eyed the card but knew better than to lunge for it. "So, what's it say?"

"I don't know. It wasn't addressed to me."

He waited.

"Well, maybe he's coming out here. To Marin County."

"Would you be so kind as to allow me to read the card?"

"Of course," she said and flipped the postcard into his lap like a playing card. His glasses were dangling around his neck with a scrap of leather thong, and he perched them on his nose scanning the postcard. The lenses might have been made from a glass brick wall in a fifties futuristic bathroom.

"What is it with him?" she asked plopping down in a canvas chair and fanning her brow. "You know we've never talked about this, but he made most of my bridesmaids crazy. I thought during the whole week there was going to be some sort of crazy orgy – like a grade C teen sex movie. It was real edgy."

"Edgy? That sounds very now. Why didn't I see all of that?"

"You were crazy in love and blind."

"Yes, there was that," he said after a moment. Any other comment would have been incredibly foolish.

"What's he all about?" she asked now leaving the canvass chair and squirreling into his lap. "You've never much talked about him. But I know you guys were close friends."

"I guess we were. But with Jack it's hard to tell. I always had the feeling he would go to the wall for me, you know, but the next day he might be gone."

"Doesn't make much sense."

"With Jack it did," he said and thought for a moment. "He was always about eighty percent there. Nobody knew that other twenty percent, not that it might have really amounted to anything dramatic. And hell, at college relationships aren't really that deep, so most guys took him for what they saw."

"Do you think the hidden twenty percent was by design?"

"Good question. I don't know if he was aware or not.

Also Jack was a classic 'shoot yourself in the foot' kind of guy but the sweetest, nicest guy you'd ever want to meet. Do anything for you," he said scanning the postcard.

"The night before this championship handball match, big deal, NCAA finals, he spends the night with some bimbo,

Kimi or some damn name, shows up late the next morning and forfeits. Against a guy he would have smoked. Absolutely smoked. I thought the coach was going to kill him."

Dannie snuggled into his lap.

"Did I ever tell you what Linda Lou and Patsy said? After our wedding?"

"What? Jesus, I barely remember Patsy? Linda Lou comes through loud and clear."

Dannie poked him in the ribs.

"Everyone remembers Linda Lou. But Patsy was the hot ticket."

"Okay. I got a picture of the two of 'em. So what did they say?"

She squirmed a little and hesitated. This was excellent information and needed to be treated with respect.

"They both sidled up to me at the reception and put it out there."

"Put what out there?"

"Like if I could somehow arrange it, they would like to share him."

TJ lurched to the left and almost dumped her onto the flagstone.

"What! Like a ménage a' trios?"

"Yep."

TJ melted into the chair and smiled.

"Jesus, Patsy *and* Linda Lou. That's got to be every man's naughty dream."

Dannie poked him in the ribs a second time. Only harder.

"Men are such filthy beasts."

He laughed at the ceiling for a moment and then shrugged in agreement. They both looked at the commuter traffic for several minutes although Dannie's interest was much more passive.

"Do you think he might really show up?"

TJ thought about that for a moment, finger combing his beard. "Yeah," he finally said. "I think he might. Could be fun, don't you think?"

* * *

SIX

Everything Teal had left unattended on the balcony was gone in the morning – ravens and chipmunks had dined well and left only strips of cellophane behind. Teal decided on a punishment breakfast to start his new life. Nothing with a wisp of sugar or interesting taste. Lots of fiber, minerals and elements touted on late night TV and understood by few. His mind assured him of their positive effects – his stomach disagreed.

When he finished and left the restaurant under the pitying looks of the wait staff, all of whom seemed strangely keyed into the drama. He went to his room, changed into running clothes and started with a moderate jog to the south. After a mile he stopped and threw up the fiber and minerals, hanging on to a picket fence for support, while his stomach turned inside out. When he looked up, wiping his mouth with the back of his hand, he saw a little boy sitting in a sandbox twenty feet away and staring at him with open mouth. They locked eyes for a moment as Teal tried to smile. The effect must have been ghastly. The boy's eyes widened and he scrambled to his feet, picked up his dump truck and high tailed it back to a house set well off the road.

Jeez, poor kid's going to have awful dreams tonight!

He ran for three more miles, stumbling and staggering the final one before collapsing on the railing outside his room. The cleaning staff watched with alarm.

The following days he repeated the pattern. The maids and the staff watched everyday. He had become their obsession.

Whatever his focus, his problem, his final destination – it became theirs. Doubters wagered against him and supporters covered. None knew what they were really betting on, but all agreed they would know when it was over.

Teal ran all the compass points from the motel, finally finding the trails and paths that suited and challenged him. One of his favorites was up a steep trail in a state park. Serious runners frequented it and tourists rode to the top in a funky tram complete with fringed surrey top and canned travelogue. When Teal reached the summit after his first ascent, he thought his heart would burst. A runner, who had passed him on the way up, nodded and without hesitation started his jog back to the parking lot. Teal trudged after him with trembling legs. Less than two weeks later Teal came close to matching him stride for stride. At the summit the runner who was barely breathing hard held out his hand.

"My name's Ben. Hang in there."

"Jack," was all he could answer between gasps.

Ben smiled, and they jogged side by side down to the lot with lean tanned legs and contented smiles.

The following day Teal said goodbye to the manager and maids, checked out of his home of three weeks and headed north. His body was fit and his mind was clear.

* * *

SEVEN

His planned route was simple. He would drive north skirting Phoenix and on through Prescott and Sedona on his way to Flagstaff where he wanted to take a look at the museum at The University of Northern Arizona. From there he would be heading due west to San Diego where Koontzman kept his suite of offices. It was not the most direct route and that played a part in his plan. He would check into a motel to sleep when he felt tired or drive and play tourist when something piqued his interest. The freedom to act on an impulse and choice was a supreme luxury.

The Porsche ran flawlessly through the hot desert badlands and the pockets of cool air lurking in the canyons, as he edged around the western flank of Phoenix. There was little traffic on the secondary road as it wound through a shallow pass, and Teal increased his speed on some of the cambered turns. Out of the corner of his eye he was just able to catch a glimpse of a sign cautioning fifty-five at the entrance to a blind curve and started to bring the car down from seventy. When his eyes readjusted to the road ahead in what must have been less than half a second, he was staring at the tailgate of a stalled pickup in his lane with a woman and a young boy standing well off on the shoulder.

He yanked the steering wheel to the left feeling the rear tires break traction throwing the car into a backwards skid. Careening past the pickup, he caught a glimpse of pure terror on the woman's face. In the next instant the Porsche snapped back in the opposite direction while he fought to gain control. The car skidded up an embankment and bounced over a rocky outcropping, then performed a lazy three-hundred-sixty-degree spin and slowly backed down to the highway.

Teal's hands still gripped the wheel and shook violently for a moment before he opened the door and ran, half stumbled, over to the woman and boy.

"Are you all right?" he asked and touched her shoulder. She was shaking badly and flinched at his touch. Teal kneeled in front of the crying boy. "How about you?"

The boy nodded vigorously, hair flying, and looked terrified.

"I th-thought you were g-going to crash into our truck. But you j-just crashed your car," the boy said with a stammer looking back and forth between the truck, the Porsche and Teal. Teal wondered for a second if he was doomed to spend the rest of his life scaring the crap out of little boys.

"My God, I'm so sorry you wrecked your car," the woman said in an almost whisper. "The truck just stopped and wouldn't move. I don't know what happened. I called for a tow truck, but I didn't know what else to do." She was wringing her hands.

Jack ran back to the Porsche and found flares in the trunk, which he lit and laid one about fifty yards on either side of the truck, then trotted back to the woman. At the same time a tow truck slowly rounded the turn from the north and pulled in next to Teal. He carefully studied the truck and the Porsche and finally, Teal.

"Had yourself a wild ride up that hill looks like to me."

He had the broad brown face and careful eyes of a Navajo.

"Yep. Scared the hell out of me."

"You look the other side of that hill, you gonna be real scared," he said slowly. "Goes down, oh, about two, three hundred feet and ends up in a dry creek bed. Don't think that pretty little car would look so good down there."

"I don't think I'll look. Already have the shakes."

"You want me to call you a tow?"

"Let me check it out while you're hooking up the truck. Don't think I hit anything, so it may be okay."

The driver nodded and positioned the wrecker to hook up the truck. Teal started the Porsche and backed across the road. The engine sounded strong and ran without any hiccups, but there was a tiny shudder he felt through the steering wheel.

"I think I can probably limp into Phoenix," Teal said to the man who had completed his hook up. "Is there someone in town who can take a look at it?"

"Yeah, there's a Porsche dealer in Scottsdale. Ain't too bad from what I hear."

"Wait a minute," Teal said, remembering. "Isn't there an independent guy, can't remember his name, works on Porsches."

"Probably thinkin' of Jason's place. Jason Easy," the man said with a broad smile.

"Yeah. That's it. How 'bout him?"

"Well he's the best – no denying that. But you're going to have a hell of a time gettin' in. He's backed up for months from what I hear."

"Well how 'bout I follow you, and see how far I can get."

The little caravan started down the road after the driver gave Teal the address and directions for Easy Motors. Teal found that below fifty the Porsche was comfortable, but above, the front suspension began to shake getting worse with each additional mile per hour. The procession limped into Phoenix and when the tow driver pulled into a Ford agency, he waved Teal past, and they honked farewell.

Teal shuddered along for another mile, hooked two quick rights and found a low-lying building fronting a large fenced lot in the rear. The sign in the front proclaimed 'Easy Motors'; and in smaller letters 'If we can't fix it, you shouldn't own it!'

Teal pulled into the front parking area and entered the tiny waiting room. It was clean, had an interesting array of current magazines and a coffee maker that didn't smell burned. It was also empty. Teal looked back into the shop through the glass door and saw five Porsches, some on lifts, and all being tended by men in shop coats. A radio was playing *Desperados* by The Eagles and two of the mechanics tried to match the harmony while a third laughed, said something Teal couldn't hear and shook his head. He turned for just a moment to see if his car was still where he had left it and when he turned back a woman was leaning over the coffee pot filling two Styrofoam cups.

"With you in a sec," she said over her shoulder.

"Sure. No hurry," he answered trying not to stare at her blue jean hip pockets.

She turned around with the two cups of coffee and smiled.

"I'll inform Mister Easy he has a customer," she said in a neutral voice that somehow sounded sexy.

Teal tried to say 'sure' and 'okay' and maybe 'fine' at the same time. What came out sounded vaguely Middle Eastern and possibly obscene. She grinned and left him standing rooted to the floor. The vision of her face had blasted through his eyes, slashed through his optic nerves and been branded into his brain in a split second. If he lived another three hundred years, locked away in a home for other three hundred year-olds, he would remember the instant he first saw her face. Large wide-spaced green eyes, high cheekbones and a full lower lip.

A pile of dark blond hair carelessly piled high and held in place by a silver barrette. Nose a shade off center – maybe broken when she was a little kid and set by the local vet. Absolutely no makeup and no need for it. Beautiful was not the right word. All the other one-word descriptions seemed pathetically inadequate. She was all of them and much more. Most probably a one-person category. He scratched the back of his neck and wiped his hand over his lips. Had he been drooling? Probably.

He laughed and quickly looked around to see if anyone had heard him. A stocky man was walking across the garage floor wiping his hands on a red shop rag. Entering the waiting room, he smiled at Teal and stuffed the rag in his shop coat.

"Can I help you?"

"Yes, are you Mister Easy? Your secretary said she was going to fetch you."

The man laughed quickly, and his eyes crinkled at the corners.

"Sloan? Sloan's my daughter. You call her a secretary, and she'll tear your tongue out. Sloan doesn't take any prisoners."

"Sloan?" Teal asked liking the sound of it while curious about the prisoners comment.

"Yep. It was her grandmother's name. We both sort of liked it."

Teal nodded and quickly outlined what had happened and asked if Easy could check out the car.

"Wish I could, but I'm out about two to three weeks. You can leave it if you want, and we'll let you know when we get into it."

"Shoot, I was hoping to get to the coast sometime next week."

Easy shook his head. "The Porsche agency might slip you in. I could give 'em a call."

Teal thought for a moment. "Well, Bet over in Kaycee said you were the best, so I thought I'd try."

Easy grinned slowly and scratched his cheek.

"You been to Kaycee? Jesus." He nodded slowly and looked at the ceiling. "Arnie still cooking and grousing?"

"Yes to both. I had the Cowboy Stew for lunch."

"Good Lord! And you're still walking around?"

He laughed again and hollered back into the shop. "Hey, Sloan. This fella's been visiting Kaycee. Ate that damn Cowboy Stew, too."

She came out of a side office and walked into the waiting room with a smile.

"This is my daughter Sloan. Couldn't run the place without her."

"Hi. Jack Teal." Her hand was cool and strong and her green eyes direct and seemed slightly amused. Teal wondered if something from breakfast was stuck to his lip, and he unconsciously rubbed his chin.

"I'll tell you what," Easy finally said, breaking the handshake, which had gone on a tick too long. "I'll take a look at it first thing tomorrow, and we'll sort of go from there."

"Thanks, Mister Easy. I'd really appreciate that," Teal said while secretly hoping that the repairs might take two weeks. "Can you recommend a motel I can cab to?"

"Yeah. Crazy Horse Lodge is just up the road. Great digs if you got a couple of bucks on you – it ain't cheap."

"Sounds great," Teal said.

"Well, bring your rig around back and take what you need out of it."

"Dad, I can run him up to Crazy Horse," Sloan said slowly like she was making up her mind at that moment. "I'm done with the accounts and have to do some shopping up north anyway."

"Okay, but don't scare him, sweetheart. He might be a paying customer," he said and chuckled. "I'll let you know tomorrow – leave a message if you're out," he said to Teal.

Jason filled out a work order, and Teal drove the Porsche into the fenced area behind the shop. He pulled out his duffle and suitcase just as Sloan was slipping into the seat of a silver Carrera 4 convertible. Teal joined her scrunching into the passenger seat and tossing his bags in the back.

"Thanks. I really appreciate this."

"You're welcome," she answered with that same amused look in her eyes. Teal thought that if keeping her amused meant keeping her close, well, that would work.

With fluid movements she started the car, dropped the shift lever into first, and they shot out of the parking lot like a dragster. Teal caught a glimpse of a wide grin on Easy's face, as they rocketed by.

For the next four or five minutes Teal had trouble breathing. She drove faster than Teal had ever ridden in a car, much less in downtown commute traffic, and the performance would have put any New York cabbie to shame. Convertibles, SUVs and sports cars disappeared in their slipstream like so much flotsam and jetsam. Teal had a death grip with one hand on the lip of his seat and the other on the dash. He was only slightly comforted by the thought that at this speed they most certainly would be killed instantly. Body parts strewn over the roadway like the leftovers from a McDonald's bag. No lingering comatose and pain racked bodies lying in some critical care unit with sobbing relatives and somber clergy lurking in the shadows.

When she finally tapped the brakes and downshifted, they entered the hotel's circular drive at a modest pace. Teal was still blinking away tears.

"Do you always drive like that?" he finally asked.

"I just don't see any sense in dawdling along. Life's too short. Plus," she added with a grin, "I know every cop in town."

Teal felt his breathing returning to normal but would be willing to bet his blood pressure was still off the charts.

"Anyway, thanks for the ride," he said unfolding out of the seat and collecting his bags. "Do they have a restaurant here or is there a better place to eat near by?" he asked quickly not wanting her to leave.

"No and yes, a bunch. La Mesa's the best though. As a matter of fact, I'm going up there for dinner tonight."

They stared at each other for a long moment. His heart had ceased beating.

"Maybe you'd like to tag along," she finally said.

"You mean like a date?"

"Too soon to tell," she answered with a laugh.

"Sure," he finally answered. "One condition."

She cocked an eyebrow – waiting.

"I get to drive."

She laughed again. "I thought you were going to say you'd buy me dinner or something dumb like that. Be nice to see the scenery from the passenger's seat for a change. I'll pick up at seven."

She started the car still looking at him. "Do you have any cowboy duds?"

He shook his head – worried.

"Good," she said. "I think they look stupid."

And then she was gone.

* * *

EIGHT

Teal shaved twice and nicked himself four times. Looking at his toilet paper-festooned face in the bathroom mirror was not pleasant. He looked like a yacht regatta, and when he laughed, the scraps of paper fluttered like tiny butterflies. After glancing at his watch for the fortieth time, he stripped it from his wrist and flung it on the bed where it bounced high and landed on the plush carpet.

What in the hell is going on here? She's just a girl. Well, a woman. But I'm acting like a pimply kid.

When he saw her drive into the motel circle, he had been waiting in the lobby for fifteen minutes reading a months old *Time* magazine article about vapid looking girl named Paris Hilton. He hadn't the faintest idea who she was.

The Porsche burbled quietly as he pushed opened the door, flustered, pretending he had just raced from his room thinking he might be late. It was a weak charade.

"Hi," she said surrendering the driver's seat.

"Hi," he answered afraid to offer another word.

Strong and quiet. A brooding man carrying a world of problems on his broad shoulders.

She directed, and he drove. He enjoyed the suppleness of the car and its incredible power although all that was overshadowed by the sense of Sloan's presence and the sensation she was staring at him. When he looked over, her eyes would slide away and that smile would flit across her lips. She was wearing a silver satin dress that was cut to mid-thigh, a teal blue sweater across her shoulders, and a pair of matching medium heel pumps. She was also wearing very subtle touches of makeup and perfume. She was so extraordinarily beautiful, Teal knew if he kept glancing over he was going to jump the road and plow into a burro or a saguaro.

So mostly they rode in comfortable silence; Teal enjoying the scents of the desert and the pockets of warm air tucked away in the cooling evening. Sloan leaned back in her seat, humming something and letting the wind play with her hair. Occasionally she held her hand out in the wind stream like a kid letting it swoop and soar. Teal thought that if they were embarking on a two thousand mile trip, all would be right with the world.

The restaurant seemed to be perched on the edge of creation with a sensational view of the valley below. Teal opened the heavy oak door set in multihued sandstone and adorned with Mimbres figures, and it moved as light as a screen door. He noticed that every male eye in the bar followed Sloan's movement through to the dining room. Some furtive, like a couple of the guys in her dad's shop, afraid that they might be caught in the act and some bolder, fueled by Jack Daniels or single malts.

"Why the big grin?" she asked over her shoulder.

"Nothing. Well, I guess it sort of looks like every guy in here would like to be your friend."

She laughed. "And it appeared to me as if every woman was looking at your fanny."

They ate steaks, baked potatoes, sautéed mushrooms and a Caesar salad; a glass of Pinot Blanc with the salad and an excellent Cabernet Franc with the steak. Everything was perfectly prepared and served. They talked about the food, her dad's shop and Scottsdale. When she asked, he gave her the expanded version about the loss of his job in Atlanta and his trip to California. She seemed satisfied and asked few questions. As the evening flowed by, she seemed to change slightly; became somehow softer, gentler, less with the smart mouth. Teal wondered if the wine was kicking in. Whatever the reason, he liked it. He liked her and found himself staring when they weren't talking or eating.

A man came in from the bar, greeted her, and she allowed him to kiss her on the cheek but offered no introductions. He chatted for a moment before joining his friends in the bar where there was a round of laughter.

"Ex boyfriend?" he asked slightly amazed that he had felt a solid whap of jealousy.

"Doesn't he wish," she said, playing the hardass again.

Sloan drove back to the motel easing the Porsche through long sweeping turns and shifting with such fluid ease, it created the illusion the car was floating on air. At one point while Teal was telling her a funny story about an old friend, he touched her on the arm making the punch line. They both laughed, and he left his hand there a few extra seconds.

"I'm going to rent a car and drive up to Flagstaff tomorrow. I'd like to see the museum up there," he said when they pulled up before the motel "Would you like to join me?"

She tilted her head slightly as if picturing the trip. "Sure. But let's take this buggy."

He agreed and slipped out of the car having figured out how to do it without looking like an arthritic giraffe. When he turned to say goodbye, she was standing next to him, her face flushed and her eyes luminous. She kissed him lightly on the lips and brushed a hand over his cheek, stepped quickly around the car and disappeared into the night like a rocket sled.

In the morning Teal took a quick run around a small park next to the motel and showered. He pulled the suitcase down from the closet, unlocked it and checked the bundles of hundreds and the SIG. Perhaps it was the morning light filtering in his window that made the bundles look dusty and used. He picked up a packet, hefted its weight and squirreled it back into place.

When he called the shop, he was surprised Jason Easy answered the phone.

"Oh hell, we always get here early. Get some work done while it's still cool. And your rig doesn't look bad at all. You got a bent rim and wasted tire and we'll need to replace the right strut and bushings. Good news is we can have it Monday – early afternoon – bad news is that it's going to run you right around fifteen hundred. Maybe a little less."

"Sounds good to me," Teal answered thinking that Koontzman's credit card could pay for that. He was also wondering if Easy knew where his daughter would be today.

When he came out of the motel, Sloan was just getting out of the Porsche, and he touched her shoulder before sliding in the car. She wore hiking shorts and a t-shirt that said 'EASY MOTORS' on the front with 'Don't even go there!' in smaller red letters below. Teal laughed and she joined him, a little embarrassed.

"So what do people call you? Any nick names?" Teal asked as he adjusted the passenger seat.

"They call me Sloan. But there was a kid at high school who called me Slo'An'Easy. Thought he was a comedian."

They drove for a few miles. "So what happened with that?" Teal asked.

She sighed. "They found him in the spring. Not much left – you know with the coyotes and badgers."

He stared at her until she started laughing.

They drove through several small towns, finally stopping in one to have coffee. They sipped a scalding brew at a table overlooking the main street with a table of teenagers as the only other customers.

"Are you guys scouting a movie site?" the boldest finally asked with some peer prompting.

"Why do you ask?" Teal said with a Dirty Harry scowl.

The bold one wilted but his female companion pressed the issue. "Because you're a fox, and you guys are driving a Porsche Carrera."

Teal winked at Sloan. "You guys have to keep it under your hat. Competition, you know."

There was lots of jostling and 'told you so' while Teal dropped some bills on the table, and they made a quick exit.

They visited the museum of Northern Arizona and enjoyed the world's finest collection of Anazasi pottery. Later they were caught kissing beneath the famous cliff dwelling, Montezuma's Castle, by a gaggle of Brownies. The little girls giggled and were sternly hushed by a woman with a walking stick and permanent scowl.

"You know they have motels locally," the woman said with a hiss.

"How long have you been living with your dad?" Sloan was driving, and they were sliding through a canyon, playing hide and seek with the sun.

"About four years now. I was getting my masters at Arizona State in archeology. Then Mom was diagnosed with cancer and four months later she was gone. Hell, we hadn't even adjusted to the fact that she was sick."

She cleared her throat, and Teal put his hand on her shoulder.

"Dad just flat crashed. He lost it. We were all scared to death," she said taking off her dark glasses and swiping angrily at her eyes. "Finally I couldn't watch it anymore. I packed up all my crap and showed up on his doorstep. He pretended he was pissed, but his eyes would have torn your heart out."

She looked over and smiled. "Been there ever since, and I couldn't be happier."

Outside the motel and hidden between two pickup trucks, they kissed with such a feverish intensity, it left Teal slightly dizzy. He gently pulled her hand leading her towards his room, but she shook her head, and they stood quietly holding each other.

"What are you doing tonight? We could catch dinner and maybe a late movie," he asked.

"Oh, I've got plans," she said and smiled.

"How about tomorrow? Maybe a hike or something."

She shook her head. "Sorry, I can't."

Teal considered hunting down his competition and drilling him with the SIG. Of course, someone who had major problems offing a skunk probably wouldn't make a great assassin.

"But if you're not otherwise engaged and can fit me into your busy calendar, perhaps you would like to join me and papa and watch the Cards kick the crap out of the 49ers on Sunday."

Teal thought he might reply with a clever rejoinder, but it was easier to say 'sure' and smile like a brain-dead hayseed.

She blew out the parking lot with her standard exit scenario, and he stood in the cooling evening wondering what in the hell he was doing. His simple plan had become complex, but it was hard for him to find fault in the radical change. They would have to talk. At some time she would have to know who he was and where he had been. And what would that mean to her? He didn't know, but he did know the lies would have to stop.

* * *

NINE

Saturday seemed like one the longest days in Teal's life, made doubly agonizing by a spike in the temperature. All of Phoenix and Scottsdale retreated behind mountains of wheezing, whistling and clanking air conditioning units. He checked his locked suitcase stashed on the high shelf of the room's closet. The lock was solid, and the leather appeared to have a very thin coating of dust.

Teal had never really had a home since graduating from college. When he had a job before meeting and working for Koontzman, he lived in an Atlanta apartment building that was eminently forgettable and all it inhabitants strangers to each other.

When he was working for Koontzman, there had been a network of ultra safe houses scattered across the southwest and Pacific Coast states, which could be used for a night or two and some as long as a month or longer. He had stayed in several for short periods and always found them comfortable and well stocked if somewhat bland.

His parent's house in Colorado where he had been raised had never been an option after his incarceration.

When the DEA and Texas Rangers assisted by the local police popped him, and he was quickly sentenced to prison, there was very little for the authorities to confiscate. There was the leased BMW M3 of course, but no big screen TVs, expensive sound systems or gold chains. And no Rolex. He also carried very little money and a single credit card that matched

the false name on his driver's license, a misdemeanor that the
DA tossed out.

He always traveled quick and light, like a hummingbird,
never spending time in any house or county he could call home.
His future, as he had always seen it, laid tucked away in a safety
deposit box, and the key placed in trusted hands. That had
always been his focus.

Sloan picked him up mid morning, and they drove east
out of Scottsdale and up into the plateau country, some of
which was being developed into ranchettes.

"What the hell is a ranchette, anyway?" he asked looking
at a sign in front of some of the new construction.

"Sort of like an expensive house with some acreage. Of
course, no livestock. Well, maybe a llama or a pygmy goat."

Teal nodded pretending it all made sense.

"You have fun yesterday?" he asked.

"Sure," she said arching an eyebrow. "How 'bout
yourself?"

"Peachy. I went to a mall where they sell God awful
expensive things that nobody needs, meaning everybody has to
have them."

"Have you been living in a cave?" she said and laughed.

Jason Easy's ranchette was all adobe, stucco and tile
and conformed to most of the local architecture. The roof
was peaked with extended eaves while the house was low and
sprawling and determined to take maximum advantage of the
spectacular views. While Jason swore at the barbeque, Sloan
and Teal toured the house. Every time they entered a darkened
room or found themselves tucked behind some massive piece

of Mission furniture Jason seemed to favor, they caressed each other and kissed for as long as Teal thought would be safe. When they joined Jason on the patio, he looked at them and smiled.

"Air conditioning not working in the house?"

Teal swallowed and stared at the television, while Sloan smiled and kissed her dad on the cheek.

They watched the game until San Francisco was up by three touchdowns and driving for a fourth. Jason finally slammed the off button on the remote and threw it at the couch.

"Enough. How much can a man take for Christ's sakes?"

Sloan grinned, and he smiled at her with a tenderness that almost made Teal feel like an interloper.

"Okay then. Let's go see what really makes the world go round," he said slapping the arms of his chair. "Ribs are gonna take a while longer."

The garage behind the house was as clean and neat as his repair shop in Scottsdale. Along one wall was a well equipped machine shop with more tools than Teal had ever seen in a private garage. He couldn't even guess as to the function of some of them. Another wall was dominated by an enormous glass case filled with trophies, silver plates and bowls, racing programs and ribbons. Teal scanned the plaques, most of which were for first place. Some of the names sounded vaguely familiar: Laguna Seca, Riverside and Phoenix International Raceway. Others: Willow Springs, Torey Pines and Vaca Valley meant nothing.

"I don't see too many second place trophies here," Teal said.

"They're all tucked away behind the first place ones," Sloan said, and Jason chuckled.

Finally Jason proudly pulled the cover from his gleaming, sky blue Porsche 550 Spyder, which he had driven in vintage races throughout the western states.

"I got her cheap," he said and caressed a fender like a lover. "Some LA bozo bought her years ago after she won the European Hill Climb Championship and kept her squirreled away in a collection out by Oxnard. Then he sold her years later to a wannabe racer out of San Diego. He tried her out at Willow Springs and came in white as a sheet after ten laps. Said the car was a death trap – and I happened to be standing right there with a pocket full of money and little brains. My lucky day.

"Sloan named her Baby Blue after a song some guy sung. You know – that guy who sounds like he's been drinking battery acid and sort of talks his way through it?"

"Would that be Bob Dylan?" Teal asked, and Sloan beamed.

"Dad why don't you take Jack out for a little spin," Sloan said with something in her smile. "Baby Blue hasn't been worked out in a while. Probably could use the exercise."

"Peach of an idea," Jason said winking at her and opening the driver's door. He slipped into the seat with practiced ease.

"Do I need a helmet or goggles or anything?" Teal asked, more than a little concerned with Sloan's broadening grin.

"Naw, Naw. We're just going to putter around for a couple of minutes. Won't even muss your hair."

Jason fired the engine, and the bellow from the single stinger pipe was deafening. Jack sat with his knees tucked up into his chest and gave Sloan a forlorn wave as they backed out of the garage. Moments later they were moving through the warmth of the late afternoon, the little car snarling and clinging to the road. The pace was not leisurely, but neither was it frantic, and Teal began to enjoy the ride. There was no conversation.

They had almost completed a broad loop of four or five miles and were headed back in the direction of the house. The speed had picked up dramatically, and Teal cast a tearing eye at the dash trying to find a speedometer. Ahead of them was a long stretch of perhaps half a mile, followed by a long gradual left hand sweeping turn leading to a short straight before the house. As the speed increased, and the turn galloped towards them, every muscle in Teal's body began to strain as he braced himself against the door and the skimpy dash. They could not make it at this speed his brain shrieked, as they entered the turn. The spyder, cocked at an angle, drifted through the turn, neatly clipping the apex of the corner and straightening out. Jason downshifted three times in quick succession with the exhaust howling and popping and leisurely crept into the driveway.

"I heard you go through Hillcrest turn," Sloan said walking up to the car. "So don't come limping in here like you're on a moped or something. You know Ned's going to be on the phone in a minute or so complaining his head off."

"We were just loafing," he said as he corked the stinger pipe and pulled the cover over the car. Sloan shook her head and sighed.

"I looked at the dash and the speedometer said we were going seventy," Jack said. "Felt a hell of a lot faster than that!"

"No speedo in this car," Jason said with a grin. "That's the tach. We were just loafing along at about seventy-five hundred RPM."

"That's about a hundred and thirty five," Sloan said, calculating quickly, then looked at Teal's face and tried to hide the giggles behind her hands.

"I think I've just found religion," Teal stuttered.

Jason slapped him on the back and crowed. "Well, by God, that's what I thought the first time I drove her!"

The three of them gnawed barbequed ribs and sipped a zinfandel on a veranda overlooking the valley, watching lights blink on like wakening fireflies. They talked about Arizona, vintage sports car racing, the Porsche repair business, and danced around politics the way strangers will.

"Friday night me and Sloan went to see that new spy thriller? Couldn't figure the damn thing out."

Teal suddenly realized who his alleged competition was and grinned at Sloan in the dark. She nudged him in the ribs and scowled.

They talked for more than an hour, and Teal sensed that the relaxed conversation was a personal routine between Jason and Sloan. He felt privileged to be within their circle, and thought about the kindness of Bet in Kaycee while wondering why more of these people had not entered his life before now.

When Sloan drove him back to the motel, they were quiet, content and consumed with their thoughts. He kissed her by the car and trudged up to his room knowing sleep would not come easily. He opened the door, closed it behind him and stood motionless in the darkened room for almost a minute. When he reached towards the light switch, he heard a sound at the door – a light tapping or hesitant scratching.

He listened until his ears ached, finally turned and opened the door. Sloan stood in the muted light from the hall with her eyes downcast and shoulders shaking. Teal thought she might have been crying. He took her shoulders and brought her to him and into the room. They backed across the room until tumbling onto the bed while grasping at buttons and zippers and laughing like children. A button popped and caromed off the nightshade with a loud ping. The only light in the room seeped through a slit in the curtains and Teal's early suspicions were absolutely correct – sleep did not come for a long, long time.

Once he awoke in the middle of the night and stared at Sloan lying next to him, body slight curled with hair tousled and hiding her face. He was staring at something – a small tattoo – low on her back. It was a rearing black horse no more than two inches high with its mane flaring off its arched neck. When he glanced at her, one green eye was staring at him though the tangle of hair.

"I was looking at the horsey tattooed on your butt," he said somewhat apologetically.

"That's not a 'horsey'. It's a proud stallion. And that's my hip not my butt."

Teal could see part of a smile through the hair. "Isn't that the Ferrari symbol?" he asked.

"If you knew any thing about anything you would know the Porsche badge has a rearing horse just like this one. Much better looking than that Ferrari nag."

Teal grinned at her and said, "So do you think it would be alright if I kissed the proud stallion."

Sloan made a sound deep in her throat and said, "That would be nice."

When he awoke shortly before dawn, Sloan was gone but the memory of the past six hours had tattooed his soul.

* * *

TEN

Everything: thoughts, plans, intentions, had been thrown into a vortex of confusion. Suitcases of money, vaguely anticipated meetings in San Diego, a renewed future in California and the world meant nothing. Teal had never in his life felt this way. He felt stupid, yet incredibility elated like a fantastic drug high, giddy and giggly like a fool. He wanted to be with Sloan. In his mind, it was really as simple as that. Together they would travel the world, have babies who squealed and smelled of powder, go to granddad's races and celebrate a dream life forever.

He checked out of the motel and, with his two suitcases took a cab to Easy Motors a few minutes before noon. In the waiting room he saw Jason walking towards him across the shop floor with several papers in his hand.

Watching him approach, Teal felt a chill slide down his spine as if he had kicked off his blanket on a cool night. Jason entered the room walking stiffly and would not meet his eyes.

Jesus, he knows about last night!

But Teal knew that he could put all of that to rest. He loved Sloan and wanted her to be the touchstone of his future. Jason would certainly understand that.

"This is your bill. Are you going to pay by credit card?"

"Sure..."

"Well, I hope to fuck it's good."

Teal handed him the card trying to fathom what was happening. Jason ran it and handed Teal the slip. While he was signing it, he noticed the quiet in the shop. Everyone was watching the waiting room, and two men had stepped forward as if waiting for something to happen.

"Do you know what this thing is?" Jason suddenly asked holding a small plastic box in his hand. Teal looked at it and shook his head. Jason placed it carefully on the coffee stand.

"One of my guys tells me it's a very sophisticated satellite tracking device. GPS he called it with a motion activator. I wouldn't know it from a turkey's asshole, but he sure did. He did three tours in 'Nam, and I think he hung out with some spooks in Central America. He said this is very sophisticated and high tech and placed so the driver would not know. What I want to know is why it was hanging underneath your car?"

Teal stared at it without comprehension.

"I don't know what's going on here, and I don't really know diddley squat about you," Jason said, clearly very angry. "I know how Sloan feels about you, and I can't stop that. But you will not see her in my shop or at my house. She's not here now because I sent her out on a parts run. So what ever you're involved in, I sure as shit don't want my daughter hurt."

One of the two men in the shop had moved closer to the waiting room. He had a grim expression like a man spoiling for a fight.

"I want you to pick up your car and get out of my life and leave my baby alone."

Teal picked up the device from the table and looked at it without really seeing. Then he dropped it on the floor and crushed it under his heel. With everyone in the shop watching him carefully, he stepped out of the waiting room, loaded the car with his suitcases and pulled out into the flow of traffic that swept by the shop, with each and every one of his thoughts and concerns having nothing to do with the small tiled repair shop shimmering in the mid day heat.

* * *

"Sloan, it's Jack."

"God where are you? I've been worried something happened to you." Her voice sounded concerned and a little frightened. For a moment he could not speak past the restriction he felt in his throat.

"Sloan, I've got a problem I have to handle. I need to go somewhere for a while."

"What do you mean go somewhere?" she asked with her voice cracking. She was starting to cry.

Teal stared at the ceiling of the phone booth and felt a desperation he had never known. "There's a problem…"

"Jack you said that. What is it? Are you married? God, don't tell me you're married."

"Sloan, I'm not married, but I haven't been truthful with you. I've been in trouble with the law. I just got of prison."

He could hear her ragged breathing. "Did you hurt somebody?"

"No. That's not it."

"Jack, I love you. Whatever it is, we can face it together," she said in a rush.

"It's not that simple Sloan. I need to settle it – to get my head screwed on right."

"I'll help you," she said sobs racking her voice.

The conversation was driving a cold, stainless spike through his body.

"Sloan, I'm just outside of Las Vegas. I'll call you within a week. I love you…"

"Las Vegas! Oh my God…"

He gently placed the receiver on its cradle hearing her sobs fade away and then brutally cut off with a dull click. He slumped in the booth, dizzy and disoriented, angry and confused, his breath coming in gulps. Someone standing outside the booth started to lean in and say something. What he saw in Teal's face caused him to shrug and walk quickly away.

Teal shuffled back to the car in a stupor. He could reach San Diego in the very early morning. There would be time for sleeping then.

* * *

ELEVEN

When Teal awoke he felt as if the left half of his body, jammed against the door handle and arm rest, was paralyzed. He opened the door carefully to keep from sprawling on pavement of the parking lot adjacent to Old Town, San Diego. After rubbing some feeling into his arm, he watched his hand turn from a death pallor gray to rosy pink. From where he was parked he could see the building where Koontzman had his office on the eighth floor facing west towards the Pacific. He had watched the lights wink out shortly after he arrived in the dead of night – the last lights to extinguish in the building, with the exception of the stairwell security spots. Now the building, with the sun rising behind it, appeared as a bland, stone-colored structure devoid of architectural promise or civic dignity. It served its purpose; nothing more, nothing less.

He stared at it for almost half and hour knowing where the windows were and which room lay behind each, although he saw nothing except featureless reflections off the glass.

What would he say to Koontzman? In his mind it had always played like some sort of a reunion, long time friends or classmates getting together to revive old times and make some sort of plans for the future.

Would Koontzman even be there? He had houses in Mexico City, Santa Barbara, Paris and, of course, San Diego. There were apartments and suites in New York and London and probably others Teal never knew about. And if he were here, would he even want to see Teal. Of course, the question above all others: why had he bugged the car? Wasn't more than three years of Teal's life and silence worth a modicum of trust? He hated the feeling of hurt and betrayal that chewed at his gut.

What could I have been thinking? That we're fraternity brothers tried and true? Am I truly that naïve? Jesus – has my thinking process eroded to a point where reality is what I choose it to be?

He stared at the building until his eyes started to tear from the glare of the sun as it cleared the horizon. Even at this early hour the lot was starting to fill with tourists and joggers and people on their way to work, to breakfast or to see the sights. It was a strange combination of scrubbed children in striped tee shirts and jeans being prodded along by parents wearing clothes which had been buried in a trunk in Des Moines for at least three years, now sharing the sidewalks with three-piece suits, sports coats and jogging shorts. Cell phones and iPods squelched natural conversation. Even though they all had dissimilar destinations firmly in mind, most seemed to be eagerly looking forward to what the morning offered.

Teal watched the crowd for more than an hour wondering about their past lives and their futures. Were they happy? What were they looking forward to? Could any remember the exact moment they fell in love? Had any of them been to prison?

The sun was warm on his face and shoulders, and he knew he had to go somewhere to think – to slow down his mad rush towards what now seemed to be a fool's quest. Finally with a decision having been made through a process in which he seemed only a spectator, he slipped into the Porsche seat, sighed deeply when the vision of Sloan's laughing face floated through his mind and headed towards the San Diego Freeway to follow the stream north.

* * *

TJ and Dannie Fitz were waiting for him when he pulled
up in front of their house in Marin County the following day.
Teal had called them from a Travel Lodge in San Francisco, and
TJ sounded genuinely excited to hear his voice.

"Get your ass over here," he had said laughing. "Dannie
and I both get back from work around four. Anytime after
that's great."

TJ gave him a bear hug while Dannie stood back with
knitted fingers and smiled. Teal had forgotten how pretty she
was – almost luminous in this late afternoon light.

"So what the hell have you been up to?" TJ asked pulling
back and looking like a young Richard Dryfus. He had never
combed his hair a day in his life.

"Like everyone else. Just trying to get by on a buck and a
bottle of beer."

It was an old Michigan State saying, dumb even back
when he first heard it, but Dannie laughed along with them.

They had a glass of white wine on the tiny deck
overlooking the freeway between the house and the Bay.

"You're in marvelous Marin County now. We sip wine.
We don't chug beers. Well, not tonight anyway."

The Richmond-San Rafael Bridge arched away to the
eastern shore surrounded by earthquake refitting cranes which
looked like giant mantis tending a nest.

Their conversation was the type that happens when two
friends have not seen each other for a long period of time,
so the dead spots were filled with 'do you remember when?'
and 'So....' Each was vaguely aware of things left unsaid and
questions avoided, perhaps because there was so much to tell
in TJ's case and certain things, which couldn't be told in Teal's.
But it was still comfortable, and Teal felt his strained muscles

begin to ease. The intense highs and lows of the past few days had taken a toll on his body, and he felt exhausted.

The conversation was further fractured by TJ's fascination with the commute traffic.

"Jesus, look at that bozo in the Hummer!" TJ said excitedly while trying to arrange his glasses on the tip of his nose. The lenses sported several solid fingerprints and looked like something a child might wear. "God I love Hummers – the ultimate road rage vehicle. Wait, is she talking on a cell phone and tending a baby at the same time? Might be a first!"

"Some people build model airplanes or carve religious icons out of cheddar cheese," Dannie said dryly, leaning out of the kitchen. "You know, to ease their tensions. My husband likes to watch road rage." She was preparing pasta and keeping close track on the conversation.

"Yeah," he reminded wagging a finger at her, "as long as it doesn't involve extreme violence."

"And we thereby enter the extremely complex world of semantics. Your definition of extreme?" she asked cocking an eyebrow and nodding at Teal.

"I guess anything short of mace and chain," he mumbled with a shrug.

They refused to listen to Teal's requests for a good local motel. After a dinner salad chocked with chilies, chicken strips and avocados and the pasta laced with enough garlic to forever banish the Prince of Darkness, they wandered into the house. TJ cleared back the few pieces of furniture in their tiny den and pulled out a sofa bed, which Dannie made up in crisp sheets printed with lilacs and daffodils. His exhausted mind thought he heard her say, 'Welcome home, Jack' a second before quietly shutting the door. Several minutes later his mind was swept away in a deep, rippling sleep, haunted by the scent of Sloan's body.

Teal heard Dannie in the kitchen early, humming and opening cupboards. It reminded him of being at home on the weekends when his father was out of the house early to play golf, and his mother was preparing breakfast. The humming stopped, and Teal caught a faint whiff of coffee before drifting off again.

When he awoke, he found TJ sitting on the tiny deck, morning paper in one hand, mug of coffee in the other and one eye never straying far from the freeway.

"Morning," Teal said scratching his head.

"Hey, you sleep alright?"

"Big time. That little foldaway's pretty comfortable," Teal answered looking through the cupboard for a mug. He poured a cup and joined TJ on the deck. There was barely room for the two of them and the barbeque.

"She sits in my lap when we have company," TJ said reading Teal's mind. "Dannie didn't wake you, did she? When she's in the middle of inventory at the store, she tends to crash around in the morning. I suppose I could read something shrinky into that."

"No, she was fine. A little humming was all."

"I guess they must be about done then."

They sat and enjoyed the morning sun and coffee. TJ handed him part of the paper, and they read and sipped in comfortable silence.

"So how's San Diego and LA?" TJ finally asked.

"Jeez, you need to ask?" he answered, and TJ laughed.

"I was just passing through anyway. On my way from Texas," he added.

"Texas. There's another wonderful excuse for a place not to live," TJ said and snorted into his coffee mug. "So what have you been doing for the last – what is it – six years?" He was getting down to it now.

Teal sipped his coffee and stretched. "Nothing worth talking about. But I've saved up a couple of bucks, so I can be fancy free for a while. I'm thinking of running up to Seattle."

"Nice town but shitty weather. You'd do better to hang here for a while. Lots of sights to see. Good folks."

"Right now I'm enjoying a cup of coffee and watching that Mazda van drifting into another lane!"

"Where? Oh Jeez!"

They both watched the van snap back into its lane accompanied by the braying of a dozen horns. TJ grinning and shook his head.

"Boy, that got my blood going." He was a happy man.

"Tell me more about the restaurant?" Teal asked. TJ had mentioned it the night before, and Dannie had changed the subject. "I thought you wanted to be a shrink. Weren't you a psyc major?"

TJ put his mug on a table between them and shook his head sending curls in every direction. "Yeah, yeah. Too much school, too little money, too weird. I wanted a little hands on."

"Yeah, but a restaurant?"

"You know. You had some experience in 'em back in Michigan. They can be fun and some hit gold."

"Yeah TJ, but they're all a hell of a lot of work. And most of them turn out to be real heart aches and end up in the dumpster."

TJ looked at him and smiled an almost gentle smile. "You are certainly right there. Tell you what," he said in a brisk voice, which meant he had a plan. "Why don't you follow me down there and see what's going on. Maybe have some breakfast."

They finished their coffees, and Teal followed TJ's compact down the hill and into the small town of Larkspur. TJ motioned for Teal to park on the street while he maneuvered the compact down a narrow alley. Several seconds later, he trotted out of the alley and joined him on the sidewalk. He had a huge grin and was swinging his arms. Several people on the sidewalk greeted TJ or nodded.

"You're going to love this place. Just like that bistro where you slung hash back in Michigan."

"TJ, that was a god damn fraternity house!" he said, but it fell on deaf ears.

Magnolia Street was lined with freshly planted trees protected by white bricks and fancy wire, and the restaurant was tucked between what looked to be an upscale bookstore and a wine shop. MAGNOLIA CAFÉ in shaded brown block letters was painted on the window with 'fine food' below looking like a remnant from a previous venture. TJ pushed open the oak door, and they entered a room that appeared to be at least three times longer than its width. The walls were used brick with casually applied mortar, which had darkened over the years. They appeared to be the original walls of the decades old building. The room was well lighted with hidden spots, highlighting the tables scattered throughout the length of the room while landscape watercolors graced the walls. The kitchen occupied the final quarter of the room with a narrow corridor leading back to a storeroom and what appeared to be a small office with file cabinets.

Before he could look at any other details of the room, a teen-aged girl came towards them. She was skipping.

"Hiya boss. Who's the stud muffin?" she asked studying Teal close enough to be a clear violation of his personal space.

"Good morning, Ginny. I'm glad to see you way up today. And this is my friend Jack Teal."

"Well hi there, Jack," she said batting her eyes. "You can follow me home any time."

"Ginny..." TJ started to protest, but she was gone skipping back towards the kitchen. It was only then Teal realized most of the customers at scattered tables were chuckling. After watching in amusement for a few moments, they turned back to their breakfasts and morning papers.

"She's our hostess," TJ said scratching the back of his neck, his eyes drifting along a wall over Teal's shoulder.

Before Teal could respond, there was a burst of Japanese from the kitchen sounding like an assault rifle on full automatic.

"I'll be right back," TJ said as he rushed back towards the kitchen. Teal heard urgent whispers, and the chattering slowed, and then ceased.

"Well, let's have some breakfast," TJ said feigning a relaxed attitude but rubbing his hands like a pawnbroker.

They sat at a deuce, and a young man as thin as a lodge pole pine approached them, laid two menus on the table and then stepped back and stood at attention.

"Thanks Tim," TJ said, "Give us a minute to look at the menu. But why don't you pull us a couple of espressos."

Wordlessly the young man turned and shuffled back to the espresso stand, and Teal could hear the clatter and hiss of the machine.

"Pulls the best lattes you've ever had," TJ said looking everywhere but at Teal. "Jump starts your heart for the next two days."

The chattering started again in the kitchen followed by a credible soprano with a stirring rendition of La *Marseillaise.* TJ glanced at a table back by the kitchen and a young man with a rugby pullover folded his paper and strolled into the kitchen. The chattering and singing stopped, followed by several giggles. The rugby player strolled back out, sat and unfolded his paper.

Tim brought back the espressos, set them down carefully and stepped back turning into a statue and staring at the wall above their heads with the unfocused eyes of a four-year-old watching Saturday morning television. TJ studied his menu as if he had never laid eyes on it, while Teal waited for the next surprise.

"Sammy's scramble is dynamite," TJ said, "Signature dish for the restaurant."

"That's good enough for me," Teal said and slapped his menu on the table. Tim flinched and reached over gingerly to retrieve the menu giving Teal a wide berth.

"And the regular for you, TJ?"

TJ nodded and passed over his menu. He now suddenly seemed defeated, and Teal felt a wave of sympathy sweep over him. "Really a nice looking restaurant," was all he could say. Even to his ears, it sounded lame.

After breakfast TJ stayed to operate the restaurant, and Teal left to take care of errands. The Sammy Scramble had been excellent, but everything else in the restaurant had been off by several degrees. Teal felt as if he had stepped through Lewis Carroll's looking glass. If TJ asked his opinion, and he knew he would, Teal would be trapped. To lie or not to lie. He didn't want to think about it.

Teal found several repair shops in a Marin County phone book specializing in Porsches. He wrote them all down and picked up a map at a local Seven-Eleven. The first shop seemed too upscale with an impressive neon sign and brightly lit shop. The second, in a worn down part of south San Rafael, appeared to be perfect.

After a minute in the waiting room, a mechanic came in wiping his hands. The shop and the manager bore little resemblance to Easy Motors. And that was what Teal wanted.

"Help you?" The man was lean and sly looking with a greasy spot of hair on his chin.

"Yeah. I need someone to check out my car for something that shouldn't be there."

"Shouldn't be there? Like what?" the man asked tilting his head. Interested.

"Like a tracking device. Some bullshit like that."

The man wiped his already clean hands and looked out the roll up door.

"I might could look at it day after tomorrow."

Teal pulled out five hundred dollar bills and fanned them. "It'll take you less than half an hour for five bills right now. Off the books."

The man glanced out the roll up a second time, and then shouted back into the shop. "Clear that 911 off number three!"

Five minutes later Teal's car was on the hoist, and they were under it with a trouble light. Two other mechanics glanced over but said nothing.

"You had some recent work done on the front suspension. Good clean work," he said and nodded while probing with the light. In ten minutes he was done and snapped off the light.

"Well there was something there, but it's been torn off. See here – way back up in the fender well. I missed it first time around. Just two screws and a shard of plastic."

It was almost impossible to see, and Teal felt it with his fingertips.

"Then up here on this strut there was something about the size of a cigarette lighter that's been cleanly removed. You can still see the outline. So you really had two 'somethings', about the same size," he said with sleepy eyes.

He checked inside of the car for another five minutes peering in places Teal would not have thought to look.

"It's clean," he finally announced, and Teal handed him the bills.

"Pleasure doing business," the man said making the money disappear. "You got any other business you want me to handle, I'll be here."

Teal drove over to a small bayside park serving as a bird sanctuary and sat in the car watching the birds wade, bobbing their heads and searching for food. A young woman with two small children dressed in quilted jackets against the cool of the afternoon was feeding some mallards in the parking lot.

There were probably two trackers Teal realized; one relatively easy to find and one well hidden. One had been torn off in the accident, and Jason Easy's crew had found the second. And there was little question about their intent. But why?

Teal stared at the marsh wondering why they had done it. None of it made sense, and all of it left him uneasy. He felt certain that Rukka was behind it, but that didn't ease the anger. His feelings of betrayal merely pissed him off, but he couldn't shake it.

TJ and Dannie were waiting for him later that afternoon.

"We were worried that you might have taken off after one night on that foldaway," TJ said with a nervous grin.

"Naw. I just drove out to the coast. Beautiful! Beats the hell out of most places I've seen."

"Well, get in here then," Dannie said. "We're putting some steaks on the barbie."

Teal and TJ sipped Coronas on the deck while Dannie prepared a salad but was never far from the window or door where she could hear their conversation. TJ talked, babbled really, about everything except the restaurant. He also paid little attention to the freeway traffic.

Finally Teal put both his hands in the air. "Time out," he said, "what's going on here?"

Dannie came out of the kitchen and deposited herself in TJ's lap. TJ let his shoulders slump, and he stared at the bottom rung of the railing.

"I think it's time you fess up, don't you? Make you sleep easier and stop poking and kicking me," Dannie said.

TJ sighed deeply. "Jack, what do you think of Magnolia Café?" he finally asked. "Straight shot – no bullshit."

Teal was aware of the intensity of their eyes on him. He glanced down at the freeway hoping for a massive accident to divert their attention.

"Well Jeez, TJ, what can I say? It's a pretty nice layout, and the scramble was great. But everything else seems – like a little off kilter – out of step. Staff seems to need a little training." He hesitated for a moment. "But most of all you seemed very nervous to have me there. Maybe that was just my imagination," he finished with a wave of his hand.

To his surprise both TJ and Dannie seemed to relax and smile at each other. Finally Dannie poked TJ in the shoulder.

"Okay, okay," he said trying to protect himself. "God, where to start." He looked down on the freeway traffic until Dannie gently turned his face back towards Teal.

"Well, it is a restaurant, and I think serves some damn good meals." Teal nodded his agreement. "But that's not its reason for being – that's not its main purpose. Its main purpose lies in helping others cope with problems you and I can only begin to imagine."

Teal furrowed his brow but nodded his encouragement, once more wondering exactly where this was going.

"The staff, well about eighty percent of them, have had psychotic breaks – many of them have been institutionalized for periods of time, and all of them are virtual outcasts from conventional society."

Teal stared at him speechless. He knew his mouth was hanging open, and he felt powerless to snap it shut.

"Magnolia Café is the pilot project of a Marin County non-profit agency called Marin Advocates for Mental Stability," TJ continued. "Nothing like it anywhere in the country. We work with these kids and try to teach them a meaningful trade while helping them work through the darker phases of their illness. Nobody has ever tried to do this, and we are starting to see some rays of sunshine in an otherwise gloomy world."

Teal continued to stare at him while both he and Dannie waited for a comment.

"You mean you are trying to run a restaurant, already one of the most unforgiving, toughest gigs in the world, with people who are…"

"Crazy? Yes, if you choose to use medieval nomenclature."

"TJ, I didn't mean to sound like a jerk, but…"

TJ waved away his apology. "We even use the word in the restaurant although we're not fond of hearing it from outsiders. The kids almost use it as a badge of courage and defiance." He leaned forward, his eyes shining and intense. "We are teaching them social skills and how to control themselves, and some of them can do it now. Also we teach them how to deal with the public while learning a meaningful trade."

"Yeah, but you've got customers coming in. What do they think about all that?"

"For the most part they're very supportive," Dannie said sharing TJ's excitement. "Did you see the little blurb on the menu that describes the program and what it's trying to accomplish?"

Teal shook his head. He could remember the menu in Kaycee better.

"See I told you it should be bigger," she said nudging TJ.

"But there's crap on lots of menus," TJ said. "You know stuff about our beloved founder or why the silly name or our special dedication to food preparation. Nobody reads that stuff."

"I tend to agree with TJ," Teal said. "I never read that stuff. But still, how do your customers deal with the – weirdness?"

TJ and Dannie both laughed until their eyes were tearing. "You couldn't possibly understand but welcome to Marin County," TJ finally said while he and Dannie slapped a high five.

They talked for another hour, and TJ told him about how the restaurant had been set up and how he was hired to manage its operation as well as perform the duties of head clinician. He talked about the tiny steps forward and the depressing setbacks. Lack of funding haunted them and constant revision of their approaches and policies left them dizzy and often depressed. But the tiny steps forward always refocused their effort and filled them with new resolve. Of the non-client staff with which TJ opened the restaurant, only one had left in frustration. Five had remained.

They were currently administering to forty-three clients, many being able to handle no more than an hour a month, while three worked forty hour a week shifts, and two were being prepared for placement. They were TJ's shining stars, but neither wanted to leave.

"You know what would be fun?" TJ asked rubbing his hands together. "Why don't you help us out for a week or so? You could show these kids the ropes. You'd be good at it. You said yourself you're not doing anything. What the heck, you might enjoy it."

Teal had always loved TJ's enthusiasm as he did now, but his mind was screaming he would most certainly hate working there. He would be scared to death.

"Oh come on, TJ. I wouldn't know how to act around your...clients. I got a D- in psyc at Michigan!"

"No, no, you just come in and cook. Show 'em some recipes, how to handle a knife and like that." Teal shook his head all the while thinking of lunatics with sharp knives. "I don't think so TJ. Besides I don't have any place to live."

"Aha, I think I got that all worked out," TJ said triumphantly. "But just do this. Come back down for lunch and meet everyone, staff and clients, before you say no for sure. Will you do that?"

Teal shrugged. He and TJ had done some interesting things at Michigan, and he seemed to have survived most of them. And some of them *were* fun.

"All right! Come down at about eleven, and I'll give you the full tour.

At nine o'clock the following morning Teal was one of the first in line at the San Rafael branch of Wells Fargo Bank. He opened an account with five hundred dollars using TJ's address, turned down the offer of a credit card and rented a safe deposit box were he unceremoniously dumped the folded duffel filled with banded bills and the SIG.

At a few minutes past eleven, Teal walked into Magnolia Café and found it bustling with energy and customers. Ginny skipped over to him and winked.

"Heard you were coming in today," she said, "probably looking for me, right?"

Teal felt the heat rise in his face, as she skipped away like a pixie.

"I'll hustle up TJ for you," she said over her shoulder. Tim watched from the espresso bar like he was witnessing a bank robbery.

Moments later TJ strolled out of the kitchen with, what appeared to Teal, forced calm.

"You want a cup of mud, or do you want to meet the folks?"

Teal smiled and shrugged. "Let's get right to it," he said, and TJ laughed.

"You sound like you're at the doctor's office and want to get your shots over with," TJ said. Teal did not smile.

They walked towards the kitchen with TJ offering a running commentary about the building, its age and historical significance and the legal confrontations the organization had to endure to license and finally open the facility. Teal only caught bits and pieces of the running monologue while setting himself to bolt and run like a squirrel in a pen of pit bulls.

"Okay, I'm going to introduce you to the kitchen staff. Head cook is straight staff, although sometimes he acts like a client, and the rest are clients."

Teal felt like reciting the Twenty-ninth psalm.

"Carl?" TJ asked and a pasty, sloppy-looking man strolled up wiping his hands on a profoundly soiled apron. "Carl, this is an old friend of mine from college. Jack Teal. Jack – Carl Johns."

The man gave Teal a soft handshake and flashed him a nasty set of stained and crooked teeth.

"Carl runs the kitchen and brings a professionalism we need in here," TJ said as if reciting something he had read somewhere. Someone snickered in the back of the kitchen.

"Nice to meet ya," Johns said looking over his shoulder, "I've got to get back at it. Can't turn your back on 'em for a minute."

TJ cleared his throat. "Well, let's go in and meet the clients," he said. Teal felt he could have substituted the word 'enemy' for 'client'. They walked into the maelstrom which is the heart and soul of all restaurants. It was confined but not restricted, meaning all who worked together had to be aware of one another. When they were successful, it almost took on the appearance of a ballet. The equipment looked well used but very clean, and the arrangement within the limited space was perfect.

"Sammy, get your butt over here," TJ said, and a rail thin young Asian stepped over and saluted. "Sammy, this is Jack Teal, an old friend of mine. He knows his way around a kitchen so don't bullshit him."

Sammy grinned, wiped his hand on his apron and offered it to Teal.

"Back here, and certainly no less important are Beth and Nicole who ably put things right when Sammy screws up."

Sammy rolled his eyes, and the two women beamed and one curtsied.

"And which one of you has the pretty soprano voice?" Teal asked starting to feel comfortable.

Beth hooked a thumb at Nicole who stared at the floor and turned so red Teal wondered if she was having some sort of a seizure.

"And on the dishwasher is…" TJ said snapping his fingers.

Beth leaned over and whispered, "Gary."

"Right. Gary. And he's doing a great job," TJ said. Gary had lined up all the dirty forks in a neat row on the feeder tray and was starting on the spoons. They looked like columns of Revolutionary War Redcoats marching off to fight the rabble in the New World.

"Let's go out front, and I'll fill you in on the operation," TJ said while nodding at Beth to help Gary disband his troops and load them into the dishwasher.

TJ and Teal sat at a deuce, and Tim wandered over with two espressos. Before they could take their first sip a disheveled man who looked like he could be the poster boy for a homeless shelter walked in the front door and announced his arrival.

"Good afternoon ladies and germs, I just flew in from Portland and, boy, are my pits tired!"

Some of the customers laughed, TJ rolled his eyes, and the kitchen exploded in static Japanese. TJ motioned the young man over. He strolled over with a slight smirk and saluted TJ. "Reporting for duty, *sir!*" he said rolling something around in his mouth.

"You're late Mickey – way late," TJ said. "Clean up, get an apron on and see if you can help us out today."

Mickey saluted, spun on his heel and retreated towards the kitchen.

"That's the notorious Mickey Ralston," TJ said. "He's been in the mental health care system for a hundred years and knows all the angles. He's been institutionalized at least four times and escaped twice. Escaped, for Christ sakes. He's also higher on the Wechsler Intelligence Scale than anyone the system has ever tested. To Sammy he's an idol, but to me, he's a super pain in the ass. But," he added and held Teal with a look, "if anyone can help him – we can."

"What the hell's he got in his mouth? A Lego block?" Teal asked.

TJ chuckled and finger combed his hair. "He's got a full upper plate. Never content to just let it stay in place and do things like eat food. He's gotta roll it around like a set of worry beads. Freaks the girls out!"

The young man Teal had seen the first day who had restored order in the kitchen approached the table and nodded to Teal. Then he knelt and said something to TJ who nodded back, and then introduced them.

"Jack Teal, meet Rich Nestor. He's my right hand man."

After Rich left they lapsed into silence, and TJ fiddled with his silverware. "Look Jack, maybe this was a bad idea, you're working here. Goddamn place is a burnout! Go on up to Seattle and drop me a postcard from time to time. Save yourself some heartaches."

They sat quietly for several minutes while Teal studied the top of his friend's head. Finally he said, "I can't promise that I'll be here when the geese fly south, but how much do you pay?"

TJ turned his head so Teal could not see his face. Finally, he cleared his throat and stared at the polished wood tabletop. He swiped his shirtsleeve across his eyes pretending to wipe his forehead.

"You'll start day after tomorrow. We have to run you through the basics first." He was using the voice and words for all new hires, and Teal stifled a grin. "We'll work it all out at home."

Dannie met Teal when he parked at the curb, and as soon as he was out of the car, she was hugging him. "Thank you, Jack," she said. "He's worked so hard, and he believes so strongly. He needs someone to go to the wall with him. Someone he trusts to watch his back."

She started to cry, tears streaming down on either side of her smile, and Jack had no idea what to do.

"You don't have to say or do anything," she said reading his mind. "Just be here for him."

They were still holding each other when TJ drove up filling the neighborhood with acrid fumes and noise. The two-some became a three-some, and they held each other for a long time. Cars passing by on the street paid little attention. This was after all, Marin County.

* * *

TWELVE

Teal had to call Sloan. He could not endure another day without hearing her voice. Dannie and TJ refused to allow him to leave the house to make the call and went for a stroll around the neighborhood. He took the cordless out on the deck, laid it on the table and sat down. Then he stared at it until his eyes started to water. When he heard a scratching to the left, he looked up to see a robin on the deck railing no more than six or seven feet away. It tilted its head and fixed him with a beady stare.

What are you some sort of chicken? Come on we haven't got all night!

He wasn't sure if he had the thought, or the robin was performing some sort of mental telepathy. He picked up the phone and risked calling the shop in Scottsdale, even though it was late, hoping that she might answer. If she didn't, he would hang up.

The phone rang five times before someone picked it up.

"Easy Motors," Sloan said, and her voice sounded so lifeless Teal was nearly struck dumb.

"I love you," he finally said softly. He realized much later, it was the first time he had said it to anyone.

There was a sigh as if a breath of wind had traveled down the line followed by silence. He wondered if she had hung up.

"Sloan, I can't be without you. I know I've hurt you, and that's unforgivable. But please give me a chance to try to make it up to you *and* your dad."

"Thank you for calling, Jack," she finally said, and her voice was small, but the hollowness was gone.

"I'm in Marin County north of San Francisco staying with an old college friend. I'm going to stay here for a while."

"I want to see you," she said her voice gaining strength and timbre.

"And I need to see you. But I want to settle in for maybe a week before we talk about a visit. How is your Dad?"

"He's pissed. Stomping around and throwing things. He told me about what happened in the shop – about the little thingy he found under your car. But I think he's also mad at himself. You left and nothing was resolved. He never gave you a chance, and now he knows how I feel about you. He's hurt, and he's scared."

"And I've acted like an asshole..."

"Well, there is that too," she said, and Teal smiled at her returning attitude.

They talked for five more minutes, and Teal promised to invite her up when he was settled.

"Will your dad let you go?"

"Jack, I'm not a little girl. As long as he knows I will always be *his* little girl."

They listened to each other breathe for a moment and Teal envisioned her lips close to the phone like an old time movie clip and thinking he sure as hell did not deserve her love and trust. She said good-bye, and he sat holding the dead phone in his lap until TJ and Dannie cautiously entered the house.

TJ knew a woman several blocks away who had a small mother-in-law unit behind her house and had thought of renting it. TJ had already spoken to her, and she was delighted with the possibility that she might have a tenant.

"She wanted two hundred a month for it which is nuts," TJ told Teal the next morning. "It's worth every penny of eight hundred, and she could probably hold out for a grand. It's not big but it's in a quiet area, and it's got a killer view. If you like it, it yours for six bills a month," he said pleased with his negotiating skills.

Teal saw it the following morning. It was small, verging on tiny, but was clean and sunny and the view from the redwood deck was wonderful. The furniture looked as if it had come from a European country inn. Mrs. Norbalm was English and cheerful and reminded Teal of some actress from a Monty Python show. Teal practically had to force her to take a month in advance, and they struck an agreement on the utilities and the phone. She was almost afraid to touch the cash he handed her.

"I'm going to put this in an envelope and go right down to the bank," she said drawing her lips into a firm line and pulling a sweater around her shoulders. "You young folks always have so much cash around. It's not safe, you know."

He was going to respond, but she was already walking swiftly towards her car waving three fingers over her shoulder.

He moved his meager belongings into the house and followed TJ back down to the restaurant for his 'orientation tour'.

They arrived after the breakfast rush, and only a few tables had customers. After sitting at TJ's favorite table, which had a full view of the room, Tim brought them lattes and a toasted bagel for TJ in less than a minute.

"Friday's a good day for you to watch the operation," TJ said taking a sip and leaving a thin, white mustache which his tongue discovered a moment later. His glasses were hanging around his neck making them a perfect catch tray for the crumbs from the bagel. Occasionally he would absentmindedly blow the crumbs off onto the table.

"All the staff heavies are here, and we have the largest client load. Twelve kids, but most don't work the full day and some only an hour if they can even handle that. Still it's a high energy day."

He took another sip, his eyes missing nothing in the room or kitchen. "You've already met Rich. Great guy with strong skills and a good backbone. Lots of our kids are real con artists like Mickey, and Rich knows how to deal with 'em. See the table over by the wall with the two men and the black teenager?" Teal's eyes followed where he was pointing and noticed that one of the men waved at TJ before returning to his huddle.

"The stocky little guy is Peter Quinn Ryan; a very heavy-duty shrink who comes in once a week to help out. We are blessed to have him. He also comes in at least once a week to do some intakes – that's like when Marin Mental Health or some other agency wants to place someone in the restaurant. We work it up together to see if the person is appropriate and if we have a slot. Sometimes we have to place a person on a waiting list, and, as this place gets more and more recognition, the list gets longer.

"If we don't have any intakes, P.Q. still comes in and hangs out. Even worked in the kitchen once, but all the kids threw him out," he said and laughed. "But he's got a huge private practice on the outside and draws from all over the state. Along with writing papers and hanging around on the lecture circuit.

"The other guy with him works at Marin Mental Health. Nice guy and capable. But way, way overloaded. I don't know if he's going to last."

"There's that many...aahhh," Teal started, but TJ waved it off.

"Yep. You'll never see 'em because you don't know what to look for and because lots are squirreled away from the public. They're not sure how to act in public, so their social skills suck, and a lot of parents or caregivers just don't want to go through it. In England they just call them eccentric, and everyone loves them to pieces," he said with a broad grin.

"What about hospitals where they can get first class care?" Teal asked, and TJ held up his hand like a traffic cop and shook his head.

"I am not overly fond of hospitals or psychiatric wards or chemical shackles," he said slowly guarding his words. "Certainly there are those people who are so desperately ill, this becomes the only solution. But for younger people, it really becomes the court of the last resort."

He rubbed his head in frustration and drained the rest of his latte. Peter Quinn Ryan pushed his chair back and strolled over.

"Peter Quinn. How goes the battle?" TJ asked with a sigh.

"We're winning," he replied in a strong voice with more than a touch of Irish in it.

TJ introduced them. They shook hands and Teal was startled by the strength of the hand and the calluses on his palm. He had a neatly trimmed beard on a face squared off like his body, and his eyes were direct and friendly.

"Pleasure," he said pulling a chair around and sitting with his arms crossed over the chair back.

"Excuse me. Got to talk a little biz with *El Jefe*," he said with a grin and turned to TJ who motioned Teal to say seated. "Got Amed over there who's still hot to trot. I know your reservations about him, but you're just going to have to suck it up.

TJ stared at the tabletop. "Yeah, yeah."

Peter Quinn gave him his best grin. "Kid wants in here bad!"

"Peter Quinn, they all want in here bad," TJ said scratching the side of his head and sneaking a peek at the other table.

"Maybe I'll go over and say 'hi', and then we can hash it out later. Listen, Jack's going to be helping me out here. Mind if he comes over and sits in? Got an A+ in Psyc back at East Lansing," he added smiling sweetly at Teal's open mouth.

"Let me bring him over," Peter Quinn said. "That way he won't think you're some sort of a hit team that's gonna take him out."

Teal stared at TJ when Peter Quinn left the table. "Is that guy for real?" he asked with a laugh.

"You bet!" TJ said. "Little bit of shrink humor. It's how we protect each other." He grinned.

Peter Quinn returned with the young man in tow, and introduced him to TJ and Teal. Teal was surprised by Peter Quinn's memory.

The young man shook both of their hands with a smile and direct eye contact.

"Doctor Ryan tells me you still want to work in this restaurant," TJ said.

The young man nodded enthusiastically and compressed his lips.

"And you want to work in the kitchen or the espresso bar?"

Again the enthusiastic nod.

"And you're going to work hard and not flake out on me and leave right in the middle of a rush or something."

This time a vigorous headshake with a very serious look.

TJ stood and shook his hand. "Thanks for coming over. Amed. I'll talk to Doctor Ryan, and I promise I'll let you know within a couple of days."

The young man, flashing a huge grin, shook his hand a second time, shook Teal's and followed Peter Quinn back across the room.

"That was an intake study?" Teal asked not trying to disguise his surprise.

"No, no, no! Jesus. Literally dozens of hours have been spent talking about Amed. Between me and Peter Quinn, the parents and me, Peter Quinn and Marin Mental Heath, etc., etc." TJ stared off into space.

"Four years ago Amed was walking to high school with his older brother who was home from college on vacation. To say that Amed idolized him would be one of the biggest understatements ever uttered. They were going to shoot some hoops at the local high school. Suddenly a car screams by, and some crack head dude in the back seat pops his big brother in the head with a .38. He dies in Amed's arms."

TJ stared out the front window, seeing nothing. "When the police finally caught the asshole who had pulled the trigger, he said they were just playing around. 'Didn't mean no harm.' His buddies pled to lesser charges and were released to probation. The jails are overrunning like rest stop toilets. You have to be a serial killer to gain admission."

Amed's been under psychiatric care ever since it happened. Been in and out of institutions twice; last time about a year ago at Marin General. Sometimes in the past they have had him so medicated he looks like he's carved from stone"

"And you want to work with him."

"You bet. The biggest challenges are the best," TJ said and smiled.

"What makes him a bigger challenge than, say, that Mickey guy?" Teal asked and stared back. TJ's smile broadened.

"What?"

TJ looked like the Cheshire cat.

Teal slouched in his chair and looked at his friend, and the years seemed to melt between them. Finally he leaned forward.

"Jesus Christ, the kid's a mute," he said in a low voice. "He can't talk."

"Bingo," said TJ and pointed a finger at Teal's chest.

"Jesus, you're thinking of hiring a crazy kid who can't talk," Teal said with his fingertips on his forehead.

"Not only am I thinking of bringing him in, I sincerely think we can help him. Otherwise, I'd pass."

They stared at each other for a long minute. Then Teal leaped out of his chair and slapped him on the shoulder. "Jesus H. Christ! Now that's the God damn TJ Fitz I remember!"

Peter Quinn gave them a thumbs-up from across the room.

* * *

THIRTEEN

Teal arose very early and ran in the darkened neighborhood for forty-five minutes until the perspiration poured from his body. Only a few house lights were on and commuters had yet to fill the streets. Two cats, an owl and a set of glowing eyes in the trimmed bushes were alone in their solemn observation of his run. After a long shower, he shaved, put on a pair of worn, comfortable jeans, a soft cotton long sleeved shirt and a leather sleeved jacket and drove to the restaurant for the opening and the early shift. He was becoming increasingly uncomfortable driving the Porsche. It was no longer 'fun' or 'cool', and it was a hook to the past. The plan to replace it was slowly taking shape in his mind.

When he arrived at the restaurant, Sammy was standing in the alcove by the front door with his t-shirt around his ears and flapping his arms.

"Hey Sammy, you're going to freeze your nuts off out here," Teal said.

"I come from a proud line of Samurai warriors," he said thrusting out his skinny chest. "We feel no pain." His arms looked like bleached matchsticks.

"Well, maybe we can use some of your frozen remains in a special Samurai tossed green salad," Teal said peeling off his jacket and hanging it around Sammy's skinny shoulders. Although it hung almost to his knees, he admired his reflection in the front window turning left and right and preening.

A moment later Carl shuffled around the corner with a 'don't fuck with me' glare, the door keys jangling from his pudgy hand.

Without saying a word he opened the door, walked into the main room and flipped on the light switch.

"I see they got you roped into working in this loony bin," he said to Teal over his shoulder, honked a laugh and walked back to the kitchen tossing the keys in the air.

"He's an asshole," Sammy whispered. "I show you the ropes."

"Cool – as long as it's not a hangman's knot."

Sammy laughed and wheezed through his nose. It sounded like garden shears working a rose bush. Teal had to help him tie the headband around his shock of black hair stuffing errant strands back in place. It reminded him of Bet in Kaysee.

"You watch. I really run the kitchen. He's just a burned out juicehead," Sammy said nodding and slipping on an apron. Then he laughed and wheezed through his nose – snic, snic.

The front door opened and Beth and Nicole entered in animated conversation followed shortly by Tim who stopped suddenly and looked around the room as if he had entered it by mistake.

"Okay," Sammy said rubbing his hands together. "Time to rock and roll."

They worked quickly and quietly while a kitchen radio playing soft rock in the background. This week the station had been selected by Rich. Next week would be Sammy. Beth and Nicole chatted and their hands flew as they prepped luncheon salad ingredients, while Sammy showed Teal the basic moves

of the kitchen and the prep routine for breakfast. Karl was
nowhere to be seen.

All kitchens are different, some dramatically so, and
all try to find a certain rhythm and style, which suits them
best. Violating that established rhythm can create chaos and
confusion and, ultimately, failure. Teal was amazed how tightly
tuned and correct this kitchen was, although Carl seemed to
be only a remote part of the scheme. He spent most of his time
ordering lattes and cappuccinos from Tim while watching at
the front door.

"All veggie trimmings go into stock pot," Sammy said
with a neat underhand toss into a huge aluminum pot. "We
make our own vegetable stock for the soups."

Teal nodded and cut his celery and beet trimmings into
a bowl. Nicole caught his eye and nodded, then whispered to
Beth, and they started chittering like a nest of mice.

The breakfast rush swelled and ebbed with Rich and Tim
waiting tables and Carl grousing about everything. Nobody in
the kitchen paid any attention to him and soon began to prep
for lunch. Teal knew he would sometime soon have to talk to
TJ about Carl's value in the organization.

"Hey, you ain't bad," Sammy said.

"I come from a long line of WASP warriors," Teal said
puffing out his chest, and the kitchen was filled with peals of
laughter punctuated by machinegun Japanese.

"Jesus Christ," Carl said briefly snapping out of his stupor.
"Do you think we could get something done here?"

The comment was greeted with rolling eyes and silent
smirks. Carl seemed not to notice, red-rimmed eyes still fixed
on the front door.

Teal began to feel his own kitchen moves return: how to
hold the knife and position whatever was being sliced or diced,

how to stand close to the counter and balance so you could turn quickly in either direction, and how to make room for other workers and be aware of their own space. Some people called it muscle memory and others probably had terms incorporating four or five Latin words, which were unpronounceable. By any name it felt satisfying, and he started to whistle as he worked.

Near the end of the breakfast rush, TJ strolled by quickly followed by Ginny and a middle-aged woman with neat hair and careful makeup. TJ peered through the kitchen pass-though and grinned at Teal.

"Is he just getting in the way or what?" TJ asked Sammy and flipped a thumb at Teal.

Sammy shrugged his thin shoulders. "He's not too bad. We whip him into shape."

Teal noticed that Carl's demeanor changed dramatically when Ginny came through the front door. He perked up, waved at Ginny and motioned her over. When she didn't respond, he left the kitchen and strolled over to chat wiping his hands on a towel. Teal watched as she left after a moment, appearing slightly annoyed, and began cleaning and setting tables for lunch.

That's interesting.

In the next instant the front door slammed opened and Mickey stumbled in looking as if he had spent the night in a culvert with a nest of wombats.

TJ took several quick steps across the room and grabbed his elbow pulling him back towards the kitchen and out of sight of the main room.

"Mickey, I am not going to put up with this shit," he said in hushed urgency, his face inches from Mickey's.

Mickey flinched and tried to hold his own. "What shit," he whined and looked at something over TJ's shoulder.

"Get serious, Mickey," TJ said in a strained voice. "You come in here looking like you've been sleeping under a car and expect me to have you wait tables? We've gone over this a dozen times, and I'm fed up with it. There are lots of kids who would like your slot – kids who will come in here not looking like a freakin' bum."

"I didn't have time...", he started, and TJ cut him off.

"Then you, by God, make time. You shower, shave and wear clean, decent clothes, if you want to work here. Got it?"

Mickey rolled his plate until one end was sticking out grotesquely while he tried to pump up and look defiant. Finally he visibly shrunk and nodded. "I got it."

"Okay. Go home, clean yourself up and put on nice clothes, and I'll hold your slot opened," TJ said more softly now. "Hurry up." He turned him around and pushed him lightly towards the front door.

The kitchen was completely silent, filled only with the sound of chopping knifes and the clatter of pots and pans on burners.

"Jesus, why they put up with these feebs is beyond me," Carl said shaking his head. Teal put his knife down slowly and started to walk across the kitchen towards Carl, but only Sammy noticed it.

"Mickey sometimes makes trouble for everyone," Sammy said quickly stepping in front of him, "but he's still my friend. He's a very funny guy. Makes me laugh all the time," he added with a shy smile.

Mickey returned in about forty minutes, neatly shaven and wearing crisp knife-edge khakis with a faded orange polo shirt. He bore little resemblance to the person who had slammed opened the door three quarters of an hour before. The rest of lunch was busy and without incident except for an attempted whistle duet between Teal and Sammy, which had Beth and Nicole doubled over.

Teal helped with clean up and took turns with Beth and Nicole helping Gary with the dishwasher.

"Uh-oh," Gary said standing back and wringing his hands. "Uh-oh."

Teal took one look at him and thought, *Rainman*. He even looked a little bit like a young Dustin Hoffman.

"Its okay, Gary," Teal said and patted him on the shoulder. "Just helping you out a little bit here. We all help each other out."

After they had finished loading the tray, Gary shuffled over sideways to Teal and held one of his hands.

Teal, looking around the kitchen for help, saw Sammy snort through his nose and put a hand over his mouth to stop from cracking up.

Beth patted Gary on the shoulder and smiled at Teal.

"He's shaking your hand. Doesn't know how to do it very well...yet."

Gary released his hand and took off his apron figuring *his* work was done.

"How long has he been working here?" Teal whispered to Nicole gathering up the remaining battalion of forks and knives Gary had lined up to march off to war.

"'Bout five months," she answered with a sigh. "He's a tad slow."

After work Teal drove into San Rafael's auto row and visited three used car lots. It was a beautiful spring afternoon, and every tree along the sidewalk was fat with buds and the air was ripe with the scent of green leaves and lawn mulch. All the lots were busy, and, although it took almost three hours,

Teal managed to see what he wanted without being waylaid
by a salesman. He returned to the Porsche, jotted down some
quick notes and drove north, finally taking a turn off leading
into a small industrial area dominated by a large public storage
complex. He paid for three months in advance for a medium
size rental unit, as sterile but functional as a concrete block, and
doubled back to the bank before returning to his cottage. His
pockets now bulged with twelve thousand in hundreds split
between several large bricks.

He had a quick beer with Danny and TJ before turning
in early. "My butt is dragging," he said while taking a final
peek at the freeway to see if there was anything interesting
happening.

*God, I'm starting to pick up TJ's habits. I'll probably become a
client within a month!*

"Did you meet Claire today?" TJ asked him.

"Nope. Was she the dominatrix you walked in with?"

TJ laughed and spilled beer on his glasses, which he
carefully lifted up and sipped. "You aren't the first to make a
comment like that," he said wiping the glasses with a shirt tail
before Danny snatched them out of his hands and returned to
the kitchen.

"Snow Queen – Ice Maiden – she's probably heard them
all. She's a good clinician and certainly pulls her share of the
load. It's good to have different personalities in there."

Teal wasn't sure he sounded convinced.

"What about that Gary guy? The guy on the dishwasher.
Is he like a *Rainman* kind of guy?"

TJ smiled a little indulgently. "Different as apples and
oranges. Dustin Hoffman portrayed a man who was a savant, an
autistic savant to be absolutely correct, and a condition he was
probably born with. It shows up early. Gary's schizophrenic – one

of several we have as clients. His condition manifested itself when he was in his early teens. He's been in treatment ever since, and, to my mind, being way over medicated. But," he said holding up his hand and tilting his head, "that's a whole 'nother subject we don't want to get into now."

"Beth told me he's been working at Magnolia for like six months or something," Teal said.

"Five months and twelve days," TJ countered immediately. "But when he first started, we would be lucky to get him through an hour before he burst into tears. I think it was in the second month when we finally got him through three one-hour work sessions in a row. Big day. Very exciting. We all had a party after we closed. Of course he was so nervous being the center of attention, he broke down in tears and someone had to take him home."

They both pondered the freeway, keeping a close eye on a hybrid in the fast lane going the speed limit. SUVs were stacking up behind it like lumber trucks.

"You guys never talk to me about what medications these kids are on," Teal said. "Hell, I even hear them talk to each other about what they're taking. This one's cool, and this one makes you dizzy and like that."

"There's a good reason for us not telling you, and, yes, it is intentional," TJ said keeping a close eye on any new developments in the hybrid caravan. "I want you to be a teacher and leader in the kitchen. Your focus will be helping in running a restaurant to the best of our and your abilities while teaching the kids how they can help you and develop their own skills. After all that *is* what we're trying to do, and I don't really know diddly squat about the operation of a kitchen. You are a natural born teacher where Carl is not. He may be a gifted cook, but he can't lead and direct the kids.

"So I don't want you to be concerned with the level of medication on this client or that one, or should we take this guy off Geodon and put him on Risperdal. It shouldn't make any difference to you if a kid is schizophrenic or bipolar. You don't need or want those responsibilities."

They were both quiet for a moment.

"You know what?" Teal finally asked as the hybrid procession topped a hill and disappeared from sight. "That Carl is one of the biggest assholes I've ever had the displeasure of working with. And that's a one day observation. I have a bad feeling that it won't get any better."

TJ squirmed and looked at the freeway for help. "He is somewhat personality challenged," TJ said. "But he has cooked in some well known restaurants and brought in a pile of great recipes." After a moment he said with a resigned nod, "And, bottom line? It's hard to get non-clinical people to work in here."

"Well, buck up, old buddy," Teal said. "Now you got me to kick around." He got up, stretched and slapped TJ on the shoulder. "I'm going home and talk to Sloan."

"You can use our phone," Danny said from the kitchen.

"Thanks but I got a deal working with Mrs. Norbalm. Plus I think I'm going to pick up a cell phone, so I can look important like the rest of you clowns."

Just before leaving, he looked back from the front door. "Now tomorrow, I'm taking you guys out for Mexican food. All you can eat and drink, and I'm footing the bill.

It'd probably break me if it weren't for this cushy, high paying gig I just fell into."

Dannie chucked a carrot at him from the kitchen, but he was already out the door.

Seeing a light in Mrs. Norbalm's living room, he tapped on the front door.

"Jack, how nice to see you. I hope everything is alright," she said. She was holding a needlepoint in her hand with some colored yarns trailing off one corner like tiny fireworks contrails.

"Good evening, Mrs. Norbalm..." he started, but she waved her needlepoint at him.

"Please call me Emily. It makes me ever-so-much more comfortable."

"Thank you, Emily. I have a request but please be honest with me, if you're not happy about it, and I'll certainly understand."

She smiled and tilted her head.

"I have this friend – a girl friend. Well, she's more than that. And I was going to ask her to fly up for a visit and see Marin County and Magnolia. I think you'd really like her," he said hurrying on.

"And you would like her to stay with you."

"Yes Mrs. – Emily."

"Well I think that would be lovely," she said without hesitation. "Ed, my late husband, and I used to think the cottage was our little love nest, even though it was really just his office. Sometimes we would sleep out there and pretend we were kids again." She smiled at the ceiling for a moment and laid her needlepoint on the hall table.

"We always thought the little cabin sort of liked the idea. That probably doesn't make any sense at all, does it?"

Teal took her hand, and they both smiled. "It makes all the sense in the world to me," he said.

Even though the phone in the cottage was an old-fashion black table model with a dial face, the cord managed to reach out to his deck. If TJ's deck was small, Teal's was miniscule. But it had a wonderful view of San Pablo Bay and the hills of the East Bay beyond and had probably been built in a time when everybody had wonderful views and thought little about it. There was only one wooden slated chair on the deck, some sort of Adirondack knockoff, but it was surprisingly comfortable.

Sloan answered the phone almost immediately.

"Are there any good looking blonds hanging around there?" he asked.

"Not that aren't taken," she answered. "Try the Chevy dealer down the street. Or better yet the motor scooter store over on LeGrand."

Teal grinned into the phone. His aunt would have said that's certainly a cheeky little girl you've got there.

They talked for almost an hour. He would have to warn Emily so she wouldn't have a cardiac arrest when she opened the bill. He told her about the restaurant and TJ's deep commitment to helping his clients.

"Sound like you're enjoying it."

"You know, so far I am. I really didn't know what to expect, but I wanted to help TJ out. He's really a good guy and hasn't changed a lick."

They made plans for her visit, and she refused to let him pay for her plane ticket.

"See in that way, if I decide I really don't like you after all, I can just fly on home."

Teal smiled although it was sometimes hard to tell when she was joking. After he hung up, he heard a scrabbling in the Texas privet bush next to the house. In the next moment a robin hopped down a branch and jumped onto the deck railing.

"What? Are you following me?"

The robin tilted his head and stared. Couldn't be the same bird, Teal thought. That was five blocks away.

The robin puffed his feathers out, and then smoothed them with his beak. Or her beak, he thought. They all look the same.

And, of course, he or she probably wouldn't be able to tell the difference between me and TJ. Now there's an unsettling thought.

Teal walked into the kitchen, and the bird scuttled back into the bush. He brought out a crust of toast, placed it on the railing and went to bed. In the morning the crust was gone – replaced by a bird dropping. Teal grinned. Everyone's a critic.

The following morning Teal picked up a simple combination lock at the local hardware store, reluctantly passing on the key lock with eye-catching graphics showing how it refused to be breached while being viciously blasted by bullets from a .30-.30 rifle. He drove the Porsche to the public storage unit, parked it inside and locked the door without looking back. The car had played a part in the betrayal and, as Teal saw it, no longer had a soul. The manager called a taxi and less than ten minutes later he was back on auto row.

Starting with the dealer furthest to the north which also happened to have the car he like the best, he planned on working his way south. It had taken him one long afternoon to isolate the several cars of interest in three different lots. The first lot was busy, but a salesman came slipping sideways between cars in a minute.

"Beautiful day to buy a car," the man said. He had an odd, spiked haircut and a black leather vest over a graying yellow long-sleeve shirt.

Teal nodded in his direction without really looking. "What's that Taurus – a two thousand six?"

"Oh seven, and I'll say you have an eye for fine automobiles. That is *the* creampuff on the lot."

Teal idly ran a finger along the hood where there was a fine skein of dust.

"Looks like it's been here a while. Probably because it's brown."

"Actually that color is chestnut. Special order color," the man said carefully ignoring the first observation. "Nine thousand miles and still on warranty. They just don't come any better."

"Boy I don't know. The color didn't bother me at first..."

"We have some other terrific cars," the man said quickly looking around the lot. "But none as clean as this puppy."

Teal opened the door and peeked front and rear. It was spotless and had no lingering traces of cigarette smoke. But he already knew that.

"So what are you trying to get for it?"

"Nine thousand, nine fifty."

Teal let his flinch show. "Almost ten large for a brown car?"

"Chestnut," the man reminded him.

"That your boss in there?" Teal asked nodded towards a man watching them through the plate glass window.

When the salesman nodded, he said, "Why don't you bring him out here, and let's see if we can work a deal."

The manager strolled out and introductions were made. "Well you're looking at the pick of the litter," he said and let his stomach balloon out over his belt. "nine thou, nine fifty, and you'll have years of trouble free driving pleasure. It's got every known option for that year."

"Well, let me tell you what I had in mind," Teal said looking from man to man as if to take them into his confidence. "I'm buying this for a friend of mine, and, well, I don't want my wife to know, if you understand what I'm saying. So it will have to be a cash deal," he said pulling one of the wads of hundreds partially out of his front pocket. It was the size of a grown man's fist.

Pot Belly looked at it the way a bluegill stares at a worm on a hook, never questioning why it's suspended mid-water and not safely burrowed down in the mud.

"And does your friend have a figure in mind?" he asked with a weak attempt at camaraderie.

"Eight and a half. Out the door."

"Oh boy, I can't do that," he said and sucked in his gut. "Could see my way clear to nine two fifty, and I'm not makin' more than a couple of bucks on that." The gut lost its battle with gravity.

"Okay, here it is," Teal said once more pulling out the hundreds. "Nine even, out the door, cash, or I'm outta here," he said. "There's a couple more of these down the block that'll do me fine," he added and 'accidentally' dropped the bundle at the man's feet, and he moved exceedingly fast to retrieve it and hand it back. The warmth of the bills lingered on his palm.

"I think your friend will love the car," the man finally said and hitched up his pants on the way back to the office.

When he coasted to a stop in front of the Fitz house, they tumbled from the front door like puppies; Danny pointing with her hand over her mouth and TJ running both hands through his hair as if he were trying to put out a fire.

"What the dickens are you doing with a brown car?" she asked laughing, her thoughts only partially deflected by the bouquet of flowers he handed her.

"And what happened to the Porsche?" TJ asked.

"Firstly," he said to Dannie with a waggled finger, "It's not brown. It's chestnut. A very desirable color. And secondly,

I told you the Porsche belonged to a friend, and he wanted it back. Personally I thought it was very small mined of him."

The lies were smaller and fairly innocuous now.

"Anybody for tacos and Coronas?" Teal asked, and TJ and Dannie piled into the back seat laughing like children going to the beach.

* * *

FOURTEEN

"Sloan's flying up Thursday. Gonna stay through the weekend," Teal said casually while mopping up the remaining tomato sauce on his plate. TJ was kicked back in his chair letting the owner's teenage daughter flirt with him under the guise of teaching him correct Spanish pronunciation.

"Oh Jack," Dannie said, grabbing and holding his hand. He had spoken of Sloan so often, Dannie felt she almost knew her. She was anxious to meet her.

"Does this mean you're going to bug out on me?" TJ asked, clearly not as enchanted with Sloan's impending visit.

"TJ, you are about as romantic as a case of warts," Dannie said and punched him in the shoulder.

"Owww, Jesus, Dannie. I was just having some fun. Come here, Maria, and *besame*...what's the word for shoulder?"

"I know the word for ass," Dannie mumbled glaring at the confused teenager, while Teal almost choked on his beer.

"How long will she be here?" Dannie asked on the way home in the Taurus, which she had nicknamed 'Brownie'.

"Just through the weekend," Teal said. "But if we can get our act together – if I can get *my* act together – she can spend more time, more often."

"Does she know?" TJ asked.

"Know what?" Teal asked, his scalp prickling.

"About the loony bin you're working in," TJ said. He was feeling his three free Coronas.

"A little bit," Teal said relaxing. "She knows how I work tirelessly for almost no money and in daily fear for my life."

"Did you tell her you went out and bought yourself a brown car?" Dannie asked sweetly.

Before driving out to the airport, Teal stopped by a cellular store and bought a cell phone. The girl who waited on him was tiny, scarcely over five feet and with a helmet of black hair that feathered around her face, dark brown eyes and a nose that turned up at the tip. Teal thought she looked like one of Santa's helpers. She was wearing a dark blue blazer and gray slacks and brown walking shoes. She explained the range of phones they offered, and Teal settled on a mid-range model. She was a toucher and a talker, but he had no interest in taking pictures with his phone or listening to stock market reports.

"It's a great model and very reliable," she said. "I would recommend getting a hands-free if you want to use it in the car," she added taking off her blazer.

Whoa, thought Teal, that's definitely not one of Santa's helpers, all the while trying desperately to maintain eye contact.

"I get off in half an hour for lunch break," she said while writing up the order.

"Well shoot, I'm off to the airport," he said and favored her with a broad grin. "Sure wish I could stick around."

She sighed as he strolled out the door. Slipping on her blazer, she trudged out to meet the next customer in line who had two gold rings in his nose.

Teal parked in the short-term parking and strolled into the airport and towards the security station which serviced all Southwest arrivals. He was forty-five minutes early, but sitting around the cottage was making him crazy. The first three days

of the week at the restaurant had gone much faster than he
had anticipated. On one afternoon, he sat with Claire and Rich
for ten minutes, laughing about politics and politicians while
drinking lattes and hot chocolates. He liked Claire but felt a
slight sense of insecurity and doubt in the way she spoke about
the restaurant and the clients. And although she was probably
twenty years older than Rich, it appeared they had become close
friends and were at ease with each other in their conversation.
Teal discovered whenever he left the kitchen for any reason, Carl
would grumble and take his absence out on the clients. So he
cut his breaks short for the sake of the kitchen crew.

Teal and Sammy were beginning to jell into a smooth
duo, particularly when working the Wolf range. They
anticipated and complimented each other's moves while
building their speed. Pans slid across burners with the speed
of oversized hockey pucks and burner flames leapt and danced.
After a particularly difficult lunch rush, which they handled
smoothly, Beth and Nicole gently tapped empty pots in
acknowledgement. Sammy and Teal swept off their chef caps
and bowed deeply, while Rich and Ginny clapped and Mickey
cackled and rolled his teeth with such fury, they fell out and
bounced on the carpet.

Carl was absent the last two days of the week, and
Teal noticed an entire attitude adjustment. The kitchen ran
smoothly and considerably quicker while Gary proved to be the
biggest surprise of all; working the Stero dishwasher as if he
had invented it.

Teal, after watching cool Gary handling the machine
with ease, made big eyes at Sammy who turned to the wall, his
shoulders shaking and making his shears sound. Snik, snik.

When Carl finally showed up for work the last day of the
week, his rumpled clothes smelled sour, and he was swigging

from a bottle of cranberry juice. Teal looked around the restaurant in vain for TJ, and by the time he came through the front door, the dining room was packed, and the restaurant was in the middle of a major rush.

Carl chose that exact time to go off on a rant and flushed what ever good mood existed down the toilet.

"I can barely make ends meet with the piss-poor salary they pay me," he mumbled. "I gotta get outta here."

Teal assumed he was talking to himself since no one was near. But he saw Sammy stiffen and knew he had heard.

"And while they're not paying me a dime, they're always poor mouthing everything and looking for handouts. 'Give me a break on the price, cut my rent, give me some money.' It's enough to make me puke." Even though he was looking at Teal, he still seemed to be talking to himself. Everyone else in the kitchen was intent on what they were doing. Nobody spoke and the atmosphere was as still as the predawn.

Carl walked over to the soup steam table and opened one lid after another. He lifted the ladle out of the last one, sipped from it and put the ladle back in pot. Teal immediately walked over to the steam table, brushed by him and lifted the pot out of the table. Carl watching in amazement, as Teal poured the soup into the sink and took the pot over to the dishwasher.

"What in the hell do you think you're doing?" Carl sputtered, his eyes popping.

"I was disposing of contaminated food," he said calmly. Everyone in the kitchen was watching including Mickey at the pass-through.

"You cannot sip from a ladle and put it back into the soup. That's about as basic as kitchen rules get."

"Don't you dare to teach me about proper kitchen etiquette," Carl said pointing at him with a shaking finger. "I was cooking in gourmet restaurants before you were born."

"Well, somebody has to teach you. Might as well be me," Teal answered pleasantly.

Carl tore off his apron and hurled it at the wall above the sink and stalked from the kitchen. When Teal looked around the room, everyone was smiling.

* * *

Teal sipped a latte and stared at the security gate, willing the flight to land ahead of schedule. When it was finally announced, he felt a shortness of breath and wondered for a moment if he was having a heart attack.

Jeez, that'd be great! Sloan gets off the plane, gets all the way down the corridors and ramps and finally sees me sprawled on the floor with all the gum wrappers and used Kleenex and probably, what, toenail clippings.

The corridor on the opposite side of security was crowded with every size and color of human being, baby carriages, suitcases and cosmetic bags, the elderly and crippled in wheelchairs, airport jitneys and children in backpacks, front packs; running, walking, crawling and creeping towards the security exit.

In the middle of this mass of humanity, Sloan walked with the snappy gait of a woman anticipating an interesting day shopping in Manhattan. She was wearing designer jeans (which caught the eye of every living male within two hundred yards), a sleeveless starched white top with a beaded buckskin vest and pink tennis shoes. She stepped around people as if they had blown head gaskets, her hair, in a French braid, whipping from side to side like a metronome.

She saw Teal and her pace quickened and she dropped her small carryon. Their bodies collided, and she drove him back against the wall. Wedged between the frame for the restroom door and a soft drink dispensing machine, they held each other for a long minute, sensing each other's breathing and heartbeat and muscles moving smoothly beneath their skin. When they finally kissed, it was almost shy and chaste.

"God, I missed you so much it made me feel...stupid!"

Teal laughed.

"No I mean stupid, really. Like some dumb little high school kid that doesn't have a brain in her head."

Her hair was against his chin, and she pulled back angrily to swipe at her eyes.

"Sloan, I'm so, so sorry for what..."

She put a finger on his lips. "We are starting today. What happened in the past stays in the past."

He thought for a second. "Does that mean we can't do some of the things we did in the past?" Teal finally asked with a loopy grin.

"We can talk about that when we get to the cottage," she said sensibly while straightening her braid.

"Agreed," he said. "But before that, we are going to sit down, and I'm going to tell you who I am."

"Jack, I know who you are."

"But you don't know some of the stuff that I lied to you about. You need to know."

She nodded and kissed him again while a group of teenagers, looking like a traveling basketball team, whipped by hooting and hollering and running in circles and shooting imaginary hoops. Teal took her hand and led her to a sitting area at the convergence of three hallways. Several large World War Two fighter planes of about a quarter scale hung over them and swayed slightly in the blast from the air conditioning. He bought two coffees from a kiosk, and they sat facing each other.

"There was this guy at college, Michigan State, who was a good friend of mine," he said after a moment. "Very smart, very funny guy and very popular. He used to do things to make people laugh. Not mean stuff either. Had a gift for it like no one I've ever known."

He took a sip of coffee, scowling at the heat, and Sloan reached over and held his hand.

"When we started our senior year, he started selling dope, grass, you know to friends and like that. He always seemed to have the best. I smoked with him and some other people a couple of times, but I really didn't care for it. Seemed like sort of a waste of time and made me feel goofier than I already am."

He took another sip, braving the heat and continued. "One night he asked if I could help him out by delivering a bag of stuff because he was studying for a big midterm. I didn't want to, but he talked me into it. Turns out it was more than a bag, more like a suitcase. He said he was also returning some books to this guy," Teal said looking down the concourse. "I guess I knew what it was all about. Anyway, the next day he thanks me and gives me three hundred dollar bills. Just about blew me away. I was the poster boy for a struggling college student. Didn't have a dime, and I was working two part time jobs."

Sloan held both his hands for a moment and waited for him to continue. Teal thought she was the most beautiful woman he had ever known.

"Anyway, we graduated, and I went off to work in Colorado and Chris went down south somewhere around

Atlanta. Not a word from him for a couple of years. Then
he blows into Denver just about the same time the company
I'm working for runs into a stone wall and starts to downsize.
We go out to dinner in a limo and, of course, he has a suite
at The Brown Palace, and he's dressed to the nines with
designer labels. I felt like a ground squirrel sitting with him
at dinner."

"You can stop whenever you want," Sloan said, but Teal
shook his head.

"No, I need to get this all out. It can't be in our way."
She nodded and waited.

"Of course I knew what he was doing so when he pitched
me, I wasn't surprised. 'Just like back at State,' he told me, 'but
one hell of a lot more money involved. And I need somebody
around me who I can trust.'

"I turned him down that night but when I got laid off
three weeks later, I gave him a call. I told him I would help
him out for a couple of weeks until I got on my feet again.
He was so happy and grateful, it made me feel like a jerk for
turning him down in the first place."

Teal took time to gulp down the rest of his rapidly
cooling coffee.

"Anyway he flew me down to Charleston and put me
up in a hotel. Picked up the tab for everything including new
clothes. Hell, all I had were a pair of blue jeans and my best
khakis!"

Sloan smiled. "Do you know this is the most talking
you've done since I've known you?"

"Yeah, and I'm getting parched. Let's go into that bogus
looking little pub over there."

They found a corner table looking out on an empty
concourse and ordered two beers in frosty mugs.

"The first run I made for Chris involved driving a car cross town and into a parking garage, leave it unlocked and walk around a department store for half an hour. When we hooked up that night, he gave me a thousand dollars. A thousand dollars! For shopping in a department store for half an hour."

He topped his beer and took a long sip. "Of course the two weeks stretched into two months," he said skidding the glass around the slick on the table. "I had more money than I had ever dreamed of. I knew it wasn't grass. There was too much money involved. I should have walked, but I was lazy and stupid and my life up to then seemed to be going down a steep slide into a dumpster."

Sloan scooted her chair around the small table so she could be next to Teal and laid her head on his shoulder. Her hair smelled of freshly blooming wild flowers.

"Then there was a turning point. At a party in Los Angeles, a big charity affair with all the high rollers there, by absolute chance I met the head of the organization Chris worked for, a very wealthy guy by the name of Hector Koontzman. At first I didn't even know who he was nor, do I think, did he know who I was. We just seemed to hit it off. He had a sense of humor, and we had some shared interests like handball and favorite writers. We ended up talking for about an hour with another group of people. At the time I didn't think much about it, but when I got back to my hotel room the phone flasher was going ballistic. All three messages were from Chris. Knootzman had called him wanting to know what I was all about. How he found out who I was and what I was doing is still a mystery."

He breathed into Sloan's hair and closed his eyes. "I never understood the dynamics between the three of us but the more

time I spent in Knootzman's company – at his request – the
further Chris and I seemed to drift apart. I think he was jealous
of Koontzman"s interest in me. It was all so weird."

"You make it almost sound like he's gay," Sloan said.

"I thought about that at first although he never gave off
gay vibes," Teal answered after a moment. "Much later I met
one of the women he had dated in the past. Couldn't have been
over twenty five. She was now going with a guy I knew, and she
told him that Koontzman wore her out. Wanted to screw about
four times a day. Plus he sort of scared her."

Sloan frowned.

"You said he was wealthy. How wealthy?"

"Very. He had about five houses that I knew about. There
certainly could have been more. There were office buildings
in Mexico, a string of polo ponies, a Mexican soccer team and
apartments and condos all over the place."

Suddenly Teal got up almost spilling both of their beers.

"I gotta walk," he said. "Let's go grab your bag before
some bozo takes a hike with it.

They found the lonely bag sitting off to the side of the
carousel with no one near it. He picked it up, and they headed
towards the garage.

"We were as different as two people can be. He's a
Mexican national and I'm the poster boy for WASPs...

"Not really, Jack," Sloan said but grinned.

"He's loaded," Teal continued, "and I was penniless.
Hell, we're not even the same generation. He's at least thirty
years older than I am. He spoke English, Spanish, French and
could probably find the best hotel in any town in Germany. My
English is lame.

"But we do have the same sense of humor. I told you he
played handball, but I never had the opportunity of taking him on."

Sloan took his hand as they walked through the parking structure.

"I started taking some orders directly from him. Silly stuff like delivering cars or having lunch with some guy and sort of scoping him out and reporting back. The amount of money he paid me for these gofers was almost obscene. And addictive. I still worked with Chris, but less and less. Some of the guys in our group started teasing both of us about it. Just kids stuff. They didn't mean any harm and certainly weren't jealous. But Chris blew up one day, and it almost came to blows. So that was the end of it."

Teal could see the Taurus ahead and shifted the bag to his other hand.

"Eventually I was so comfortable with Koontzman and the whole setup, I got careless. One night I made a last minute decision to attend a get-together with some people in Dallas I didn't know very well. Unfortunately the DEA had been watching the house and monitoring their activity. They raided it that night. I had been on my way to make a delivery somewhere else and planned to stay only a few minutes. I took the fall with everyone there."

When they arrived at the Taurus he put the suitcase down and opened the trunk.

"Is this your friend's car?" she asked brightly.

"It's another long story," he said a little defensively.

"There was a good chance I could have beaten the charges," Teal said as they drove out of the garage and onto the freeway. "My uncle had talked with a lawyer who was convinced I would never go to trial."

"So what happened?" Sloan asked. "Couldn't he deliver?"

"We'll never know. I refused to allow him to be hired and pled guilty."

Sloan thought about it for a moment and watched the scenery skid by.

"So you wanted to punish yourself, and this was the easiest way of doing that?" she finally asked.

Teal stared straight ahead and drummed his fingers on the steering wheel. "Well yes and no," he finally said carefully.

"I hope this doesn't sound too weird, but I wanted to punish myself for being stupid and getting caught. Not for doing something illegal. Does that make any sense?"

"I don't know," Sloan said staring at the side of his face. "Do you feel that way now?"

"You know it's funny, but I don't. I'm not clear on exactly what I feel about the past because I don't dwell on it. I know it's there, and one day I will have a proper perspective on it. And, of course, most of the time I'm thinking about you," he added and favored her with his most engaging grin.

"Well that works okay," she said with an evil smile and dropped a hand in his lap. He quickly retrieved it and placed it safely on her side of the car.

They drove back north through Daly City, South San Francisco and finally Golden Gate Park in the City itself.

"Oh my God," Sloan said as they finally reached the Golden Gate Bridge. "Is the whole area as beautiful as this?"

"Better," Teal said. "A lot of people go to Los Angeles or San Diego and think they've seen California. What they *have* seen is Southern California which is as different from the Northern California as Manhattan is from Bridgeport, Connecticut."

Sloan was watching sail boats clustered and then fly away from each other and tack off in different directions, their sails ballooning and slapping in the breeze. Her eyes were bright as she tried to see everything at once, Teal wondered if she was holding her breath.

With everything Teal had told TJ and Dannie about Sloan, he would have been shocked had they had not been waiting for his arrival. Formal introductions were made and everyone stood around shyly for a moment before Dannie grabbed Sloan's arm and they ran off giggling towards the house like sisters. TJ followed, looking over his shoulder once to arch his eyebrows at Teal and make an exaggerated hourglass sign with his hands.

They drank Coronas with limes while mutual lap sitting was in order and talked until Teal's leg went to sleep, and he nearly dumped Sloan over the railing. By the end of dinner, it was as if they had known each other for years. Dannie and Sloan went to wash dishes while TJ and Jack stayed on the deck.

"Man, those are two fine looking women," TJ said and made a clicking sound through his teeth. "Makes me feel like having a cigarette."

"I didn't know you smoked," Teal said trying to see him clearly in the dark. The night had cooled the porch, and sounds from the emptying freeway were muted. The scent of a night blooming jasmine waved over them for a moment and then was gone.

"I don't," TJ finally said. "Never have. I guess it must be the power of advertising."

Teal nodded slowly. It sounded about right.

Teal left early the next morning to help with the morning prep.

"I'll come pick you up at about ten thirty, and you can have the car for the rest of the day," he said to the eye that was watching him from a tangle of hair. How could a woman look and smell so good in the early morning, Teal wondered and started to get back into bed with his clothes on. She laughed and shrieked and pushed him out.

"If my landlady comes around, be nice to her," he said through the half opened front door.

"How will I know who she is?" a muffled voice asked.

"Well she looks a lot like a young Pamela Anderson," he said and ran for the car.

Teal heard from Claire when he got to the restaurant that, Amed, the black teenager, was starting the following day. Although she was very excited, the mood in the kitchen was very quiet, almost somber, and Teal wondered if it had something to do with Amed.

"What's up?" he asked Nicole. Sammy had just shrugged when Teal asked him.

"Oh...bad day yesterday," she finally said.

"Can you tell me?" he asked getting an omelet ready for its ingredients.

"What it's always about," she whispered, and the skin turned blotchy around her face and neck.

"You don't have to tell me if you don't want too," Teal said, worried now.

"It's Carl. It's always Carl." The blotching intensified. "He was saying something to Ginny she didn't like and was laughing. I think maybe she went in the back and was crying later."

"What?" Teal could feel his anger spiking.

"Please don't say anything. Please! I love working here. I don't want to get in trouble."

"Nicole, Nicole," he said and started to touch her slumping shoulders, then stopped, unsure. "That's not going to happen, alright? But I'm glad you told me."

Half and hour later when Carl went to the rest room, Teal gathered the kitchen crew together.

"I'm bringing my girl friend by for a visit in a few minutes, so you guys better be on your best behavior." He hoped it would pull them out of their funk.

Finally Beth smiled a little and looked at Nicole and Sammy made the snik-snik sound through his nose and actually blushed. Gary came over and held his hand for a moment before Teal could direct him back to the dishwasher.

When he brought Sloan in, Sammy, who had been watching the door motioned Mickey over and they both stared openly and giggling like schoolgirls.

"I want you to meet my buddies," he said with his arm around her shoulders. She was wearing Khaki walking shorts and a bright yellow Polo shirt. You could have fitted a medium sized dog in her purse. When they walked into the kitchen, Sammy was actually hiding in one of the corners, giggling uncontrollably, which even coaxed a grin out of Gary. Teal introduced Sloan to Nicole and Beth, and they shook hands and laughed about something only new women friends could understand. He introduced her to Sammy, who was feigning nonchalance. When he turned she smiled thinly and said, "*Dozo Yoroshiko*" and bowed sharply from her waist. Sammy's lower jaw dropped like a dumb waiter with a severed cable. When he regained control, he repeated the greeting, bowed deeply and smiled. Teal saw Carl returning from the bathroom and quickly spirited Sloan back into the main room. Sloan took the keys and agreed to pick him up at two thirty, and Teal went back into the kitchen to prep for lunch.

The mood had definitely elevated, and the rest of the day went smoothly. Just before Sloan was due, TJ motioned Teal out of the kitchen. He was huddled at his favorite duce with an older couple who stood when Teal approached.

"Jack, I'd like you to meet two of my favorite people, Sissy and John Barrington. Sissy's president of our board."

They shook hands all around, and TJ pulled up another chair.

"TJ has been singing your praises," Sissy said. She was an attractive brunette in her sixties with wide set blue eyes. Both had deep tans causing Teal wonder if they were avid tennis players.

"Must have been a short song," Teal said with a grin, and they both looked at each other and then chuckled.

"We hope you will be able to stay with us a while," Sissy said. "We are very grateful for your help."

"You're welcome," Teal said. "But I have to tell you a little secret. I'm having a good time."

Sissy clasped her hands in front of her. "I'm so happy to hear that. They're quite lovely people – our little kids. And they need so much help."

John patted her knee, and she put her hand over his.

"To be honest with you, they're more interesting than most people I've met in my life," Teal said, nervously eying Mickey, who was strolling toward them.

"Mr. and Mrs. Barrington. How nice to see you again," he said pleasantly and shook both of their hands. When he walked away, TJ expelled his breath and mopped his brow.

"Oh come on, TJ," Sissy said and laughed. "He can be very sweet."

"Yeah, when he wants to – which isn't very often."

The Barringtons and most of the crew had left when Sloan returned, her cheeks flushed and eyes bright.

"Boy, I thought Scottsdale had some good shopping! Wait 'til you see what I bought you."

Teal and TJ looked at each other dead pan to see who would break first.

"Emily's very sweet," Sloan said. "She's obviously very fond of you."

Teal kissed her on the neck.

"Hey, I'm trying to talk to you here."

Teal sat on the sofa and put his hands under his butt.

"By the way, where did you learn Japanese?" Teal asked. "You flat blew Sammy away. I'm going to have to deal with him for the next couple of weeks."

She laughed. "I have a girlfriend I've known since grade school who was a foreign correspondent in Japan before getting married. She gave me a couple of phrases. I only hope Sammy doesn't want to have a long conversation. I'll just have to keep saying 'pleased to meet you'.

"All those kids you work with are sweet," she said. "They all seem so shy and quiet. And that one boy was holding my hand. I wasn't quite sure what to do."

"You did just fine," Teal said. He was actually proud that she didn't flinch or become frightened, but he didn't know how to tell her.

"When you told me about the restaurant, I couldn't imagine how it could even be possible. I guess I have the same hang-ups lots of people have about mental illness. I mean I'm not trying to preach or anything."

"It's true, Sloan. When TJ told me what he was doing I was almost afraid to go down there. Not to say that things don't get a little weird sometimes, but probably the scariest person in there is the head cook, Carl."

Sloan shook her head. "I don't think I saw him."

"Good thing. He probably would've drooled on you. And I think he was drunk when you were there. He went to the bathroom for a long time, and when he came back, he seemed unsteady. Always drinking cranberry juice."

"Oh boy," Sloan said. "Working man's cocktail. Dad had the same problem with a guy a while back in the shop. Took him a long time before he was sure enough to let him go. You know you get sued if you look at an employee sideways now days. Speaking of which," she said snapping her fingers, "do you remember Dutch?"

Teal shrugged.

"No, you wouldn't, but he's one of the mechanics in the shop. Good mechanic and a hell of a nice man. Dad hired him about three years ago on the recommendation of an old racing buddy. Dutch was having trouble finding a job because...he had just gotten out of prison." She did a little ta-ta with her hand.

"Jesus, you're kidding."

"Nope. And he's turned out to be one of the best wrenches to ever work there. And it was Dutch who knew about the thingy under your car, the tracking device."

"I can see why your dad went ballistic. All sort of piling up on him," he said and then grinned. "You want to see a naked jailbird?" he asked.

"Why the hell not," she said after a moment, got up from the chair and tugged him towards the tiny bedroom.

Teal drove into San Rafael early before Sloan was awake. He bought a disposable cell phone at a convenience store and returned to the car. He dialed a number from memory and listened to the rings.

"Hello." A low voice with little inflection. Teal thought it might be Rukka but wasn't sure.

"Is Hector there?" he asked.

"You have a wrong number," the voice said, but the line was still opened.

"Do you recognize my voice?" Teal asked.

There was a long silence, and he could imagine he heard breathing.

"Yes," the voice finally said.

"Good. I have a message. I have something which was loaned to me and which I no longer want," he said, unconsciously falling into the same odd rhythm of speech, which was native to the man on the line. He gave the man the address of the public storage and the combination for the lock.

"Do you have all that?" Teal asked.

"Yes," the voice said, and the connection was terminated. Teal tossed the phone in a trash can and drove Brownie back up the hill playing Tommy Lee drum riffs on the steering wheel.

* * *

FIFTEEN

The plot of land six and a half miles north of Santa Barbara had long been considered unsuitable for building, fabulous ocean views not withstanding. In the nineteen eighties, a few had tried to put a package together and lost heart when the pre planning costs escalated into the stratosphere. So the land owner had really ceased trying to market the turkey and was seriously considering giving it to the coastal commission and taking an obscene write-off.

Enter a reclusive dot comer who had hit it on not one but three separate ventures and cashed in at the peak. He was said to have more money than most European nations, and, with very wise investments, it multiplied faster than fruit flies. When he saw this lonely jut of land, he said, 'this is where I'll build my home.' The locals snickered, but contractors left off business cards just in case.

After buying the property, he hired soil engineers, structural engineers, hydrologists, botanists, surveyors, architects (four) and a water witch. He personally went on a campaign to meet and schmooze with every politician of note in the state of California. He remembered wife's birthdays, passed out tickets to sporting events, symphony openings, sold out Broadway mega hits and had the uncanny ability to make everyone feel they were, indeed, entitled.

It took much, much longer than Hitler rolling into Poland, but it was just as effective. Two years later he broke ground on his thirteen thousand square foot 'home', and the

tickets, the glad-handing, the high school grad presents and
all the rest of the wonderful fluff disappeared overnight like a
Sahara waterhole.

Even Paige Rence, the editor of Architectural Digest, had
pulled all her considerable strings to gain admittance – and to
no avail

When it was discovered that the house was to have but
three bedrooms, the snickering began anew.

"Doesn't have any friends, so no need for bedrooms," said
one of the local contractors whose bid had been tossed. Many of
the other comments were somewhat more libelous.

So, when the dot comer went for an evening drive up
Highway 101 in his latest Ferrari and missed the second curve
from his driveway gate, plunging into the Pacific Ocean, there
wasn't a wet eye in the community.

The estate he left behind was the largest to be probated
in California history. Relatives arrived by the plane load and
lawyers by the busload; it was shaping up to be everyone's big
jackpot. Nobody wanted the house, which was considered the
biggest white elephant in real estate history. Someone slapped
an arbitrary price of 17.5 million on it, and everyone thought it
would rot away, unloved, and fall into the Pacific.

When a representative from Matador del Sol International
took a walkthrough, nobody paid much attention. When his
offer of sixteen, five came less than three days later, the local
collective consciousness said, 'What the Hell!'

Cash offers in real estate put the closing on a fast track,
and Matador Sol International became the legal owner in a
matter of weeks.

After escrow had closed, pick up trucks descended in
endless convoys bringing workers, lumber, roofing supplies,
plumbing fixture, fully grown trees and starter plants of every

description and mountains of boxes of every size and shape. The house was essentially rebuilt from the inside out and, word had it, bore little resemblance to the original. The landscaping was terraced and planted and looked as mature as the Tivoli Gardens.

Of course, in a matter of several more months, the house was on the cover of Architectural Digest and the feature story within flowed over twelve pages. The house and grounds were now said to be on the fast track for several design awards, and other magazines were scrambling in an attempt to pick up some crumbs.

Hector Alviso Koontzman, the sole shareholder of the company that owned the company that owned Matador Sol International, sat in the sunny open gazebo enjoying the sights and sounds of the ocean some three hundred feet below. Rukka sat with his back to the ocean and, even then, could feel the ticklish fingers of the pounding surf dragging down his spine and beckoning him to an icy grave.

"Whom do you wish me to send to pick it up?" Rukka asked. He was pulled up so tight to the table in fear of the cliff edge, there was little room left for him to breath.

"There is no hurry," Koontzman answered taking a deep breath from the breeze, which carried the scent of salt, seaweed and damp sand and soil. He wore no shoes and wiggled his toes in the warming afternoon sun.

"I'm surprised he found both trackers and curious why there was a three day gap," Koontzman murmured softly. "We know the car was in an accident, and I have to assume that one was torn off then. Remind me to call Mr. Barka and thank him personally for calling about the accident. The second must have been discovered during the repairs. I don't believe he found either of them, although perhaps he knows." Then he corrected himself. "I would be most certain he knows. And it has made him angry."

They were both quiet for a moment as a particularly large roller slammed the cliff face below them and the ground shuddered almost imperceptibly. Rukka closed his eyes briefly and felt nauseous.

"And if he knows, what will he think? What will he do?" Rukka asked. Talking made him think less about a watery grave, and his stomach settled somewhat.

"I think his anger is causing him to make a statement. I must say that I find it hard to blame him. I would have been angry as well."

He took a sip of lemonade and squinted into the setting sun. "I will wait for a while and then perhaps contact him. Or have him 'accidentally' come into contact with someone of us he would remember. That would have more class, don't you think?" He knew how Rukka felt about Teal and enjoyed a sadistic pleasure probing his discomfort.

"Maybe he is content working with his *locos.* Maybe daily wages will satisfy him."

"I think I know Jack Teal far better than you. He will wish to come back," he said with a confident smile. "And perhaps the two of you can work together." He was a trifle ashamed of *that* comment but not enough to make amends, as he took another sip of the lemonade and wondered how long he should keep Rukka hanging on the edge of a cliff before releasing him for other duties.

* * *

SIXTEEN

Their road trip up the coast on 101 was leisurely and interrupted by quick stops for anything appearing vaguely interesting. Sloan had bought a bag of Kodak throwaway cameras and insisted on portraits at virtually every point of interest along the way. When she tired, Dannie picked up the cause and pestered people. The two women were like twin sisters, to the point of anticipating what the other was going to say. That morning before they got on the road, Dannie and Sloan had switched clothes and served TJ and Teal breakfast. Teal caught on first and almost collapsed laughing while TJ sat stone still looking from face to face with his forehead furrowed in confusion and concentration.

"I'm getting a headache," he said. "And I can't for the life of me figure out why."

When they could catch their collective breaths and tell him, he said, "I think I'm going to have some very strange dreams tonight."

"Are you guys ever going to open for dinner," Sloan asked. They were poking along riding family style, and Teal would ease off onto the shoulder when anyone came up behind him. Fortunately the turnouts were numerous.

"Well, of course we talked about it. But that's a long rung on the ladder. We have to keep in mind what we originally set out to do, and we can't help people if we're scrambling around and working two shifts. You have to remember, for us, two shifts are twice as expensive because of the clinical staff it requires."

"How about dropping breakfast?"

"Can't do that," TJ said. "It's my favorite meal."

"Seriously," Sloan said poking him, while Dannie grinned her encouragement.

"Because breakfast is simpler, not easier, simpler. Do you understand the difference?"

"I think I do," Sloan answered after thinking a moment.

"These kids are not going from here to be a sous-chef somewhere. Nor do we give them any encouragement to pursue that. But if they can handle the breakfast pressure and turn out some good food while maintaining their composure, they can hold a good paying job. Then maybe, just maybe, with good training and a lot of luck, some might climb the ladder and take that next step. And we've got friends in other restaurants who are willing to give them a chance.

"Same goes for the dishwashers and wait staff. Those are good steady jobs and, at least in the case of the wait staff, can be a source of serious income."

"Dannie's been telling Sloan about the rest of the organization," Teal said once they were back on the road and headed for Sea Ranch. TJ was scrabbling through everything in the glove box and not finding anything of interest.

"I think she knows more about it than I do."

TJ shrugged and stared out the window.

"So, what, is it some sort of a white slavery deal?" Teal asked sounding peeved.

TJ started to look through the glove box again, and Teal reached over to close it.

"You want to share this with me?" Teal said swatting TJ's hand away from the glove box.

"It's a very complex organization, Jack," he said and
sighed deeply. "There are other projects under the umbrella of
the organization and..."

"But there is only one Magnolia in the entire country,"
Dannie said leaning over into the front seat. "The other projects
are residential houses and things like art and pottery classes
taught at high schools after hours, and they're about as common
as ticks in the forest. I'm not knocking them mind you, but
they sure as hell don't measure up to Magnolia."

"As I was saying," TJ continued slowly while Dannie sat
back and stewed. "Marin Advocates is a complex organization
involving lots of clinicians and clients – I am just a small part
of the whole." He ignored the snort and whispered comments
from the back seat.

"The organization was founded by some concerned
residents of Marin County when it became apparent mental
health issues were not high on the state and the federal agendas.
Cut backs were looming and then became reality. Kids were
having trouble getting any sort of adequate and enlightened
treatment. Some people like the Barringtons and others put up
seed money and put together a lay board."

"A lay board?" Teal asked. "What's a lay board?"

"All non pros – that is to say no clinicians. Just concerned
and worried human beings who are putting their money where
their mouths are."

He started to reach for the glove box and then thought
better of it.

"You will also find many on the board have had their
families touched in some way by mental illness," he continued.
"If not a family member then perhaps a close friend."

Sloan was whispering something to Dannie and once
again a wave of giggles erupted from the back seat. TJ turned

to scowl, and they both sat bolt upright with serious faces which threatened to crumple starting with the corners of their mouths.

"I'm just part of it," TJ said and scorched a warning glance into the rear seat. "We've got two residential houses with a third in the works for the end of the year. Generally three to five kids to a house with a program director and a counselor. We also have three other counselors who we call floaters. They rotate between the houses and occasionally come into Magnolia. In the houses we teach living skills and what it takes to survive in the real world. Many haven't the faintest idea. It can be as basic as how to correctly brush their teeth and clean themselves in a tub or shower. You would think parents would have taught them, but many give up. And some of the kids have been institutionalized so long, they have lost the basic skills you and I take for granted.

"So it's very difficult to find a community that will accept one of our houses in their neighborhood. Most of the time it works great but sometimes not, and we have to close it down."

Teal pulled into a vista overlook parking area, and they all got out stretching their legs and letting a long stream of cars go by. And more pictures were taken of people, flora and fauna and even the stream of cars. Gulls circled the beach far below and pelicans strafed the crests of the breakers.

"MAMS has a director who is the man at the top," TJ said propping a foot on the guard rail and staring into the surf below. "His name is Lawrence Gorman. Never Larry to anyone, as far as I know." He scraped his shoe on the railing as if he had stepped in something.

"Sounds like the two of you aren't very tight."

TJ cocked his head and snorted. "You might say that.

But," he held up his hand like a traffic cop, "he is very important to the organization. He carries heavy credentials and lends a strong sense of legitimacy to MAMS. Also we hope he will open some funding doors for us."

Teal stared at him for a moment then said, "Christ, TJ, that's the most rehearsed party line I've ever heard come out of your mouth."

TJ nodded almost imperceptibly and cocked his eyebrows. "We tolerate each other as long as he stays out of my fucking facility," he said with sudden rising vehemence in his voice. His face turned bright red, and Teal backed up a step. Dannie came up next to him quickly and put an arm around his waist. "Shh – shh," she said mothering a child, now rubbing his back. "No more talk about Larry. You know it's not your favorite subject."

TJ smiled at her use of 'Larry', and the red drained from his face leaving it looking waxen.

"Let's go up to Sea Ranch and walk on the beach," she said taking his hand and walking back to the car. "Maybe we can find a treasure chest or something."

"Well at least some nice artistic driftwood," he said grinning and following her meekly while Sloan looked at Teal with arched eyebrows.

When they were back in bed at the cottage, Sloan lay curled next to him stroking his hair.

"How come you never talk about your folks?" she asked making little ringlets of black hair at the nape of his neck.

"I don't know. You don't talk about your dad all that much."

"Oh foo, I've told you heaps about him. And Mom. Plus I live with Dad" As if that somehow made a difference.

Teal figured he knew less about women than the average human being. But he did know an unchallengeable statement when he heard one. He at least prided himself on that.

"Don't you think about them? Worry about them sometimes?" she asked.

"Sure, I do, but maybe not in the same way you do."

"So if your mom passed away, would you go to take care of your father?"

He had never thought of that before. The other way around certainly. But his father seemed so…indestructible.

"I don't think he would need taking care of."

"But say he did. Say he was like my father, and his grief took control and started beating him down. And he was really lost and needed someone. Then?"

"Maybe, if he wanted me there. Sure, then I'd help."

"What if he was too proud to ask? Would you go then?"

"Yes."

"Good. Do you want to fool around a little bit?"

Much later Sloan said, "I worry about TJ's health. Has he said anything to you about high blood pressure?"

Teal shook his head and kissed her palm. "He's never said anything, but the way he looked today scared me."

She snuggled against him and said, "I know you will keep him safe. And by the way did you know you have a robin hanging out on your deck. I gave him some old dried oatmeal, but you should really get him some robin food."

Robin food? Where do you shop for robin food?

Sloan flew out on Sunday morning already making plans for the next visit in two weeks. She had also invited Dannie down for a visit to Scottsdale, and those plans were beginning to jell. Although he felt a bit guilty about it, Teal

was considering more pressing matters. Not plans for the
distant future but plans for Monday morning. Monday would
be Amed's first day.

Teal and Sammy reached the restaurant at the same
time, and Teal opened the front door with a spare key TJ had
slipped him. Sammy did the bug eyed look, and Teal winked at
him. They were turning on the kitchen when Nicole and Beth
walked in looking around for Carl, then smiled and shrugged
and got to work. They talked in low voices stealing looks over
their shoulder at Teal.

It would be a perfect time for Amed to start. He would
be working with Tim on the espresso bar, and, if it worked
out successfully, would take over on Friday, the day Tim was
scheduled to leave on a vacation to Southern California with his
parents. On his return he was scheduled to start in the kitchen
and had been talking about it for the last two weeks. Teal
hoped they wouldn't give him a knife for a while. Maybe a very
dull one would be okay.

Carl blew through the door moments later looking
rumpled and angry. "Hey, hey, how the hell did you clowns get
in here," he shouted throwing his coat into the hallway behind
the kitchen.

Teal dangled the key from his little finger, and then
dropped it back into his pocket. "TJ wanted me down here
early," he said mildly. "He's expecting a big day."

The only other sounds in the kitchen were the chopping
of knives and clattering of pots and silverware.

"This is my kitchen," Carl said, his voice rising with each
word. "TJ and me are going to have words about this, you can
bet your sweet ass."

He stormed out of the kitchen, scooped up his coat and tromped out of the restaurant. The two girls clapped just as Gary came in the front door. Thinking it was for him, he smiled, bowed deeply and high stepped it into the kitchen.

Teal shook his head.

This is going to be one hell of a day.

Ginny and Rich came in together laughing, followed shortly by Mickey, looking like an advertising executive and Clair, cool and collected. TJ, looking rested and excited, strolled through the door and waved at the kitchen crew. It was very early for him, and Rich looked at Teal and wiggled his eyebrows.

"Man, is everybody pumped today or what?" he said and awkwardly tried a high-five with Clair.

Then Peter Quinn Ryan came in with Amed who was practically walking on his tiptoes he was so excited. Peter Quinn looked like a proud father after a successful piano rehearsal. His beard was freshly trimmed.

Tim and Amed were introduced and immediately went to work setting up the stand and pulling espressos for the staff. Tim had even written down basic operating instructions and slipped them into plastic sleeves. Amed hung on every word, his eyes wide and his hands sure.

"Where's Carl?" TJ asked looking around the kitchen.

"Ummm…maybe he's going to be talking to you later about something," Teal said waving his hand behind his back at Sammy who was about to add his two cents worth.

"Seems he was a little pissed I had a key to the restaurant. Said it was his turf and blew out the door."

Then, almost under his breath, "Probably went to find a bar."

"What do you mean by that?" TJ asked and seemed genuinely surprised.

"I can't prove it, but I think he's drinking at work."

"Oh fuck, that's great. Just great!" TJ said with his hands on his temple.

"Look, TJ, let me worry about him."

TJ gave him a wary look.

"Please don't worry about it. I'm not going to punch him out or something." He put his hand on TJ's shoulder. "I don't know if the kids suspect anything, but I wouldn't be surprised. They're pretty perceptive."

TJ nodded and Teal thought if Carl made a drunken scene or in any way threatened anybody, he would kick his ass around the block.

"How did your first day go?" Teal asked Amed who was helping Tim clean up at the end of the day. Ginny was cleaning the hostess stand and chattering to both of them. Tim would nod wearily while Amed would smile and encourage her with head shakes. Amed gave Teal a huge grin and pumped his hand vigorously. At least he doesn't want to *hold* hands, Teal thought.

TJ was packing his briefcase and motioned Teal over.

"You know about the Tuesday night roundtable, right?" he asked.

Teal nodded. "The kids talk about it some. I get the impression most of them like it."

"It's designed for clients and clinical staff. Occasionally we invite people who fit neither category; Sissy, for instance attends from time to time." He ran his hand through his hair and scratched his ear.

"What I'm getting around to is asking you to attend next Tuesday."

"Boy, I don't know, TJ…"

"You don't have to. It's, like, not in your job description or anything," he said and flashed him a big grin. "I ran it by Peter Quinn, Rich and Clair, and they all liked it. Rich said the kids really like and respect you – although I can't imagine why," he added with a bigger grin.

"Jesus, you're still the sweetest talker on the face of the planet," Teal said. "What time does it start?"

The day went very quickly although the lunch rush was strong, and Teal nodded to returning faces he recognized. Carl who had returned near the end of the rush was quiet and efficient as long as people stayed out of his way. Sissy and John came in for breakfast, and Teal stepped out to talk with them.

"How is Amed doing?" Sissy asked. "He's just darling."

"He's doing terrific," Teal said. "Very smart kid. Pretty much mastered the whole setup in a day. And today I gave him the go ahead to experiment with flavors. I think he's envious of the Sammy Scramble."

John laughed. "When I order one of those, I eat half here and save the other half for lunch – and even then I sometimes can't eat it all."

"Plus it makes you pokey on the courts," Sissy added and patted his hand.

Teal went to a pet store on his way home and searched through racks of seeds stuck together in the shapes of trees, footballs, stars and kittens.

Kittens? Why would a bird want to eat seeds from something shaped like one of their mortal enemies?

A young man stopped stocking the shelves long enough to ask if he could help.

"I need food for a robin, but I don't know what they eat."

"A robin? I don't think we sell no robins."

"No, I don't want to *buy* a robin. I *got* a robin. I want to feed it."

"You got a robin? Where did you buy that?"

An older man strolled over and smiled. "Can I help you with something?"

"Yeah, I need to find out what robins eat."

The man beamed. "Haven't you heard the saying 'the early bird gets the worm'?"

"Sure."

"What sort of a bird do you picture when you think of that saying?"

The image popped up in Teal's brain so fast, it startled him. "A robin," he said remembering the book his mother read him when he was two or three. Several pictures of a fat bird on skinny legs trying to pull an even fatter worm out of the ground. It was as if he had seen it yesterday.

"I'll be damned. Worms. I'd forgotten that. You got any?"

"Nope. We got some mealworms for lizards and like that but for earthworms you have to go to a bait shop. There's one by the yacht harbor on fourth. Can't miss it."

Teal drove over to the bait shop and found pint and quart containers of earthworms as well as containers of various and sundry other exotic baits. The nightmarish creatures called pile worms looked absolutely lethal. He picked up two pints of earthworms and strolled up to the check out.

"You got yourself a farm pond all staked out, I'll bet ya," the grizzled owner said with a smile.

"No, no," Teal said and smiled. "These are for some robins outside my house."

"Whatever you say," the man said and chuckled, ringing up the charges. "I don't let anybody know where my favorite spots are neither."

When he handed Teal the plastic bag he said, "Hope you come back in for all your...bird needs."

On the way back to the cottage Teal realizing he had forgotten to pick up Amed's recipes. He had intended to study them that night and the following morning recommend which ones had possibilities. When he arrived at the cottage, he selected a soup bowl, dropped in a pinch of worms and put it on the rail. The worms immediately beat a hasty retreat, bailing out over the rim and dropping into the weeds below, while the disbelieving robin watched from a tree branch. After thinking for a moment he retrieved a barren redwood planter from outside the front door, carefully placed it on the railing and dumped in the second pint of worms. From inside the living room, he watched the robin pick off the slow ones while most of the others burrowed into the soft dirt and temporary safety.

He started to sit down and have a beer, but realized how disappointed Amed might be if he didn't have any suggestions for him the following morning.

Damn it, he thought and put the beer back in the refrigerator. It would probably be flat when he got back.

When he reached the restaurant, there was ample parking in front, generally a rarity, and he walked to the front door tossing his keys from hand to hand. He opened the door and walked quickly to the espresso stand without flipping on the lights. He knew the layout so well, he could have done it in pitch dark without tripping over a table or chair.

He found the notes where Amed had left them and started for the front door when he noticed a sliver of light from

the back hallway. Someone had left a light on which happened
to be one of TJ's greatest phobias.

"Christ, we got bills coming out of our ass without
having to leave lights on so the mice can see what they're going
to have for dinner."

Teal slipped around and through the chairs and tables
seeing that the light came from the storeroom. He opened the
door and was reaching for the switch when he saw Carl and
Ginny and froze. Ginny was lying back against a pile of aprons
and towels, her shirt was opened and brassiere pulled down
revealing tiny breasts that looked red from mauling. Her hair
was in disarray and her eyes had problems focusing. The room
reeked of alcohol.

"Hey what the fuck are you doing," Carl shouted. "Get
outta here." He was trying to pull his underwear and trousers
over an erection, which was rapidly wilting.

Teal had trouble breathing for a second; his anger had
escalated so quickly it caught him by surprise. He stepped over
to Ginny and handed her his leather jacket.

"Come on, Ginny," he said quietly. "Put the jacket on,
and I'll take you home."

She nodded dumbly and rearranged her brassiere and
blouse before slipping her arms through the sleeves.

"My car's out front. Remember which one it is?"

She nodded.

"It's open, so go ahead and hop in. I'll be along in a
second."

She fled through the restaurant and was gone.

"You stupid, asshole," Carl said, his face contorted with
rage. "You can kiss your fucking job goodbye."

Teal backhanded him. His left hand started from below
his beltline and hit Carl on his left cheek and nose and spun

him backwards over a bag of potatoes. He pulled down a condiment shelf as he fell. Coriander, pepper, salt and cayenne bounced and rolled and popped.

"Are you crazy, you son of a bitch?" Carl screamed. "You're going to jail for assault and battery."

Teal grabbed the front of his shirt and pulled him upright. When he was standing, he backhanded him a second time and Carl slid down a wall and slumped. The pain in Teal's hand extended from his knuckles to his neck, and he gritted his teeth.

Then he reached down and pulled Carl up, sitting him on the sack of potatoes. There was a flicker of confusion in his eyes.

"Listen to me very carefully, you fucking prick," Teal said softly. He was no more than six inches from Carl's face and could smell the blood flowing from his nose and the reek of alcohol on his panting breath.

"You are done here," Teal said. "When you walk out that door, you will never be coming back. After you walk out that door, you will walk out of this county and never come back. Are you with me so far?"

Carl shook his head and started to get up. Teal grabbed his hair and slammed his head back against the brick wall. Now fear had replaced confusion in his eyes.

"You threaten me with jail, you stupid piece of shit. I've been to prison," he shouted into his face. Carl flinched and tried to turn away, but Teal pinched his chin and held him fast.

"I saw things in there you could not imagine in your worst nightmares," he shouted with saliva spotting Carl's face. "Ways to hurt a man so badly he loses the desire to live. Ways to disfigured and maim…Are you listening, you sorry piece of shit?"

Carl nodded, his eyes wild and fleeting.

"You will call TJ tonight and resign. I don't care what the excuse is – tell him your dog died. Tell him you will send him an address where to mail your severance check when you get resettled. And," he said pinching Carl's chin until he whined, "you will have mysteriously forgotten all of what happened here. If one word, one tiny word, gets back to me, I will find you and seriously fuck you up. When I'm finished, you won't be able to boil water."

Teal stood up. "Do you think you can remember all that?" he asked. "Because if you're unsure…" he said stepping forward.

Carl put a hand in front of his face and cringed. "I'm leaving, I'm leaving," he said quickly. "Let me just pick up my knives and recipes."

"Pick up your knife box, but the recipes stay here. I know you stole them from other restaurants."

Carl cleaned his face with a towel, picked up his knife box and started for the door. Teal stopped him halfway across the room. Carl visibly shrunk from him.

"Just remember, Carl," he whispered into the man's face. "If I ever, *ever* see you again, you better be behind bullet-proof glass."

After Carl left, Teal closed the restaurant and got into the Toyota. Ginny was curled in the passenger's seat and looked like a tiny pile of discarded laundry.

"Where do you live, Ginny?" he asked in a soft voice.

"Up on Blithedale – Blithedale and Harrmon," she answered.

"Is there someone there for you to talk to? To help you clean up?"

"Yeah, my roomy, Diane."

"Okay, keep my jacket, and you can bring it in tomorrow."

She nodded and started to cry, and Teal was startled with such immense sobs from the tiny frame.

Teal stopped in front of a small house with a light on by the front door. He saw the door open, and Ginny leapt from the car and ran up the pathway. A woman met her and put an arm around her shoulders and closed the door gently behind them.

By the time he returned to the cottage, his shakes had dissipated, and his blood pressure had started to level off. As he stepped out of the car Emily saw him from her back door and waved.

"I have a letter for you," she said waving an envelope. Teal walked over to her with a curious expression, thanked her, passed the time of day for a moment and then went into his cottage. He had rented a post office box in San Rafael for what meager mail he received which consisted mainly of bills from his cell phone provider.

His name and Emily's address had been printed on a label and stuck on the envelope. There was no return address but a Los Angeles postmark had canceled the stamp.

He slit it open and shook out a single six by four glossy photograph with no markings on the reverse side other than the word 'Kodak'. It was a photograph of him and Sloan standing next to a Porsche Carrera with the saguaros dotting an Arizona desert stretching out behind them. He had his arm over Sloan's shoulder and she had her arm around his waist as they walked and smiling towards the photographer. In the background was a troop of Brownies.

Teal felt a chill start between his shoulder blades and spread through his system like a fast acting poison. There was absolutely nothing sinister about the photograph. On the contrary, it was well composed, the color was true and, other than being very slightly fuzzy as if taking through a telephoto lens, it might be the perfect photo a young couple would use to grace their next Christmas card.

Teal sat on the bed and stared at it while his emotions ran the gambit from fear to fury. What was the point and what was the message, he wondered. No warning was implied or even hinted, but its mere presence coupled with the method of delivery was confusing and ultimately disturbing. He stared at it for a long time before finally tucking it beneath some clothes in the dresser and going into the bathroom to try to soak the pain and swelling out of his hand.

TJ called earlier than Teal had expected, the cell phone playing the first few notes of *Purple Haze*. It seemed as if he had just gone to bed after soaking his hand, which now had settled into to a dull throbbing rhythm. If it had been his right, he would have had a problem working in the kitchen.

"Teal? Teal?" TJ asked as if he had dialed the wrong number. "Jesus Christ, Carl called me up and quit. Said he's leaving town tonight, some sick relative or something. I don't know what we're going to do."

"We're going to open the restaurant tomorrow and have a great day," Teal answered stifling a yawn.

"Jesus Christ Jack, we just lost our chef. We lost our credibility."

"Oh come on, TJ. You're selling yourself and your clients short. They are far better than you think they are and far better than what Carl's been telling you."

"You don't seem to be that torn up about it," TJ said, but he was calming down. Teal imagined Dannie was scared to death.

"TJ, it's no secret that I couldn't stand the guy. He's no loss at all because your crew can and will do the job. Plus," he added cheerfully, "You can shave his salary off your bottom line."

Teal gave him a few seconds to absorb that thought. "Hey, do you mind if we chat about this in the morning, so I can get some beauty sleep? Or maybe we can talk after the party we'll have when everyone hears he gone."

He heard TJ sigh. "You better show up, you bozo," he finally said, and Teal chuckled.

"Oh I'll be there, and probably bring my agent. We'll have to be talking about a new pay scale." He hung up on TJ's laugh.

Teal arrived at Magnolia early, left the door open and started to clean up the storeroom. Sammy came in several minutes later – early for him – and stared at the mess.

"Hey what happened in here?" he asked. "Look like a bomb went off."

"That damn shelf came down and sprayed stuff all over the place. Go on in and get started. I'll be done in a couple of minutes."

"What's with this bloody towel?" Sammy asked holding it up.

"Oh I hurt my hand a little bit," he said holding it up for Sammy to see. Sammy looked at the hand, at the dried blood on the towel, chewed on his lip for a moment and went into the kitchen. Teal could tell he was trying to put it all together in his mind. And it didn't quite add up.

When the crew was assembled, Teal called them over to the corner by the dishwasher.

"Carl's no longer working here," he said. "I heard someone in his family is ill, and he had to leave right away."

There was silence, as they seemed to be waiting for him to say something more.

Finally, Nicole timidly raised her hand. "Can we go back to work now?" she asked. Beth stood behind her and nodded in agreement.

"Yep," Teal said slapping his hands together and wincing from the pain, which almost took his breath away.

The morning rush came and went, and the main topic of conversation was Carl's resignation. Rich and Claire both asked him what he knew and when Peter Quinn came in, he did the same. His answer was the same for all of them.

He didn't see Ginny come in but noticed her cleaning tables and seating people. She was subdued, all the usual chatter missing, and everyone seemed to be giving her space. Also she looked about fifteen years old. When Teal glanced back at the coat rack, he saw his leather jacket hanging among the jean jackets, the cords and the hats.

"You know," Peter Quinn said conspiring with Teal. "I never really cared much for that guy. I think the kids were afraid of him."

"Know what you mean," said Teal munching on a stalk of celery. "He didn't do much for me either."

In the middle of the rush, Teal put up an order and called for Ginny to pick up. When she did, she gave him a small smile before looking away. Over her shoulder, Teal could see TJ and Peter Quinn sitting with a man and a woman while Rich hovered nervously and Clair cast glances from her position by the front station where she was talking with Mickey.

The man was tall and very thin, almost skeletal, and had a thin, neatly trimmed goatee and small rectangular glasses, which looked old fashioned. He was wearing a medium gray suit with a European cut that looked very expensive. When he spoke, he tilted his head back slightly so he was literally talking down his nose at people. His eyes rarely blinked behind the thick glasses, which under certain light appeared to be nearly opaque. The woman sitting next to him was quite pretty in a severe, tailored way. She might have passed for Clair's younger sister, except for her body movements, which seemed too controlled and careful. He realized he had seen movements like that before when his mother had been under heavy medication for a severe back injury. Weird.

"Who's the guy sitting with TJ?" he asked nudging Sammy. "He seems to have everyone on edge."

Sammy looked up and made the snic-snic sound through his nose. "That's Lawrence," he said pronouncing it like the young Bedouins in *Lawrence of Arabia*. "He da man."

"I take it you're not a fan," Teal said dryly.

"How could I be? He's never said one word to me. Like I'm some sort of Samurai ghost."

"How about the woman?"

"Her name's Ann somethin'. She's sorta strange!"

Teal slapped him on the back and said, "Well come on spooky. Let's get these sandwiches up."

"Okay, okay. I just wish I knew which one Lawrence ordered." Snic-snic-snic.

Teal hoped to be called out to meet Gorman, but TJ never looked his way, and after the couple left, his complexion was ashen. Teal stole away from the kitchen and sat down across from him.

"Hey scout, you look like someone just peed in your briefcase," Teal said looking for at least a chuckle.

TJ sighed deeply. "Lawrence and I don't see eye to eye on some things. He can be...difficult to work with. He would rather me say 'work for', but I don't work for him. I work for the Board of Directors."

"Well, he must understand that," Teal said unconvincingly.

"He might know it, but he chooses not to accept it. He makes life tough for all program directors, but the more Magnolia gains recognition, the more he wants to have a hand in its operation. And that, I can tell you," he said wrinkling his forehead, "won't work. Not even."

"Have you talked with the board about it? Sissy and John seem like very savvy people."

"We've danced around it, particularly me and Sissy, but we had to jump through monster hoops to get the guy in the first place. So now they're reluctant to try and rein him in, much less anything more dramatic."

"I'll watch your backside partner, so he can't sneak up on you."

That garnered a weak smile, which was far better than the death mask. "If you stick around here long enough, you'll probably be summoned out to The Center."

"What the hell is The Center?" Teal asked not liking the sound of it.

"The Center is his headquarters out on Lucas Valley Road. It's where he lives. He also has meetings and conferences out there – probably human sacrifices."

Teal laughed when some of TJ's color came back, and he grinned. "By the way, I've been meaning to tell you the board is having a meeting next week on Wednesday, and I suspect Sissy is going to invite you to attend. They'll have their board meeting, and then you and a couple other people will show up for the cocktail party afterwards. They do this with almost all staff, Carl being the most notable exception. I think Sissy despised him. He came out of the kitchen once when she and John were having breakfast and extolled his virtues and went on about all the magnificent restaurants courting him."

TJ laughed. "The most amazing thing was his inability to pick up the vibes. I was across the room and the vibes almost knocked me out of my chair. And he just sits there and blah, blah, blah. It was really sort of funny."

"Yeah, Carl was a real card," Teal said.

"Anyway, keep Wednesday open. I'll let you know." He had his full color back and was packing his briefcase. "So what'd you do to your hand?" he asked not looking at it.

"My hand?" Teal had been caught off guard and was stumbling.

"Yeah, your hand. That thing on the end of your arm." He had finished packing the case and was eyeballing Teal.

"Oh yeah, I smacked it between the chair and railing on my deck. Hurts like a son-of-a-bitch."

"Did you go see a doctor? We have a health plan for employees, you know," he said still pinning Teal with a stare.

"Oh it's alright. If I have any problems with it, I promise I'll go see someone."

"Hmmm..." TJ said and hooked his briefcase under his arm. "Remember Tuesday night. It's rough and tumble, but..." he looked down at Teal's hand, "I suppose you can handle it."

When Teal got back to his cottage, Emily came out to meet Teal wiping her hands on a towel.

"How was work today?" she asked smiling and tucking the towel into her apron.

"It was fine, Emily. Thanks for asking."

"I used to ask my husband, and he would always say everything went just fine. You know men aren't great communicators," she added taking Teal into her confidence.

He smiled because Sloan had said the same thing on several occasions.

"You have a phone message," she said. "A man called from a public storage place and wanted you to call. Do you need the number?"

"No thanks, Emily. I've got it, and by the way I've gotten a cellular, so I won't be a bother anymore."

"Nonsense," she said patting him on the shoulder. She sounded disappointed. "I'll look forward to Sloan's next visit. She is absolutely the sweetest child."

Teal decided it probably wouldn't be appropriate to share Jason's 'prisoner' comment. "Yes, she is, isn't she," was all he said.

Teal fed the impatient robin, pulled a beer out of the refrigerator and took the cell phone out to the deck. He was not comfortable carrying the phone with him, although he seemed to be the only person in Marin County not packing one.

The manager of the public storage facility told him the Porsche had been picked up that afternoon.

"Great. Then the unit is all yours. I won't be using it anymore."

"You got two more months paid up on it, and I can't give you no refund. Against company policy."

"Oh well," Teal said cheerfully after he gave him the combination to the lock, "Merry Christmas."

Sloan answered on the second ring. She had become accustom to the time he generally called and probably hovered over the phone, not allowing anyone in the shop to use it.

He wanted desperately to talk with someone about the incident with Carl. It was gnawing at him, and he was wondering if he hadn't way overreacted.

"That son-of-a-bitch," she said with a typical Sloan assessment of things. "You should've beaten the crap out of him and buried him in a dump!"

That must have been the attitude her father mentioned.

"Poor little Ginny. She's such a sweet little thing and has something nice to say about everyone. My Mom used to say, 'If you have nothing nice to say about a person, say nothing at all'."

"Which is probably why she never mentioned Carl," Teal said and heard her giggle.

Then she said, "Wait a minute." Then in the background he heard, "Dad, I'm talking to Jack. I know. I'll get to it in a few minutes. Thanks...yes, I love you too."

"Hi, I'm back," she said a little breathless from shouting across the shop. Teal was happy to hear her tell Jason she was speaking with him, and he hadn't come over to tear the phone out of her hand.

"Seriously, baby, you and Sammy and the two girls can handle that kitchen. Food will probably be better, and it certainly will be a nicer place to work. I thought he was real sneaky. I caught him a couple of times looking at my breasts."

"Well, Sloan, that doesn't in itself make him a bad person," Teal said reasonably, and Sloan snorted loudly.

They spoke for several more minutes before making kissing sounds and hanging up. The robin stared at him hard for a moment before shaking its beak in apparent disgust and hopped back into the bush.

On Tuesday afternoon, Teal helped set up the dining room by pulling all the tables along the walls and all the chairs in a large circle. Everyone was allowed to go home until four to clean up or attend to personal matters. The meeting started at four sharp and anyone arriving after that time was turned away. TJ told him that the first half dozen meetings were a joke, with people arriving and being turned away, and confusion reigned supreme. But TJ and Peter Quinn were firm with their rules

and set limits to which clients and staff alike would have to
adhere.

Finally, as if someone had waved a magic wand, it all
came together one night. TJ and Peter Quinn looked at each
other and thought, 'well, all right!' And it had worked ever
since.

"You're going to see some new faces tonight," TJ told
Teal. "The program directors from the houses will be here
and bring a couple of their kids and everyone who is currently
working here will be present. We should have around forty,
forty-five," he said rubbing his hands. "It'll be great!"

At three forty-five people started to arrive in clumps, and
the sidewalk outside the restaurant was more crowded than
during the busiest of days. It was obvious everyone had gotten
the message about being late. People started taking their seats:
some sitting in groups and chatting and some sitting singly and
staring at the floor. Teal wondered if he could accurately tell the
clients from the clinical staff. Without using the age difference,
he was sure he wouldn't be able to do it.

At four sharp, TJ, looking at his watch said, "Okay, let's
get started." Somebody Teal did not recognize locked the front
door.

"Okay," TJ said. "I'm going to go over the rules again
tonight." He held his hand up against the grumbles.

"We have some new people who need to hear them. But
first I want to make a couple of introductions."

He looked around the room and found a woman sitting
close to the door. "Betty Shelton has just joined us and will be a
floating counselor working out of The Center."

Everyone turned to stare at her while she sat stone still
like a deer in the headlights.

"I might add that she is a tough cookie with lots of experience. So your scams will not work on her," he said carefully directing his comments to Mickey. There were a few giggles around the room.

"Amed is our capable new person on the espresso bar. Tim will be leaving for a two week vacation, and Amed will handle those duties." He motioned to Amed who stood with a huge grin and bowed. The kitchen staff clapped and did a lopsided spectator wave, which left Gary still standing. Sammy reached over and pulled him down.

"The other new person, and most of you already have already met him, is Jack Teal in our kitchen."

The kitchen crew started clapping and saying 'hoo, hoo, hoo' until TJ shushed them with his hand.

"The only other announcement I have is that our head cook, Carl Johns has resigned. He had pressing family matters."

Someone said, "Awwww." TJ looked around the group and was met with a sea of blank faces.

"Now a recap on the rules real quick," he said with a stern face. "You folks, who have heard the rules a bunch of times, just put a cork in it and respect those who have not."

There were some chuckles around the perimeter. Teal was watching one young girl who looked terrified.

"Our sessions start at four o'clock sharp. Those who are late do not get in and will have to explain later, why. We take a five-minute break at quarter of five, and we close it down at five thirty – sharp! Makes no difference if we are in the middle of something or just diddling around. It stops right there."

He cleared his throat and looked around the room. "You can talk about anything you want, but there will be no personal attacks, and..." he said pointing at Mickey.

"What is said here, stays here," Mickey said in a bored voice, and then added, "just like Las Vegas."

"Thank you, Mister Ralston," TJ said. "I'm sure everyone present appreciates your editorializing."

Teal couldn't help from smiling.

"Okay," TJ said. "If you like, we can all sit here quietly for an hour and then go home."

There was a long silence while people shifted in their chairs. Finally a tiny little girl raised her hand and Teal thought, 'God, bless you.'

"She's doing it again, and I think it's disgusting," the girl said.

"Oh shit, here we go," Mickey said, and TJ scalded him with a look.

"We're working on that Reba. We're doing what we can, but it will take some time," TJ said. "Please be patient."

Teal noticed Peter Quinn jotting something in a notebook.

"Anybody else?" TJ asked.

Mickey raised his hand and TJ said, "The floor is yours Mister Ralston."

Mickey stood and looked around the group catching several eyes.

"What I would like to know is who is in charge of the kitchen? With Mr. Johns gone, who will pick up the reins and provide the leadership to carry us forward."

Mr. Johns?

Teal stared at him in amazement. What a shit disturber, he thought and then raised his hand.

TJ nodded at him with an anxious look.

"I'm glad Mr. Ralston brought that up because the concern for continuity in a restaurant is very important.

Fortunately, we have a superior staff at the restaurant, and we work without the need for labels. On some days I may appear to be directing the action and on other days it may be Sammy. But remember who ever is responsible for that day could not do it without Nicole, Beth and Gary."

Nicole looked pleased and turned blotchy while Beth nodded and smiled. Gary heard his name and looked around to find its source as if he had been fingered in a conspiracy.

"And that doesn't even include the front staff: Ginny, Amed, Tim, Rich, Clair and, yes, even Mickey.

"My point is this," Teal continued. "I cannot run the restaurant and neither can Sammy. Rich can't wait on all the tables and neither can Tim or Mickey. We all count on each other for better or worse. There is no way any one person can do these jobs alone.

"So I've worked it out with Sammy. When we have a really good day, Sammy's the head cook and if we blow it big time, I'm the head cook," he said and sat down to a round of laughter. Teal looked over and saw Peter Quinn give him a nod and a tiny thumbs-up.

The rest of the meeting was remarkably even keeled with some people airing their complaints, announcement of coming events and program directors giving quick sketches on their facility over the past week. A few clients spoke, one making almost no sense to Teal, but most were content to sit – some quietly and some restless. The terrified girl never changed expression and Teal found he could no longer look at her. The boy seated next to her stared off into space with his mouth open. He looked brain dead. TJ would later explain to him this was a perfect example of chemical shackles.

"Why even try?" Teal asked. "If he's that fucked up on medication, how can you help him?"

"Jack, I don't know if we can. But nobody else will try. He's at least due a shot at getting better." He scratched his beard and squinted at Teal. "Is Beth helpful in the kitchen? I mean can she carry her own weight?"

"Are you kidding? Yeah, sure! Why?"

"Less than two years ago, that person you called brain dead could have been Beth."

Teal stepped back visibly surprised. "Bullshit." He said and snorted.

"Nope, no bullshit. Ask Peter Quinn. When we took over on Beth from Marin Mental Health she was so medicated she could barely function as a human being. She couldn't take a pee without help, for Christ's sake."

Peter Quinn looked over quizzically. Almost everyone else had gone home, and the restaurant had been quickly rearranged.

"She's manic depressive and considered a high suicide risk, so the easiest treatment was to whack her out on meds and walk away. We put her into our most secure house with our most experienced program director and started creating a life for her. We taught her basic living skills, drew strong limits and goals for her and gave her positive reinforcement...and we started weaning her from medication. This is where Peter Quinn is a master. He understands the balance better than anyone I know."

Peter Quinn strolled over to listen. "She is still on meds," Peter Quinn said, "but they are vastly reduced and she functions better than a lot of people I know who aren't even ill. It takes strength and willpower, and, believe me, beneath that calm façade, is a very strong, very committed young lady."

"I'm embarrassed," Teal said. "After working in the kitchen with Sammy and the girls, I sort of forgot that they all are classified as mentally ill."

"Don't be embarrassed," said Peter Quinn with a wide grin. "That's the greatest compliment you could have given us. Hell, I look at guys like Sammy and tend to forget how far down he was before we got our hooks in him."

The three sat alone at a table in the partially darkened restaurant, and Teal pulled them some decaf espressos.

"How could a kid, say like Sammy, get so far down when the potential for a better life is lurking beneath the surface?"

TJ and Peter Quinn looked at each other and grinned. Peter gestured to TJ. "You want to field that one?"

TJ poured some cream in his espresso and stirred slowly. "The mental health field is littered with booby traps and disappointments. Staff burnouts are more common than any profession or business I know of. Violence, drug abuse and suicide are real and bizarre behavior is commonplace.

"You only have to wonder how you would react if you were totally convinced someone was following you with the intention of stabbing you. And no one's listening to you.

"Imagine your fear when you hear voices telling you to do things – like jump in front of that car or the only way you can stop that pain in your head is by tearing the skin off your forehead."

"Jesus," Teal said in a shocked voice.

"Now, Jack, imagine you are the parent of one of these kids," Peter Quinn said and put a hand on his shoulder. "You can't control your child, you might even be afraid of him, and county or state mental health says there's nothing they can do. Because they are under funded or understaffed or just don't give a shit. So they raid the pharmacy and lo and behold, the child is no longer tearing their skin or shrieking in terror. Of course, it's hard to tell the difference between the child and a potted palm, but at least the parents are not afraid of them anymore.

"And even worse is when they are left to fend for themselves," he added tracing his beard with an index finger. "Family has given up, mental health community has given up, and they are no longer adolescents, so it's difficult to put a hold on them. So they end up living under freeways in cardboard boxes getting beaten and raped. And feared."

"Nobody's really to blame and everybody's to blame," TJ added. "But we would be the worst offender, if we didn't try. And sometimes that means taking on some really tough ones. Mickey's a perfect example of someone who's been bouncing around the mental health halls for years. He knows all the tricks and all the scams. And since he's so bright, he's really tough to keep up with. Keep in mind that the Mickey Ralston you've seen bares little resemblance to the Mickey Ralston when he's on a tear. In the early days, you couldn't have Mickey in your house – well, at least your bathroom. He'd take every drug in there."

"Well, he might leave you your aspirin," Peter Quinn added, "but anything with a prescription label would be long gone. Wouldn't make any difference if it was for migraine or insomnia or crab lice, he'd take it."

"I think I need a raise," Teal said with a weak smile.

Peter Quinn laughed and clapped him on the back. "Jack, you're doing just fine by being who you are. We wanted a strong presence in the kitchen and someone who has little clinical training to get in the way. After all, it *is* a restaurant and we *are* teaching them skills. It's not like cooking for your friends. You're cooking for strangers who are paying hard earned money for their food. That's front line stuff. Can't get any more real world than that."

* * *

SEVENTEEN

Teal picked up Sloan at the Marin airporter in Larkspur after work on Friday. She had refused to have him continue picking her up at the airport.

"I don't want to be responsible for wearing out poor Brownie," she had said.

"We're going right over to pick up TJ and Dannie and run out to this restaurant in Tomales. I discovered it about three weeks ago and been back a bunch of times."

"We can't go to the cottage and freshen up? Maybe take a shower together?" she asked putting her arm over the back of the seat and loosening two buttons. Teal glanced over and almost rear-ended a pickup full of lawn waste.

"Jesus, don't do that. TJ's probably watching us from the deck right now."

Sloan quickly buttoned up. "God, you're probably right," she said and giggled.

TJ and Dannie piled into the back seat, and there were kisses and hugs over the seat back.

"What's the big rush?" Sloan asked reattaching her seat belt.

"Because it's Friday," Teal said, "and it's an oyster bar."

"An oyster bar? God, you didn't tell me it was an oyster bar. I love oysters," Sloan said bouncing in her seat like a child. "Do they have Samish Bay? Steamboats? Royal Myagris?"

Teal looked over at her mystified. "You're a high desert girl. You eat flank steak and Mexican food. How would you know about oysters?"

"San Diego. Remember I told you I went out to watch Dad race?" she asked.

"Oh right, the time you got...Oww!" as she punched him in the arm. "I'll tell you later, TJ," he said, and she punched him harder.

TJ leaned over the seat back and said to Teal in a stage whisper, "I think this is going to be a very expensive evening."

Sam Keller greeted them at the door to the restaurant and kissed the lady's hands. "Nice to see you again, Jack, and welcome to your friends. I practically had to kill a couple of truck drivers to save you that table by the window," he said with a grin. He was a big, burly man who looked more than capable of mixing it up with a couple of truck drivers.

"You don't think he was serious?" Dannie asked after they were directed towards the table.

"Oh, I think so," Teal said. "Friday? Oyster bar?"

Keller seated them at the table, which had a view of the bay shoreline. Birds were working the mud flats below the window finding sea lice and worms and leaving modified peace symbol prints in the sand while fishing boats threaded their way home through the red and green marker buoys. The sun was low and would set over a ridge on the opposite side of the bay. Sloan, ignoring all the scenery, had her face buried in the menu and was humming to herself.

"I think I've died and gone to heaven," she said to no one in particular. "Look at this menu. I want to live here."

Keller slipped a tray on their table with nine oysters nestled in a bed of ice. In the center was a pot of tart dipping sauce. "A little something to get your taste buds going," he said. "Hog Islands here, Kumamotos and Royal Myagris," he said pointing to the different types.

"Thank you, Sam," Sloan said with a bright smile. "Will you be bringing something for the other three?"

He had to look at the other faces to be sure, and then he walked off laughing and shaking his head.

It was a feast of monumental proportions: Dungeness crabs, five kinds of raw oysters, oyster Rockefeller, oyster casino and sand dabs for Dannie. All of it washed down with IPAs and a crisp Sauvignon Blanc.

TJ finally pushed back from the table and looked down at his stomach in dismay. "God, I think I just broke my belt buckle," he said with a moan. "I may need a stretcher."

"Are you guys done?" Sloan asked. "What a bunch of lightweights." Then she burped.

The crowd had thinned, and the sun was setting in a blazing show of power. When Keller came over to ask how their meal was, Teal asked him to sit down.

"Take a load off, I'll buy you a beer."

"Wouldn't mind that at all." He went to the cold box, pulled out a beer, popped the cap and sat down.

"This is the guy I've been telling you about," Teal said nodding at TJ. "TJ Fitz and his wife, Dannie. And this lady who I might have mentioned a time or two is Sloan Easy from the great state of Arizona.

"Keller smiled and shook hands all around. "Truth be told," he said, "Jack doesn't talk about anything else but you three. I'm pleased to meet all of you."

He raised his beer to TJ. "And you, TJ, I admire greatly. I heard some time ago about the café. What you are doing for those kids is special. I know I couldn't do it."

"I'll share a secret with you, Sam," TJ said with a chuckle. "I wasn't sure I could do it either." He finger combed his beard for a moment, thinking. "But you believe that someone has to do it, so you just start and work hard at it and listen to the pros. And a couple of weeks go by, and you think, whoa, two weeks have just gone by. So you go back to work, and you see some kids getting better and you think, success. And some not getting better, and you think, failure. And then one morning you wake up and someone says, 'Congratulations on your one year anniversary', and you look at him like he's gone bats. Didn't I just start two weeks ago?"

Teal almost couldn't look at Dannie as she watched TJ, she was so heartbreakingly beautiful. Like a sweet angel. Then he turned slightly and saw that Sloan was watching him in much the same way.

"Tell me, Jack," Keller said. "Would you ever want your own restaurant?"

"Sure," he said. "I've thought about. Love to have a place just like this. Fresh crab and oyster. Sand dabs for the ladies," he said gesturing to Dannie.

"I'll sell it to you," Keller said.

"Man I wish I had the money," Teal said. "But why would you want to walk away from this. You've got a great reputation, place is packed all the time, beautiful setting, lots of regulars."

Keller leaned back in his chair. "Oh I guess I'm not really ready to sell, but, damn, do I miss Seattle. I miss my Seahawks, I miss sailing on the Sound and I miss bitching about Gates' house. Hell, I even miss the original Starbucks."

"I always thought you were from around here," Teal said. "You seem to know everybody."

"Well, I have been here for a spell, but I grew up in Seattle, and I've always sort of thought about it as being home."

"Doesn't it rain all the time?" Sloan asked. "I went up there with Dad for a race, and it rained the whole time. All these people walking around and looking all white and pruny."

Keller laughed and took another sip of beer. "See that's the problem with all you people who live in California. You see the sun so much you don't really appreciate it. Up there, when the sun comes out, we all have a great big party."

On the drive home, Sloan had her head on Jack's shoulder, and Dannie and TJ were curled up sleeping in the back seat.

"He's really a nice guy," she said while fiddling with the radio dials.

"Yeah, he is. I've spent a lot of time out there when you're not around. Sam's really the only guy I know outside of the Marin Advocates people."

"I think he likes you too," she said.

"Well, I don't see why not. I'm a very likeable person."

"Some of the time," she said and snuggled closer.

Teal opened the restaurant early and left the front door ajar. Sloan had left the day before taking the airporter from Larkspur. It was getting harder and harder for them to say goodbye, and Teal knew he was on the verge of doing something which was foreign to him – planning for the future.

Teal's life had been like a person growing up in an enormous building with thousand upon thousands of rooms. He had no direction as to where to go nor did he want any. None of the rooms were labeled, so you really had no idea what they contained until you entered. Some of the rooms held wonderful surprises and some held misery and pain while many were bland and completely forgettable.

This was his life. Wandering from day to day and only
mildly curious about what might happen. Until he went
away to college, his mother did all his planning, much to
his father's displeasure, and that was all right with him.
Once he entered college, he was like an untethered balloon
drifting from one class to another, one girl to another, one
day to another. There was always someone to pick up a class
assignment for him or to turn in a paper because he was too
busy playing handball.

One girl in his junior year had made it her project to pick
him off like a ripe plum and make him commit to her. She
was a classic midwestern beauty and had a flawless figure. And
added to that, she was smart and her family had serious money.
There wasn't a man on campus who wouldn't have thrown
himself in front of a bus if it would have gained her attention
and sympathy. But she wanted Jack, and she knew she could
get him.

By midterm she had lost some weight and close friends
detected stress lines around her eyes. She was also cranky much
of the time. Two weeks before finals she threw in the towel and
admitted defeat. When a friend of hers much later asked what
Jack was like, she said, "I don't really know. He was never really
there."

But now he was planning for the future, something
in which he had little experience. He had flashes of Sloan in
a wedding dress, maybe Dannie as her maid of honor, both
dressed in white and maybe touches of fuchsia. He had visions
of Sloan pregnant and giggling with Dannie over something
making sense only to them.

"Jesus, this is a little scary," he said to himself and saw
Sammy watching him from the front door.

"Not good, boss. Talkin' to yourself. That's what we're suppose to be doing."

TJ had warned him a new person would start in the kitchen and would be closely monitored by Rich.

"He's a little weak," TJ confessed in his throwaway voice he used when he didn't really want you to hear.

"What does that mean…a little weak? Like he can't pick up garbage cans, or he's going to have to move around in a wheelchair?" Teal asked, not allowing the squirming TJ off the hook.

"Well, he's up to his eyeballs in meds and is low functioning. He'll need a lot of direction and support."

"Jesus, TJ, we're up to our nuts in work, and we've got it floatin' along pretty good now. Why another person?"

"Because he comes in fully funded, and we need the God damn money," TJ said turning pink.

"Okay, okay, what's his name?" Teal asked.

"His name's Dan. Just have him on pickup and some light cleaning. He's not even ready for the dishwasher."

"Oh terrific," Teal mumbled, and then turned to the kitchen. "Hey, get in here Sammy. I want to talk to you about something."

Sammy walked over slipping on his apron.

"We got a new guy starting today," Teal said tying his apron. "Lightest of all possible duties, okay? And keep an eye on him. And there's something else I want to tell you."

Sammy slipped into an apron and put his traditional headband in place. "So what's up? Something so important that you're talking to yourself?"

"You just don't want to answer yourself," Mickey said from the front door. He had been coming in early and was helpful in setting up table and vacuuming.

"I've been thinking of adding some new dishes to the menu. I don't know if they would replace something or just be an addition."

Sammy nodded. "Where do the recipes come from?" he finally asked.

"You," Teal said.

"Me?"

"Yeah, you and Beth and Nicole and anyone else who wants to take a crack at it," Teal said, excited now. "If someone has a recipe, they write it down and submit it to me and TJ. Then, if we think it can work, we'll help you fine-tune it. Cost it out. Then you make a small batch, and we'll try it out in house. If it passes that test, we'll get the board in here and maybe Peter Quinn and some other guys and see what they think. Then – and only then – will it be placed on the menu. What do you think?"

Sammy tilted his head from side to side. "Maybe it will be cool."

Teal was surprised and disappointed with the reaction and didn't quite know what to make of it. He had considered the plan for some time, and thought the clients in the kitchen might have some fun with it, and word would get around to everyone at least by the next meeting. Additionally it was excellent training if they decided they wanted to continue cooking in another restaurant out in the big, bad world.

Teal went back to prepping for breakfast feeling keenly disappointed. It appeared there was still much for him to learn about the clients.

Beth and Nicole came in and launched into the prep, chattering and laughing followed by Rich leading a young man who was about six feet seven and ducked entering the kitchen. He didn't have to, but was programmed that way.

"Dan, this is Jack," he said by way of introduction. "He's a very busy man, so do what he wants."

Dan nodded looking around the kitchen like a forward looking for a fast break.

"Okay, Dan what I want you to do is keep the floor clean. Anything on the floor you pick up and put in the garbage can, right over here. Okay? Any questions and you come to me."

At that moment, Sammy dropped a celery trimming destined for the crock-pot, and it bounced on the floor. Dan went for it like shagging a grounder, scooped it up and slam-dunked it into the can.

"Very good, Dan," Teal said patting him on the back. "You don't have to run and make sure you don't get in the way of the cooks." Teal looked at Sammy who shook his head in weary resignation.

Gary wandered in, filled up a tray with leftover utensils, slid it into the Stero and cycled the machine. Teal put down his knife and stared. Gary glanced over, smiled and gave him a little wave.

The day was predictable and strong. They ran out of two soups and most of the sandwich ingredients. With another dozen customers, they would have been wiped clean.

"Perfect planning," he said jokingly to Sammy who was staring at something over his shoulder.

"What you mean?" Sammy asked, now squinting at something.

"Well, we ran out of customers at the same time…what are you looking at?" he asked turning around just as Sammy launched into a barrage of Japanese, tore off his headband and flung it against the wall.

Dan had finished his work, and the floor was almost as spotless as when they had come to work. But to him the items he found on the floor were treasures and were not to be destined to the cruel fate of a garbage can. Instead he had arranged them carefully, even with a modicum of artistic flare, on one of the shelves of the refrigerator. There were carrot peelings bursting joyfully from a carefully poofed crepe, tiny ridges of cream cheese creating a happy face on a beet slice and shrimp tails, caper and blintz mix describing a tribal mask on the ridge of a Romaine lettuce leaf.

Rich rushed in, saw the display and Sammy's tirade, and left the room with Dan gently in tow. For months afterwards all that anyone could talk about was Dan-Dan the Garbage Man, and he was well on his way to becoming a Marin County legend.

When order was restored and they set about to clean the refrigerator, Beth sidled up next to him wiping her hands on a towel.

"Sammy told us about the recipe contest. Well, I guess it's not a contest," she said flustered, looking over at Nicole who gave her the 'go on' movement with her hands.

"Sammy's so excited, he couldn't talk about anything else, well, except for Dan. He told Mickey about it, and I think he's even going to try."

"Sammy's excited about it?" Teal asked putting down the grill scraper. "When I told him about it, he acted like he could care less. I thought he was going to fall asleep."

"Oh, Jack," she said and pushed his arm with the tips of her fingers. "You are so funny some times. Sammy always acts that way when he really gets excited about something. He calls it 'getting in the zone' or something like that."

Teal shook the cobwebs out of his mind and laughed. "Well, what do you guys think?"

"Everybody loves it," she said, and Nicole nodded vigorously behind her.

"Okay, I'll tell you what we're going to do. First I want to talk with TJ and all you guys who are interested, and then we'll figure out exactly how it goes. But I want to make sure that everyone knows it's not a contest. You are not competing against each other. You are simply helping to make the restaurant better and more unique."

"Yeah, I'm glad they're pumped. I think it's a cool idea," TJ said when Teal started to bring it up. They were sitting on TJ's deck enjoying the traffic.

"So you know all about it?" Teal asked mystified.

"Sure. Mickey told me when I first came in at nine. Everybody's pumped, talking all day about it. Hell, I think even Ginny's got something she wants to fine tune."

"Where was I when all this conversation is going on?"

"Vaguing out in the kitchen, I suppose. Maybe helping Dan create," TJ said with a wide grin. Then he cuffed him on the shoulder. "You have just witnessed first hand the underground form of silent communication – like muffled tom-toms. I don't know how they do it, but if you haven't seen it before, it will blow by you like a hummingbird."

Then TJ shifted in his chair and craned his neck. "See the blue Chevy ragtop slowing down? In the second to the slowest lane? She's going to decided she wants that next turnoff about two seconds too late."

They watched and in a matter of several seconds, the convertible swerved across lanes towards the off ramp to an accompaniment of braying horns. TJ turned and wiggled his eyebrows at Teal.

"How did you know that was a she?" Teal asked.

"Simple. That's the turnoff to Nordstrom's."

"Sloan wanted to come up to meet the board Thursday night," Teal said. "But her dad wants her to do the quarterlies, so that's that."

"By the way, how do you get along with him?" Dannie asked. They were now having a light dinner on the deck, scrunched together like they were riding on a subway. TJ was picking things out of his salad and tossing them over the railing while Dannie pretended not to notice.

"That's the million dollar question," Teal said. "I left under less than ideal circumstances, so I'm not really sure."

"What happened? You two get in a beef?"

"Well, sort of. I'll tell you the whole thing when I get it sorted out in my head."

"I hope that's soon," she said and smiled. "Sloan is real serious about where this is going." Then she reached over and took something out of TJ's hand, which was about to be heaved overboard.

"She couldn't be more serious than I am," he said, and Dannie grinned to herself in the dark.

Teal rode out to the Bennington's house on Thursday night with Paul Landers who was the program director at one of the residential facilities. He was a small, quiet man with a quirky sense of humor, and Teal liked him. It was the first time Paul had been invited to the after meeting cocktail bash as well.

"I've heard that the restaurant is doing well. I need to get in there more often, but I never seem to have the time," he said with a deep sigh.

"I haven't even been to *one* of the residentials yet," Teal said.

"Well, there's nothing to see there. Just a bunch of naked crazy people trying to jump out the windows."

When Teal's head snapped around, he chuckled and said, "Just kidding."

The house was in Kentfield and built high on the slope of a hill adjacent to Mount Tamalpais. Its setting was such that whoever lived there could look directly across at the mountain. Teal could clearly see several hiking trails or access roads working their way through the trees and brush towards to summit. The fire lookout station at the peak was clearly visible.

The house itself was single story and rambled comfortably across the hillside as if part of nature's original plan. Teal could see it was constructed of real adobe bricks painted a flat white. The door and window trims had the look and color of mission furniture while the red Mexican tiled roof drained into copper gutters with the patina of a rich moss.

John Bennington met them at the door and graciously introduced them to the other eight people in the room. TJ had gone to the meeting with Peter Quinn, and they were standing in front of a massive picture window talking with an attractive Asian woman. She was telling them something with graceful animation, which elicited genuine laughs from both.

The room in which they stood reminded Teal of Jason's adobe outside of Scottsdale, or more properly, what Jason's house would look like in thirty years or so. The furniture consisted mostly of dark woods and burnished leather all processing a sense of grace rather than solemnity, and the oriental carpets were intricate and deeply piled. The artwork was interesting and eclectic and challenged the eye. Their tastes were dictated by old money and dignity.

Sissy came across the room and greeted them warmly. She took them on a tour of the house and explaining some of the artwork when they expressed an interest. TJ lifted a beer with a smile in a quiet toast.

"Anybody for a martini," John asked rubbing his hands briskly.

"Sure, I'll try one," Teal said while Paul asked for a beer.

"Careful of his martinis," Sissy whispered as she walked by. "They've floored bigger guys than you."

Teal and Paul answered questions about their respective facilities for the next hour while Teal sipped perhaps the best martini he had ever had. The questions were astute and the individuals asking them were interested. It wasn't polite cocktail chatter.

"TJ tells me you play some handball," John said. The party was winding down, and one person had already left.

"I played a lot in college, but I'm probably pretty rusty now."

"Perhaps you would care to join me down at the club sometime, and we could work up a sweat."

"That would be terrific," Teal said. "There don't seem to be a lot of public..." And he stopped and stared.

"John Bennington. I mean you're not *the* John Bennington," he said stuttering.

"Well, I am *a* John Bennington," he said laughing.

"No, I mean *the* John Bennington who won back to back to back NCAA handball championships. Went to Yale or some place."

"Actually, it was Penn State," John said and sipped his martini.

"Good God," Teal said looking around the room almost wildly. Did these people know they were in the presence of a sporting legend? Apparently not, as he watched them stand in their individual groups and talk of new wine releases, city government scandals and mental heath funding woes.

"I hope I'm not sounding like a weird groupie or something," Teal said trying to maintain control, "but I've read about you for years. They even named a maneuver after you. The Bennington Wall Slash."

"Oh dear," John said. "I sort of hoped that nonsense would go away after a few years."

"Excuse me, sir, but sporting legends in whatever sport they compete, never go away. They are never forgotten," Teal said and then became embarrassed with his statement.

Then the two of them huddled and talked about some of the great matches and rivalries of the past and present, different styles of players and the future for the sport. Teal could have continued the conversation for hours. But when he saw TJ crooking a finger at him and looking at his watch, he thanked John for his hospitality.

"Don't forget," John said as they shook hands, "that's an open invitation for a game at the club.

"I wanted you to meet Beverly before she leaves," TJ said when Teal walked over. "Jack, this is Beverly Sukano. Beverly this is Jack Teal."

"My pleasure," Jack said shaking her slender, cool hand. She was dressed in an elegant black silk dress highlighted by discrete touches of jewelry. Her completion was flawless.

"The pleasure is mine, Mr. Teal," she said, almost formally looking up at him with a ghost of a smile. Her eyes seemed to sparkle with unknown humor. "I have heard wonderful stories about you. I hope in the future we will have an opportunity to speak at length."

TJ strolled over before Teal and Paul drove down the hill. "See you bright and early tomorrow?"

"You bet. Half the day will be gone by the time you get there." TJ laughed, and Teal started the car.

Before he rolled up the window, he said, "Beverly seems like an interesting lady. Is she a board member?"

"Yes, indeed. One of the founding members along with John and Sissy. They've been very close friends for years. She's a very bright and charming woman. I don't know if I mentioned it or not," he said putting his elbows on Brownie's windowsill and carefully finger combed his beard, "but she's Sammy's mother. See you tomorrow."

* * *

EIGHTEEN

Teal was waiting for TJ when he came in the following morning at a few minutes past nine. He took off his apron, dropped it on the counter and walked into the main room with Sammy watching him quizzically. TJ was sitting at his favorite table and when Teal walked over, he looked up from a writing tablet.

Teal's irked feeling dissipated almost immediately, and he almost took a step backwards. TJ's face was ashen, and there were smudges under both eyes.

"I know. I look like shit; don't remind me."

"Jeez, TJ, I'm sorry," Teal said. "Maybe you should head home and catch some zees. We can handle it here."

"No, I'll be okay. Now, you came over with fire in your eye like you were pissed off at something. What is it?"

"Well I guess not so much pissed off as curious," Teal said.

TJ pulled the opposite chair out with one foot and nodded at it. "Why don't you sit down?"

Teal sat, and TJ put his writing tablet back in the briefcase and snapped it shut.

"I guess I was sort of wondering why you didn't introduce me to Beverly Sukano earlier last night. I would love to have talked with her for a while."

TJ nodded and looked at Teal for a moment with his head tilted to the side. "You like Sammy a lot, don't you?" he finally said with a mild tone of voice.

"Well, yeah. Pretty hard not to like the kid."

"Would you say he's probably your favorite client?"

"I guess. Where are we going with this?"

TJ sighed and pursed his lips. "Peter Quinn and I had a long talk about you and what you have meant to our operation," he said and then held up a hand as Teal started to bristle. "You have been a much needed breath of fresh air in here. Neither P.Q. or I knew it until Johns was gone and you had taken his place."

Again he held up his hand.

"Please let me finish. You have done a wonderful job in here, and the place has never felt so secure and supportive. When I hired you I had hopes it would turn out the way it has. We needed someone with restaurant skills and, more importantly, no clinical agenda. We wanted someone who would push people into learning and performing their jobs just as any company manager would. Peter Quinn and I have purposely shielded you from the everyday jargon that we babble to each other: clinical diagnoses of this client or that, worrisome retrogressions, medication levels and all the other crap *we* were hired to do. I've told you before you don't need to know this stuff, and it was always our feeling that it could only get in the way of your thinking and judgment."

"But?"

"Yes, but," TJ said and fiddled with the lock on his briefcase without looking at it. "There is one thing I must counsel you on and warn you about, and it's a difficult thing to grasp clearly."

He cleared his throat and took a sip of water. Even his movements had slowed since the night before, and he appeared to have aged ten years. "You cannot have favorites among the clients. You must try to react to all of them in the same manner. It is very difficult to do because it really is contrary to human nature."

"Come on, TJ," Teal argued. "It's not like we go out and tip a few, you know."

"And I'm glad you don't," TJ responded sharply. "That would be a gross violation of the rules, and you know that.

"All our clients need and deserve to be treated equally. Many have fragile egos and have for years thought that no one gave a shit about them. We don't need to reinforce that here. And just as important," he added staring at Jack, "and I hope this doesn't sound sinister, clients often use those situations to their own advantage and to your disadvantage. This is particularly true of people suffering from borderline personality syndrome. They like nothing better than to pitch two people against each other and then stand back and watch them go at it."

"And lastly," he said with a voice that was clearly starting to tire, "the pain of losing a favorite to a psychotic break, or worse, is excruciating. A person you've grown to care for suddenly becomes a ranting, screaming harridan is a scene out of your worst nightmare."

Teal felt chastened and said nothing for a moment. "Are you telling me you don't have a favorite?" he finally asked.

"Of course not. But do you think you could guess who it is? You and I have worked together for a long time now."

"I would guess either Ginny or Amed," he said after a moment. "Probably Ginny," he said with finality.

A faint smile passed over TJs lips and disappeared as he stared back at the kitchen with unfocused eyes. "It's Mickey," he finally said and watched Jack's face.

Teal could not contain his surprise. "Mickey!" he whispered. "He's the biggest shit disturber on the face of the planet."

"Be that as it may..." he said rubbing his eyes. "Sometimes you don't have the luxury of choice. It just happens. By the way," he said tapping a finger on his briefcase, "Claire quit – said she was going to Omaha to take care of a sister who has cancer."

"Boy, I'm sorry to hear that. I sort of liked her," Teal said wondering how much this contributed to TJ's insomnia. "Are we going to be shorthanded?"

"I don't think so. We can shuffle things around until we replace her. She really faded in the past few months and hasn't been much help. I suspect it had nothing to do with worry about her sister. She just flat burned out."

"She sure seemed chipper to me," Teal said.

"Yeah. Too chipper can also be a sign of a flame out."

TJ opened his briefcase, and Teal had started back towards the kitchen. "Jack, speaking of people who have recently left, the emergency room at Marin General billed our health provider a while back for services performed on one of our staff. They're always a month or two late, so I just got notice. It wasn't too serious – out patient stuff. Wondered if you knew anything about it."

"Noo..." he started to say, then remembered and froze.

"Yeah, it was Johns. He told them he had been in a car wreck. Got a broken nose, four stitches in his lip and a couple of wobbly teeth. Knot on the back of his head. This was before he resigned, so technically he was still covered. Isn't that a weird set of circumstances? I mean the same day he leaves?" he said shaking his head in amazement.

Teal looked at him and offered a weak smile. "Boy that is a weird coincidence."

Later in the day Teal was sitting with Rich, talking about hiking Mount Tamalpais and the Gold Country.

"Did you see the way TJ looked when he first came in this morning?" he asked. TJ had regained much of his color but still was going to go home early.

"Yeah, he's pissed about Claire and having real heartaches with the funding. Marin Mental Health is always threatening to pull back. I think they do it just because they've got nothing better to do." He shook his head and snorted. "I guess you could say I'm not a fan."

"What about the Finessen Fund? I hear you guys talking about it like it's the second coming."

"I guess you could say it is," Rich said. "At least to non-profits it sure is."

"How much money is involved?"

Rich looked at the ceiling thoughtfully. "Probably enough to fund Magnolia into the year three thousand and not make a dent in the fund."

Amed came over and placed a tall, steaming mug in front of each. His recipe had been finally accepted on the menu as the Amed's Delight, and it was a strong seller. Teal loved them but limited himself to one a week.

"So we're talking millions?"

"Probably closer to billions," Rich said, wiping some foam from his upper lip. "Jesus, if I have any more of these, I'll have to enter myself in the Macy's parade."

Teal took a sip. His contained half the cream called for, but he still considered it was a very dangerous drink.

"I guess Finessen was a piece of work," Rich continued. "Arms dealer between the first and second world wars but seemed to be courted and loved by all. I guess when you've got the good stuff, everyone loves you."

Teal nodded, remembering some of his own stories.

"He was also somewhat of a stock market wizard and tripled his fortune with shrewd investments. Then he started buying stamps and gold coins and squirreling them away in banks. He lived over in Ross in a very modest house and drove a five-year-old Buick. Loved going to Little League games."

Rich had finished the Amed's Delight and burped quietly while looking at the espresso stand and trying to make a decision.

"Anyway..." Teal said prompting.

"Yeah. Anyway when he dies suddenly and somewhat mysteriously, he leaves behind this huge fortune with a very simple will. To paraphrase it: 'all the money is to be used for the enrichment and enhancement of Marin County as deemed appropriately by the foundation board'.

"So what do you think would happen with a will floating around that appears so open-ended and vague?"

"Enter the lawyers?"

"You got it. By the packs. There were some surviving relatives although it was claimed he hadn't seen or corresponded with any of them in years. Of course, they all claimed to be his favorite, you supply the appropriate title, and forthwith hired legal representation."

Amed looked over expectantly, and Rich shook his head with a great deal of apparent remorse.

"But the foundation board says, 'Wait a gol-durn minute. You don't even live in Marin County. You live in Paris or Bangor, Maine or wherever."

"Man, what a mess," Teal said.

"Yeah, and you've got to remember this was back in the early eighties. Lawyers have been shootin' it out ever since."

"I assume MAMS has been waiting in line while the lawyers get rich," Teal said.

"Oh yeah. We hired some fancy grant writer out of LA and have been beating on their door for almost three years. They have little interest in the residentials regardless of how you argued your point. Then Magnolia came along with a lot of fanfare, and they decided they wanted some of that limelight. We've gotten a few dribs and drabs, but no year to year long term commitment."

The kitchen crew was leaving and had turned off all the lights except the one by Teal's table.

"So that's the pressure TJ has to endure every day," Rich said taking his glass into the kitchen, rinsing it out and putting it by the dishwasher. Teal followed him and did the same.

"What are the odds of getting any money?" Teal asked.

Rich laughed as they swung open the front door and flipped off the lights. "Jesus, if I knew the answer to that, I'd be in Vegas playing craps."

Teal stopped by TJ and Dannie's on the way home, but TJ was already in bed. He and Dannie sat out on the lawn in front, drank some fresh lemonade and nodded at the neighbors. Dannie knew everyone: old duffers puffing along and getting their constitutionals, young mothers jogging with streamlined baby carriages and people coming home from work.

"Is there anybody you don't know?" Teal teased.

"Not that's worth knowing," she said, and Teal laughed. She had the same quick wit as Sloan, and the two of them had engaged in semantic duels several times, which should have been taped and sold to The Comedy Network.

"TJ's got to start taking care of himself," Teal said, and Dannie looked away quickly. "If there's anything I can do, I'll do it. Just ask."

She turned back and her eyes were glistening. "Just do what you're doing. If you hadn't come along when you did and took some of the weight off, I don't know where he would be right now." She wiped her eyes with the back of her hand.

"Sometimes I just hate that damn restaurant!" she said suddenly angry. "I just hate it! And I hate Gorman for being such an asshole and hindering rather than helping. And sometimes I even hate all those poor people he's trying to help who suck energy out of him like a vacuum. Sometimes I just hate the whole thing."

He patted her on the knee and she rested her head on his shoulder. "I'm just so glad you and Sloan are around. I don't know what we'd do without you."

They sat like that for half an hour and watched the sun go down, while little kids rode bikes and skateboards down the empty street on their way home for dinner.

Saturday morning promised a beautiful day, and Teal first called Dannie to check on TJ.

"He had a good night and looks much better," Dannie said, and her voice sounded chipper and bright. "I'm going to take him for a drive down to Carmel. We can walk on the beach and have a nice lunch, then come back. He can sleep both ways, or hang out the window like a big, homely spaniel. I just want to get him the hell out of this county for a while."

"Have a nice drive," Teal said. "Tell TJ I'll see him Monday."

Then he called Rich. "You still got that spare mountain bike you told me about?"

"Yeah, sure. Just put a new chain on it."

"Well, if you're not doing anything we can go out, and I'll whup your ass."

He heard Rich break up on the other end. "Meet me at my house in half an hour – sucker."

They packed the bikes into Rich's pickup and drove to the north side of Mount Tam, parked and unloaded. Rich was long gone up a trail before Teal had his seat adjusted. He tried to catch him for an hour and finally got just a tantalizing hundred yards behind but could never close the gap. They finally reached an overlook with a spectacular view of the San Francisco Bay and the city of San Francisco beyond. Hawks and seabirds were taking full advantage of the thermal updrafts around the mountain. When Teal reached the overlook, Rich was comfortably seated on a flat rock, his bike propped up against a stunted tree.

"I was about to send out search and rescue," he said with a grin. Teal flopped next to him trying to catch his breath. His legs were shaking visibly.

"Alright, alright," he said between gasps. "So I misspoke. For the love of God, have mercy on me!"

Rich laughed and took a long drink from his canteen. "We'll hang here for a while and dig the view. It doesn't get much better than this, right?"

Teal nodded hoping his legs would stop their Saint Vitas dance. Rich handed over the canteen, and Teal took a long pull watching his legs in fascination.

"They'll calm down in a while. We'll ride down a little bit different route and stretch out, then go get a bite to eat."

Teal nodded dumbly, looking at Rich who was breathing normally and chewing absently on a twig – not a worry in the world.

Teal leaned back and enjoyed the warmth of the sun as it soaked through his jersey and seem to calm the trembles in his legs. He glanced over at Rich who appeared to be asleep.

"You awake?"

"Mmmmm."

"What are you going to do with all this – working at Magnolia? I mean do you have any plans or goals?"

Rich sat up and rubbed his eyes. "Me? I'm not going to be around that long."

"What?" Teal said surprised. "You do a great job there. You're really needed."

"No," he said shaking his head slowly with a faint smile. "I'm good. TJ is great, Peter Quinn is even greater, and Clair was very good before she started to fade. But me, I'm only good. Don't worry; I'm okay with that. It actually would worry me if I were great. Then I'd be stuck in something I'm not really comfortable doing."

Teal thought about that and watched a large sailboat tack beneath the Golden Gate Bridge.

"What about Gorman," he finally said. "You never mentioned him."

Rich snorted and flipped the twig down the path. "Shit, I'm better than Larry. That guy's an enormous fucking fraud."

"Does that go for his assistant, Ann what's her name?"

"Ann Bock?" he asked. "She's okay. We went out a few times, but the dope thing always got in the way for me."

"Dope thing?"

"Shit they smoke dope out there like there's no tomorrow. Half the time she's stoned, and the other half she's terrified she'll lose her job. They're all a bunch of dopers. There's even rumored that they've smoked with clients."

"Jesus, does TJ know all this? He'd go ballistic."

"I don't know, maybe. But TJ's like a rat in a maze. He's trying to do the job as he sees it while fending off Gorman who wants to control Magnolia. He's schmoozing with the board that hired Gorman, pleading with the foundation for more money. It's never ending."

Rick thought for a moment and bowed his head over folded hands. "When I first hired on, I thought TJ had the job of a lifetime in this industry. After half a year or so, I thought, boy I don't know. Now," he said and thought about it for a few seconds. "There ain't enough money in the world for me to take that gig!"

They enjoyed the sun for another half hour, then picked up their bikes and lined up on a trail back down the mountain. Rich turned around and looked at Teal while putting on his helmet.

"I'll tell you one thing, and I don't mean it to put any pressure on you. But your friend TJ is on the front lines without so much as a bulletproof vest. He needs all the help he can get."

They rode to the bottom of the hill and loaded the bikes. After having a hamburger in Tam Junction, they drove back to Rich's house.

"Thanks for being candid with me," Teal said opening Brownie's door.

"You seem like a decent guy, Jack. I don't really know who you are, but I've watched you relating to the kids. They listen to you, and you really can't ask for more than that."

Teal went back to his cottage and sat on the deck for a long time. The robin hopped out of the privet and stared at him with a beady eye. A moment later a second bird, a shade lighter and smaller hopped out of the privet and stood behind the first.

Got to be a girl robin, Teal thought as he went into the kitchen to get the worms. Probably going to have to stock in lots more if there's going to be dinner for two.

Sleep was elusive, as he knew it would be. Am I a decent guy, he wondered, and will Sloan stand behind me or is this just a happy illusion doomed to failure?Finally he thought about Sloan's tattoo, the proud rearing stallion and her impossibly green eyes peering out from a tangle of hair, and, slowly but surely, sleep came.

* * *

NINETEEN

The following weeks settled into a rhythm – pleasant and peaceful on some days and challenging on others. Days sped by like a calendar being riffled in an old time black and white movie clip. Rarely was he bored. His new recipe plan was wildly successful with Sammy working up a new recipe to compliment the Sammy Scramble, which was his in name only, and Beth and Nicole about to pass the first hurdle with their sandwich entry. Mickey, as secretive as only he could be, claimed his proposal would 'put the restaurant on the culinary map – maybe get a Michelin nod', although there wasn't a hint as to what it might be.

New clients were admitted into the program, always on a temporary basis, but few for any more than an hour or two a week. A teenager named Brian was working with Beth and Nicole two hours a day and doing well. He had blown through the dishwashing job like a strong wind in less than a week and now was efficient on salad prep. The girls seemed to like him, and the three worked together well. There was a new girl named Daisy helping the wait staff and appeared to be learning quickly. She was bright and cheerful, and Ginny didn't like her.

"I'm glad that's your problem," Teal told TJ one afternoon. "Although a little hissy cat fight might lighten things up around here."

"Jesus," TJ snorted and turned away to hide his smile.

Others came and left, several only lasting an hour before it became apparent the fit wouldn't work at this time. Mindful

of what TJ had told him, Teal formed no attachment, not that
he really had time, and some were in and out before he knew
their names. They always worked with a counselor, sometimes
TJ or Rich, but often someone from a group home or from
Marin Mental Health. There were some weeks when the
restaurant seemed to resemble Grand Central Station, and any
introductions were summarily forgotten.

Teal had started sitting in on the intake sessions to
determine whether or not their placement was appropriate.

"You look at it from a practical point of view," TJ had
said. "And I'll look at it from a touchy-feely point of view." He
stared at the ceiling for a moment then grinned at Peter Quinn.
"But of course, my point of view will always prevail," he finally
said, and Peter Quinn nodded somberly.

The Tuesday night session had become a highlight of the
workweek and was attracting the attention of others in the Mental
Health community who sat in from time to time. They were
always carefully screened and told what to expect and not expect.
They were always introduced, but told by TJ in confidence to keep
quiet. Lawrence Gorman and Ann Bock had asked to attend and
TJ kept finding reasons for denial. Gorman had complained to
Sissy, and she was beginning to corner TJ on the issue.

Some of the sessions were rough and tumble, keeping TJ,
Peter Quinn and all other counselors walking on tiptoes. Others
were like an old man's coffee group where everyone talked about
their ailments, the doctors and their meds.

When a representative from the Finessen Foundation
requested a visit, TJ and Peter Quinn agonized long and hard,
finally agreeing on a night that wasn't close to a full moon.

The representative, a mousy little woman in her forties
who acted as if she had drawn the short straw, sat on the
edge of her chair the entire hour and a half. Although it was

an absolutely mellow session, she looked convinced that soon they would be tearing at her clothes in savage blood lust and fighting one another for the choicest body parts. The grisly front-page story the following morning would be sure to make titillating reading.

Teal shook her hand when she left, and it was cold and clammy. TJ and Peter Quinn looked at each other and grimaced.

Mickey approached Teal several weeks later after one of the sessions with a battered briefcase he shifted from hand to hand as if the handle was hot. "I was wondering," he said, then hesitated and gave his denture a good roll. "Well, I was wondering if you'd like to read something I wrote. I heard TJ say you liked to read."

"Sure. What have you got?"

"It's a novel I've been working on," he said and turned looking at the front door as if he might change his mind. "It's probably a piece of shit."

"Mickey, you'll never know what it is unless you let someone else read it. Because I like to read doesn't necessarily make me a good critic. Maybe you could take it to one of those creative writing classes over at The College of Marin. I hear they got some good ones."

Mickey looked at him almost desperately, and then handed the briefcase to Teal. When he took it, Mickey fled through the front door.

Teal pulled some decaf espressos for TJ and Peter Quinn and sat down.

"You packing a briefcase now?" Peter Quinn asked which got a weary smile from TJ.

"Naw, Mickey gave it to me," Teal said. "Some novel he's writing or something. Wants me to read it."

Teal caught TJ and Peter Quinn exchanging a meaningful glance.

"What?" Teal asked.

"The Ralston novel," Peter Quinn said and laced his fingers over his stomach. "He's been writing it for about ten years. Sometimes you can't get him to shut up about it and other times he denies it – claims it's all a big joke."

"Well, there's something in the briefcase. What's it all about?"

"Nobody knows because nobody's seen it. Some think it's all a bunch of bullshit."

Teal hoisted the briefcase up on the table and started to open the clasp, but Peter Quinn stopped him.

"Let's wait a minute here," he said. "Mickey trusts you enough to read it. The whys behind that aren't important right now, but the sense of trust he's placed with you, is. As much as I'm dying to see what he's written, violation of that trust could be a very serious blow to Mickey's support values."

TJ was nodding, but still had an eye fixed on the briefcase. "I have to agree, but I have to admit I'm a little jealous."

"I don't know if I'm really comfortable with this," Teal said slowly shaking his head.

"Come on, Jack, no sweat," TJ said. "You don't have to tell us what's in it, but just what you think of it when you're finished, and we can figure out the best way to respond to Mickey if and when we need to."

"I don't know," he repeated.

"If you do that, I'll give you a chance at becoming a TV star," TJ said and winked at Peter Quinn.

TJ then brought them up to date on a mental health television special being put together by a production company in Boston. Teal had heard dribs and drabs of it, but always that it probably wouldn't include the restaurant.

"I had been told by the assistant to the producer that Magnolia would not be included," TJ told them. "They pretty much had it all shot and edited and had no room. But then, guess what happens? That little mousy lady who was here a couple of weeks ago from Finessen? Apparently she is somewhat of a big deal and knows lots of important folks and started calling around."

"You mean the one who looked like she thought we were going to rape her?" Teal asked.

"Yep. And now the guy in Boston is reassessing things and will let me know within a week."

"God, that's fantastic," Peter Quinn said. Whenever he became enthused about things, the Irish brogue became thicker, sometimes to the point where TJ and Teal were asking 'What? I'm sorry?' and trying to slow him down.

"If it happens, when would it happen?" Teal asked.

"Probably within a week after we know," TJ said.

"Jesus," Teal said scratching his head. "And I haven't got a *thing* to wear."

Teal wanted the kitchen crew to be exposed to the other duties they might be facing if they wanted to find a job in another restaurant.

"You know there are a lot of crossover duties they need to learn. Managerial stuff." he said to TJ one night after work. "They have to understand portion control, produce and meat buying and storage...hell, bill paying for that matter. I'd like to show them some of this stuff."

"Give me a scenario," TJ said watching a beat up foreign sedan pull off to the side of the highway with a flat tire. "Oh, this is going to be fun."

"Keeping in mind the little talk we had the other day, I'd
like to start with Sammy. Take him to the Produce Mart in San
Francisco so he can see the enormity of the food distribution
process."

TJ squinted with one eye and said, "Just the Mart,
right? You're not going to take him to Swan's Oyster Bar or
anything?"

Teal was so uptight about the process of having to ask, he
almost missed the sarcastic zinger TJ fired by him with a sweet
smile and arched eyebrows.

Two days later, at two in the morning, he picked up
Sammy at his home, and they drove to South San Francisco.
Sammy was so excited his conversation snapped back and forth
from English to Japanese and back. There was almost no traffic
on 101 going south and little in San Francisco as they worked
their way to South City. The closer they got, the heavier the
traffic became, until it was a jostling honking major traffic tie-
up. TJ would have loved it.

"All these people here to buy veggies?" Sammy asked his
eyes wide in astonishment.

"Yep. Stuff comes in from all over the west in vans,
pickups and eighteen-wheelers. Probably some of the rare stuff
in cars just like Brownie."

They parked and walked to the mart, which was as busy
as anything downtown during lunch hour. Men in coveralls
were offloading pallets of boxes, some dripping from the early
morning dew and packing ice.

"Most of the independent markets and lots of restaurants
will only buy their produce here – never through a wholesaler,"
Teal said. "You know why?"

Sammy thought for a moment. "Because it's fresh."

"You bet. The freshest. Lot of these veggies were in the ground yesterday afternoon."

Teal recognized another chef, and they nodded to each other.

"That's George Snyder from Georgie's in San Rafael. You ever eat there?"

Sammy shook his head vigorously. "No way! Too expensive for me."

"Well, let me tell you. It's terrific, because he takes the time to buy only the best ingredients. Now let me ask you. If you buy crappy ingredients what are you going to end up with?"

"Crappy meal," Sammy said quickly as he danced out of the way of a forklift loaded with cases of strawberries. "But you still can have crappy meal from good veggies unless you have swell cooks like you and me."

Teal laughed and said, "You know you're going to have to learn all this stuff because you will not be a line cook all your life. You're too good for that."

Sammy looked worried as they walked back to the car.

In the ensuing weeks, Teal brought Sammy, Beth, Nicole and occasionally several others into the mysterious inner circle of restaurant operation. They were all curious.

He asked them all to stay after work one afternoon which they did with a minimum of grumbling. He retrieved an accordion file from the office and brought it out to the largest table in the dining room where he unceremoniously dumped the content. Bundle after bundle of banded invoices and lists bounced on the table with some finding their way to the floor.

"This is what all restaurant managers hate to deal with," Teal said flipping several packets back on the table. "And next to the quality of the food, there is nothing more critical. You can cook and serve the best food in California, but if you don't have a handle on keeping on top of expenses, you're going to be toast."

He picked up a bundle and flipped it to Sammy. "What have you got there?" he asked.

Sammy slipped off the rubber band and shuffled through the papers. "Veggie bills," he finally said.

"You got it," Teal said. "But what about the bills? What does this mean down at the bottom of the most recent?"

Sammy looked and shrugged his shoulder.

Teal showed the invoice to the rest at the table.

"It says three percent discount," Beth finally said, and Teal gave her a thumbs up.

"We had been paying our veggie bills in sixty to ninety days," Teal said. "The terms are for thirty days and the supplier was not happy. So I talked with him and asked if we paid within terms, would he be willing to give us a discount. He was more than happy to oblige."

Sammy was nodding his head. "It's just like us working together here in the kitchen. We have to work with our suppliers because we're all sort of in this thing together."

Teal stared at him dumbfounded until Beth finally giggled. "Sammy," he finally said, "you are the sharpest Samurai I've ever met." And they bumped knuckles.

Teal picked up Sloan in Larkspur on Monday afternoon. The plan was for her to spend four days and fly back on Friday.

"Dad's thinking of buying some stock in Southwest," she said and grinned. "Might be cheaper if we just shacked up somewhere together."

Teal smiled and pulled her over next to him. "I owe your dad, you know that. I know he can't shackle you and stop you from seeing me, but he could make things really unpleasant. But he's not, so I owe him."

Sloan reached over and touched his cheek. "You two guys are a lot alike. We'll work things out."

Back at the cottage, Teal brought her up to date: including his ride with Rich, taking Sammy to the Produce Mart and the possibility of the television special.

"Did you ever think you might like to have a nice quiet job, like maybe a CPA or driving a school bus?" she asked.

"I know you're kidding. But what Rich said really stayed with me. TJ is really flying solo out there, and if I can help him, I will. Plus," he added, "it might be my chance to be discovered by Hollywood."

"Oh, and you'd like that, wouldn't you?" she said frowning at him. "All those brainless bimbos with big boobs saying 'Oh, you're so cute. I just love the way your hair falls over your eyes.'"

"Sloan, if you don't stop poking me in the ribs, I'm going to throw up, and it's gonna be all your fault.

"By the way did you bring your Nordstrom's charge card?" he asked, and she nodded.

"Now Dad wants some fancy California threads. He's all hooked on Tommy Bahama. I'm beginning to feel like a sales girl – excuse me, sales associate."

"The reason I'm asking is John Barrington has invited me to play some handball with him at his club in The City. Maybe you can do some shopping at the Nordstrom's on Market Street, and, after I smoke his ass, we can hook up for some dinner."

Later that night as they lay in bed with a quarter moon lighting the deck and the back wall of the bedroom, Sloan asked, "Do you ever think about your old friends and what you were doing? Do you think about Koontzman?"

Teal was lying on his back with his arms beneath his head. The moonlight washed across his face turning his hair to an inky black.

"I don't think about the crew much anymore. I still mourn Chris, and I think I always will."

"Do you think he would have mourned over you if things had been reversed?" she asked.

"Maybe, I don't know," Teal said realizing he had never thought of it in those terms before. "Probably not."

"How about Koontzman?"

"That's a whole 'nother issue," he said looking out the window and thinking about the photograph in the dresser. A pleasant scent of honeysuckle drifted though the screen.

"I'm not entirely sure I could explain it. I'm not sure I understand it myself. He always seemed to be interested in what I was doing, what I was thinking. He was always advising me to make plans for the future. Before I got busted, I saw more of him than I did of Chris and the rest of the gang."

Sloan said, "Mmmm." And snuggled closer.

"I think he knew I was on the verge of quitting, and he was wondering why. And he knew if I did quit, we would probably not see each other again."

"It almost sounds as if he thought of you as family," Sloan said.

"I don't know. Perhaps he did in a distorted way," Teal said. "But in that business everything is distorted and magnified. Your friends can become your enemies overnight, and you live with the thought of death or prison everyday. Maybe that is one of the things I admired in him. He seemed to live a normal life. He was a voracious reader and had a curiosity about everything. He was having a wonderful life by all appearances and was happy to share it with you. It's hard *not* to like a person like that."

He could feel her breathing slowly and regularly next to him and wondering if she had fallen asleep.

"Jack," she finally said in a sleepy voice. "There's some bullets in your bedside table. When we have babies, I don't want any guns in the house."

He tilted his head to look at her, but she had fallen asleep.

On Wednesday, Teal left the restaurant early and Sloan picked him up in Brownie. She drove down the freeway at barely subsonic speeds while Teal braced a hand against the dash knowing that it would snap like a matchstick when they collided with something, but unable to stop himself.

"I'll tell you what, Sloan," he said his voice almost a croak. "If you slow down to a normal speed, so I'm not about ready to pee in my pants, I'll get rid of the gun."

She turned in her seat and gave him a thousand watt smile, then patted him on the knee. "Thank you, Jack. It will really make me feel better," she said and dropped the speed down about four miles an hour.

John met them in front of the club and instructed Sloan on a short cut to Nordstrom's and a recommendation on where to park. Then he and Teal walked into the club.

Teal had been in many men's clubs when he had been in business with Koontzman, and he had a brief prickly moment of fear they may meet someone with whom he had dealt in the past. But he realized that men's clubs, such as this one, were different. Physically they may look somewhat the same, the members resemble each other, but beneath the surface, they

could be far different. The clubs he had been to in the past,
for the most part, had been a little too glitzy with people too
aware of themselves. They would have called John's club stuffy
or boring. Subdued rooms with the slight click of dominoes and
quiet hallways and a restful protectiveness, all of which Teal
found very pleasant.

When they entered the area with the handball and
racquetball courts, that peacefulness shifted to an almost
tangible sense of combativeness. In the locker room, John took
off his long sleeved shirt and trousers to change into his
t-shirt and shorts and Teal thought, uh-oh. John's arms and
legs looked like tree limbs twined with vines of muscle. There
was a tiny faded tattooed high on his right arm that said,
Simper Fi.

The first game went quickly and savagely and Teal was
almost shutout. John played a style of game popular with older
tennis players; try to stay in one place and make your opponent
run his ass off from the very first shot. Teal never felt his
rhythm and if he started to find it, John would shift his.

"Try another?" John asked. He was breathing normally,
and his shirt appeared to be bone dry.

Teal took a sip from the water fountain and said, "You
bet."

This time he fared better. He was still beaten, but it
wasn't embarrassing. A small group of men had gathered
behind the glass and were enjoying themselves.

"You're very good," John said, "but very rusty. How about
a third now that you've warmed up?"

John was beginning to tire and Teal pulled out all the
tricks he could remember: back spins, nasty little dropping
shots that died coming off the wall and corner shots that came
back at you like a rocket.

Teal won the point with an evil wall shot, which appeared it would drive the opponent back against the base line. Because of the vicious spin, it instead climbed the wall and then dropped straight down like a fallen walnut. John had no chance, and the crowd behind them clapped enthusiastically.

John laughed, and they shook hands. "Where did you learn that God damned shot? You'll have to teach me some day."

They had iced tea in the reading room and then waited out in front for Sloan. A few minutes later she sped up the street, making Brownie perform maneuvers not in his repertoire and pulled to a smooth stop in front of them.

John clapped Teal on the back and opened the passenger door. "Let's do this again some time. I haven't had any competition for years." Again the hearty laugh. "And you, young lady," he said with mock severity. "You should be racing in NASCAR and not scaring the pants off my handball partner."

John had called in a reservation for dinner at a small French restaurant near the top of Nob Hill. Teal couldn't pronounce the name correctly, and Sloan ordered the entire meal speaking flawless French. The waiter was in love and pestered them throughout the meal. Teal thought he might try to follow them home.

Emily and Sloan and Dannie had all become close friends, which took a worry off of Teal's shoulders. He didn't want her to become bored and restless while he was at work. At length he realized he was wasn't giving her due credit for who she was and never thought about it again.

His current worry, and it was like a bad toothache getting worse, was the urge to tell TJ and Dannie about his

past. Well, at least TJ and *he* could tell Dannie. Teal wasn't sure
he could face the two of them together and for the first time he
felt shame and guilt.

He asked Sloan, and she thought for a moment. "I think
you're selling both of them short", 'she finally said. "But I also
agree with your chicken shit method of doing it; tell TJ first
and let him tell Dannie."

As usual Sloan was brutally blunt.

"I think I would like to take you into the shower and
rinse your mouth out with soap."

She arched her eyebrows. "I'll bet if we go in the shower,
I can convince you not to do that," she said.

"Well, if we hurry, we can take TJ and Dannie out for
Mexican food."

"Hurry?" Sloan said and smiled at him thinly. "I – don't -
think – so."

It was a beautiful evening, so they chose to sit on the
restaurant's back patio. The dinner crowd was starting to build,
and they were lucky to get a table. The owners treated them
like royalty and ushered them to a table on the veranda beneath
a bay tree laced with tiny lights. The teenaged daughter stared
at TJ as if he were a pair of Guess jeans in just her size.

"How're you feeling," Teal asked TJ who had to take
almost a minute to chew up and swallow the enormous piece of
burrito. Dannie frowned at him with down turned lips.

"I'm feeling good," he finally said wiping his lips with a
cloth napkin. The rest of them had paper napkins.

"Long as I get my sleep and things seem relatively stable –
and, of course, I have the love of my sweet woman."

The usual table-hopping was in full swing and several
people came over to say hello and were introduced to Teal and
Sloan. A woman came over and asked Dannie if she would

come over and meet her niece who was attending Dannie's alma mater.

"She's thinking of rushing a sorority and could probably benefit from your input," the woman said with the barely hidden plea.

Dannie got up, grabbed Sloan's hand and towed her in her wake. Sloan, looking over her shoulder, pointed her fingers at the two of them and then touched them together. Teal had a clear idea what the movement meant and treated himself to a long pull on his beer.

"TJ, I need to talk with you about something," Teal started wondering about the timing of the whole thing but more fearful Sloan would blast him if he didn't.

"Shit, you're not going to tell me you're quitting are you?" he asked but not very concerned.

"No, but in many ways, it's probably worse," he said starting to writhe in his chair.

TJ yawned and stretched his hands over his head. "You mean about your being in a Texas prison?" he asked mildly.

Teal carefully put down his beer and openly stared at TJ. "How long have you known?" he finally asked.

"A while, just after I got your postcard, I guess," he said easing forward in his chair until his elbows were on the table and their faces no more than two feet apart.

"I've kept up with a bunch of the guys we went to school with – particularly a couple of guys who entered the same field as me. One of them lives in Texas and has a buddy in law enforcement. The cop guy hears about some guy being kicked free who had gone to Michigan State and calls my buddy to needle him. And my buddy calls me – it's hardly top-secret stuff you know. Matter of public records." His eyes searched

Teal's. There was no distrust or judgment in them, just a trace
of concern as to how Teal would process this information.

"And you hired me anyway," Teal said.

"Sure," TJ said. "I'm a believer in people and the fact
that most people don't really change over the years. Oh sure
they mature and look at things differently, maybe become
Republicans when they were Democrats before. But the core
of the person stays the same. Evil people stay evil, good people
stay good. You're not an evil person, Jack. That much I knew at
college."

"I don't know what to say," Teal said quietly. "I feel
humble and stupid."

Dannie had started back towards the table when Sloan
took her arm, and they walked off to talk with the owner for a
moment.

"Does Dannie know?"

"Sure, I told her, although not right away. That would
have been a setup. Unfair to both you guys."

"And she's..."

"Dannie is a loving and trusting human being. How I
ended up with her is a mystery of the age. She has grown to
love you the way I do. It's something neither of us is prepared to
admit even under extreme torture by the CIA."

Teal smiled faintly. "How about Rich and Claire?"

"Nope."

"Sissy and John?"

TJ squinted. "I don't know. But if they know, it's not from
me." He took a final sip from his beer. "John is phenomenally
well connected even though he's retired. He knows just about
everyone who's anyone. For all his mellow appearances, he has a
network the FBI would die for." TJ looked over to see what the
two women were doing, and then turned back.

"When I hired Carl, we did a background check, of course. But that's not as easy as it sounds. Everyone is afraid to say something negative about an ex employee because they might get sued. John certainly doesn't operate under those restraints. He never liked Carl from the beginning. Not that Carl is overflowing with charm, but still it seemed out of character for John."

TJ stared over Teal's head for a moment lost in thought. "So I would say if he knows about your past, and that's a big if, his silence I take as acceptance. So the long and short of it is don't lose any sleep."

Teal nodded, and then asked, "How about Gorman?"

TJ laughed so loudly several people turned around and grinned. "Larry? Shit he's too dumb to know if his shirt's on fire, and I'd be the last to tell him."

Almost a week later, Teal set aside the time to start reading what Mickey had given him. Mickey had never pestered him in the interim. He had looked in the briefcase the first night he brought it home, and the manuscript appeared to be pitifully slim for ten year's work.

After feeding the robins, that must have been feeding all their friends because Teal was absolutely blowing through quarts of worms, he arranged himself on the deck with a beer and a good light over his shoulder. When he finished at a little past two in the morning, he placed the last page on the table next to him and stared out at the diminishing lights across the bay.

It was a novella really, just over two hundred pages, and titled *Cold Echoes.* It was professionally typed with sensible font and spacing, and the grammar was spot on. It was also one of the most touching and deeply felt manuscripts Teal had ever read, reminding him of Norman McLean's *A River Runs Through It.*

It told about a young boy growing up in a family in turmoil. Everyone had too many agendas, meetings, luncheons and club dates to pay attention to a boy who was quiet, shy and afraid of the world. There wasn't really a conclusion, leaving Teal with the impression it might not be finished. Although when he thought about it, maybe it was.

When TJ came in the following day, Teal waited a few minutes, then took off his apron and joined him at his favorite table.

"Hey what's the haps?" he asked when he saw Teal. "Hitch up a chair."

Teal sat down and stretched his legs out getting comfortable. "I read Mickey's book last night. It's not really a book – more like a novella."

"Bunch of gobbledygook, right?"

Teal fidgeted for a moment, then leaned forward. "I'm not a critic. I wouldn't even be able to qualify as an assistant professor at a community college." TJ was watching him now.

"But I read a lot, at least when Sloan's not around, and my tastes are fairly eclectic although I prefer fiction. I got my first library card when I was eight." He leaned forward and rested his elbows on the table, so there faces were close.

"Mickey's novella is absolutely one of the finest pieces of writing I've ever read." TJ leaned forward further and cupped his chin.

"He writes with the passion and sensitivity of McLean and has the wordsmith abilities of a Gardner or Cheever. It's simply phenomenal and eminently publishable. It could damn well be a best seller."

"But a novella?"

"Sure. Think *Brokeback Mountain*. It was a short story."

"Jesus," TJ whispered and sank back into his chair. "This I didn't expect." He chewed on his lower lip for a moment. "Peter Quinn and I had multiple scenarios how to progress after you reported back. This was not really one of them.

"I'm going to go back in the office and call P.Q. and see what he thinks. He's not scheduled today, but I don't want to wait. Give me a couple of minutes."

Mickey had just walked in and was tying on a waiter's apron while joking with Sammy in the pass-through. Teal walked back into the kitchen and greeted Mickey like any other normal day. Several minutes later, TJ nodded at Teal who once again joined him at the table.

"P.Q.'s going apeshit. He wants to get over here badly, but he's in sessions all day. He recommended that you tell Mickey what you feel and see what his reactions are. I mean if it's really that great, I would love to see him publish it. Rich and I will be around for backup and moral support. Wait until the end of the day when everybody's gone."

Teal was nervous and wired for the rest of the day. There were few things he could do right and finally flipped a blintz that missed the pan and almost landed on Sammy's shoulder.

"God damn," Sammy said, and then muttered something in Japanese. "We're going to have to get your girlfriend back up here before you kill someone."

Teal smiled while scraping the blintz off the range.

When the restaurant had finally closed, and the crew was starting to head home, Teal approached Mickey. "Can I talk to you for a second before you're out of here?" Mickey nodded appearing curious, and Teal went back into the office where he had left Mickey's briefcase. When Mickey saw him approaching, his body language went through a dramatic shift.

Rich and TJ were lounging at a table across the room and appeared to be paying no attention.

"I've read your book, Mickey," Teal started.

"It's a piece of shit, right?" Mickey said quickly, his heel beating a rapid rhythm on the floor.

"No it's not," Teal said calmly. "As the matter of fact I think it's beautifully written, and I loved reading it."

Mickey stiffened and laughed harshly. "Then I really pulled the wool over your eyes," he said. "I didn't write it. I found a book in the library and copied it word for word. Ha-ha, so the joke's on you."

TJ and Rich were watching closely now, and the restaurant was still except for the sound of the dishwasher going through one final wash cycle.

"No, I don't believe that," Teal finally said. "I believe you wrote it, and you're afraid someone will say it's a piece of garbage. Perhaps you didn't hear me Mickey," he said leaning forward and speaking softly. "It's a wonderful piece of writing and should be shared with other people. It's that good."

Mickey seemed to deflate before him. His shoulders hunched and his head lowered and the heel tapping ceased. Finally he looked at Teal briefly and then lowered his eyes.

"You really liked it?"

"I loved it, Mickey. It's one of the finest pieces of writing I've been privileged to read. Some authors write for a lifetime and never produce something like this."

Mickey got up quickly and grabbed the briefcase. "I gotta go home. Got lots to do tonight."

"I hope we can talk more about this later," Teal said to his retreating back.

"Maybe, perhaps, but I've got lots to do right now," he said and was out the door.

Rich and TJ waited a minute then rushed over to the table.

"Could you hear anything?" Teal asked.

TJ nodded. "Particularly at the end, just before he left."

"Jesus, why would he deny writing it? Say that he copied from a library book?"

"How do you know he didn't?" Rich asked.

"This is sort of goofy," Teal said after he thought for a second. "But the writing sort of sounded like him. I mean when he's not wigging out and making an ass out of himself. I have no idea how you could tell if it's copied from something. But my feeling is something that good in print would get noticed, would get some play and end up on some lists. It is that good, folks."

"I don't suppose you made a copy?" TJ asked.

"Nope. And it wasn't because I didn't think of it. And when I did think of it, I felt ashamed."

TJ and Rich nodded. "I heard him deny writing it at first," Rich said. "Terrified of success." TJ looked at him remembering what he had said to Dannie.

"So what happens now?" Teal asked.

"I need to talk with P.Q. and get his input," TJ said. "I personally feel that we should help him do something with it. Talk to an agent – something."

"How about, John?" Teal asked. "You guys are always telling me he knows everyone who's anyone. Probably knows an agent or two. I hear they're all over Marin County."

"Good idea," TJ said and nodded. "But first let me huddle with P.Q. God, I am so pumped!"

The television producer in Boston contacted TJ two days later at Magnolia. It was a go. When he came out of the office, he was literally dancing. He grabbed Ginny, spun her around.

"What's wrong with him?" Sammy asked thumbing at
TJ.

"I don't know," Teal said calmly. "Got a bug up his ass, I
guess."

When the final customer was ushered out, TJ gathered
the staff and they all huddled with Peter Quinn who was
outlining the manner in which it would be presented.

"To most of them, it won't mean anything. But to those
who are scheduled to be working here that day, it could be a
big deal. Keep in mind that some clients who are not working
here, or never have, still might want to see the action. So we'll
have to deal with that."

"How about kids who are scheduled to work but feel
threatened?" Rich asked.

"We'll have to shift them around. The ones who can't
handle it will trade with those who like the idea. But it's really
important there is no stigma attached to not wanting to be
part of the action. We need to be clear on that. Now," he said
rubbing his hands, "we have ten days,"

* * *

TWENTY

The dining room was packed at five o'clock and after everyone settled, TJ rose to begin his presentation. He hadn't uttered a word when Lawrence Gorman and Ann Bock strolled casually through the front door, which someone had left unlocked and took seats outside the circle.

Mickey leapt to his feet a second later. "Don't we still have a rule about people arriving late?" he asked TJ, and his glare never wavered.

"Sit down please, Mickey," TJ said staring at Gorman who glared back.

"Mickey, we can talk about this issue later, but right now I have a far more important issue to discuss."

Mickey twisted in his seat, and TJ and Peter Quinn exchanged glances. Thanks to Gorman, they would have to perform some serious damage control later.

Teal started once more. "What I'm going to tell you is perhaps the most exciting thing to happen to Magnolia Café in a very long time. A production company on the east coast is making a television special about the status of mental health in the United States. They have decided they would like to incorporate our restaurant in the special."

A murmur of voices sweep around the room – all from clients, since all staff and the board already knew. Most of the clients appeared to be excited and eager for TJ to elaborate. One young girl stared at the floor and seemed on the verge of tears.

But Teal remembered her from past sessions, and she almost always looked the same.

"They will be filming in the restaurant on the seventeenth. That's only nine days away, and we've got lots to do around here."

"What happens if someone is scheduled to work and doesn't want to be here that day?" Peter Quinn asked. TJ and Peter Quinn did this so seamlessly, it almost fooled Teal.

"Good question. If you don't want to be here talk with your counselor, and we'll have you switch places with someone. Also if there are some of you who are not scheduled but would like to be here, please let us know and we'll try to fit you in. But keep in mind it will be extremely busy – Mickey would say a zoo." There were a few titters and Mickey looked pleased, and TJ may have partially defused the earlier issue.

"When will the special be on TV?" someone asked.

"I've been told the show had been almost completely edited when they decided to add the segment about Magnolia," TJ said. "Our part will be significant – between four to six minutes."

"Doesn't seem like much to me," Mickey said.

"Believe me it is, although to someone like you Mickey with a limited attention span, it might seem like forever," TJ said.

There were snickers and laughs around the room and Mickey cackled. It was their "Bob and Ray' routine at its best, and Teal had seen it often enough in the past.

There were other questions about timing of the filming and the showing and what it all meant. Many were excited by the idea or by the fact others were excited. Some were confused and detached. Others, anxious by the heightened emotions and excitement. To some it meant virtually nothing.

When the meeting was adjourned and people started to
leave, Gorman approached TJ. He was walking stiff legged, and
Teal drifted over to be close to them.

"You need to have more control over your meetings," he
said with controlled anger, "and exercise some sort of restraint
in your relationship with Ralston. He's skating a fine edge."

TJ stared at him for a moment before taking his glasses
off and allowing them to dangle from the cord.

"As always, I appreciate your input, Lawrence," TJ said
with remarkable aplomb. "But I must remind you that you are
an invited guest – who by the way was late in violation of our
well established rules."

Teal watched Sissy and John drift closer.

"I would also remind you who is in charge of this facility
and who is responsible for its operation and well-being." TJ's
cheeks were touched with color.

"And finally I would remind you of discretion which you
have not, in my opinion, exercised this evening. If you wish to
speak with me in the future about the operation of *my* facility
or about one of *my* clients you will do so in an appropriate
manner. I hope I have been completely clear about this."

Gorman stared down his nose at TJ, who looked like a
furious bulldog returning the stare. Teal stepped forward and
put his hand on TJ's shoulder, and it was as if he was touching
a rock outcropping. John, who was holding his hands in front of
him as a universal peace gesture, also stepped in quickly.

Gorman turned to them dismissing TJ and said, "Rest
assured we will be talking about this on a later date."

He turned and strode through the front door, slamming
it behind him. TJ sank into a chair, his arms and hands
shaking and his face pale. Teal sat with him, his hand on his
friends forearm waiting for his color to return.

Sissy was speaking to John in a low voice and he was nodding his agreement. They approached the table, deep concern apparent on both of their faces.

"TJ we want you to go home immediately, take a nice warm shower and go to bed," Sissy said. "John's calling Dannie right now to tell her you need lots of TLC tonight and maybe a big mug of hot cocoa. I would like Jack to drive you home..."

TJ shook his head. "Thanks Sissy. I'm okay to drive. Beside," he said with his traditional grin, "Dannie has a breakfast date with an old friend and would kill me if I left the car down here."

Sissy looked doubtful.

"No really, I'm fine," he said touching her arm.

They all left together, being the final four out the door, and Teal flipped the light switch. Sissy hugged both of them and took one last concerned look at TJ.

"Please take care of yourself, dear," she said. "Your health always comes first."

John opened the door for her, and they drove down the darkened street. Teal followed TJ home and watched Dannie meet him at the door and bring him into the warmth of their house.

* * *

When Teal heard the opening notes of Dire Straits playing *MTV,* he was puzzled. Hadn't they broken up? They hadn't done a tour in years, so where was he? It wasn't until he rolled over and his pillow fell on the floor he realized he was in bed, and his cell phone was ringing. He changed the ring every other week or so to another favorite rock standard.

He punched it on and the face told him it was two thirty-five in the morning.

"Hello."

"Jack, this is John Bennington." A prickle of fear raced down his spine. "I'm at Marin General. TJ's had a heart attack. You'd better come down right away."

Teal was dressed and out the door in less than twenty seconds. He tried to drive quickly and sensibly but failed, all the time wishing Sloan was with him, not only to handle the driving but also just to be there. A cop picked him up two miles from the hospital and followed him into the emergency entrance before pealing off and disappearing.

Teal burst through the emergency room door and into the brightly lit room almost colliding with a young couple who were leaving. Sissy and John were holding hands and John was trying to smooth his sleep-roiled hair. Dannie sat on a couch with Rich who was holding her hands and speaking softly. She saw Teal and leapt into his arms crying.

"Oh God, Jack, I'm so scared. I've never been this scared."

When Teal looked at John over Dannie's head, he stepped over and put one hand on Teal's shoulder and one on Dannie's.

"The cardiologist is with him now. We don't know anything," he said quietly.

"He took a hot bath when he came home," Dannie said with her voice shaking so badly Teal had to listen closely.

"Listen, Dannie," he said. "You don't have to talk about it right now."

"I have to," she said. "If I don't…if I just have to sit here, I'm going to lose it."

Teal nodded.

"He didn't want to have any dinner, just go to bed. Didn't even want a beer," she said and her voice choked.

Teal stroked her back and some of the shaking eased.

"A couple of hours ago he woke me up and said something like, 'I think I'm in trouble'. I flipped on the light and he was drenched in perspiration and shaking. I called 911 and promised myself I would wait five minutes before loading him in the car." Her voice broke, and Teal held her tightly.

"They made it in less than four."

"How long has he been in there?" Teal asked.

"About an hour and a half," John said looking at his watch.

They heard the sound of voices from behind the E.R. door, and a moment later a man in a doctor's scrubs walked out and looked around the room. He saw Dannie and walked over to her with a smile.

"Well you must be Dannie," he said taking both of her hands. "He's been talking about you so much in there I feel I know you."

She was trying to be brave and hold it together.

"I'm Peter Wilkins. Call me Pete if you'd like. Let's sit over here so we can talk, and all your friends can gather around and listen."

He nodded at everyone but made it clear he was speaking with Dannie. "TJ's a tough young man, and I don't see any reason why he won't be fine," he said with a smile.

"That's the good stuff. And now the not-so-good stuff. He has suffered a cardiac infarction – not a serious one but a definite wakeup call. For now he needs bed rest and absolutely no exposure to pressure."

He held up his hand and nodded. "Now I know what TJ does for a living. I've eaten at Magnolia any number of times. He has to take a break and smell the roses," he added with a grin.

"If he takes care of himself, I envision him returning within a month – maybe less," he said and held up a finger. "And that will be at reduced hours for a while."

The front door burst open and Peter Quinn rushed in, his hair wild and one shoe unlaced. He looked at the faces and relaxed somewhat.

"Pete," he said nodding. "How is he?"

"He's in there babbling about this lovely young lady and I must say, I can't blame him," he said winking at Dannie.

Peter Quinn's shoulders slumped with the tension release. Sissy had walked outside the building and was talking on a cell phone and gestured him to join her.

"I'll want to see TJ twice a week for at least two weeks, and, of course, immediately if anything arises. And that means anything, at any hour of the day."

"May I see him?" Dannie asked.

"Yes, but for just a minute or two. I'm going to keep him here for at least three nights. Then we'll see about his going home."

Dannie followed him through the doors while Teal and Rich stared at each other.

"Jesus," Rich finally said. "Is this fucked or what."

Teal nodded in agreement. The conversation outside between Peter Quinn, Sissy and John continued, and they seemed to be agreeing.

John and Peter Quinn came through the door while Sissy waited outside. "Jack, Sissy would like to have a word with you."

When he stepped outside Sissy was just hanging up her cell phone. "I am so distressed about TJ. And just when he was on the verge of seeing something he had worked so hard for. I'll have to call the producer in Boston."

"What? You're not thinking of canceling?" Teal was surprised.

"I don't see that we have a choice. To be brutally honest, we don't have a program director."

"Sissy, this is TJ's dream," Teal said. "We can't take it away from him."

"Well, what do you suggest," Sissy asked looking confused. "I see no alternatives, do you?"

"Sissy, we have a wonderful group, and they're all really looking forward to this. I think we can pull it together and do it."

"But we have to have a program director," she said her brow furrowed in thought. "I suppose we could bring in Lawrence. He has always expressed an interest in wanting more control over the restaurant. That might work."

"I could take over and fill in," Teal said quickly. "I think we could pull it off. And it would just be for a few weeks."

Sissy held her chin in her hand and thought about it.

"Well, that *is* an interesting thought," she said as John walked through the doors.

Sissy motioned to her husband. "John, Jack has an interesting idea," she said and as he strolled over, Jack had an odd but very pervasive feeling he had just been well and truly finessed.

While Rich stayed with Dannie, Teal, Peter Quinn and the Barringtons ended up at an all night restaurant drinking stale decaf and working out some of the details.

"As soon as TJ comes back, he will be the main man again," Teal reminded them for the fourth or fifth time. "These responsibilities have temporary written all over them."

"Absolutely," Peter Quinn agreed. "And I don't think you're going to see much change in your day-to-day activities.

I will be lurking around an extra day, and we will get help from a floater if we need it."

Sissy and John nodded in agreement.

"We have to present it to the restaurant clients in a positive manner, so they don't become afraid," Sissy said.

"Or combative like Mickey," Teal added.

"So why don't you open tomorrow like usual," Peter Quinn said. "And after I arrive we can have a quick talk with the group. I'll get there as soon as I can, and you'll probably have to stay a little later."

They talked until it was apparent they were starting to repeat themselves. Sissy dabbed at her lips with a napkin and said, "Well, I think we have all our ducks in a row."

The shooting gallery image was not one Teal would have chosen, but he smiled weakly at the group and nodded. He was practically asleep on his feet.

An hour after he climbed into bed, his alarm rang and he swept it off the chair and laid there with his eyes burning. After a quick scalding shower and putting out a wad of worms, he trudged out to Brownie and drove down the hill.

"Hey, boss, you look like shit," Sammy said and followed it with his snik-snik laugh. Teal was late, and they were all waiting. "Did that pretty girl keep you up all night?" he asked. He always called Sloan 'that pretty girl' behind her back and Miss Easy to her face, and she was powerless to correct him.

"Nope, faced with another day working with you bozos left me tossing and turning all night," he said and put his arm around Sammy's thin shoulders. The girls giggled.

They worked quickly and had nearly finished prep by the time Peter Quinn arrived. Teal went out to meet him, and they

spoke quietly in the front room. After Rich came in looking
equally as exhausted, they all laughed at each other.

"How's Dannie?" Teal asked, and Rich nodded.

"She's okay. I took her home to shower after she saw TJ.
Then she was going to go back down. She's taking a cab –
wouldn't let me drive her."

Peter Quinn gathered the clients together.

"I want you to give the initial explanation," he said
pointing at Teal. "I want to be able to watch everyone in the
group. Soft soap it as much as you can, and I'll step in to add or
clarify things. Then we'll go straight back to work."

"No break?" Teal acted surprised.

"No. We are facing a real world situation, and we have to
handle it in a real world manner. Sometimes you are faced with
disturbing news and then are asked to go back to work. No
different here. Rich and I will be watching."

They brought the kitchen staff out into the main room
and everyone grabbed a seat sitting haphazardly around the
room.

"I need to talk with you guys real quick this morning, and
then we're going back to work. TJ is sick and won't be in for a
couple of days. It is not serious, but he's had a heart attack."

The color drained from Mickey's face as if he was the
product of computer animation, but he was quiet and attentive.
Ginny had her hands folded in front of her chin and her elfin
face looked like it was in danger of crumpling inwards. Peter
Quinn quickly walked over and started talking to her softly.

"You guys know there are all different degrees of heart
attacks, and this was a mild one," Teal continued. "But he needs
to take care of himself and that means no tension. And we all
know this little restaurant can be tense at times." Nobody so
much as twitched.

Teal nodded at Peter Quinn who had raised his hand. "I will be coming in an extra day until we can get TJ back in here. Ginny will probably have me waiting tables. What a sight that will be!" he added, and Amed smiled timidly.

"Can we go see him?" Beth asked.

"Not for a few days," Rich said. "But we'll let you know when and sort of make a field trip out of it."

Body language was easing, and Teal noticed a line forming outside the front door.

"One last thing before we open," Peter Quinn said raising a finger. "In TJ's absence, Jack will be our acting program director. Remember we have to have someone to blame everything on." That actually got a couple of laughs.

"You're my hero," Sammy said and fluttered his eyelashes when they were back in the kitchen, and Teal ruffled his hair and messed up his neatly tied headband.

"There's one thing we forgot to mention," Teal said. "The filming will go on just as it was planned. You know TJ wouldn't have it any other way. So when we get done cooking, the real work begins. We're going to make this place shine." There were groans but followed with grins.

The word had gotten around quickly, and a number of people came in concerned about TJ. Peter Quinn was gracious in his thanks of their consideration while somehow slipping in the thought that further and perhaps more active support of the restaurant would be a good thing. Most people left feeling satisfied and probably proud of themselves. Teal and Peter Quinn had roughed out a list of priorities and specific duties for clients. Most importantly he would call all the suppliers and have them channel their requests and plans through Teal.

"God, are we supposed to put them up and entertain them?" Peter Quinn said wondered about the production crew.

"Naw, those guys have budgets for everything," Teal said wondering if that was the truth. "Anyway, I'll take care of anything they need."

They all sat around after cleanup, no distinction between clients and staff and talked about what was needed and who would handle it. The carpet would have to be professionally cleaned; Teal's job, eke out a little more from the budget for new flower vases and arrange for cut flowers; Nicole and Beth, cleaning the kitchen, sharpening the knives, cleaning all of the pots and pans to a luster they hadn't seen in months and arranging the storeroom; Sammy assisted by Gary, front window, front door cleaned and tables and chairs waxed; Ginny, make the espresso bar look better than anything you could find in North Beach; Amed and Tim.

Teal knew hundreds of other details would spring up over the next few days, and there would be plenty of work for everyone. The trickier task of determining who would work that day was more daunting and left to Peter Quinn.

"So far I don't know anyone who *doesn't* want to be here," he told Teal. "Even after I've explained this is a special about mental health and, if on camera, they would be identified with that. Made no difference," he said and stroked his beard.

"I think when the day arrives some may change their minds, so I've allowed for back up."

"You know with the excitement of all this I almost completely forgot about Mickey's book," Teal said. "How do you think we should play it?"

"I talked to John and he's going to put some feelers out. See if he can find someone in the business to at least read the thing." Peter Quinn said and looked at his watch. "I gotta get out of here pretty soon," he added apologetically. "Got a session I absolutely cannot miss."

"For customers we're putting a sign in the window and tent cards on the tables," Teal said ticking off things in his own mind which needed attention. "They'll be in place tomorrow, so we have almost a full week of warning."

Teal looked around the restaurant sensing and enjoying the excitement. "I'm going to see Dannie when I leave here, maybe TJ if they'll let me."

Teal slumped in his seat suddenly feeling the fatigue. "You know what Gary wanted to do?" he asked Peter Quinn. "He wanted to clean all the mortar between the bricks on the walls. Jesus, it would have taken him about a year!"

Peter Quinn rolled his eyes and smiled. "Magnolia will never be this clean again."

Teal called Dannie on her cell, and she met him at the hospital. "They won't let anyone in yet," she told Teal. "Gorman even tried this morning and got turned away. Can you imagine trying to deal with Gorman the day after you've had a heart attack?" she asked and even laughed.

"You look good this morning," Teal said. "How does he look?"

"He looks good – already starting to be a pain in the ass with the nurses, but they love him anyway."

Teal related everything being done at the restaurant and the sense of anticipation everyone was feeling. "What are the chances he can sit in? Like in a real limited capacity," Teal asked.

"Oh, believe me, he's already angling for that. They think it looks good but only if he can get some rest now and responds favorably to treatment. They're making no promises to him."

"I called Sloan this morning and she wanted to fly up right away, but I told her there was nothing she could do," Teal said. "She sends her love. Of course, she'll be up next week for the filming and maybe stay through Saturday."

Dannie nodded and took Teal's hand. "Jack I'm sorry we didn't tell you about TJ's blood pressure problems. I wanted to, but he wouldn't hear of it. Said you could be a worrywart, and you had enough on your plate.

"I'll forgive you as long as he gets better in a big hurry. You need him. Magnolia needs him, too."

The producer, David Gilly, called Teal that night on his cell phone, and they talked for half an hour. A packet of information regarding the filming at Magnolia was being sent overnight, and Peter Quinn would have it the following morning.

"I've included everything I feel is relevant, but let me know if I haven't," he said. "There's an outline of the entire special which I think you know has already been shot and edited. We have a slot of right around five minutes we can allot to the restaurant. If we use less, we have a bunch of filler shots we can cut back in. Also we've hired Nicky Stressler to be the interviewer."

"Stressler?" Even Teal knew of Nicky Stressler, goddess of the syndicated talk show circuit. "How did you get her? She's a pretty busy lady from what I hear."

"Come on, Jack. By now you know how many people are deeply invested in the mental health care system in this country. Some have a son or daughter or niece or just a friend of the family who's been through it. Could be anything from bouts of depression to post traumatic stress syndrome to full-blown manic depression. Very few people escape a brush with it. Nicky's younger brother was in Iraq. Came back with two purple hearts, a commendation and a brain that's way fucked up. He's getting better but it will be a long road for him." And Teal thought; a long road for all of them.

They agreed on the two best times of the day to call and hung up. Teal took a beer from the refrigerator and sat on the tiny deck. Both the robins hopped out of the trivet and watched him until he brought out a squirming mass of worms and gave them an extra helping. He thought one of these nights he would have to watch and see just how many animals he was feeding.

The birds slurped and Teal sipped and eventually when all three had their fill, Teal stripped off his clothes and climbed into bed, and the robins hopped back into the trivet.

* * *

TWENTY ONE

The carpet cleaners came after work on Wednesday and completed their job quickly and efficiently. All the furniture was piled in a jumble in the kitchen and back hallway.

"You need to let it dry overnight," the cleaner said while making out the bill. "I know you guys open early, so you could get here at five and start putting it back together." He smiled when he saw Teal wince and then handed him the bill.

"This isn't the amount we agreed on," Teal said looking at the man.

"Yeah, well, we gave you the professional discount rate – thirty five percent off."

"Thanks, man," Teal said. "You didn't need to do that."

"Yeah, I did," the man said after thinking for a moment and folding his billing book. "If you guys had been around ten years ago, you might have been able to help my little brother. There was nobody else. Everybody had given up. So he did too."

Teal helped him pack his gear out to the van, and the man climbed into the driver's seat.

"Thanks," Teal said. "I wish we *had* been here ten years ago."

He walked back into the restaurant remembering what Carl had said several days after Teal had started.

"These guys are like beggars. Always have their hands out wanting more, more, more."

Teal wondered for a brief moment where Carl was and sincerely hoped he was having a lousy life.

A little fat kid who looked to be no more than twelve or thirteen was touching up the window sign. He came from one of the residential houses and had never worked in the restaurant. His chubby hands worked with infinite care, and he mumbled the entire time.

"Shoulda' done it in gold leaf. I told them a million times, shoulda' done it in gold leaf."

The counselor who had driven him over from the residential was kicked back, enjoying one of Amed's creations before he shut down the bar. "Take your time, Eric my man," he said looking up from the swimsuit issue of *Sports Illustrated*. "Take your time."

Teal drove TJ and Dannie home from the hospital on Saturday, then sat and brought both of them up to date on the restaurant. It was a beautiful, clear day but with little traffic on the freeway, which was somewhat of a disappointment for TJ.

"So are they going to let you participate?" Teal asked.

"Yep, I responded very well to treatment, so doc said to have at it. But always remember to stay calm."

"So, I guess my main duty will be to keep you-know-who away from you," Teal said. Gorman's name had been banned in TJ's presence.

TJ smiled calmly. "How are you getting along with Gilly?" he asked.

"Seems like a very decent guy and a good planner. I can't see anything he's missed. He and the crew get in Monday afternoon, and I'll huddle with them for dinner. You want to join us?"

"Better not," TJ said. "I told Pete I'd take it easy. I really don't want to shine him on."

"I'll drop by after dinner and fill you in," Teal said. "Of course, the commute traffic will be long gone by then. Won't have a damn thing to talk about." TJ smiled.

When Teal picked up Sloan in Larkspur, her bus was late, and he paced the waiting room like a badger.

Sloan was last off the bus, most of the other riders practically running to their respective cars when they spied Teal stomping around outside. Sloan looked spectacular. Teal wondered how that could be. When he got off a flight from San Francisco to Los Angeles, he looked like he had spent the night in a drunk tank.

"Hi, sweetie," she said breezily. "You look like you just got out of jail."

I knew it.

"They feed you on the plane or would you like a bite to eat?"

"I had a cardboard sandwich on the plane, but I'm not really hungry." Then she cocked a hip and ran a hand through her hair. "At least not hungry for food," she said, and the driver of a Nissan watching her plowed into a Mercedes sedan. Teal laughed and shook his head.

They drank beers on the deck, and Teal brought her up to date while the robins hopped onto the railing and watched. Sloan got up at one point and looked closely at the privet.

"Do you ever see them come from any place other than this bush?" she asked prying the limbs gently apart.

"I don't think so," he said.

"Well, come here and look at this," she said softly while the robins waited patiently at the opposite end of the railing. She parted the limbs further and Teal could see a nest holding four bright blue eggs.

"You know, we've never really talked about children," she said after a moment and gently let the limbs back into place. Teal grinned weakly and looked at the robin. He would swear later to friends, it was grinning.

Teal picked the crew up at the airport Monday afternoon and, rather than get stuck in commute traffic, they ate at a restaurant close by. There were three in the crew: a typical Bostonian sounding man who handled the video camera and was dressed straight out of a Land's End catalog, an ephemeral woman who seemed to be in charge of everything else from lights to paying for the meals and in person as he was on the phone.

"When we get there in the morning, I'm going to look for setups with Glen and Lilly's going to be scoping people out who she thinks have the look," Gilly said. "And don't worry. They won't even know she's looking at 'em."

"Sometimes it's sort of hard to tell the staff from the clients," Teal said which got a chuckle from all three.

"We've been working this project for almost six months now," Gilly said, "and everyone told us the same thing. I'll have you to sort 'em out for us."

"Me!" Teal said and acted surprised. "I can't tell them apart myself." That got a good laugh all around.

Teal dropped them off at their motel and set a time for the morning. There was a note on the door when he got home: 'Over at Dannie and TJ's'. He changed his shirt and walked over, finding them all crammed on the deck.

"Cal Trans has a lane closure just before the Nordstrom's turnoff. High drama!" TJ was a happy man.

"No 'can I get you a beer' or 'how did that important meeting go'?" Teal asked.

"Jack, Jack, Jack," TJ said. "There will always be meetings and there will always be beer but there might never again be a lane closure before the Nordstrom's turnoff. You need to get your priorities straight."

Dannie brought out a wide range of snacks that constituted a meal when all was said and done, and Teal washed them down with two beers. They talked about the following day, and Teal made it sound like a cakewalk. When he and Sloan finally left, Dannie gave him a hug. "Thank you, buddy," she said and kissed him on the cheek.

Teal and Sloan arrived at the restaurant at the stroke of five in the pitch dark. Other than a gray and white cat rolling an eyeball at them and fleeing down the alleyway, the street and sidewalks were deserted. Teal flipped on the lights and set to work in a room that already was as clean as a birthing center in a hospital. Sloan looked around and laughed.

"What, you're just going to do a little last minute tidying up?"

They had no more than gotten their coats off when the crew started to show up, way before their allotted time. Teal always figured it was the underground telegraph thing. If someone saw something happening at the restaurant, everyone knew about it seconds later, and since several lived in residential hotels close by, someone would trigger the telegraph throughout the county.

By seven everyone was there, and the sidewalk was becoming crowded. Rich had been appointed door monitor and was making sure everyone signed a release.

"You've missed your calling," Teal told him. "You could be a maitre d' accepting all those twenties and fifties. You'd make a fortune."

"Just what I was thinking," he said with a wide grin.

The filming crew had set up and was shooting general shots of the restaurant. Sammy was putting the finishing touches on a Sammy Scramble and called it up to Ginny who pranced over to pick it up wearing something which looked suspiciously like a modified matador outfit, minus the hat. Amed was pulling several espressos and serving all of them lined on his arm while Teal held his breath.

TJ and Dannie came in around nine and were immediately seated at his favorite table. Dave Gilly liked the table as well because it would afford him two different filming angles with a minimum of setup. Much of the interviewing would be held there.

When Nicky Stressler arrived, the intensity ramped up a notch. There were few people who had not seen her on television.

After quick introductions, she interviewed TJ for almost twenty minutes with the cameraman working in tight on both her and TJ. He calmly and professionally told her the history of setting up the restaurant and what it was designed to do and the everyday operation.

"Of course, it's difficult to operate a facility such as this without additional funding," he said and launched into one of his standard spiels while Teal mugged and tried to catch his eye.

"How about the oriental boy in the kitchen?", Lilly asked Teal.

"He's a client and assistant cook. Damn good one too."

"Alright, I think we'll try him next and you to follow."

"Me? Why me?" Teal felt dread course down his backbone.

"Why you?" she asked rhetorically. "Because you run the damn place, Jack. We'll be gentle," she added and reached out to squeeze his arm.

Sloan was drinking coffee and tea with Sissy and John, balancing their cups on the railing before the front window.

"They're going to interview Sammy and then me," he said to Sloan with a pleading look, hoping she might find a way to get him out of it.

"I'm going to be watching you very closely, buster," she said, "and if there's any schmoozing with that Nicky woman, you will find a very cool bed this evening." Then she turned back to her conversation. No help there, he thought morosely.

"I'm taking lover boy on home," Dannie said. "That woman got him all charged up, and I might get something off the bounce." She wiggled her eyebrows and whisked him out the door.

Sammy was at the interview table and looked as cool and collected as a junior executive. He actually had Nicky giggling over something he said. When they finished, Sammy retied his headband and returned to the kitchen while Nicky's eyes searched the restaurant before finding Teal huddled in a corner, a pathetic lump of a man. She crooked her finger, and he stumbled over hoping an eighteen-wheeler would lose its brakes and crash through the front window.

"Jack, for God sakes don't be so nervous," she said and touched his arm. He looked up to see Sloan glaring at him and brushing something imaginary from her sleeve.

Stressler *was* good, and it was much like chatting with someone you've just met and find you have mutual interests. She led him where she wanted to go, and he followed like a simple mule trying to please. He was barely aware of the cameraman, and finally not at all.

"Thanks, Jack" she said. "Now that wasn't so bad, was it?"

Jack mumbled his thanks and stumbled away from the table like his feet were shackled. His back felt damp with perspiration.

The restaurant was now packed with people, many of whom Teal recognized: loyal customers and some strangers, board members, counselors from other facilities and projects, the town mayor and, of course, Gorman and Bock.

Nicky interviewed Sissy and John, Nicole, Mickey and Ginny. They were asked if they wished to interview Gorman, but Dave Gilly declined.

"From what you guys told me, I could never see where he fits in," Gilly said. "Besides, we've got more than enough right now. I'm just going to wrap it up with a couple of quick customer interviews, and then we'll get out of your hair."

Nicky interviewed three casually dressed businessmen who were regulars and when she was finished, she selected a younger couple who Teal didn't recognize.

"Hi, I'm Nicky Stressler," she said with an infectious grin. "I wonder if I might ask you a few questions about Magnolia Café."

"Sure," the young man said. He was wearing a letterman jacket with a capital T underlined with twin footballs. His companion was cute and small and nervous.

Nicky pulled up a chair and sat shaking each one's hand. The boy was the picture of aggressive teenage confidence when faced with speaking to an attractive stranger.

"Do you come here often?" Nicky asked.

The young woman started to answer, but he cut her off.

"Well, she does, I guess," he said hooking a finger in her direction. "I don't have much time with football and all."

"But you do like the food?"

"Oh yeah, the food's great. I had one of those Sammy Scrambles. Dynamite!"

The cameraman had moved in tighter, while Gilly was standing just outside the picture watching intently with his head cocked to the side.

"Then it probably goes without saying that you support this project?"

The boy looked confused for a moment, and the cameraman was in very tight now.

"I don't know about no project, but hell yes, it's a great restaurant."

"Have you ever heard of Marin Advocates for Mental Stability?" she asked, and the director seemed to be holding his breath.

"Yeah, I've heard the name, but I don't know much about it. I think they work with people who are nuts."

"Then you probably don't know that Magnolia Café is one of their projects and is operated in part by their client base."

The young man looked thunderstruck and then angry. "You mean to tell me there's crazy people working here?" he asked, now looking furious and frightened.

"Yes. As the matter of fact the young man who made your scramble is one of them."

He looked at the half eaten scramble for a moment before sweeping it off the table narrowly missing Stressler.

"What the hell are you people trying to prove doing something like that? Well, you're not going to fuck with me and my girl friend," he shouted and slammed his chair against the wall. He pushed his way out of the room with his mortified friend following in his wake.

The silence in the restaurant was absolute and profound before Nicky smiled up at the cameraman and director and quietly said, "It's a wrap!"

When order had been restored, and Amed was pulling drinks on the house, Dilly quietly explained.

"He was a key we've been looking for. Someone so fearful and angry and naive about mental health, he becomes almost a caricature. We have thousands of minutes of wonderful people doing and saying wonderful things in the name of mental health. And, of course, that's all well and good. But there is another side to the picture that's bleak but often hidden."

"And that's the fear," Teal added.

"Yes. But the interesting thing is trying to find that fear in raw, undiluted form as you just saw it," Nicky said. "You can ask a dozen people, who you know for a fact do not support mental health initiatives or funding, what they feel about the issue. And you will never find one react the way our friend did. They'll hem and haw and couch it in acceptable terms. We couldn't have done better with an actor."

"And we actually thought about that at one point," Dilly said, and they all laughed together. "God, I hope you got a release on him," he said quickly looking round the room. Rich stood with a grin and waved a sheet of paper.

All the clients, extra staff, Nicky Stressler and onlookers had left, and the crew was finishing packing. Teal pulled some cold beers out of the refrigerator and put them on a tray. Peter Quinn came in to help and gave him a loopy grin.

"What?" Teal asked.

"Man, Sloan is something else," he said and sighed deeply. "I mean look at her: cargo shorts, lime green Tommy Bahama collared T and hair in a French braid. I thought *my* heart was going to blow a valve."

Teal peered over at the table where she was laughing with the crew. "Yeah, she is something," he said absently.

"And how about Stressler? She's even better in person."

"Mmmm," Peter Quinn said and nodded. "You know what she asked me before she left?"

Teal was popping the tops off the beer bottle and waited.

"She asked me if you and Sloan were, like, an item."

"An item? She said an item?"

"Yep, but the best part was when I told her you were. Know what she said?"

Teal waited for the punch line.

"She said 'pity'."

"Pity? That's it?"

"That's it. Oh, and she left me her card, just in case," he said pulling out a business card and flicking it with his thumbnail.

"P.Q., I don't want to see it or have it anywhere near me," Teal said backing up and holding up his hands as if to ward off a bloody switchblade. "If Sloan even heard about this, she'd kick the shit out of me. I'm serious!"

Peter Quinn roared with laughter, and they carried the beers out to the group waiting at the big table in the center of the room.

* * *

TWENTY TWO

What passed for normalcy settled on Magnolia Café for the next few weeks. TJ was coming in twice a week for short periods and always accompanied by Dannie as his chauffer. She had taken a leave of absence from her job and didn't miss it. Gary was a full-fledged waiter doing a wonderful job and was actually building a following. Mickey tolerated him but seemed to be stepping up a bit more himself.

Tim went on another vacation with his family and never returned. His father had accepted a promotion, and they were relocating to Arizona. Teal found himself missing the teenager with the startled look.

Teal spent more and more time at Bodega Bay, and he had become friends with Sam Keller. Sometimes he went with TJ and Dannie, always with Sloan when she was visiting and often alone. He and Sam played a 'what if' game. What if you had a restaurant, what would it look like or what kind of food would you serve or where would it be. What would the tables and chairs look like? Would they just serve wine and beer or go for a full liquor license? Breakfast and lunch? Lunch and dinner?

"I would always want nifty bathrooms," Sam said. "I hate going into a place that has smelly, dirty or, even worse, uninteresting bathrooms."

Teal agreed. "Yeah, nice lighting, good soaps and towels. Maybe the sports section pinned to the wall over the urinals. And none of those air blower things they've got in airports. I always leave a restroom feeling like I've peed on my hands."

And so it went.

After one of the Tuesday night round tables and most of
the group had drifted out the front door, Peter Quinn clapped
Teal on the shoulder and said, "They've got this little pub over
in San Rafael where I hang out sometimes. Want to catch a
beer tonight?"

The pub was boisterous and as close as one could be
to the United Kingdom and still be standing on U.S. soil. It
was packed with people who all seemed to be of one extended
British family. Virtually everyone acknowledged Peter Quinn's
entrance and squeezed an opening at the bar for the two of
them. A barmaid swept the sparkling wood before them with a
clean rag.

"Petey, my love, what will it be this evening?" she asked
and fluttered her eyelashes.

Teal drew back from the bar in mock astonishment and
stared at the side of Peter Quinn's face.

"One word, Teal," he said softly out of the corner of his
mouth, "and I will personally have you flogged and then drawn
and quartered and your parts strewn willy-nilly across the Bay."

Teal had to look away and go through a series of throat
clearings.

"Two large Harps, and put a dab of ground glass in my
friend's mug, if you don't mind," Peter Quinn said, and the
corners of his mouth turned up. It was not a smile.

They drank their Harps and talked about local politics
and customers and clients.

"Tell me," Teal said. "The first time I shook your hand,
I thought I had latched onto a gnarly tree branch. All calluses
and tendons. Are you a logger in your spare time or what?"

Peter Quinn laughed and skidded his beer in lazy circles.
"I'm a weight lifter. It's something I've done all my life, and if

you ask me why, I'm going to give you a blank look. I simply don't know. But I love it."

"Have you ever competed?"

"Oh hell yes! High school level, which made me a freak, college level and then on to Olympic try outs for the summer games."

"Cool. How did you do?"

"Okay. But the real problem was I didn't come from a stan country."

"Stan country?"

"Yeah. Kurdistan, Uzbekistan, Afghanistan. They have the world's greatest weight lifters. Particularly in the lower weight classes – like me. They eat all that yak meat and walk seventy kilometers to school and like that. No way I could compete."

"Too bad. Did it bother you?"

"No. I'm way better looking than those dudes. I'm dialed in," Peter Quinn said, and Teal grinned.

Then Peter Quinn sucked him into a game of darts and thoroughly embarrassed him with his final shot, which was backwards over his shoulder while sipping his Harps. It was great entertainment for all except Teal who was beginning to question his athletic skills. He had been smoked in handball by someone who was almost three times his age, ridden into the dirt by a contemporary and now humiliated in a dart game by a shrink!

When the pub began to clear slightly, they grabbed a table and sat sipping their third Harps. Teal seemed to be doing most of the talking and Peter Quinn the listening. Teal was relaxed and comfortable and feeling the beer. The conversation had turned exclusively to Magnolia: its operations, its future, client problems and money woes.

"How do you feel about that?" Peter Quinn asked, and Teal felt a shadow flit through his thinking.

"That's like...what...the fourth time you've asked me how I feel about something. It's almost like..." and his voice trailed off.

They stared at each other before Teal groaned and said, "Aww, shit. You're doing a shrink number on me. You're wondering if I'm going to freak out under all the pressure. Right? Am I right?"

Peter Quinn sighed. "What's the answer to that? Yes, no and maybe?" he said and pursed his lips. "You're working in an industry where raw emotions get tangled up everyday, and the walking wounded are out there to prove it. So, yes, we check on each other and, yes, sometimes we do it in an oblique manner."

Teal wasn't sure if he was disappointed or pissed off.

"You're behind it?" he asked, and Peter briefly shook his head.

"No, it was John and Sissy."

"John and Sissy," Teal said feeling a familiar tinge of betrayal.

"Now don't get all hot on me, Jack. They asked me if I would just poke around and make sure you were okay. Sometimes tension builds up without a person even realizing it. A little loss of sleep, not eating very well, lethargic, daydreaming and a whole host of other niggling little problems can suddenly become something very significant. Believe me when I tell you that their concern is well founded, and they're doing this out of the most pure intentions – because they like you and want to protect you."

Teal felt some of the tension leave his body. "Is this standard procedure? You pull this on other people?"

"Oh sure. Rich, Claire when she was here, Paul, some
of the other guys. It's sort of second nature to me, I guess you
could say. Part of my charming personality." He smiled at Teal.
"TJ's gotten so good at seeing it develop, I really can't shrink
him anymore. So we sort of do it back and forth to each other,
like a game of darts but more serious."

Teal thought about it for a moment and skated his
own beer mug in lazy circles. "You get paid extra for this? For
tonight?"

Peter laughed. "Hell no. I do it out of the kindness of my
charitable little heart."

"Well in that case," Teal said. "Let's have another round.
You're buying."

With Magnolia Café on such an even keel, Teal and Sloan
started planning a vacation together, and it was natural they
selected Seattle. Sam thought he might get away for a couple of
days and fly up. Show them the town.

Three of the four robin's eggs had hatched, and Sloan
pined over the fourth, which had disappeared. The three babies
were fast growing eating machines and kept their parents busy
and Teal broke. The bait shop owner now believed him.

"You can't catch that many small mouth in Marin
County," he finally grumped.

The television special was to air in less than a week and
other than the excitement it engendered, it was like the dog
days of summer. And that in itself worried Teal, making him
think that another shoe was about ready to drop.

Then on a lovely Monday morning near the end
of September, it did. But in a manner no one could have
envisioned.

Teal opened the restaurant and within minutes the
crew was tumbling through the door like a farmyard of geese
shoving and bickering and laughing over a shared silly thing.
The morning crowd was busy, and Teal took the time to go out
and schmooze with two city council members. When he walked
back, he passed the espresso station where Amed was working
as fast as his hands could move.

"Morning, Amed," he said as he walked by and patted his
shoulder.

"Good morning, Jack," Amed said softly with a grin.

Teal continued into the kitchen walking like a
mechanical man who's been over wound. He walked around
the kitchen nearly bumping into Sammy and Beth, and then
lurched into the hallway. He caught Rich's eye and gestured
frantically.

Rich walked over quickly, his eyes questioning.

"Amed just spoke to me," Teal whispered. "He said 'good
morning'".

Rich's eyes sprang open as if his toe had been slammed
into a wall socket.

"What?"

Teal repeated it. "Listen I'm going to call Peter Quinn
and TJ. You go over and chat with him like nothing's
happening out of the ordinary."

"Fuck. I don't know if I can do that."

"You got to. We got to keep everything on an even
keel until P.Q. and TJ get here. Okay? You can do it," he said
slapping him on the shoulder.

Teal walked into the office and left the door ajar so he
could still see the front room.

"Hi Dannie. It's Jack. Is Mr. Wonderful up?"

Seconds later, "Hey, man, what's happening?"

"You sitting down? It's a good thing, not a bad thing."

"Yeah," he said very cautiously.

"Amed just said 'good morning' to me."

There was a sharp intake of breath, and Teal could hear Dannie say something in the background. "Oh my God," TJ finally said. "We were just about out the door."

"I'm glad I caught you. You might have croaked in the main room or something."

TJ laughed. "Your concern is touching. Who's with him?"

"He's working alone, and I've got Rich over there acting like nothing special's happening. I hope he can hold it together."

"Okay, we're on our way. Call P.Q. and let him know. Man, would I love to see his face," TJ chortled.

Teal got Quinn's office secretary. "Is Peter Quinn in session?" he asked.

"No, but he didn't want to be disturbed."

"He'll want to be disturbed for this. Tell him it's Jack Teal calling from Magnolia Café."

"Jack, what's up," Peter Quinn's voice was guarded.

"Amed's talking. He said 'good morning' to me, and he and Rich are having a good old chat right now."

There was a very long silence.

"Well, Sister Mary Joseph," Peter Quinn finally said and started giggling. "I'll be down there right away."

They hung up, and he watched Rich and Amed talking like the world had not just shifted on its axis. So he went to join them, and the three talked about espresso recipes, coffee beans and customers until TJ and Peter Quinn appeared on the scene playing 'no, you first' at the front door.

"The thing he's really sad about is leaving the restaurant. He knows he'll have to go soon," Peter Quinn said much later. Everyone had gone home except for Rich, TJ and Teal.

"He's really quite a remarkable young man. Extremely bright and personable. He wants to go to San Jose State starting in the winter term. We're going to help his family by pulling some strings. But he said it's okay if he doesn't make it right away. He'll go to a JC and then transfer over."

"And rest assured, he will get in sooner or later," TJ added. "He's one determined kid."

They all sat for a few moments, drained and lost in their own thoughts.

"You know what Mickey said?" Teal asked, and everyone looked at him. "He asked what the big deal was. The kid didn't want to talk, so he didn't talk. Now he wants to talk. No big deal. And even stranger, I think all the rest of the kids sort of agreed with him."

Peter Quinn nodded and stared at the ceiling. "I've always wondered about this weird form of understanding and communication they seem to have. I can't dial into it, but I know damn well it's there."

"Sometimes I think we should all wear numbers and pass out programs to the customers so they'll know who's who," Teal said expecting a laugh. But everyone sat quietly and nodded in agreement. They had covered this ground many times before.

Later that night when he told Sloan about Amed, she started crying softly over the phone. Maybe it was the late hour, or he was overly tired. Teal wasn't sure, but he soon found himself joining Sloan, and they listened to each other cry some nine hundred miles apart.

* * *

TWENTY THREE

When Teal called Dave Gilly in Boston to tell him about Amed, all that Gilly could say was 'shit'.

"The thing's edited and virtually in the can as they say. Christ we air in, what, a week?"

"Five days," Teal said and then thought of something.

"You know those Star Wars movies where they roll a storyline like a great scroll or something? How about something like that? Just casually mention Amed is now miraculously cured due to the strength and guidance of Jack Teal."

"Humm," Gilly said which was followed by a long silence. "Like at the end of *American Graffiti*. Maybe we could tip that in – of course without the strength and guidance shit. It would only be maybe five, six seconds."

Before the evening the special was to air, Marin Advocates made a decision that whoever wanted to watch it together should do so. And since there were literally dozens who wanted to, the restaurant was selected as the only place large enough to seat everyone.

Naturally, John with his connections was able to borrow an enormous wide screen, and the restaurant was already hooked up to cable and had a tiny set in the office. Nobody watched it except for Ginny watching soaps on her break. She thought *General Hospital* was a reality show.

"Watch TV? With all that's going on out here?" TJ once said to Rich. "You'd have to be...crazy!"

Teal picked Sloan up in Larkspur two days before the airing, and she was ecstatic when she got off the bus.

"Guess what?" she asked and before he had a chance to said hello, she continued. When Sloan was happy and excited, her face became animated and her gestures almost theatrical. Every male within range smiled and nodded as if privy to her thoughts and actions. Women, on the other hand, became wary and slinky.

"Dad's been accepted to the Historics at Monterey. Well, I think he's known for a while and just told me now.

And," she added poking a finger at his chest, "he's thinking of taking some extra time and visiting the restaurant."

Teal liked the idea and told her so although he had no idea what the 'Historics at Monterey' were.

"Anyway while he's here, I'll probably have to sleep in a motel," she said hugging him. "I'm still his little girl."

"Well, come on," Teal said taking her hand. "We'll have to put some snuggling in the bank in advance of his visit, don't you think?"

They had breakfast the following morning with TJ and Dannie who made some cinnamon rolls that were perfect.

"When I die, I want to be buried in a cinnamon bun," TJ said with a dreamy voice. "Just hollow out one huge sucker and stuff me in."

Teal nodded. It sounded good to him.

"Are we ready for this afternoon?" Teal asked. It was a question lobbed back and forth for almost a week.

"I don't see what else we can do," TJ said. "We've talked with all the clients who will be there and told them what to expect. Got a feeling about how they might react."

He was watching the commute traffic out of the corner of his eye while Sloan and Dannie were giggling about something in the kitchen.

"We'll have fourteen clients and eight staff. I'm pretty pleased with the match up, and both P.Q. and I don't foresee a problem." He picked an edge off the remaining roll and popped it in his mouth.

"Granted we haven't seen the special, but Gilly thumbnailed it for me," TJ said. "We've covered any number of scenarios with the fourteen, so they won't be blindsided by something they don't expect. I think were cool."

Teal drove to the restaurant while Sloan stayed with Dannie and TJ. All of the morning crew were there: Mickey splendid in a new Tommy Bahama shirt and Ginny in a variation of a ballerina outfit. Sammy had a new headband with black symbols on a scarlet background.

"What does your headband say?" Teal asked Sammy.

"Can't tell you."

"Aww, come on. Aren't we buds?"

"Okay," Sammy said reluctantly and with a solemn face. "It says 'Die Yankee Dog'." He went back to chopping with his shoulders shaking – snic-snic.

Teal laughed and elbowed him in the arm. With Sammy sometimes you really weren't sure.

The television was against one wall and had already been tested, and the seating would be haphazard and casual. Everyone went home after clean up, and Teal returned at a few minutes after six with Sloan, Dannie and TJ. They had picked up some snacks: corn chips and dip, popcorn, potato chips and mixed nuts along with two cases of assorted soft drinks. People were already loitering around the front door and cheered when they pulled in.

When they finally closed the front door there were an even three dozen people settling in their seats and arranging bowls of chips and soft drinks. Everyone was animated and excited and conversation swirled from group to group – no lines were drawn, and the blend was total. TJ was so pleased he was beaming – possibly because of the blend and possibly because Gorman and Bock were not in attendance, and possibly because he had chugged a Corona before coming down.

They tuned in the local public broadcasting station, KQED, ten minutes before the show, and people settled down in anticipation. There were a few comments about potty breaks, but by the time the special started, the room was quiet.

The opening scene showed Dave Gilly from the knees up leaning against a fence with activity in the background. He introduced himself and quickly out-lined what the special was about and only in the most general of terms.

Then the camera pulled back to afford the viewer a better picture of the activity behind him, which showed a small number of people working in a large vegetable garden. He went on to identify the group as adolescents who were working through their problems with mental illness. The manner in which the people were dressed and the general surrounding scenery gave no hint as to a date or location. It might have been shot twenty or thirty years ago, or the day before, and it might be England, the United States or Canada.

It had a pleasant relaxing feel to it: sunshine and fresh, ruddy cheeks, shy glances and hard work. But there was always the quirkiness playing around the edges like an elf dancing just out of sight. Nothing displeasing or annoying. Just...different.

Teal recognized the feeling in the first few seconds. He had felt the same the moment he had walked in the doors of Magnolia Café. Nothing scary or morbid or edgy. Just a few degrees off center.

The special went on to talk about the efforts of the farm and some of the problems and successes they had experienced.

It then described several residential facilities, some large and some modest in different parts of the county and the everyday life of those who lived there. This was followed by the description of a mechanics shop somewhere outside of Detroit populated with young males and females both working on car and truck transmissions. It was active and rough and tumble and made Teal think about Easy Motors. He hugged Sloan closer, and she hugged him back, and Sammy nudged someone and pointed at them. Snic-snic.

The theme was consistent from facility to venture and back to facility. Strong, supportive counselors, adolescents, some of whom were confused and frightened in a tangible manner and, of course, funding woes. Always money problems while trying to accomplish something governments were reluctant or incapable of backing.

Teal snuck a look at his watch. Six minutes left, and, at that moment, the front of the restaurant popped on the screen, and everyone cheered and a bowl of chips was spilled.

Teal had wondered about the choice of Nicky Stressler, but with her first words that doubt vanished. She was totally sincere and earnest, her beauty somehow not distracting from the power of her words.

She explained the purpose of the restaurant and its history while the camera wandered through the dining room and kitchen. Whenever an employee appeared in a close-up, everyone cheered and some blushed.

Sammy was stellar in his interview, and even though Teal had watched the taping, he had not heard the words.

"You really like it here don't you?" Nicky asked.

"Sure," he said embarrassed to look at her. "Great restaurant, good food." Choppy sentences like he was ready to lapse in one of his Japanese tirades.

"And how long have you been here?"

"Little over a year," he answered after a moment

"Where will you go from here?"

"I don't know," he said and his forehead furrowed.

"But I have to go so someone can take my place. Somebody who's crazier than me."

Peter Quinn added the clinical presence, his brogue so rich Teal started laughing.

"Jeez, it's become a travelogue of Ireland," he murmured.

TJ was mellow and distinct. Teal could almost hear the underlining demand for public support. Subtle but there.

When Teal appeared on the screen, the kitchen staff went into prolonged hooting and palm slapping, and someone dropped a soft drink that fizzed all over the carpet. Teal thought the flickering images made him appear to be a cardboard moron. The camera cut back and forth between Teal and Stressler with an easy, relaxed rhythm, each time bringing a barely suppressed hiss from Sloan when Nicky smiled sweetly into the camera or at Teal.

The voice that Teal heard could not possible be his; it sounded so adenoidal, and he finally held his hands over his eyes until the scene blessedly came to an end.

Amed featured his fifty watt grin and pulled espressos and lattes like he had ten arms while Ginny danced through her hostess chores and actually winked at the camera when Nicky spoke to her. Gary with his crisp white shirt and black

vest could easily have been mistaken for a waiter at Swan's
Oyster Bar in San Francisco while Mickey, teeth firmly in place,
looked and acted like a young investment broker or venture
capitalist.

When the three businessmen were interviewed, Teal felt
his shoulders tense knowing what the next scene would be.
Sloan put her arm behind his neck, knowing it as well.

"You know, of course, the purpose of the restaurant?"
Nicky asked the three men.

"Sure," one answered. "To help kids with mental illness.
Teach 'em a trade. I think it's terrific. A lot of the local business
people come here for lunch." His friends nodded in agreement.
They all looked well fed and comfortable and completely at
ease.

When the young couple appeared on the screen, there
was total silence in the room. All the clients knew what was
coming, having been well versed by both TJ and Peter Quinn.
Still, Teal could see TJ and Peter Quinn tense in their chairs.

The camera showed the couple at medium distance and
then, inexorably began to creep forward, first isolating the
young man's face, supremely confident, as if he were receiving
the league trophy for his team. Then a cut to the young woman
showing her discomfort, eyes and smile flitting. This time the
camera shots were almost jumpy and nervous setting up the
viewer for what was to follow.

Nicky drew them into conversation, and as it progressed,
each cut of her face showed someone who was increasingly
aware she had the opportunity to sculpt the signature scene for
the special.

When the young man leapt to his feet and swept the
luncheon plates from the table, there was a gasp from someone
in the room and then silence in both the rooms, video and real.

Nicky turned to the camera, her face concerned and saddened in a scene shot after the young couple had stormed from the restaurant and some order had been restored.

"You have just been introduced to the face of fear and ignorance," she said. "It is a prejudice and mindset often encountered by those who work in the mental health field. Everyday these dedicated people fight such ignorance with education and sensibility and pray the fear will dissipate. Some nights they sleep very poorly."

The screen went black, and the credits began to roll. At the end was a tag line:

Amed Bequari, the young man working the espresso bar, has miraculously regained his ability to speak after being mute for four years. Through the support of Magnolia Café, he has completely regained his speech and is planning on attending a California college in the spring. Some small steps forward are truly miraculous.

And the screen went to black.

There was applause, some weeping and not all from clients, hugging and handholding. TJ and Peter Quinn circulated; talking to groups, taking a collective pulse and saying good night to those leaving. Teal sat slouched in a chair with his legs stretched well in front of him. He couldn't remember when he had felt this comfortable and quietly tired. Sissy had kissed him on the cheek when she and John left, and Sammy had hugged him, then flushed bright red and fled through the front door.

Suddenly Sloan was at his side, her face pale. He gathered himself thinking she must be ill, and a tendril of fear crept into his bowels.

"Jack, I need to talk to you outside."

He followed her out to Brownie where they sat beneath one of the streetlights.

"Someone left today's copy of *The New York Times* in the restaurant," she said holding it out to Teal. "I think you better read this."

The dateline was Associated Press, Mexico City.

Hector Alviso Knootzman, reclusive Mexico City billionaire, was gunned down by a hail of bullets in the midst of a lunchtime crowd in downtown Mexico City. He was pronounced dead at the scene after being shot numerous times by two hooded gunmen who stepped from a black sedan, fired into the crowd and sped away. Flying glass and bullet fragments injured six other people, and one onlooker likened the unbelievable scene to something from a Hollywood movie. Koontzman, who had alleged ties to the Mexican and South American drug cartels, was fifty-six. The police have no suspects in custody.

Teal stared through the windshield and let the paper slip though his fingers and drift onto the floorboards. "I need to go home," he told Sloan. His voice was very tired. "Please take me home."

They exchanged seats, and he slumped with dull eyes and parted lips. She stroked his hand and his shoulder and whispered to him gently. "It's okay. Everything will be fine. You'll see. I'll make it so."

By the time they reached the cottage, he was leaning forward with his head against the padded dash, hiding his face so she could not see the stream of tears and his face contorted in utter anguish.

* * *

TWENTY FOUR

Teal woke and looked at the luminous dial of his watch, trying to make some sense of it. Two o'clock or three? Sloan was spooned to his backside with one hand on his cheek.

"You were freaking out and thrashing," she said softly. "I was afraid you'd fall out of bed."

"And probably bawling again," he said angrily whipping the sheets around him.

"Just a little."

"I don't really fucking get it," he said and punched his pillow. "He was a dope dealer, and I was a fucking runner for him. Is my life so piss-poor pathetic that I lose sleep and mourn someone like that? I think I'm crazier than the kids at the restaurant!"

He got up and stood looking down through the inky darkness to the bay and the quiet hills beyond. The only lights visible were from the gasoline cracking plants and storage sites in the East Bay hills. San Pablo Bay was an enormous black footprint.

Sloan slipped up behind him and wrapped her hands around his waist. "He was your friend, and you liked him. Now you're trying to deny it, and your brain's going nuts with the confusion."

He turned and held her, feeling her heartbeat against his chest. "Maybe I could help you get a job with Peter Quinn," he said. "He loves that kind of psychobabble." He could almost feel the corners of her mouth turn up.

"Want to sit on the deck?" she asked.

They wrapped themselves in a comforter and watched the occasional car speed down the nearly empty freeway, coming home from a swing shift or going to work very early.

"When I was a teenager," Sloan said, "I had this friend who was really sort of a bad girl. She did all the stuff the rest of us gossiped about. She would tell me about it in this casual off-hand manner but never tried to hook me in. I liked her, but I really couldn't tell you why."

Teal pulled the comforter close. "What happened to her?"

"She died, and I think I cried for days. She and her boyfriend were snorting coke with some other people. One of them had some bad heroin. She shot up – end of story."

Teal stroked her shoulders and kissed the top of her head.

"I think my parents were relieved. My mom was still alive then," Sloan said. "They never said anything, of course, but I could tell. And they went to the funeral with me. I think it was the first time in my life I realized how classy my parents were.

"The point I'm trying to make is the choices you make in life are not always conscious and perfectly thought out. They just...happen, and then they sort of have a life of their own."

They stayed on the deck for almost two hours, finally seeing some lights begin to wink on, far across the bay. Probably stock brokers Teal thought, trying to get a leg up on the market and make a buck.

They slipped into bed for a couple of hours before Teal finally called Rich and told him he wouldn't be in.

"What happened to you last night, man?" Rich asked. One minute you're there, and the next you're gone."

"I felt this cold coming on and just bugged out without saying goodbye," Teal said.

"Yeah, well, if I were hanging out with Sloan, I'd probably bug out early too." Teal could picture the grin.

Teal and Sloan went out to Bodega Bay and spent the day with Keller.

"Who's running the store while you're out screwing around with us?" Teal asked.

"I may have a live one on the hook," he said, and his eyes crinkled. "He wants a restaurant in the worst way, and I'm trying to show him how mine is a total cash cow."

"So you let him play with it during the slowest time of the day?" Sloan asked.

"God, beauty and brains," Keller said. "Very, very scary!"

After he showed them some trailheads and good hiking paths with beach access, they had lunch at a restaurant featuring fresh fruit and vegetables and filled with locals, all who knew Keller and wanted to share the latest gossip.

"Close to vegan as we're going to get out here," Keller said consuming a mushroom with more dipping sauce than mushroom meat. "And that's a good thing!"

"Those are good folks," Sloan said on the way home. "Pop would like 'em."

"Yeah, and he could take them for rides along the coast highway and scare the crap out of them," Teal said.

"I wonder why I didn't meet people like this when I was growing up. Instead I fall in with Chris and the Dog Pound and all that junk."

"Your life probably would have been way different. And you might not have met me," she said with a bright smile.

"Wow," Teal said after a moment. "That almost makes me glad I went to prison."

She gave him a sour look, but no jabs or punches.

Teal looked forward to the next two weeks, aside from the fact that Sloan wouldn't be able to come up. Intakes were scheduled with three new applicants, and Peter Quinn wanted him to handle one of the Tuesday night meetings.

"You can do it. It's a breeze," Peter Quinn said. "And I'll be there to save your sorry ass when you fail miserably."

On Monday Sissy and John came in and had lunch with another couple who looked ready to bolt and run at any moment. Sissy went into the kitchen to chat with Sammy and Beth, and Sammy made her put on an apron and hairnet. She did it willingly and bowed to an appreciative audience.

"Jack," she said in the kind of voice she used when she was going to ask a favor. Teal could identify most of the tones, which exasperated her, so now he played dumb.

"Lawrence Gorman is going to have a retreat on Thursday evening, and he has requested that both you and Rich attend," she said.

"Boy, Sissy, I don't know. I'm just a damn cook here, and there's a lot happening in the next few weeks," he said squirming and trying to meet her gaze.

"Well, certainly not at night, Jack," she said. "I know Sloan's not due up for a couple of weeks. She told me herself," she added with a faint smile.

If anyone else had made the same request, he would have fought them to the death. But this was Sissy's request.

"Okay, but I can't guarantee I'll stay awake," he said churlishly. She patted his arm and kissed him on the cheek, which made him feel like a stupid little boy.

The Tuesday night session at the restaurant was raucous and fun. When Peter Quinn announced Teal was to be the moderator, there were jeers and laughs, and Mickey was center stage. But everything went smoothly, and the little girl who always appeared to be on the verge of tears, grinned at the jousting. TJ was there; he had started attending the Tuesday sessions but was expressly told to stay out of the give and take.

"You're sort of like Switzerland," Mickey said and cackled.

As Thursday rapidly approached, Teal became more and more anxious. He wished Sloan were there to tease him and divert his thinking. He also created a scenario in which he went to the meeting and was assailed by Gorman and his minions only to be saved by Sloan who flew in the door and kicked their asses. The thought made him feel considerably better.

"So what's all this retreat shit about anyway?" he asked Rich for the fourth or fifth time.

Rich, patient as ever, would explain it to him again adding a few new details. "It's Gorman's way of saying he's the director, and everyone else needs to listen up. Get on the same page. His page."

"If he's the director of the whole thing and gets paid the big bucks, how come he spends all his time squirreled away out in Novato? Why doesn't he hang with us folks?"

"He hangs with some folks," Rich said.

"Well, he doesn't come in here very much. What, maybe half a dozen times since I've been here."

Rich smiled indulgently. "In case you haven't noticed, he and TJ don't really hit it off – and that's a good thing."

"Well, what does he do? Where does he go? To the bat cave?"

"He spends a lot of time at the residentials," Rich said. "Makes those directors crazy. We're having troubles keeping them around because he interferes in everything they do."

"Doesn't make much sense," Teal said. "I'd think the board would get that straight in a hurry."

Rich nodded. "I think they're getting pretty weary of the shit. They had high hopes when he first came in. Heavy credentials and the big rep. But the board's on a very different page, and now they know it. So what to do?" Rich asked and shrugged. "Beats the hell out of me."

Teal thought for a moment. "You seem pretty relaxed about going," he finally said.

"Jack, I'm just a little fish. Gorman doesn't care about my kind. We're as interchangeable as peanut M&Ms from a jumbo bag, and he knows it. He wants to control the big fish – the program directors and such."

"What? And I'm a 'such'?"

"Probably," Rich said giving him a sad smile and a pat on the back.

"Terrific," Teal said grumbling. "I hope I get food poisoning and croak."

Rich nodded in silent agreement. "That would probably work," he finally said and scratched his goatee.

When Rich arrived at the cottage in the late afternoon on Thursday, Teal was reluctantly ready to go, and they took Brownie. Teal thought the driving might calm his nerves. They drove down to 101 and headed north taking the turnoff to Lucas Valley Road and continued west.

"You've been to these things before," Teal said hoping he wasn't starting to sound whiney. "How do you get through them?"

"Oh, I generally smoke a fat one," Rich said casually.

"Bullshit, Teal said and laughed. "I've never smelled weed on you. Never."

Rich rolled his head and shrugged. "Like I said before, I'm a little shit. I don't squeak, and they don't pay me no mind.

I smile and say 'yassir' and nod and go home. It's as easy as
that."

He pointed through the windshield. "You're going to
want to turn right up there by that big bay tree."

"I don't see any God damned road," Teal complained,
then jabbed the brakes. "You mean that? Looks like the
Overland Trail."

"That's it, wagon master," Rich said. "Pull up next to the
mansion and find a place to park in the well attended, well lit
and architecturally correct parking lot."

They drove out of a copse of trees into a darkened area
surrounded by trees draped dark with moss and mistletoe.
Without the headlights, the area would have been as dark as
the bottom of a well. The single story main house was weary
and complicated looking – as if someone, and never the same
person, had added bits and pieces to the main structure over
the years without the benefit of a plan or competent architect.
There were shingles missing from the peaked roof, and those
remaining were covered with moss and lichen. An insurance
underwriter's nightmare.

The yard displayed a halfhearted vegetable garden,
which had no chance of growing anything in the shade of the
surrounding trees. Maybe mushrooms.

Five late model cars were parked in front of the house
– the only visible sign of life. Ten feet to the right of the house
was an unattached two-car garage leaning precariously. An
elderly Volkswagen van with a happy face painted on the front
and propped up on concrete blocks seemed to be holding up the
structure. The slat fence surrounding the yards was within days
of paying a permanent visit to Waste Management.

"You know," Teal said slipping Brownie between two
sedans, "if Hansel and Gretel came running out of the woods

following a trail of Reese's Pieces, I'd pop 'em in the back seat, and we'd beat it the hell out of here."

Rich smiled and stroked his goatee. "Oh, it gets a lot worse than this," he said and poked Teal in the shoulder.

They stumbled down the front path, lit only by some faint light from one of the front windows. Rich knocked on the front door and then entered. No one was there to meet them.

"No one home," Teal said cheerfully. "Let's go get a beer."

A door opened at the end of a long hallway, and Ann Bock walked down to meet them. She said nothing but kissed Rich on the cheek and beckoned for them to follow. They walked past several closed doors, one with light and muted television sound seeping through the gaps, and finally stepped into a large, dimly lit room. It was about thirty feet square and had drapes or sheets hung over the windows and a high two-story ceiling peaked in the center.

There was no furniture – merely a collection of large pillows and throws in bright slipcovers. The only light came from several recessed spots set on dim. Gorman was standing with half a dozen other people and nodded to them.

The only one who approached them was someone Teal had never seen before.

"Rich," the man said. "Nice to see you again. Ummm, I assume this is Jack Teal?" he asked examining Teal as if he were an interesting postage stamp.

Rich introduced him as Gerald Cooper, and Teal shook a damp, limp hand.

"Gerald is a facilitator to assure the meeting runs seamlessly," Rich said in what sounded like a clipping from a brochure. The flat look in his eyes told Teal this was a verbal high wire act without a net, and he had walked it before.

"Ummm, well put," Gerald said. His glasses were almost opaque and looked like they had been handled by a child with sticky fingers. He was dressed in a Pendleton knockoff in strange, almost tropical colors and buttoned at the wrists and Adam's apple. The temperature in the room did not warrant it. Teal glanced at Rich whose gaze was fixed rigidly on the far wall.

"Let's meet, ummm, the rest of the ensemble," Cooper said, and Teal wondered if he was trying to emulate William Buckley. He concentrated hard not to despise him.

Teal was introduced to the program director from one of the living facilities and his female assistant and a second young woman who seemed to have no affiliation with anything. They were offered tea and some sort of dry cracker.

"We have Darjeeling, chamomile and some Celestial Seasonings," Cooper ticked off on his fingers like a waiter in a trendy San Francisco bar. Teal could think of half a dozen snappy rejoinders but graciously declined the offer.

Rich had a cup of Darjeeling and wrinkled his nose with the first sip.

After everyone had been served by 'My name is Gerald and I'll be your server this evening', he clapped his hands vaguely reminding Teal of an emperor who had just witnessed a Christian being eaten by a lion and found it somehow disappointing.

"Let's all sit and get comfortable," Cooper said and folded onto a huge pillow with colors clashing dramatically with his shirt. Teal wondered if he were colorblind.

The rest of the group settled, the lines of affiliation being as distinct as a school lunchroom.

"My duty this evening, ummm, as it always has been is to mediate and direct the conversation and exchanges. We are free to say what we feel here," he said but shaking a finger and grinning, "as long as we remain civilized."

That produced a chuckle from Gorman and a nervous smile from the residential program director.

"Lawrence, is there something you wish to say?" Cooper asked.

"Yes, thank you Gerald," he said leaning forward and fixing each in turn with an intense stare. "I would like to welcome you all to The Center, whether you are newcomers or have had the opportunity of visiting us before." He relaxed slightly and shifted his weight on the cushion.

"We call this The Center because it represents the hopes and aspirations of what Marin Advocates for Mental Stability is trying to achieve in the mental health field. We feel The Center is the heart and brain of this organization, and it has been entrusted to us, the task of directing this organization through often choppy waters."

"Ummm – ummm," Cooper said in apparent agreement.

Gorman's voice had a rhythmic, sonorous tone, which coupled with a few more degrees of temperature, would be guaranteed to put Teal to sleep. He snuck a glance at Rich who was looking transfixed at a crack in the hardwood floor.

"Sometimes we have jolly, amusing times which are always balm to the soul and provide us with a pleasant night's sleep. But sometimes we must dig beneath the façade to correct slippage."

Slippage, Teal wondered. *Like a landslide? What?*

He looked at Rich who was still locked into the floor.

"Grace, how are things going with your neighbors?" Gorman asked, and the young woman's head snapped up hard enough to cause whiplash. Teal started to grin but squelched it. This was going to be a zinger of an evening, he thought.

"Much better," the woman replied in a strong voice. "We had some representatives over from the neighborhood for tea and a look around the place. The kids were on their best behavior, so I think we diffused a time bomb."

"Were they some sort of block leaders?" Gorman asked.

"Yes and that's why it was so important for them to see there's no mystery in what we're trying to do. And the kids came across just like any other teenagers would."

"That's wonderful to hear," Cooper said with a thin smile. "It's, ummm, too bad it took you so long to reach a meeting of the minds."

Teal was startled and thought: *what the hell is that?*

What could possible be achieved by pulling the rug out from under her and diminishing something in which she took pride. He looked at Rich and saw him shake his head almost imperceptibly. The young woman, exhausted, sank into her pillow probably wishing it were fifty feet deep.

"And welcome, John and Katherine," Gorman said. "I'm glad you could both come. I trust you have someone tending the store," he added and chuckled. Bock's smile was wan as fleeting moonlight. No one else moved an inch.

"Now you've had very few problems with neighbors if I remember correctly," Gorman said.

"That's right," John answered, "but we have an advantage in having some land around us. People tend to be more tolerant when they have a buffer zone. And I think people in the country are more tolerant anyway."

"And why should they not be tolerant of your facility?" Gorman asked quickly and scowled.

John looked confused for a moment and answered carefully. "Well...it is common for people to protest a facility such as ours coming into their neighborhood. They consider it an invasion, and it dredges up all those horror stories they've heard all their lives. It's quite natural for them to display some resistance."

"It's a sure sign of small minds," Gorman snapped and flushed a dark red. "It really pisses me off!"

"Ummm, it certainly is a frustration," Cooper said watching Gorman carefully and defusing the situation.

Everyone in the room seemed frozen in place except for Gorman, Cooper and Teal who was still having difficulty getting settled in his cushion. His knees were begging to be stretched out, and he was trying to focus his mind on anything but running out the door.

"And John," Gorman continued with his color returning to normal, "how are all your charges doing? I've been hearing good things through the grapevine."

"They seem to be progressing nicely," John said. "Brad is sleeping much better and his grooming skills are improving. Jane is still frightened and wants to go home, but both her parents and I are holding firm."

Gorman was nodding his head as if bored and trying to move the conversation along. Cooper looked from face to face and seemed eager, anticipating something to come. Bock now looked stoned or drunk and had trouble focusing on anything but the fingers laced in her lap.

"And how about Bitsy?" Gorman asked quietly with a seemingly sly tone in his voice.

Rich stiffened next to Teal and gently cleared his voice. John looked frozen in place and finally coughed into his hand.

"Bitsy is doing much better..." John started to respond before Gorman cut him off.

"So, none of those problems from the past?" Gorman asked while Cooper looked from face to face. Teal felt very uneasy and shifted his weight once more.

"Bitsy has had some problems adjusting and was having some affection transference problems," John said in a stressed voice. His assistant shifted her pillow slightly away from his in a subtle and damning statement.

"Affection transference," Gorman mused. "Is that the same thing as saying you're fucking a client?"

Teal realized the breathing he heard was his own. His mind was racing out of control while the silence stretched for several seconds. If he hadn't been there to hear it, he never would have believed the story.

"Ummm, let's try to work through this," Cooper said, rubbing his hands like a man watching a great cockfight.

"Bitsy is a deeply troubled young girl," John said ignoring Gorman's profanities, only to be cut off once again.

"And therefore a perfect candidate for someone to manipulate," Gorman said with an angry flip of his hand. "These young girls are as easy to pick off as overripe blackberries," he said with a sneer. Bock was breathing deeply through her mouth and staring at the ceiling as if in a trance.

"Now wait a minute," John said. His face was white with anger, and he struggled to get up from his cushion.

"Sit down, John. We're going to work through this, and we're going to do it now," Gorman said pointing at him.

Teal was on his feet almost without realizing it and with his anger barely in check. Everyone stared at him as if he had just fallen through the roof.

"What the hell is going on here?" Teal asked looking from Gorman to Cooper and back. "I'm not interested in listening to something best discussed in private and not a God damned open forum."

"Jack, please sit," Cooper said. "Ummm, it will all work out for the best. This is a process which is very effective and positive."

John had settled back in his cushion looking stunned and exhausted.

"Bullshit!" Teal shouted. "I'm not going to sit and listen to character assassination or intimidation or mind fucking or whatever it is you're doing here. Life's far too short."

"Teal, sit down," Gorman said angrily. "I'm not interested in what you want or do not want. And when we have finished discussing John, we are going to have some dialog about you and your so-called abilities at running an important facility."

"Not a chance, Gorman," Teal said suddenly very calm. "I'm outta here, and please don't bother to stand. You people are way more fucked up than the kids working for me at Magnolia."

"Please sit down," Cooper said reaching out to touch his arm.

"If you so much as lay a finger on me," Teal said, "I'll knock you on your fat ass!"

"Teal, if you walk out of here, you'll be walking out of Magnolia and leaving all those clients behind," Gorman said shaking with rage. "I'll have the board fire you and get you kicked out of the county."

"Until that time, Larry, I suggest you barricade yourself in here and play your mind fuck games with Gerald.

"If you set one foot in Magnolia while I'm there, I will call the police and have you arrested for disturbing the peace. And you know what? I will have at least half a dozen witnesses who will back up everything I say."

Gorman was scarlet with rage, and the tips of his ears were so white, they appeared to have been frostbitten. He was struggling to get out of his pillow.

"No really, Larry, don't bother getting up," Teal said. "I can find my own way out of this hellhole."

He started for the door and heard Rich behind him.

"I came with that guy," he said with no apology in his voice. "He's my ride home."

They drove all the way to highway 101 in silence. At a Park and Ride Teal pulled in and got out of the car. He was still shaking. Rich followed him over to the guardrail where they could look down on the highway and watch the streams of traffic going north and south. Teal wondered if any of the commuters had just lost their jobs.

"Well, that was fun wasn't it?" Rich finally said.

"Stupid fucking thing to do," Teal finally answered.

"Yeah, but still sort of cool," Rich said and laughed a little hysterically. "Jesus, that's going to be *the* number one topic of conversation in the mental health field for weeks and weeks. And I was there to see the whole show! How long were we there? Five or six minutes? Wild, wild shit!"

Teal kicked a pebble and it banged off the metal railing and trailed off into the underbrush. Something squeaked and scurried away.

"They'll can my ass, won't they?" Teal asked, knowing the answer. "What have I done? Who's going to run the place? TJ's not ready for full time."

"Jack, with all due respect, we'll muddle through," Rich said and put a hand on his shoulder. "I'm not saying you didn't do a hell of a job, but life goes on and things adjust. We'll make it."

Teal nodded while feeling miserable for betraying Sissy and TJ and Sammy. "Son of a *bitch*," he shouted.

"Yeah, it is," Rich said. "But I'll tell you one thing, Jack. I'll never forget that scene as long as I live. Whenever I'm feeling really down, I'll remember this night and the looks on all those faces. Shit, Jack, you're my hero!"

Teal sighed. "What in the hell was that all about tonight? I just lost my job over something I know nothing about," he said with a wan smile.

"It's been going on for a while," Rich said leaning forward and putting his hands on the railing. They could feel a very faint breeze from the cars whizzing past below them.

"Bitsy was admitted into John's facility about three months ago. He didn't want her but got coerced into taking her. She's eighteen and absolutely gorgeous. I mean a total knockout." He scratched his goatee and smiled.

"Coupled with being a gorgeous woman, she's got this thing about latching onto older men. Actually got preggers by some old fart who's a bartender in Sausalito. She's a borderline schizophrenic and extremely bright, which all in all makes her a handful.

"Well, of course, from day one, she's working poor John like a cow pony. John's a very cool dude, and I really don't think anything happened between them, but who knows. I would have caved in a heartbeat," Rich said and laughed loud.

"But the weird thing is – and I heard this from several people – they think Gorman had his eye on her and was jealous. Wanted her for himself."

"God, that's sick. Does the board know?"

"If they do, it didn't come from me. I haven't got the balls for the court intrigues."

They returned to the car and drove the slow lane with
traffic screaming by them to important destinations. When they
reached Teal's block, they saw a Mercedes sedan with a wisp
trickling from the exhaust pipe idling in front of Rich's pickup.

"Oh boy," Rich said quietly. "Sissy and John. News gets
around fast."

Teal parked and walked over to the Bennington's car.
Rich waved to all of them, gave Teal thumbs up and drove
slowly down the hill.

Sissy was getting out of the sedan as Teal approached.

"Do you have any tea in your cottage?" she asked and
when he nodded, she took his arm, and John followed them.

John and Sissy sat quietly while Teal prepared the tea and
served it on a beaten silver Navajo tray Sloan had brought up
from Scottsdale. He didn't have the range of teas offered by The
Center, but the Bennington's didn't seem to mind.

"I do not approve of vulgarities," Sissy said after taking
a sip. "And I heard quite a few were bandied about at The
Center tonight."

Teal nodded numbly trying to think how he would tell TJ.

"However, having said that," she continued, "I have no
intention of firing you – just to remind you vulgarities are not a
substitute for proper English."

Teal stared at her.

"Please close your mouth, dear. I can practically see your
lungs." John sat next to her trying to control his mouth twitches.

"In our industry, and it is an industry," Sissy said,
"sometimes we spend so much time helping others and telling
them how well they're doing, we forget to treat each other in
the same manner." She took a sip and smiled. "The job you
have done at Magnolia has been simply magnificent. The clients
adore you and, more importantly, they trust you. That trust is

very hard to earn. As you know, these are not stupid people but often very wary.

"It is very difficult for me to imagine whatever transpired at The Center was of your making. I believe I know you well enough to feel you reacted to something, which I'm quite sure everyone will be terrified to mention in my presence."

"Thank you, Sissy. Thank you, John." Nothing else needed to be said.

"I trust you will continue to do the job you started," she said. "We have always been dedicated to a practical approach to help solve complex problems, and we've been successful. But some have a 'vision' which is not entirely compatible to our way of thinking, and it is obviously time for us to reevaluate some of our employees," she said with a sweet smile laced with traces of acid and resolve.

They talked for a few more minutes before John looked at his watch and smiled at Sissy. "I think we should let this man get some sleep," he said.

"Goodnight, Jack," Sissy said. "It's nice to know you can keep that temper of yours in check until it's really needed." She started for the front door and then said over her shoulder in the sweetest voice imaginable, "Like that time with Carl." And made a tiny fist.

Teal punched the number for Rich on his cell phone speed dial a minute later.

"You asleep?"

"Not really. Sounds like you probably didn't get canned."

"Nope, but Gorman might not be so lucky."

"Cool. Maybe you can take over his job," he said laughing and broke the connection.

* * *

TWENTY FIVE

For the upcoming sports car races in Monterey, Sloan
and Teal did much of their planning long distance, and Teal
dreaded the next phone bill.

"I'll drive up with Dutch and Dad, and I think Bill
and Janie are going to fly up the day before. Or maybe Bill
will drive up with us. I don't know." She sounded giddy with
excitement.

"Dad got a section of rooms at the Double Tree Inn
where lots of the drivers stay. The awards banquet will be there
Sunday night. Anyway you'll get to room with either Bill or
Dutch – probably Dutch, so you guys can swap prison stories."

"Jesus, cut me some slack here," Teal complained, but
he was laughing. Then he suddenly remembered Cline, his
cellmate, and the three years of silence.

"I'm just kidding, baby," she said. "Dutch is one of your
champions, and Dad listens to him. You'll see. He has this
quiet way with no wasted words. When he talks, other people
shut up and listen – and not because they're afraid. It's because
they don't want to miss anything."

"Okay, I believe you. Who's Janie?"

"Janie hangs out with Dutch. She's as tough as a horsehair
rope. But when she's talking about Dutch or to Dutch, her
whole face changes like some sort of trick photography, and she
just looks...adorable."

Teal remembered seeing the same thing in Dannie when
she spoke of TJ.

For the two weeks leading up to the race weekend, Teal pestered Rich and TJ to near distraction.

"Come on, gimme some good race car makes I can sprinkle in my conversation," he asked Rich for the fifth time. "Some of the hot drivers and some of that good gossip. I'm going to come across as a total nerd unless you guys help me. Sloan will probably leave me."

"Okay, let's see," Rich said, pondering the request with fake gravity. "I'd say AMC Pacer, Borgward and Buick Reatta. Drop those names and you'll be home free," he said and went back to reading the sports section.

"Help me out here, TJ. Is it Porsche with an 'ah' at the end or not. I can never get that straight."

"You're asking me about cars? Someone who nobody would team up with in shop class? Someone who can't remember the brand name of the car he currently owns? You're pathetic," he said and walked away laughing.

"Well tell me this," Teal said running to catch up. "Should I go down Friday night or Saturday morning and go right to the track. I mean you're the traffic man, help me out here."

TJ shook his head as if the weight of the world had pounced on his shoulders. "If you leave Friday night, you'll be driving in Friday rush hour, and God only knows how long it will take. I'll probably get to watch you from my deck for a good fifteen minutes or so. Jesus Teal, get it together man.

"Didn't you tell me your ticket passes and such were going to be a will-call trackside? Just drive down early Saturday and go straight to the track and pick 'em up. Okay? Now leave me be. I got reports out the butt I'm late with, and you're making me bonkers."

Rich looked over from his table and grinned.

Teal got up at four in the morning and shook his head
in amazement. This was early, even for him. The bird nest was
quiet and Highway 101 almost empty. He showered, quickly
ate a toasted bagel, left a pinch of worms and took a mug of
coffee for the road.

He cruised down 101 to San Francisco, Brownie
humming along happily as if he knew he was going to where
the big guys played. In San Francisco, Teal hooked over to
the 280 down through San Jose and the valley south towards
Monterey and the old military base of Fort Ord.

Even at the early hour, the roads became more and more
congested as he neared the racetrack. But it was if he had
entered a different automotive dimension where Toyota pickups
and Honda minivans and Cadillac SUVs had been banished.
Teal had to concentrate on the highway not to be distracted
by the flashes of color and snarls of exhaust from four wheeled
works of art. He had only the faintest idea what any of them
were.

He could pick out some the Ferraris and the garden
variety Porsches; the Ferraris because of their rearing black
stallion badge, which really didn't look like Sloan's Tattoo and
Porsches because he figured there might be a million of them in
Marin County.

He saw some Jaguars he knew and a Cobra. But the
others? They were blurs of colors, some with rooflines barely
reaching Brownie's windowsill. The morning was filled with the
tang of hot oil and scorched rubber from impatient burnouts.
He felt like a deer pellet trying to adjust to a Shreve's window
display. Brownie chugged along without a worry in the world.
Oil and coolant temperature gauges planted solidly in the green.

At the will-call gate he picked up his ticket and parking
pass, trying not to pay attention to the young girl's obvious

disdain as she put the pass on Brownie's windshield. He parked in the preferred paddock and surveyed the acres of cars. Brownie was the least expensive car there by perhaps as much as a hundred thousand dollars. Maybe more.

Teal trudged towards the pits to find Sloan and her dad. Despite all of Sloan's encouragement and stories about how her dad was coming around, he had slept poorly the past several nights and was now scared almost witless. He wanted his relationship with Sloan to work so badly; the thought of losing her scared him. And he knew her dad was an important part of the package.

TJ and Dannie, of course, had been lots of help.

"For God sakes, man. Just be you," TJ said. "And know that if you fuck it up, you can't come back here."

Dannie tried to jump on his back. "God you're of no help *what-so-ever*!"

Teal was about half way through the competitor's pits when he saw where they had parked. Their tow truck, trailer and Porsche were parked with several other racing cars in a compound of motor homes, trailers, pickups and racecars. Shade was provided by multihued awnings canted from motor homes or freestanding and tethered in place with sand bags or cinder blocks. There were car parts and tires and tool boxes everywhere but neatly placed and arranged.

Sloan was standing with a group of five people, one of whom was describing something involving lots of hand movements while the others laughed. Sloan was wearing hip hugger jeans, an Easy Motors t-shirt and a billed hat on backwards. Teal always wondered why it was women looked so cute with gimme hats on backwards, and guys looked like morons.

Sloan said something, and they all laughed, and
the man standing next to her pecked her cheek, which
made Teal a little stiff legged. At that moment, she saw
him and started to run across the open access road. She
lost her cap and had to run back laughing to retrieve it,
narrowly dodging a Shelby Mustang who honked and
waved. She hugged Teal long and hard, and he knew eyes
were on them. Several people in the group smiled, and Teal
felt a glimmer of hope. Maybe he wouldn't be beaten to
death with monkey wrenches and dragged behind a
Corvette for everyone's pleasure.

"I really missed you," Sloan said taking his hand and
pulling him urgently back towards the group. "You gotta meet
these folks. They're the best."

Sloan made introductions, and they stood talking about
the weather and the competition and the condition of the track.
Sloan never relinquished his arm, and one of the men seemed to
be studying him as if thinking; so this is the guy.

Sloan led him over to a gigantic motor home sporting a
huge awning shading a barbeque sizzling with sausage, bacon
and a flat grill with several kinds of eggs.

"You haven't eaten yet, have you?" she asked, then
suddenly kissed him.

"I'm afraid if I eat anything, I'm going to barf."

One of the guys looked up from the grill and said, "Hey,
it's a great course. Nothing to worry about. You're really going
to like it."

It took Teal a moment to understand. "Oh no, I'm not
driving today. I've got to meet up with Sloan's dad."

The two guys looked at each other, and one of them said,
"In that case, I wouldn't have anything to eat either."

"Thanks a lot," Teal said with a sour face.

"Let's walk around a bit and get you calmed down," Sloan said and took his hand. "Dad's out for a warm-up, so we'll catch up with him later."

"Don't you want to watch him now?" Teal asked wanting to make sure he did everything right.

"Oh, we'll watch the races, but practice is pretty boring. And I want to walk around and show you off."

They strolled from one end of the paddock to the other, stopping for introductions or to look at some interesting cars. It was no surprise to Teal that Sloan seemed to know everyone, and there was a fair amount of bantering – some at his expense. When they passed one group without stopping, Teal asked why.

"Corvette drivers," she said and wrinkled her nose.

When they got back to the compound, Baby Blue was sitting propped up on jack stands with two pairs of legs sticking out from beneath. As they arrived, one of the sets of legs was trying to scrunch out from beneath the car, and finally Jason's head popped into view.

"Well there you are," he finally said squinting.

"Good morning, sir," Teal said hoping he didn't sound too much like a West Point cadet.

"Hand me that eight millimeter open end, will ya," Jason said nodding at the toolbox. Teal looked into a tray holding at least fifty or sixty tools and blanched. Suddenly a pink tipped nail slid over the rear of the box and pointed. He grabbed the tool and leaned down to Jason who took it, grunted and slid back beneath the car.

Teal threw his arms in the air as if he had just scored in the Super Bowl and did a silent victory dance as Sloan watched and laughed.

"Hey, stop kicking up the dust out there," a voice warned from beneath the car.

Jason was busy trying to correct something and had little time for conversation with anyone except Dutch who represented the second pair of legs.

"Jack, don't call me sir," Jason said from beneath the car. "Makes me feel like an old fart."

Jack could see the point scored with the proper wrench selection being erased from the board.

"Don't worry, baby," Sloan said and giggled. "He's always cranky before a race."

In the early afternoon, with the skies threatening, Jason drove Baby Blue out to the grid with two dozen other cars in a wide variety of shapes, colors and sizes. Dutch and Teal were hitting it off, and he patiently answered all of Teal's questions.

"I didn't know diddly poop about all this stuff when I first come out to one of these things. I know how you feel," he said with a soft Arkansas twang. Teal thought it would probably be unwise to tell Dutch he knew diddly poop about cars, period.

When the race started, Teal couldn't remember ever hearing anything quite as loud.

"Oh, Christ," Dutch said. "Wait 'til you hear those Cobras and Can-Am cars have at it." Then he spat a stream of tobacco juice.

Teal had no idea what was going on, and Dutch pointed out there were races within the race – different classes of cars with smaller engines which would run back in the field. They concentrated on winning their class, not to be first overall. However, Jason, who was in one of the smaller classes, didn't think that way. Baby Blue was very well suited to the track, and he was running in the top three cars – the other two having engines triple his size.

Teal was fascinated by how Jason flew by the larger cars going into turns, only to be passed on the long straight-aways. Yet, the next time around, he would be at it again, buzzing around their exhausts like a pissed off hornet. Teal shouted encouragement along with others standing bunched along the fence.

"We've got trouble up in the corkscrew," the announcer said two laps from the finish. "Larry, are you up there on six?" Teal could see dust swirling behind a hill.

"Yeah, we got a mess up here," another voice said cutting in. "Looks like maybe…five cars involved."

Teal saw an official rush to the start/finish line and wave a red flag."

"Shit, they're stopping the race," Dutch said. "I hope Jason's not involved in that.

Sloan was looking anxious, and Teal put an arm over her shoulders.

"We've got a real mess up here," the second announcer said. "Doesn't look like any injuries…except to some wallets."

Wreckers and an ambulance were charging up the course, as a few racing cars trickled down the hill and into the pits. Dutch ran over and leaned into one car, spoke for a moment and trotted back.

"Your dad's okay, but he was right in the middle of it. Blue's taken a pretty good hit," he said. "Gonna be a long night."

One wrecker was coming down the hill with a car hanging from its boom. The car looked as if everything behind the seat was missing in a tangle of wires and steel.

"Jesus," Teal said and whistled. Sloan was shaking and holding his arm.

When they finally towed Jason's car into the paddock, he was still steaming, and Baby Blue was well and truly crumpled. He leapt out of the tow truck and went over to speak with Dutch. Then the two of them unhooked the car and positioned it beneath the awning.

"Sonofabitch!" he said standing with his hands on his hips. "I'm lapping him and have the line, and the little pissant shuts the door on me. They ought to ban that little fucker from ever driving here again."

Nobody said a word. To ask a question would have been suicidal. A couple of drivers wandered into the area and looked at the car.

"Sorry to see that, Easy," one said. "I saw the whole thing. Wasn't your fault."

"Thanks," Jason grumbled. "But it sure won't help fix Blue."

"Well, we better get started," Dutch said. "We got you, me and the kids. We'll get her done."

Dutch and Jason worked on the car while Sloan and Teal helped in any way they could. Teal blasted into Monterey to pick up a part and then had to return because they had given him the wrong thing. At seven thirty it started to rain and at eight thirty the wind came up and shredded the awning and spread pieces of it throughout the paddock.

Teal held up umbrellas until they turned inside out and then sheets and tarps and anything he could find to keep Jason, Dutch and Baby Blue dry. Sloan handed down tools and pulled broken pieces off to the side. Both she and Teal were soaked. Teal thought she looked like a mermaid and figured he looked like a downed rat. When Dutch and Jason finished with the car and looked them over, they both broke into fits of laughter.

"You ever see a sadder looking bunch of kids in your life?" he asked Dutch who shook his head and spat.

Two minutes after taking a hot shower, Teal was sound asleep at the Doubletree. He didn't even try to stay awake for dinner.

The following morning, Teal discovered a fully dressed Sloan shifting around at the end of his bed trying to paint her fingernails blue. He thought it might be a dream until he smelled her perfume.

"Blue fingernail polish?" he asked.

"Ah, it speaks. It lives," she said. "Yes. Always blue fingernail polish on Sunday at the races. Don't know how it got started, but it seems to bring good luck."

"If your dad knows you're in here, my ass is grass," Teal said.

"Dutch let me in. Everyone's gone to the track. Come on sleepyhead. We gotta move!"

After Saturday's excitement, Sunday was almost anticlimactic except for Jason's continued attempt at giant killing which had the spectators going nuts. At one point when the two lead cars bobbled, he snuck through and actually led the race for a lap. At the end he was third overall and way, way first in class. It was the race of the weekend.

At the awards celebration late that afternoon when he stepped up to accept his trophy, the room burst into applause and several started chanting 'Speech, Speech'.

"You know I wouldn't have been out there if it hadn't of been for some people who really helped me out. They're all sitting at my table," he said pointing them out. "Most of you know Dutch Breen who's the best damn wrench in the country." Some cheers. "And most of you know my daughter, Sloan." Sustained cheers. "The guy you don't know sitting

next to her is Jack Teal. Now I know a lot of you young guys
been hanging around my pit because you say you want to talk
cars. But the real reason is sitting next to Jack Teal." Lots of
laughter. "I'm sorry to have to tell you she's sitting next to the
reason she's no longer available."

He held his trophy over his head and returned to the
table to sustained applause. When he reached the table,
everyone bumped knuckles and a floodgate opened in Teal's
system and filled his veins with relief, which flowed like
molten gold.

People were talking about Christmas and saying everyone
was talking about it earlier this year; the same they had said
last year and the year before. TJ was almost back to full
schedule, and the transfer of the nebulous title of Program
Director would soon be riding his shoulders. Best of all, the
Mexican restaurant was back on his schedule.

However, cash flow for the restaurant was an increasingly
serious problem, and the single most daunting problem slowing
TJ's recovery.

"I think about it everyday," he told Teal. "I try not to, but
I just can't stop."

Rich was seeing Ann Bock again, and since he had little
to say about the matter, Teal assumed it was serious.

"She's a mole," he told Teal one morning.

"What do you mean?"

"All that good inside stuff? Like your never-to-be-
forgotten scene? She tipped Sissy on all that inside crap."

He shook his head slowly. "You gotta admire that."

Gorman had not been fired but had been 'severely'
reprimanded' by Sissy. Teal would have loved to witness the
dressing down, and his admiration for Sissy soared. He and

John had played handball twice, the second time to a draw, and Teal could barely move the following day. Sloan went shopping with Sissy at Neiman Marcus and bought Teal a suit which made him look foppish – until he smiled his wolfish grin, and then he looked like a hit man from Canarsie.

Gary had taken up tap dancing, and TJ had trouble getting him *not* to wear the tap shoes to work.

On a Thursday afternoon with the lunch rush just beginning to diminish and Teal in the back room balancing the bills against the checkbook, Rich peeked in the door and grinned.

"Someone to see you out front," he said.

"Who?" Teal asked barely looking up.

Rich flicked a business card with his thumbnail and laid it down with a flourish. It read:

SENATOR GARLAND PEARSON
DEMOCRAT NEW JERSEY

Teal dropped it on the desk as if it had burned his fingers. "He's out there? In the restaurant?"

"Yeah. He's sitting at number five in case you can't find him," Rich said with a grin.

Teal ran his fingers through his hair and tucked in his shirt before casually walking into the dining room. He heard a female voice in the kitchen say, "You look beautiful!"

Pearson was sitting at a deuce with another man quietly sipping lattes. Teal approached and Pearson stood immediately. Everyone in the dining room was watching them, including TJ, who seemed pinned against the wall and holding his breath.

"Senator, this is truly an honor," Teal said approaching the table with his hand outstretched. From the corner of his eye he saw the senator's companion stiffen.

"Jack, my God," Pearson said. "You look terrific. How many years has it been?" He held out his hand and beamed. But he appeared to Teal to be smaller as if his body was imploding.

"Far too long, sir," Teal said. "I hope my staff has been treating you well."

"Indeed. I could only wish the Washington cafeterias were as kind."

Teal joined the laughter wondering if the senator had ever eaten in a cafeteria in his life.

"Ralph, thank you," he said. "I'll just be a few minutes."

The other man stood, nodded casually to Teal and stepped outside the restaurant to talk with the driver of the stretch limo.

"Jack, I had an opportunity to see the mental health special done by the Boston group. Imagine my surprise to see your face."

He wiped his forehead with a handkerchief and tucked it back neatly into the breast pocket of his coat. Teal noticed a slight palsy movement in his hands.

"I was out here talking with Barbara and Diane about some legislation we're involved in and jumped at the chance of paying you a visit. I hope you don't mind."

"We're honored by your visit and your interest," Teal said, and Pearson nodded with a wan expression. "Are you going to be in California a few more days? I'd love to be able to show you around."

"That's very kind of you," the senator said, "but I'm flying out this afternoon." He reached across the table and patted Teal's hand with a touch like ice.

"We so enjoyed having your visits with Chris. He was very fond of you, you know. Talking about this and that and

what the two of you were up to and which young ladies you
were seeing. Denise and I loved hearing about all of it."

He straightened his tie and his collar and stared down at
the table. "When Chris was killed in the car accident, a major
part of my life came to an end," he said softly and compressed
his lips.

Teal stared at him, speechless.

"Stiffer drunk driving legislation needs to be enacted
in all states so mothers and fathers and loved ones won't have
to go through what we did. Chris never saw the drunk boy in
the pickup," he said with his jaw trembling. "He never had a
chance."

My God, Teal thought. He's created a scenario to survive
the pain and humiliation, and it's eating him alive – from the
inside out.

"People tell me I look grand, but I know they're lying,"
he said looking at Teal with vacant eyes. "Denise is living up in
Connecticut and sometimes joins me when I'm on the campaign
trail. I don't know how long that will last."

Teal saw someone approach the table from the edge of his
vision. He made a small hand gesture, and the figure drifted
away.

"Well," the senator suddenly said puffing out his chest
and running a hand through his hair. "So much to do. I had
better be running along. I so wanted to just drop by and pay
my respects and tell you what a splendid job you're all doing
here."

They stood and shook hands. "I've also heard about your
money problems and about some of the grants you've written
to the Finneson Foundation," the senator said brightly. "I know
most of the folks over there, and I'll see if I can't get things to
move along a little more briskly."

He patted Teal on the back and then pulled out a
business card and wrote a number on the reverse side.

"That's my personal number on the back. It will get
you past all the secretaries and roadblocks." The color had
come back into his cheeks, and he once again resembled the
consummate politician he had been in years past.

"That young black fellow, the one who was mute and
regained his ability to speak? Is he still working here?"

"No, he was accepted into San Jose State and will be
starting next semester. He wants to study law. I'll tell him you
asked after him. He'll get a real kick out of it."

Teal watched from the doorway as the senator waved from
the recesses of the stretch limo, and it quietly moved down the
street.

When he stepped back into the restaurant, everyone
mobbed him: customers, clients and staff. The questions came
at him so fast he started to laugh. Just as he held up his hand to
restore order, he heard a car door slam, and Sissy came running
into the restaurant losing a shoe in the process.

"Did I miss him?" she asked Teal, and when he
acknowledged she had, she stamped her bare foot and said,
"Well, damn it all to hell!"

The laughter was followed by John strolling in the front
door and hooking a thumb at his frustrated wife.

"Big fan of the senator," he said with a grin. "I told her
we wouldn't make it in time. The senator moves quickly."

A dozen of them sat at two tables pulled together, and
they made Teal recite over and over everything the senator had
said. Teal cheerfully told them over and over – always omitting
the part about Chris.

"Did he say he was going to talk with Finnesen today?" TJ asked wringing his hands.

"He didn't say, but he has a flight out this afternoon, so my guess would be he'll call from Washington."

"Did he really call them 'Barbara and Diane'?" TJ asked and when Teal nodded he said, "Jeez, all this power schmoozing is making me a little light-headed."

"How did he look?" Sissy asked. "I've heard he's not terribly well, and you rarely see him on TV anymore."

"He didn't look very good," Teal admitted. "I haven't seen him for five or six years, and the change sort of caught me off guard. He looks...used up."

"Oh dear," Sissy said. "Did he mention his wife, Denise?"

"Yes. She's living in Connecticut and only joins him when he's campaigning."

Sissy sighed, and John put an arm around her shoulders.

"Tell us about the Finessen part again," TJ said looking as if he were ready to jump up on the table.

So Teal took a deep breath and told them again.

When he returned to the cottage, Teal saw an envelope propped up against his door. It was identical in all respects to the one he had received weeks before. The only apparent difference was the postmark date which was three days prior. He thought of asking Emily how it had arrived, but her house was dark. He opened the envelope while standing before his front door and shook out an identical photograph. He stared at the photograph and then looked around him in frustration as if someone near by had invaded his personal space.

The twelve day time discrepancy between the time of Koontzman's death in Mexico and the Los Angeles postmark on the envelope was strange, and the mere quirkiness of it was unsettling.

Inside the cottage after comparing the two identical photographs, he dialed Koontzman's number from memory only to be informed by a mechanical voice that the number was no longer in service. Next he dialed information and requested numbers in Santa Barbara as well as San Diego. There were no listings for Hector Alviso Koontzman, Hector Koontzman, H. A. Koontzman but two for H. Koontzman; one turning out to be a sleepy postal worker in Temecula and the second was a Helen Koontzman in Santa Barbara who stated in no uncertain terms that she was tired of these calls and was going to apply for an unlisted number.

Teal sat on the bed and looked at the two photographs as if the harder he stared, the sooner the truth might be revealed. Other than the timing of the second, the photographs were becoming comfortable settling in his brain as something benign. The concern they had caused was drifting into the category of foolish overreaction. The first had probably been to remind him of his close association with Koontzman and the second mailed late by some underling who had left it forgotten on his desk.

He put the two photos in the envelope and slipped them back into the drawer.

Finnsen foundation notified TJ less than a week later.

"Five thousand on a quarterly basis? What the hell is that?" he asked angrily. "We gotta kiss their butts four times a year for twenty grand?"

Dannie was stroking his arm, and slowly he cooled down

"I mean really! What did that guy in Fairfax get? The guy tracing the history of that dead Indian? I think a Miwok or something – died like two hundred years ago? I heard that grant was for thirty-five thousand, lump sum for one year." He was starting to get steamed again.

"I got nothing against dead Indians, but we got live kids here. It just doesn't seem right."

"It is something you can build on," Teal said. "Maybe I should call the senator and thank him for his efforts. Then maybe hint around that every little bit helps – with emphasis on the 'little'."

TJ grinned. "Yeah, that'd be good. And while you're at it, why don't you drop that bit about the Indian and the thirty-five grand. That oughta shake up the halls of Congress."

Thanksgiving came and went without any major traumas, and TJ and Peter Quinn breathed a collective sigh of relief.

"Thanksgiving is always tougher than Christmas, at least in my experience," TJ said, and Peter Quinn gave an affirmative nod. The three were having coffee after the Tuesday afternoon round table.

"Thanksgiving is the traditional family get-together," Peter Quinn said. "People flying home from all over the country – hell, the world. Everybody eating huge meals, getting reacquainted, throwing a ball around and taking naps. And watching football games between two teams you could care less about. Couldn't get any more Norman Rockwell than that.

"The problem is most of these kids never had that kind of Thanksgiving. Theirs was spent in chemical lockdown or in hospital psych wards or in family situations you could not begin to imagine. So now along comes a holiday dredging up all those bad old memories. You might say it's not a bundle of laughs for them."

"Well one down and one to go," Teal said cheerfully, not meaning to be a wise ass, but they both glared at him.

Sloan flew up the following week and Teal whisked her
off to Carmel for a long weekend. During the races, she had
been too busy to check out the town, and her dad wanted to go
back to Arizona early Monday morning to properly take care of
Baby Blue. But in talking with other drivers wives, she knew
what she had missed and was excited.

They stayed in a small bed and breakfast, which to Teal's
thinking was terminally cute. Sloan adored it and the town and
the people. Teal wondered if her dad looked as foppish in his
new clothes as Teal did. The thought made him chuckle just as
Sloan was matching him up with a silk Tommy Bahama shirt
covered with martini glasses and tiny drink umbrellas, and she
raised a warning eyebrow.

They wandered down to Big Sur and agreed it was one
of the most beautiful spots on earth. After parking Brownie
in a one-car turnout, they hiked out to a desolate promontory
facing west over the ocean crashing against the cliffs hundreds
of feet below. Although the path was well traveled, there was
no way to reach the ocean from where they stood. Teal pulled
sandwiches and cold beer from a backpack, and they dozed in
the sun watching the pelicans and gulls cruise the shoreline and
wave crests looking for meals.

When they were ready to leave, Teal reached into the
backpack and brought out something wrapped in a soft cloth.
Sloan looked over and knew what it was. She didn't have to say
anything. Teal didn't unwrap it or have a ceremony. He simply
pitched it over the edge where it bounced once off the cliff face
and disappeared into the crashing foam. To the world of the
gun collector, the 9MM SIG had just become rarer by a factor
of one.

The bed and breakfast inn's only nod to the contemporary
world was a hot tub, which Teal and Sloan used often and

vigorously. When they checked out the innkeeper's wife murmured, "I'm so happy you enjoyed the hot tub". Sloan turned a veritable sunrise of color.

"Do you ever think of babies?" Sloan asked on the trip back to Marin.

"Just babies in general or some specific babies?"

"Oh you know, our babies," she said dreamily. "Little boys in jeans and t-shirts and little girls in sun smocks playing with a puppy."

"Those sound like children," Teal said having some fun with the conversation. "Babies have poo-poo diapers and drool."

"Jack, sometime you can be about as romantic and sensitive as an oil filter."

He reached across the seat and pulled her close. "We'll have lots of fat babies, and I'll help change the poo-poo diapers," he said.

Sloan smiled, kissed his cheek and said, "God, I wish I had a tape recorder."

* * *

TWENTY SIX

Teal wanted to have a waiter's seminar – something he had thought about and planned for months.

"Waiters seminar?" Mickey asked in a funk. "I know how to wait tables – been doing it all my life." And that was about the most positive remark Teal heard.

But he and TJ, Peter Quinn and Rich had planned it well, and it would be the essence of practicality wrapped around an understanding of human nature. Sissy had, of course, heard about the plan through her underground network and wanted in. Teal was totally convinced she would make a superb CIA agent.

The seminar was held after work on Wednesday and was mandatory for all wait staff or those wishing to become waiters. As a result of the seminar being virtually wide open to anyone who might be interested, the restaurant was crowded with a party atmosphere.

Rich and Teal set up a table in the middle of the room for maximum viewing. Two chairs were set at the table and the rest scattered through the room.

"We're going to start now," Teal said getting everyone's attention, and the room became quiet. "I'm going to play the role of the customer coming in for breakfast. Rich is going to be my waiter, and TJ's going to be the referee. We'll show you what we mean."

Teal walked to the front door, and Rich went to the wait stand while TJ stood next to the table.

Several moments went by before Teal walked towards the table with a newspaper in one hand and his shirttail pulled out. Rich went over with a menu to greet him.

"Good morning, sir," he said brightly. "Can I…"

"What's good about it?" Teal asked dropping his paper on the table. "My damn car won't start, so I had to take my wife's, and sat on her opened tube of lipstick."

"Stop," TJ yelled, and there were laughs and giggles around the room. "Okay…ahh, Mickey. What are your observations so far?"

"Well, that guy's one angry dude." Strong hoots and laughter and chattering around the room.

"Mickey," TJ said, "you're absolutely right. Sometimes we get up on the right side of the bed and sometimes we don't. So, let's see. Ginny, any further comments?"

She thought about it for a moment. "You shouldn't lay your bad trip on other people," she replied seriously.

"Excellent!" TJ said and clapped his hands. "You absolutely should not lay a bad trip on anyone. Who needs it, right?" Lots of nods around the room.

"But," TJ said holding up a finger. "This isn't a residential facility or a bunch of buddies living together in an apartment. This is an angry guy in a restaurant who wants some breakfast. So, let's continue."

"Well, your problems aren't mine buddy, so get a life," Rich said with a hand on his hip. There were howls of laughter, and Sissy was wiping her eyes.

"Stop!" TJ shouted. "Now what's wrong with *that* picture? Anybody?" Several hands shot into the air. People were really getting into it.

"How about the young lady sitting in the back over there?" he said pointing to Nicole.

She stood up with her hands knotted and color in her face rising. "Just because the customer is angry," she said smiling nervously "that doesn't give the waiter the right to be rude."

"Madam, you are absolutely correct. And that's why you're one of the best cooks we have in the kitchen," he said with a wink while Nicole practically collapsed in her chair.

"But I saw another hand over there. Mickey. Take that thought a little further."

Mickey rolled his denture furiously almost dropping them twice while working it out in his head. "If you run across a guy who's gotten up on the wrong side of the bed, ignore him. But you can't in here because you're working for the jerk. You don't have any choice."

TJ ran across the room and high-fived him. "Mick, you're the man! You're exactly right. The waiter *does* work for this man. It doesn't give the man the right to be rude, but it does offer the waiter a rare opportunity – the opportunity to serve the man a good meal and maybe help to cheer him up."

He swept his hand around the room. "All of us need to have the experience of dealing with people who are difficult. Sometimes it's easy, and you just have to avoid that person. But here you don't have that luxury. You must do the best job you can. Actors, please continue."

"Do you have fresh squeezed orange juice?" Teal asked.

"What? You think you're in a fern bar in Laguna Beach?"

The room sat in stunned silence before erupting.

TJ held up a hand to regain order, but he let it continue for a few seconds. "That was a joke, of course," he finally said. "But there is a lesson hidden in there. You need to be very careful around someone in a bad mood. Again, you are trying to serve him in a reasonable manner, and most reasonable people will respond. That's a life lesson – don't forget it. Actors, continue."

Teal looked up from his paper at Rich. "I want two scrambled hard and crisp bacon. And do you have any wagga-wagga sauce?"

"I don't think so, but please give me a moment to check with the kitchen," Rich said struggling hard to hide a grin.

"Stop!" shouted the ref looking around the room. "You will get some strange requests from time to time, and you must try to honor them. If you're unsure if something is available, check with the kitchen. By the way, Jack, *do* we have any wagga-wagga sauce?"

"No, but it's on order," Teal fired right back.

They went through several more setups and discussed the object lesson attached. Almost everyone participated.

Sissy raised her hand once and TJ acknowledged her.

"There's a little coffee house over by where we live," she said, "and we often stop by in the morning for a decafe and a bagel to share. We always sit at the same table and always have the same waitress. Sometimes now if she sees us coming in the decafs will already be on the table and the bagel toasting when we walk through the front door. It makes us feel very... comfortable. I guess that's the right word."

She sat looking uncomfortable while John grinned.

"Ladies and gentlemen," TJ said bowing to Sissy. "This is why this gracious lady is the president of our board. She is one sharp cookie!"

"Now," he said looking around the group. "Is there a lesson in there for us? Yes – the handsome Samurai warrior."

Sammy stood with a frown on his face putting together in his mind the pieces he knew where there. "We are not like people who work in an office or put roofs on houses or catch crabs out in the ocean. In our job we deal face to face every day with the people who we hope will keep us in business."

He took a second to look at TJ's face, which had an expression of utter astonishment. It made him grin.

"So we better do more than just feed him some good food. We want to make him look forward to coming in again."

Sammy sat down after acknowledging a resounded round of applause.

Then they turned the stage over to Rich and Teal and Mickey who alternated playing the role of the waiter and customer, roundly insulting one another and drawing laughter and applause. It was Guerilla Theater at its finest.

"God damn that was fun," TJ said. He and Dannie and Teal were sitting on his deck watching the afternoon commute traffic and sipping beers with thin wedges of lime.

"We should do more of that, or at least repeat it for those who couldn't make it," TJ said.

"Maybe take it on the road," Teal said with a yawn. "Or make it into one of those reality shows. Couldn't be any worse than what's on right now."

"Thanks, Jack. I'm serious – that was fun."

"So that means maybe there will be something a little extra in my pay envelope this week?"

Dannie harrumphed at both of them and went into the kitchen sipping her beer.

They had some other classes but none as successful or talked about as the waiter class. There was no question they would have to do a repeat. The class on the care of cutlery for the kitchen crew was hailed as being a real yawner, and a class on general dining room setup and decoration, which was a hit with the girls, left the guys dozing. Part of that class was devoted to setting up the espresso bar, which included water, beer and wine service. Since only those over twenty-one are allowed to serve wine and beer, Rich or TJ were often called in to help.

The restaurant offered wine by the glass which they bought bulk packed from their supplier. It was delivered in three-liter boxes containing a flexible bag of wine within. To set it up, the box was laid on it side, and the tap carefully pulled out so it wouldn't tear. Then the box could be placed upright and the wine dispensed.

Generally Rich did the wine setup, and no one was paying attention the day the espresso bar ran out. Teal saw Gary walking back towards the bathroom or storeroom but didn't notice him lugging back the box of wine. When Sammy nudged him, he looked up just in time to see Gary prying at the spout with the box upright.

"Gary," he hollered but too late as the spout tore and three liters of red wine shot out and pinned Gary against the wall. Teal had almost reached him when Gary took off running through the restaurant full of startled customers.

He slammed through the front door and bolted across the street with Teal and Rich in pursuit. Teal saw a flash of color and a squeal of brakes as a car slid by and sideswiped a parked pickup. Gary was lying on the opposite sidewalk like a crumpled doll, and Teal felt a stab of panic. When he knelt down beside him, Gary reached up crying, "I'm sorry, I'm sorry. I didn't mean to do it."

His hands and knees were scraped but he appeared to be otherwise unhurt. Teal motioned an okay sign to Rich who was trying to calm the driver of the car. Soon a crowd had gathered, and Teal could hear a siren in the distance. All the time Gary clung to Teal in desperation, his fingers almost like claws.

"I'm sorry. God, I'm sorry, Dad. I didn't mean to do it. Please don't tell Mom."

Over and over he said it and wept until Teal felt a stab of misery clutch his heart.

* * *

TWENTY SEVEN

Teal lay in bed and looked out at the gloomy pre-dawn morning. The bushes and trees were heavy with dew and maybe a little late night drizzle. Headlights from the cars of the early commuters made the highway look like a river of black coffee stretching in an endless stream from north to south. The bay was nothing more than a spill of black paint, and the hills beyond were invisible.

The three baby robins had matured enough to leave the nest, and Teal missed them and the parents. Without Sloan there, the cottage felt very small and lonely. Teal always thought it strange that a small cottage such as this would feel bigger with two people in it rather then one. He wondered if Emily and her husband had ever noticed it.

Teasing with Sloan about babies had been fun, even though sharing a dream was unfamiliar territory for Teal, and he felt himself treading gingerly. But he could not imagine a life without her – it would be barren and meaningless.

At the same time his pride had reared its ugly head and questioned him about the future. He had nothing to offer her: no fast track job, county club membership or sailboat in the harbor. All he had was a heavy safety deposit box. He didn't even have the luxury of the remembrances of past glories like some of the guys he knew in college. Having been a star quarterback or on the law review or student body president opened many doors. He imagined himself in future years with his daughter on his lap and leafing through his personal scrapbook of memories.

No, he's not your grandfather. His name is Hector Koontzman. No we can't go visit him because some very bad men shot him full of holes. Oh that big, fat woman taking care of about a dozen kids? Her name is Kimi. But when daddy knew her she was very pretty like mommy. Daddy took her out on a date and missed a very important handball match the next day, which he could have won and become, like champion of the world. And that man is called a warden. He was the boss of a place where daddy lived for three and a half years.

When Teal rolled over and put his feet on the cold floor, the shock blew away his self-pity, and he slowly dressed for work.

It was drizzling, and the streetlight in front of Magnolia Café cast dancing shadows. In an eerie way it reminded Teal of the 'two way', which he hadn't thought about in months. He flicked the thought out of his mind like an insect.

The restaurant was cool and smelled vaguely moldy, so he flipped on the space heaters, fired up the espresso bar and sat to read the morning paper. But he couldn't concentrate on what he was reading, so he folded the paper and went to pull an espresso.

He sat and thought he and Sloan would have to make some long ranged plans – something he had virtually no experience with. They could not continue to subsidize Southwest and United Airlines. He was becoming restless and he sensed the same in Sloan. As fun as her visits were, it was as if they were living the lives of teenagers. They were also spending more and more time away from the restaurant and Marin County.

Dannie had even teased them about not hanging out with her and TJ as often as the past, and the thought made Teal sad.

"Jesus, you make it sound like teenagers drifting apart and all the angst stuff," he said laughing, but the joke had fallen flat.

They had explored Napa and Sonoma valley and sampled wines and listened to the spiels until they were totally confused and returned to drinking beer.

They went to Lake Tahoe and took a tour on a fake paddle wheeler and swam in the lake, which was so cold Teal thought his heart had stopped beating. They stayed in a funky cottage on the north shore and walked the beaches for hours.

And they started making plans.

The morning crew had started to drift in looking morose and out-of-sorts – hair slicked down, wrong clothing for the weather, and all looking as bewildered as prairie dogs flushed out of their dens.

"Come on, guys," Teal said. "When it's raining out you put on an overcoat and wear shoes or boots that can handle the puddles. You guys know that."

Then, looking at their befuddled faces, he felt like a monstrous slave driver. He went into the storeroom and brought out a stack of towels and began to rub them down vigorously.

"Oww," Sammy complained. "That's the only hair I got."

Soon everyone was toweling everyone else and laughing. It looked like a high school locker room after a divisional championship, while Teal sat back and watched them.

"You sad today, boss," Sammy said sneaking a look.

"Not at all," he said trying to sound upbeat. "But we got a lot of things to do today. And I've got a bunch of drowned rats to get the job done."

"You're a piece of work, Boss. You know that?" Sammy said and began his morning preparation of scrambles.

Rich drifted in, pulled an espresso and slumped at a duce reading the morning paper. Word was circulating that he and Bock were very serious, and she had moved out of The Center. She seemed to have more and more free time, as Gorman spent more of his time working with Internet job search firms. He had finally realized that his tenure with MAMS was about over.

Teal opened the front door and customers began to straggle in, snapping umbrellas and shaking overcoats and rain slickers, with few happy faces among them. Teal hoped the staff remembered their training from the seminar. Gary had coffee and espressos before most could open their mouths, and that coaxed a few smiles. The morning rush was strong with the emphasis on hot meals. Cold cereals were poor sellers.

TJ had called Rich and told him he would be stopping by Marin General and would probably be a little late. Peter Quinn had planned on being in sessions for most of the day.

"Looks like just you and me for a while." Teal said to Rich while slipping him a less than perfect blintz, which had not survived its flip.

"Great," Rich said gloomily. "We'll probably be attacked by terrorists."

When Teal passed Ginny on the way back to the kitchen, he said, "You look terrific today. New hairdo?"

She blushed and fingered the pixie cut while Gary watched them closely and seemed to puff up slightly.

Teal thought: Ummmm.

The kitchen was into its switchover between breakfast and lunch, and the restaurant was relatively quiet. Rich was watching the door while Ginny took a break in the back. Mickey was late once again, and TJ would have to draw some new limits for him.

Sammy nudged Teal and flicked his chin in the direction of the front door. Two police officers had just entered, and Rich was on his way to seat them. They wore bright yellow rain slickers and had plastic covers on their hats.

They spoke with Rich for a moment, and it appeared as if he was asked a question. Suddenly Rich dropped the menus and slumped, catching himself on one of the chair backs while one officer stepped forward to assist him. Teal thought for a split second he had suffered a heart attack.

He tore off his apron and walked quickly to the front. Rich had now slumped into a chair and was breathing shallowly though his mouth.

"Rich, are you okay? What's happening?"

The taller of the two officers stepped forward. "I'm Sergeant Brean from the Larkspur Police Department, and this is my partner Officer Cale. And you are?"

"I'm Jack Teal," he answered. "I'm the program director of Magnolia Café." The truth would have taken too long to tell.

"Do you have a Michael Ralston employed here?" he asked looking at a rain-splattered piece of paper.

"Yes we do. Mickey Ralston. He's supposed to be on duty now, but he's late, which is not out of the ordinary."

"And this gentleman is?" the Sargent asked nodding at Rich."

"He's my head counselor. Can you please tell me what the hell is going on? Has Mickey been in an accident or something?" Teal felt a buzzing in his head, somewhere behind his eyes, like a nest of angry hornets.

"Sir, I'm sorry to have to tell you that Michael Ralston committed suicide at around three o'clock this morning."

The buzzing in Teal's head reached a crescendo, and he started to lose his peripheral vision.

"Sir, are you alright? Perhaps you should sit down."

Teal shook his head slowly, one hand on the table and one on Rich's shoulder with his fingers digging in for balance.

"Please sit down gentlemen, if you don't mind," Teal said while making a cup pouring motion to Gary who immediately went to work. Several customers who had looked over lost interest and went back to their breakfasts.

"Rich, are you listening to me?" Teal asked shaking him lightly and getting a nod. "You've got to put on a game face and get the customers outta here. Comp their meals and tell them the next one's on us as well. If they ask, tell them we have a minor problem in the kitchen, but it's nothing serious."

Rich was focused on him and nodded.

"I need you to do it right now. Then come right back here after they've all left."

Rich sucked in a deep breath and stood with an almost deathly grin on his face. With wooden movements he went from table to table assuring people there was nothing serious, but they would have to leave the restaurant. He even bantered and laughed with one table.

Teal tuned back to the officers. "What happened? Can you tell me anything?"

"His radio was playing loudly early this morning which is against house rules," Brean said. "So the manager went to knock on the door. When he got no answer, he used his passkey and went in. He told us Mister Ralston worked here, and to his knowledge, there were no other relatives."

Teal nodded, his mind racing ahead.

"Excuse me a second," he said and punched the speed dial on his cellular.

"This is Jack Teal. I need to speak with Doctor Ryan immediately," he said to the secretary who answered the phone.

"And, yes, I know he's in sessions all morning. This is a critical emergency."

"Jack, what's up?" he heard Peter Quinn say a moment later. His voice sounded curious but a little perturbed.

"We have the worst kind of crisis down here. Mickey committed suicide early this morning."

There was a long silence. "Aw, sweet Jesus," Peter Quinn said softly.

"We need as much help down here as we can get. This place might come unglued."

Hearing that, Officer Cale peered around the room, clearly worried about what might happen.

"I'll be there as fast as possible – maybe eight minutes. I'll probably bring some help," Peter Quinn said. "Get all the clients in the kitchen. Just tell them we are going to have a quick little meeting. For God sakes don't scare them, but don't let them leave either."

"As soon as we hang up, I'll call TJ and Sissy. You haven't seen TJ over there have you?"

"No. And I don't have time to look," he said and rang off.

"Can you come down to the station sometime today and make a statement?" Brean asked beginning to pick up on his partner's anxiety. "There's going to be some other paperwork too."

"I'll come in any time, but right now I'm up to my neck in a crisis, so it might be best if you guys left."

Gary put their coffees in to-go cups, and they walked out into the drizzle. Teal motioned Rich over and asked him to assemble the clients in the kitchen, while trying to be as casual as possible.

Then he punched the speed dial a second time. "Dannie, is TJ around?"

"He went to Marin General this morning but called a few minutes ago and said he was coming back to pick up some papers he forgot. What's up?"

"Oh Jesus, Dannie. Mickey committed suicide last night. The cops just came in and told me."

He heard a sharp intake of breath and then silence, and he knew she was crying.

"Dannie you're going to have to be strong here. You're going to have to tell TJ and then bring him down here if you think he can handle it. But it's going to be your call. If you think he can't, we'll work something out – whatever it takes. But don't let him bullshit you. If you don't think he should come down here, stick to your guns, and we'll get some help up to you.

"Okay. You think you can do that?"

"I'll do my best," she said her voice trembling.

"Good. I know you will. Tell TJ that Peter Quinn is on his way and probably bringing another guy. I'll call Sissy and tell her."

The clients were huddled in the kitchen, clearly not believing whatever explanation had been given them but unclear what to do about it. Sammy was trying to catch his eye, so Teal couldn't look in his direction. They all looked small and frightened, and Teal was suddenly struck with how much he cared for them and feared for their well being.

There was a squeal of brakes out on the street and moments later Peter Quinn and two other people rushed through the rain with umbrellas and briefcases held over their heads. Before they walked in the door, they slowed their pace so as not to appear in a panic. The kids in the kitchen watched, and Teal could see they knew it was something bad.

Peter Quinn introduced both people to Teal. Bob something and a woman whose name he completely missed.

"Two of us are going into the kitchen," Peter Quinn said motioning at Bob. I want Katherine to stay out here with you until TJ arrives. Nobody is to leave unless I clear it. When TJ gets here we'll start calling the other facilities and have everyone brought in here. There is a danger of someone feeding off of someone else's grief, but I'll have to take that chance. Remember – nobody leaves."

Just as he entered the kitchen, TJ and Dannie came through the front door. TJ looked very pale and slightly confused, and it scared the hell out of Teal, who made him sit instantly at his favorite table.

"P.Q. is in the kitchen with everyone. He's got some other guy from MMH in there, and we've got Katherine out here. We need to call all the other facilities and have them bring their clients down here. If they're somewhere else, we need them found and brought here. P.Q. wants to use this as a clearing-house for the whole organization."

He looked carefully at TJ. "Do you want me to make the calls? I'd be glad to do it."

TJ shook his head and looked at Dannie. "Can you please hand me the cell?" His color was seeping back into his face.

He looked at her and smiled. "I'll be fine," TJ said.

"I know you will," she answered and kissed his cheek.

"You got them on speed dial?" Teal asked, and TJ nodded punching up the first number while his eyes tracked every movement in the kitchen.

Suddenly there was a scream of such intensity Teal jumped and nearly tripped over a chair. He started for the kitchen, but Peter Quinn held up a hand at Teal and pointed at Katherine who hurried back.

TJ was already talking urgently on the phone; his voice was strong and sure. Dannie was rubbing his shoulders as if he were a boxer between rounds.

There was a crash from the kitchen sounding as if every pot and pan had fallen, and Peter Quinn motioned for Teal to come back.

"Nicole's fainted," he said. He was holding Beth who was crying and shaking violently. "Sorry it happened so fast, I didn't see it coming. We caught her before she hit the floor, but some pots went down.

Nicole was lying on the floor dazed and being tended to by Katherine. Pots and pans were strewn the length of the kitchen, and Bob was picking them up and putting them on the counter. Teal grabbed a stack of aprons and towels out of the storeroom and gave then to Katherine who gently placed them beneath Nicole's head.

Sammy was standing next to the refrigerator with his arms wrapped around his head. Tears were streaming down his face, but he made not a sound. Teal watched him in anguish, powerless to do anything. He thought his heart was going to explode. Peter Quinn watched him for a moment and then nodded him out of the kitchen.

John and Sissy had arrived looking wet and miserable and accompanied by two police officers in yellow slickers.

"We heard there was a gas leak in here," one of them said, and Teal went over to explain.

Sissy and John sat with TJ, and Sissy held one of his hands while he continued to talk on the phone. Teal wondered if the handholding was for her benefit or his. John looked at Teal – his face drawn and grim – and then shook his head in anguish and defeat.

"I've called all the facilities and staff with the exception of The Center," TJ said. "And that I cannot do."

"I'll call him," John said. "He has the right to know, but I do not want him down here. He can not be of any help."

TJ and Teal nodded in unison. Good.

A minute later a car stopped in front of the restaurant and a man with two bundled kids ran for the front door. It wasn't until they pulled off their rainwear that Teal could see who they were: Andy Crane from Sunset House and his two teenage clients.

He nodded grimly at TJ and Teal. "Carol's parking the car," he said quietly while the two teenagers swiveled their heads, eyes wide and fearful.

John was arguing with Gorman on the phone and looking worried. He held his hand over the phone and whispered to Teal. "He insists on coming down here!"

Teal gently took the cell phone from John and turned to step away from him. "Gorman, this is Teal," he said very softly. "I want you to listen to me very carefully because I won't say it twice. I do not want to see you on this street today much less in this restaurant. If you ignore my warnings, I will deal with you physically. Do you understand?"

"You fucking incompetent!" Gorman shrieked. "You wouldn't dare lay a hand on me."

"Maybe you should see if you can't look up Carl," Teal said quietly. "If you can find what hole he's living in. Ask him why he left. Oh, and Larry? Get back to me and let me know how his front caps look, okay?"

He folded the phone and handed it back to John who looked at him quizzically.

"He changed his mind, John. He's going to stay out there and play gin rummy with Gerald."

And so it went for the next hour and a half. Concerned program directors, councilors and parents brought in frightened young people until the room was nearly full.

It was late afternoon by the time the last client had been talked to by TJ and Peter Quinn. Bob from Marin Mental Health called it processing which made TJ grimace as if he might have an acid stomach. Finally all the clients had been picked up and whisked off into the stormy night and the quiet in the restaurant descended on those few who remained.

"Do you see any problems?" Peter Quinn said to TJ.

"No I don't think so. A lot of the kids really didn't know him, so, to them, it's little worse than reading something horrible in the newspaper. I guess I worry about Beth the most – she's pretty tightly wound. And am I the last person in the world to find out she and Mickey were lovers?"

"Lovers, yes," Peter Quinn said. "But not in the traditional sense of rolling around in bed and having squabbles. There was a sort of mystical aura in their relationship – she was a fair maiden, and he was a savior knight. They created that world and when they were alone together, they played those parts. Maybe I didn't tell too many people about it because I wasn't sure I understood it."

Teal stared at him. "You didn't understand it? P.Q. didn't understand something? You're always teaching us something because we're morons, and now you don't understand something?" Teal had started out jokingly but ended on a harsh, sarcastic note startling even him.

"Jesus, P.Q., I didn't mean..."

Peter Quinn held up a hand and then patted him on the shoulder. "With your permission, I'm going back to the refrigerator and cop about a case of beer, and we're all going to sit out here and talk for a while."

Bob begged off; a high school basketball game with two sons playing but Katherine stayed. Teal liked her. She was tough yet compassionate and could play either end of the good cop/bad cop setup when it was called for. Sissy and John stayed although he looked asleep on his feet.

They sat quietly for a moment, each with their own thoughts, sipping beers, which were tasteless.

"I know how you all feel," Peter Quinn said in a careful voice and looking at each one in turn. "I've been through this twice before, and they do not get any easier. If they did, I would probably quit because I would know something inside of me had died, and it would make me less effective.

"But you all knew this to be part and parcel of the mental health industry. You just never thought it would happen to you. Maybe to that facility in Fresno or the group home in San Diego or the Workshop for Living Skills in Denver – but never here."

He took a sip of beer and took stock of the faces around the table.

"So you feel shocked, saddened and disoriented," he said and pulled at his beard for a second. "And you feel angry and betrayed. How the hell could he do this to you?"

No one around the table challenged him.

"You know what? You're all normal," he said, nodding. "The problem is having all these supercharged emotions firing around your brain like a million spastic ping-pong balls and not knowing what to do about them. And that's why we're sitting here," he said pointing at the table "I'm going to shrink you a little bit," he said and turned to Sissy. "And it won't cost you a cent."

"Sissy, all you guys, life will go on for all of us. We will wake in the morning, brush our teeth, feed the dog, read the paper and laugh at some political cartoons. And we won't feel guilty about it. Why should we?" he asked with raised eyebrows.

"We have collectively worked as hard as we know how to make life better for some kids who can't handle it alone. Sometimes we have an Amed and sometimes we have a Mickey and always a lot of those who are floating somewhere in between.

"Could we have done better with Mickey? Absolutely not. And I say this with ten some odd years of first hand knowledge of the man. So I don't want anyone here to get mealy mouthed and feeling sorry for themselves because they perceive they could have done more."

He looked around the group and pursed his lips. "Most of you are also going to ask why this happened. Why would someone who had a lifetime of psychotic adventures, but was appearing to pull away from all that, take his own life? We will probably never know. Possibly Beth could shed some light on that, but I suspect her own grief will prevent that from happening. She will bottle it up and protect it forever."

The group was quiet. They had some questions, but they were too shocked and tired to pose them. Peter Quinn knew what they were because he had heard them before – all of them. They sometimes haunted him at night and slunk behind him like thieves when he walked down the street. He felt weary and lonely and wanted to go down the street to the pub where he could have a Guinness or a Harps with people who called him Petey.

"Beyond the fact of this being a personal tragedy, it is a tragedy for the organization. So now I'm going to tell you hard, cold facts. There will be an investigation as always happens in a death of this nature. The county coroner will sign off on the remains and release them to the next of kin – which in this case will be Marin Advocates. To my knowledge, Mickey had no relatives. I've known him for well over ten years, from the first day he ended up in the psych ward at Marin General. It was like he dropped from the sky, and has been floating around this county ever since."

Tears were streaming down Sissy's face, and she clung to John as if he were a life preserver.

"Some of you might even be wondering how much this will damage the organization – although you're angry, those thoughts sneak in. We will do our best to minimize that. I know Sandy Bell, the editor of *The Independent Journal*. He'll print it once as a matter of record, but it will be buried and pass from the public's memory quickly. I'm sorry if I'm sounding unfeeling and blunt. I have to be blunt, and I'll deal with my own feelings on my own time."

He took a deep breath and looked at the ceiling. "When Mickey's remains are released, we must make a determination in regards to a funeral. Perhaps we might find a will in his personal belongings, but I doubt it."

Sissy stood and John escorted her back to the restrooms.

"I'll be as blunt as you," Teal said, "which I personally think *is* healthy. My question is - how do we address the issue here at the restaurant. We have responsibilities to a lot of kids, and some of them are hurting much worse then we are."

"You're right, Jack, and it will take all of us weeks to determine whether this has created long term damage to anyone. But we need to keep the restaurant open and work through this together. These kids cannot stay at home and let this fester. And neither can we.

"Keep the restaurant closed for the rest of the week and reopen on Monday. You will have to be ready for customers coming in to express their feelings, which might be wide ranging. You will have to be gracious and caring, and let the issue diffuse itself. And it will over time."

"I'm in a little bit of a panic over the foundation," TJ said. "I hope they don't freak out and pull whatever little funding they've already given us."

"I'm hardly a fortune teller," Peter Quinn said, "but I would bet that wouldn't be the case. I don't think they would enjoy the type of negative publicity that might engender. You have to remember they are very concerned with image."

Sissy and John came back from the restroom and remained standing.

"I'm going to take my girl home now," John said. "She's exhausted. Would someone please call us tomorrow and bring us up to speed on what we've missed."

Peter Quinn nodded and hugged both of them in an oddly touching gesture, and they wobbled out the front door.

"I would recommend we all go home now and try to get some sleep – take a sleeping pill if you need it. I'll contact everyone tomorrow, and we'll set up a meeting to see where we're at."

Chairs scraped back from the table and everyone stood and stretched aching muscles.

Teal turned to Dannie and TJ. "After I call Sloan, do you think I could come over and bunk with you guys tonight?" he asked.

TJ smiled and threw an arm over his shoulders and Dannie an arm around his waist, and the three of them bumped each other out the door.

* * *

TWENTY EIGHT

In Mickey's personal effects, they did find a will. Peter Quinn and TJ discovered his room was as neat and clean as a hospital when they cleaned it out. In some papers on his tiny desk next to the window overlooking Fourth Street, they found a last will in his handwriting. It appeared to have been written some time in the past and was rumpled, somewhat discolored and a corner dog-eared. He left all his worldly processions to Beth.

"Interesting," TJ murmured. "John told me a couple of days ago the agent he gave Mickey's manuscript to called and is going crazy. Said it was the best thing he's read in a decade and thought it could be the blockbuster of the year. He's been in discussion with no less then four publishers, and it looks like it might go into a bidding war."

"I don't know what Mickey would have done with that," Peter Quinn said. "Except maybe roll his dentures."

Teal detested funerals. They made him feel strangely inadequate and stupid and turned people who he thought he knew well into people he didn't recognize. When he was thirteen, he went to the funeral of a classmate who had been killed in a farming accident. It was closed casket because of his extensive injuries. Teal sat for that hour and many subsequent hours wondering what 'extensive injuries' might look like. What he conjured in his mind resembled something from a slaughterhouse in a third world nation. But even worse was having to listen to people say he was going to a place where there was no pain, no crushing responsibilities, as if a teenager had any responsibilities at all. It all sounded frightening on one hand and boring on the other. Teal couldn't wait to get out of the church.

The second funeral was far worse. A friend at college had gone on a drinking binge, and late at night in his own bed, strangled on his own vomit. His family who were very prominent in the community pulled out all stops with the funeral arrangements, as they had felt obliged to do – including an open casket of burnished woods and gilded angels. Teal thought the casket was hideous and maudlin, but the figure lying within was what hard-core nightmares are made of.

The face looked like his friend, but then it didn't, and finally it didn't look human. When he returned to his pew he was shaken and sick to his stomach. Then he had to sit for many more agonizing minutes listening to people pontificate about this wonderful life tragically cut short, and how they were coming together to celebrate his life. Hypocrisy seemed to be the prevailing mood, and the moment the service ended, Teal fled the church as if it were on fire.

Mickey's memorial service was held on Sunday in a small church in Novato. Mickey had requested that he be cremated and his ashes spread on Mount Tamalpais. Although the request was illegal, there was little question in anyone's mind it would be honored.

Teal was surprised at the number of people who attended. Teal and Sloan stood far in the back and off to the side.

"I don't think I can handle it any other way," he told Sloan who was holding his hand.

Everyone connected with Marin Advocates was present, clients and staff alike as well as a number of people from

Marin Mental Health. He saw Sammy and Gary and Ginny
all huddled together in a pew near the front. Gary and Sammy
both were wearing three piece suits as if it were their daily
dress and Ginny looked as if she might be a receptionist in
a conservative lawyer's office. Teal saw they were all holding
hands.

Paul and Dan-Dan were there along with dozen of
others – some of whom Teal had seen for only an hour or two
and never even knew their names.

Teal recognized others in the crowd as Magnolia
customers who Mickey must have touched in some way.

He felt a great sadness sweep over him; a great sense of
futile loss. His eyes found TJ's, and he knew his feelings were
similar but horribly magnified. But he stood straight with
clear eyes when he spoke from the pulpit, his voice strong as
he captured individual eye contact with many in the crowd.
When he sat back down in the front pew, both Dannie and
Beth linked their arms in his, and both laid their heads on his
shoulders.

The minister droned on for half an hour, two young girls
sang a hymn, a prayer was said and the service concluded. Teal
felt completely exhausted, and his knees quaked and wobbled
when they walked from the church.

"I'm whipped," Teal said sitting in Brownie with the
doors still open letting in a whisper of breeze to chase out the
heat.

"I can't go to the reception or the wake or whatever the
hell it's called. I admire TJ and P.Q. and all those people who
dedicate themselves and work through these things. I'm not as
strong as they are."

"You are the strongest man I've ever known," Sloan said bringing his face down to hers. "But like most people, you have a sensitivity level, and it's just been trampled."

"You are the best thing that has every happened in my life," he said. "I don't know where I would be right now if I hadn't walked into your dad's shop."

He scowled and looked back at the church. People were getting into cars to drive to the wake. He saw John and Sissy get into a car with Sammy's mother and another woman he didn't recognize. Dan-Dan and Gary and Beth rode in an older Volkswagen with an older man.

Teal watched the cars slowly move out of the parking lot and queue up; occupants silent and staring straight ahead. The sun created shimmering waves from roofs and hoods and flashes of laser light from rear view mirrors.

"I think it's time to go visit Sam," Teal finally said and Sloan sighed deeply, nodded and settled in her seat.

* * *

TWENTY NINE

Jack and TJ were sitting at the favored table sipping hot chocolate, and the kitchen was humming with Beth in charge. Sammy grinned and gave the thumbs up whenever Teal glanced over. Gary was back working the espresso machine having just returned from a three week trip to Europe with his parents. He was very natty in a European blazer and tasseled loafers.

When Teal asked him how he liked Europe, he said, "Oh fine." Like he had just returned from shopping at Target. "But the French smell really, really bad," he added indicating with a broad smile it might have been the highlight of his trip.

Beth had created a memorial for Mickey in the front window and tended it faithfully everyday. A plain, blue vase filled with fresh cut flowers on a daily basis and a tiny rectangular plaque, which she insisted on paying for herself. It simply said:

Mickey Ralston
A mocking bird has found his final resting place.
In time we will join you.
Peace and Love

When she first put the vase and plaque in the window, Teal asked Sammy how he felt about it. They had been talking on this personal level for some time with Peter Quinn's encouragement.

"Sometimes I cry at night because I miss him," Sammy said.

"So do I, Sammy," Teal said.

"Thank you, Boss," Sammy said after a moment.
"I thought I was going crazy or something." Snic – snic.

Later Teal asked Sammy, "Mickey and Beth really had a thing going didn't they?"

"What you mean 'thing'?" he asked.

"You know. Like me and Sloan."

"You mean like all that mushy, kissy stuff?" he said fluttering his eyes.

For weeks after Mickey's suicide, notes and flowers and balloons and stuffed animals piled up outside the restaurant window and were carefully retrieved by Beth and packed in storage boxes as though something valuable or precious. Once a week Beth would arrive with a friend, and they would load the boxes in a car and drive away.

"Where do you suppose she puts them all?" TJ asked one time while talking with Peter Quinn.

"Who knows? She might be storing them, or throwing them out or burying them. It's her way of grieving, and we're not privy to those thoughts."

Beth was asking permission to leave the kitchen less and less as she had done in the past weeks, always returning from the tiny office with reddened eyes and mouth as thin as a razor slash. Being boss of the kitchen more often than the others had helped, and no one begrudged it.

They were trying a new kid in the kitchen and Teal thought he'd be a good one if he didn't lop off all his fingers. He had blown through the dishwashing stage in a couple of weeks and now was anxious to show the world how quickly he could learn to cook. Teal and Sammy were constantly telling him to slow down, and he was starting to listen.

"You won't be of any help to us if you cut yourself or you don't have any fingers," Teal warned and behind him he heard Sammy's 'snic-snic'.

Then Sammy went into his classic Benihana knife flipping display while preparing a simple chicken salad sandwich, and Eric watched open mouthed. Teal scowled, and Sammy sheepishly went back to work.

"So, where are you going?" TJ asked, breaking into Teal's thoughts. "Damn it, why can't you stay for another couple of months? Maybe a year?" Not giving him a chance to respond to the first question. He added, "You love it here...and hell, I think you might even be better than Carl."

Teal grimaced. "Idi Amin would be better than Carl. Thanks for the faint praise."

"Well, where are you going?" He already knew the answer but couldn't help asking again. Maybe if he asked enough the whole thing would go away.

"After I pick up Sloan at the Sacto airport, we'll continue up north," Teal said in a weary singsong voice. "She's got two weeks off, so we're going to dawdle along the way. We've got a bunch of maps and tour books but no plan. When she needs to get back, I'll put her on a plane in Seattle."

"Where are you going to stay up there? You don't have a job or any friends." Trying to make it sound as if they were going to Bosnia.

Teal reached across the table and patted TJ on the forearm. "Hey, TJ, I'm not going to disappear off the face of the earth. I'll always be around. Plus Sloan loves Dannie. They're almost like sisters."

TJ stewed for a moment, and then slyly asked, "Does Sloan like me?"

"She thinks you're okay," Teal said not going along on the fishing trip, and they both laughed.

"You're thinking of rotating Beth, Nicole and Sammy as head cook?" Teal asked changing the subject.

"I guess. We can't afford to hire another head cook. Hell we can't afford anything," he said turning morose. "You come by in a month or so, and we'll probably be gone."

"Aw, come on, TJ. The board will think of something. They always do." He got up and stretched. "Back to work. Try some of Sammy's sushi. Unbelievable!"

The lunch rush was strong, and they ran out of sushi disappointing some customers who were slightly mollified by a free latte. The crew was cleaning up and Sammy was going through the kitchen bills when Sissy and John came in and sat at a table squirming and beaming as if they had won an office pool. They motioned TJ and Teal to sit with them.

"Sissy has something to tell you," John said and settled back to watch the show.

"Well, yesterday afternoon," she said clearing her throat, "at about three in the afternoon, a special delivery service dropped off a letter addressed to John and me. He seemed like a very nice young man."

John was making a hurry up gesture and rolling his eyes.

"This is the long version of the story, dear," she said. "You will just have to be patient. Let's see, where was I? Well, John signed for the letter and then came in and asked if he should tip the young man. Everybody gets tipped now days. So anyway, I said yes, perhaps a dollar or two, and the young man left. He seemed to be satisfied."

John took a deep breath and ballooned out his cheeks.

"We opened the letter together because, of course, it was addressed to the both of us," Sissy said. "Inside there was a short

letter from a local lawyer by the name of Benjamin Cooper who
is a partner in Blaine, Cooper and Wallen. I believe you said
you knew him from the Bohemian Club, didn't you, dear?"

John nodded resigned, like a man who had heard the long
version on other subjects many times before. Teal and TJ looked
at each other and shrugged.

"The letter stated that the enclosed anonymous
contribution was to be used for the betterment, his words, of
Magnolia Café however the board saw fit. We called Mr. Cooper
first thing this morning to make sure there was not some
misunderstanding, but he assured us it was legitimate, and the
cashier's check was sound. He also told us his client wished to
remain anonymous, and he would honor that wish."

"Tell them how much," John said beaming. He looked
like he had just caught Teal in a crosscourt shot and left him
sprawling.

"Oh, I thought I had," she said smiling. "The cashier's
check was for three hundred and fifty thousand dollars."

There was silence in the room as Teal and TJ stared back
at her. She smiled, relishing their reaction.

"Could you repeat that figure again?" TJ asked in a voice
that could barely be heard over the pots banging in the kitchen.

"Three hundred and fifty thousand," she repeated.
"American," she added for emphasis.

TJ slumped in his chair like a sack of grain his eyes
unfocused. "Oh, my God," he mumbled. "Oh, my God." He
sounded like Froggy the Gremlin.

"That could fund us for three or four years – maybe
longer. And with no help from all our other funding sources,"
he mumbled.

"But I don't think we'll share this little piece of
information with them just yet," John said with a thin smile.

Suddenly TJ leapt from his chair and grabbed Teal in a bear hug nearly toppling him over. "New toilets!" he shouted his arms raised like a referee's. "We can get new toilets." Somebody in the kitchen laughed.

"You say you know this guy Cooper?" Teal asked John while TJ danced around the room like a drunken Welshman. "You have a persuasive style. Didn't you try to weasel a name out of him?"

"Thank you and, yes, I did. All to no avail. And all this despite the fact I believe I've bought him more than a few drinks at the club."

"Did he mention if it was from a Marin County resident?"

"Not a thing. Nothing. This man is noted for his integrity. We'll get nothing from him."

"Well, congratulations. This is wild!" Teal finally said shaking John's hand and standing to kiss Sissy on the cheek. "It should get you guys over some bumps in the road until the Foundation can manage to see the light of day."

"Indeed it will," Sissy said and then sighed. "Now, Jack," she continued with a change in her voice. "I'm terribly excited about this, of course, but I'm also very distressed about your leaving. You know it may be very unsettling for our clients."

"Nice try, Sissy," Teal said patting her arm. "We've been round and round on this before, you and me, Peter Quinn and me, TJ and me. They can handle it, and so can the kids. They're a hell of a lot tougher than we give them credit for."

"Oh, Jack, we're going to miss you so," she said taking his arm. "We, the whole board and more specifically John and I, think what you have helped to create here is magic. Optimism is at an all time high, clients are directed and excited, and we're getting new looks from the Foundation.

"Mickey's suicide was a disaster and truly put us in a corner. It made all of us realize what a difficult and sometimes unforgiving task we have chosen for ourselves. The strength shown by you and TJ brought us back from the brink, and we will forever be in your debt."

Teal thought: *I need to get out of here, before I lose it!*

"Sissy, I'm the one who should be doing the thanking. What's going on here *is* magic, and I've been honored to play a bit role in it."

They were holding hands, teenagers at their first prom, and Sissy was swallowing to keep from crying.

"I'll be back from time to time," he said. "You are all part of my life, and I never want to lose that."

He hugged Sissy and John and walked around the restaurant one last time. All the goodbyes had been said over the past week: to those in the organization with whom he had worked, liked and respected, to the clients, a far more difficult task and involving some weeping on both sides and to friends and businessmen he had met during this odd and important sojourn in his life. He was wearing the sweater Nicole and Beth hastily made when they heard he was leaving. He had worn it to work his final two days, and they beamed until he thought their cheeks might split.

And now it was done. Everyone had left the restaurant, respecting the few moments they knew he would want alone. He stood in the middle of the room listening to the echoes of Mickey's cackling and Sammy's snic-snic and Amed's soft 'Good Morning, Boss'. He watched the ghostly images of Ginny skipping across the floor and Gary lining up the knives and forks on the parade off to battle and the art sculptures of Dan-Dan the garbage man.

Then he slowly nodded, flipped the light switch and locked the front door. The last image he would have of the restaurant was fresh flowers in the window.

Back at the cabin he was in the final stages of packing. Brownie had been serviced and was ready for wherever the odyssey would take him. Teal sat on the tiny deck sipping the last of his beers and watched the evening creep over Marin County. A freighter was riding low in the water and headed north with a load of car parts or machinery or fencing material. It would return with onions or rice or grain – a circuit the ship would continue to ply until it became a rusty hulk destined for the scrap heap.

The robin's nest had been torn apart either by raccoons or nature. But it had served its purpose, and Teal had little doubt it would be rebuilt. There would be other generations of robins, and he was sorry he would not be there to see them. He hoped someone would be living in the cottage to monitor and perhaps feed them some bread crusts and birdseed and worms and protect them from marauding cats. This was one of the many thoughts he would take with him as he left this tiny cottage, this county, which had helped him redefine his life, and in a significant way, define his rebirth.

* * *

EPILOG

Two letters find their way across the country and are delivered by far different methods. At the same time two couples are enjoying the remnants of the late afternoon in Fort Collins, Colorado.

Spring has come early to the slopes of the eastern Rocky Mountains, and even the skiers, snowboarders and lanky cross-country people on snow shoes are pleased – and worn out. It had been a seemingly endless winter and the people who live in the towns and cities that string loosely along the western slopes of the Rockies are anxious to see any color other than white.

Spring has arrived in a forceful manner as if to remind the human race whose boss. One day there are light snow flurries and black ice and tangled traffic. Then, following day, temperatures crack fifty and people start rummaging in closets for walking shorts and take stock of the gardening supplies stored along the back wall of their garage.

The two couples, one in their early thirties and one in their late fifties are becoming very comfortable in each other's presence. The two men of differing ages sit in the waning light and watch the two women chattering in the kitchen. It brings smiles to both of their faces.

Meanwhile in Marin County north of the San Francisco Bay, spring has long since taken hold and is now tugging summer onto the scene. A silver haired woman stands outside her cottage staring at the retreating back of a teenager who has just hand delivered an envelope addressed to Jack Teal in her care. It appears to be the same as the other two delivered by the post office – the last almost a year ago. She shakes her head at the disappearing young man and wonders why he has to be so sullen. Generally Hispanic kids are delightful and laugh kindly at her stumbling attempts to speak to them in their own language.

She hasn't seen Jack Teal in almost a year although they had spoken just last week. Recalling the conversation with a smile on her face, she enters the cottage and starts to rummage through her desk for Jack's forwarding address.

While everyone in Colorado and Marin County is scrambling to make sure they take advantage of the sunshine, some harboring concerns it will not last, the Texas panhandle is not faring as well. In the panhandle it has been a dry winter sparking the usual debates about drought in coffee shops, markets, feed stores and gas stations. The people who live here have an excellent grasp on the ramifications of drought – after all they have been arguing about and experiencing them for decades.

A woman with springy coils of red hair is sitting at a counter in a quiet pin-neat restaurant in a small dusty north Texas town.

"Listen to this," the woman says. She's speaking to a man cleaning up the kitchen after a modest lunch rush and another much older man, a rancher, who is sitting at the farthest seat of the counter. It's debatable whether or not he understands a single word. His hearing is poor but not as diminished as he would lead people to believe.

"It's from Jack," the woman says. "Jack Teal. You remember him? The crazy kid with the Porsch?"

There is a mumble from the kitchen which she accepts as an affirmative answer. She snaps the letter open and smoothes it on the counter with her forearm.

Dear Bet and Arnie,

I'm sorry I haven't written sooner, but I've been running around like I've got ants in my pants trying to play catch up. First of all, we wish you and Arnie all the best and send our love. We're sorry we couldn't come down for the wedding. I guess you must have passed those good ideas along to us because we've gone and done the same. Sloan and I were married two months ago, and I've never been happier in my life. We want to have a family – maybe two boys and a girl. Or two girls and a boy, except they'd probably beat up on him. Two boys would protect their sister. We would like you and Arnie to visit us some time if Texans are allowed in the state of Washington.

"You hear that Arnie? We could go up and visit them sometime when they have kids," she says and hesitates. "I'm not really sure of myself around little kids. I mean what do you do with little kids? Hey, Brick," she shouts to the man at the end of the counter.

"Does that mean I would have duties? Like I'd have to buy Christmas presents and bounce the kids on my knee and all that kind of stuff?"

The man at the end of the counter mumbles something lost in the kitchen clean-up sounds.

Meanwhile the author of the letter she is reading sits with the older man and comforts him. They are sitting knee to knee

and the older man is weeping now and making futile attempts
to wipe away the tears.

"So much time we've wasted," he says in a voice choked
with emotion.

The younger man puts a gentle hand on his knee. "And
we have so much time in the future," he says softly wondering
when was the last time he touched his father. He cannot
remember.

"I have so many apologies to offer. I don't know where to
start," the older man says.

"So do I," his son says. "And sorrows and frustrations and
shame. But let's not think about those feelings – those black
days. I have buried them forever."

His father nods and covers the hand with both of his.

The woman reading the letter in Texas continues.

One of the best things happening is our restaurant. I
started it on a shoestring when I first got up here, and it
really took off. We're down by Pike's Market and have a
view of Puget Sound (that's like the ocean). My ex-boss
from California has moved up here for health reasons and
is now a partner. His wife is helping in the restaurant and
will until she's too pregnant to waddle round and wait
on customers. Anyway we've done so well we're going
to expand in to the space next door. The owner of the
building made us an offer we couldn't refuse. Just like
The Godfather. So we're taking on a third partner who
used to have a restaurant in California but was born up
here. Right now there are three of us in the kitchen. Him
and me and a Japanese kid I knew in California – best
guy with a sushi knife I've ever seen. You know that's

like raw fish and stuff. Probably not what you and Arnie would be too keen on.

"Boy, he's got that right," the woman says and pretends to stick a finger down her throat.

"You want any of that raw stuff they eat out there?" she asks the man in the kitchen who mimics her finger-down-the-throat gesture. She continues reading.

> This Japanese kid is one of the reasons we are so successful, and he's built up quite a following. He was even featured in the Friday edition of *The Wall Street Journal* about the hot new chefs in the Pacific Northwest. Bet, I've surrounded myself with people I love and trust. My partner calls it my extended family, and if that's what it's all about, well okay. I can't imagine life being better than it is right now. I miss you guys and hope to see you soon. You were the first people I met in my real life and hinted at a true direction, and I will never forget that.

"What do you suppose he means by that? His real life?" she asks, and the man behind the pass through shrugs and continues to scrape the grill.

"Beats the tar outta me," he finally says.

> Why don't you try to break away and see the Pacific Northwest. We'll take care of you and make sure you get home safely. Please write when you have time.
> Your friend, Jack Teal.

"That might be fun to go up there sometime," she says but knows Arnie will never leave the restaurant for more than a weekend. And that's really okay with her.

What? Are they going to sit around and eat raw things and have little babies piddle in their laps?

She laughs to herself and slips the letter back into its envelope. She will keep it in a box with some Christmas cards she likes and will read it from time to time over the years until her memory of Jack Teal grows dim.

And on the eastern slope of the Rockies in that waning day trumpeting the announcement of spring, the two men sitting in the lengthening shadows have achieved a new found sense of peace and quietude. They are not embarrassed or ashamed by their piled hands and take silent joy in the warmth not all of which comes from blood coursing through their veins. Jack watches his mother and Sloan in the kitchen preparing a salad and laughing like school girls. Sloan says something with elaborate hand gestures and his mother laughs until she has to wipe her eyes with the hem of her apron.

Two women so different connecting on so many levels and tumbling walls slyly built by the difference of age, background and sense of the future. Jack wonders why it is so much more difficult for men to achieve that same joy of friendship and acceptance.

Jack and his father finally stand and walk across the yard towards the kitchen. He puts his arm across his father's shoulders and gives him a little tug. His father nods and smiles, and they meet the two women at the kitchen door and, smiling, walk into the soft kitchen light.

THE END